W9-ARO-381

WAYPOINT KANGAROO

CURTIS C. CHEN

WAYPOINT KANGAROO

THOMAS DUNNE BOOKS
ST. MARTIN'S PRESS ☒ NEW YORK

THOMAS DUNNE BOOKS.
An imprint of St. Martin's Press.

WAYPOINT KANGAROO. Copyright © 2016 by Curtis C. Chen. All rights reserved. Printed in the United States of America. For information, address St. Martin's Press, 175 Fifth Avenue, New York, N.Y. 10010.

www.thomasdunnebooks.com
www.stmartins.com

Designed by Jonathan Bennett

The Library of Congress Cataloging-in-Publication Data is available upon request.

ISBN 978-1-250-08178-0 (hardcover)
ISBN 978-1-250-08179-7 (e-book)

Our books may be purchased in bulk for promotional, educational, or business use. Please contact your local bookseller or the Macmillan Corporate and Premium Sales Department at 1-800-221-7945, extension 5442, or by e-mail at MacmillanSpecialMarkets@macmillan.com.

First Edition: June 2016

10 9 8 7 6 5 4 3 2 1

For D,
who is both my toughest critic
and my most ardent supporter.
LOVE YOU WIFE

WAYPOINT
KANGAROO

CHAPTER ONE

Earth—Kazakhstan—150 km from Oskemen Spaceport
45 minutes after I was supposed to be on a flight out of here

My left eye doesn't lie. The scanning implants and heads-up display can only show me what's really there, and right now they're showing me a border guard carrying too many weapons. Standard-issue assault rifle hanging around his neck, but also a machine pistol under his armpit, a revolver strapped to his left ankle, and a high-voltage stunner in a tail holster at the base of his spine.

I saw suspicious bulges under his coat as I rolled up to the checkpoint, and he obviously wasn't happy to see me, so I activated my eye scanners. Now I can read the factory bar code off each weapon and look up the manufacturer's specs via satellite link. The stunner surprises me—it was manufactured off-world, somewhere in the asteroid belt, and delivers more energy than is legal anywhere on Earth. And the concealed firearms are Hungarian-made, military issue. Not the kind of thing Kazakh border police pick up at the corner shop.

But it's not the guns that really put me wise to Fakey Impostorov. I can also see into his body, and simple checkpoint guards don't have an unmistakable spiderweb of ground-to-orbit comsat antenna surgically implanted in their left shoulder. If this guy's not a field agent for a national intelligence outfit—a spy like me—I'll eat my shoe. And shoes taste terrible. Trust me, I know. Long story.

Anyway, what is a Hungarian secret agent doing on the Russia–Kazakhstan border?

While I'm pondering this, an actual border guard waddles up to my rented hovercar and squints at me. He's the real deal. I can tell by the way

1

he walks and the smell of coffee and whiskey on his breath. Career military, old enough to know better, bored with everything.

Not like my friend the Hungarian over there, standing by the guard house and pretending to smoke a vape-stick. Way too alert, way too serious. Oh yeah, he's on the job.

I smile at the guard next to me and hand over my legend passport.

"American?" he says. "Why are you here?"

"Visiting family," I reply. "My cousin just got married in Ridder. Have you been to Ridder? Beautiful place—"

"You wait," the guard grunts.

Right. I should remember not to talk so much. Whiskey-Breath walks back to the guard house with my forged paperwork. I continue breathing slowly and evenly, both hands on the steering wheel, stealing glances at the fake guard.

There isn't anything hot between Russia and Kazakhstan right now. I would have gotten that in my briefing, before I dropped in country. A Hungarian might be on the lookout for Chinese activity, but then he'd be on the southern border, not the northern. And the nearest spaceport, Oskemen, only supports suborbital launches, so he's unlikely to be from Mars. Martians always want to have direct escape routes.

I was actually looking forward to this operation. It's on Earth for once, where the geopolitics are centuries old and fairly well understood. Not like our colonies and outposts throughout the rest of the Solar System, where everything is always in motion and everyone's trying to outdo their ancestors in one way or another.

Or they're trying to pull off something extremely dangerous, illegal, and/or unethical where they hope nobody will notice. The neighbors might object if you start testing antimatter weapons on your home planet, but sneak a small team into the asteroid belt between Mars and Jupiter, and there's plenty of space to hide your unsavory deeds.

People try a lot of crazy things in the outback, and when it doesn't work out, somebody has to go clean it up. These days "somebody" tends to be my agency, because the United States of America is very interested in anything that happens in outer space. Ever since the Independence War, which started with asteroids boiling Earth's oceans and ended with Mars winning its freedom as a sovereign planet, "off-world events" have been a matter of national security for Uncle Sam.

Now that we all know how bad things can get, nobody wants to attract a new interplanetary conflict—but behind closed doors, everyone is looking for inconspicuous ways to improve their space arsenals. We're only human. Sooner or later it's going to come down to who's got the bigger stick.

So for the last five years, the agency has deployed operatives on a wide variety of glamorous missions, from space junk cleanup to investigating possible signs of extraterrestrial intelligence. No aliens yet, but it's amazing how paranoid people can get when you pay them to think up worst-case scenarios. Also no faster-than-light travel, though we have scavenged some pretty killer new tech from other people's failed experiments. In fact, I have a few of those derivative gadgets hidden in the pocket right now, including one very large—

Wait. Is it possible Fakey's looking for me?

Exfiltration is always the hardest part of the job. Even if nobody suspects anything, you still know you're guilty, and it only takes one slip at the wrong moment to give yourself away.

Just take it easy, Kangaroo. Don't wig out until there's an actual reason.

This is not how the operation was supposed to go. I shouldn't be flying solo. Reynaldo was the primary. He was the one who spoke Kazakh, the one who knew our contact, the one who would recognize the item we were sent to retrieve. I was just along for the ride.

But you know what they say: the best laid plans of mice and kangaroos often go awry.

Rey and I met our contact, Medet, at a hotel where he was attending some distant relative's wedding. Medet slipped us a hand-drawn treasure map, then insisted his old friend Rey and I stay for the reception. Rey was reluctant at first, but I talked him into it. And for the record, it didn't take much talking: after two hours of rough overland travel from Oskemen, where our flight landed, we were both ready for some free-flowing alcohol, drunken bridesmaids, and Balearic dance tunes.

How was I supposed to know the local Bratva were calling in a hit on the best man? We didn't get briefed on organized crime activity in this area. It's not my fault. If it's anybody's fault, it's on Intel for not providing the data and Lasher for not prepping us to handle this contingency. I'm not supposed to improvise. Lasher has chewed me out more than once for going off-script. Rey was in charge. He told me to lead the way out of the hotel. He said he was right behind me. He said he wasn't going to try anything heroic.

And now he's dead, and I'm alone. Story of my life.

The border guards are still talking inside their checkpoint shack. I could switch on my long-distance microphone implant and eavesdrop, but I wouldn't understand what they're saying anyway. They seem to be discussing my travel documents at length. I see gesturing. The Hungarian spy is outside, so it's not him making trouble. Something else is going on.

What did I do wrong this time?

Maybe a listening post logged my distress call. Maybe a friendly neighbor saw me digging in the woods. Maybe the rental company just wants its hovercar back. I won't know how I screwed up until days, maybe weeks later, after some agency analyst has gone over my after-action reports with a fine-toothed comb. I know this because that used to be my job.

Sometimes I miss working a desk. Sometimes I wish I didn't have the pocket. But then I wouldn't get to enjoy any of these wonderful sight-seeing opportunities, from the darkest corners of Earth to the deepest canyons of Uranus.

I spent most of last night sitting in this hovercar, crawling through the pitch-black mountains on low power, navigating by night vision. Couldn't risk anyone seeing headlights. I had to stop and backtrack at least a dozen times, trying to match reality to Medet's poorly labeled, not-to-scale road charts.

I could have aborted when the rendezvous went sideways. That is, as Lasher keeps reminding me, always a legitimate option. But the agency wasn't going to get another chance at recovering this item. And I didn't want Rey to have died for nothing.

After I found the cabin, I broke in and spent hours excavating the mildewed, insect-infested, probably carcinogenic ferroconcrete basement until I found the item. It was bigger than we thought, but still fit into the pocket just fine. That wasn't a problem. *I'm* the problem now. Half the population of Ridder witnessed me fleeing the scene of a massacre, which is why I'm motoring through the Altai Mountains instead of flying first class over them.

Whiskey-Breath comes back to the car, returns my passport, and asks some pointed questions about my itinerary. Fakey watches as I apologize for not having all my papers in order. I pretend to search my jacket for some missing documents and come up with three two-hundred-*tenge* bills, which I slip into Whiskey-Breath's palm.

"If anything else is missing," I say, "I may have left it in the glovebox."

He smiles, pockets the cash, and walks around the front of the hover-car. I stay very still as he leans in through the open passenger-side window, pops open the glovebox, and pulls out two small bars of dark chocolate. Small, because I don't want him to think there might be more of it stashed in my luggage. I really don't want these guys opening my suitcase and finding it full of nothing but bedsheets and towels.

The guard's smile broadens, and he slips the chocolate inside his sleeve. Doesn't want his friends in the shack to see that particular payoff. Good. I'd scanned a wedding band underneath his left glove, saw the metal worn and pitted with age, and guessed that he could use something of a bribe himself, for when he goes home to the wife and kids.

He shouts something. The checkpoint gate opens and he waves me through. I wave back, smile, and lift my foot off the brake. The hover-car glides forward slowly, out of Kazakhstan, toward home and a hot shower.

I risk a glance back at the Hungarian spy. He's not pretending to smoke anymore. He's looking right at me, with a gaze almost as intent as one of the bridesmaids at the wedding. But I would prefer not to dance with this gentleman.

I give Fakey a polite smile and a polite nod. His expression doesn't change. I turn back to face the road, but I feel my cheek muscles relaxing a split second too soon.

Note to self: work on timing. Practice in front of mirror or something.

Maybe Fakey didn't notice. Maybe I can still make it out of here. I lower my foot onto the accelerator, not too hard, pushing the hovercar forward faster but not fast enough to arouse further suspicion. I hope.

I get about half a kilometer down the road before I hear yelling. I don't look back. I just slam the throttle down and head for the hills.

The good news is, this is no longer a suspenseful game of cat-and-mouse, which I am demonstrably terrible at. Now it's a flat-out chase, and I should have the advantage.

Equipment gave me instructions for goosing the hovercar's main drive, and the chemical booster I poured into the fuel tank earlier will give me fifty percent more power. But there's only so much you can squeeze out of an old exotherm engine.

I check the rearview mirror and see a shiny blue atomic shield logo on the front of the vehicle chasing me. Great. They're driving a low-altitude skimmer: electrodynamic vectored thrust. I can't outrun them in this rented rustbucket. I have to disable their vehicle—without killing anyone. Nobody likes spies, but soldiers will hunt down assassins.

We're moving pretty quickly up and down winding mountain roads. Unlike me, the Kazakhs don't have any reservations about opening fire. The bullets whizzing past and ricocheting off the back of the hovercar make it difficult to concentrate, but I sprayed poly compound over the windows and chassis earlier to bulletproof them. All I have to worry about is driving.

I turn east toward my rendezvous coordinates. My pursuers follow. They know they're blowing through two national borders, but why should they care? Nobody in this part of Mongolia is going to complain about a Kazakh incursion into the Gobi Desert. The Mongolians are more worried about China. I'm not going to get any help until I reach my rendezvous, and that's three days out in the middle of sandy nowhere.

The battery light starts blinking on my dashboard. Not a problem. The booster I mixed into the fuel will cause electrical fluctuations. Equipment warned me about that.

But it does give me an idea for how to evade my pursuers.

This is a bad idea, I think to myself, even as I'm figuring out the tactical details. This low-rent hovercar doesn't have a self-drive system, so I'll have to keep one hand on the wheel while opening the pocket. That'll be tricky. It usually takes a good push to get my arm through the barrier, but I can't lean too far over and still maintain control of the car.

I wait until I hit a relatively straight stretch of road, then think of my reference object—a blackbird—and open the pocket. The circular portal pops open and travels with me, hanging in midair above the passenger seat.

I never thought about the physics of the pocket when I was younger, but Equipment insists that I learn the higher math to describe these phenomena—frame of reference, conservation of momentum, blah blah blah. I keep telling him it doesn't really help me in the field. He doesn't listen.

I push one hand through the glowing white force field covering the portal. It's hard vacuum inside the pocket, which means it's near-absolute-zero cold. My freezing fingers fumble against the insulated bag I'm trying to retrieve from its zero-gravity vault, sending it spinning. I can't see through the barrier, so I have to proceed by touch. I feel the bag strap touch my thumb, and I grip it tight, then wriggle my hand over the frigid material until I'm holding one end of the cylindrical soft-case.

I have to pull it lengthwise through the portal—solid matter obstructs the event horizon, so I can't open the pocket wide enough inside the hovercar to just yank out the whole case willy-nilly. My steering goes wonky. The passenger-side mirror scrapes the side of the mountain and shatters, but I manage to get the case into my lap and close the pocket, then straighten out again.

That was the easy part.

I've never actually used an electromagnetic lance in the field. Still driving one-handed, I unzip the case, pop the lid off the storage tube, and pull out the launcher. It looks like a harpoon gun, but instead of firing a flesh-rending metal hook at an endangered species, an EM lance is designed to penetrate most types of modern vehicle armor and deliver a massive electromagnetic pulse to disable any electronic systems inside. In the case of the guard skimmer, that should include the main thrusters.

I will have to file a whole stack of paperwork when I get back, since this is last-resort equipment. Setting off EMPs in populated areas tends to kill power grids and get you noticed. Spies and their bosses don't like to be noticed. But out here in the mountains, there shouldn't be too many household appliances to disrupt.

Of course, there is still the matter of a piece of high-tech weaponry that will be buried in the engine block of a foreign vehicle, which the Hungarian spy will likely have full access to examine. He won't get any forensic evidence from it, but an EM lance is clearly something from a well-funded government armory. Mercenaries don't stock many nonlethal arms, and certainly not specialized hardware-killers like this.

But there will be reasonable doubt, right? They won't know *exactly* where it came from or who I'm working for. And the most important thing right now is getting *me* out of here safely and securely.

We've already lost one agent on this op. I can still make it home with the item. Losing that, plus all the equipment in my body and the information in my head, would be even worse.

And the pocket. Can't forget the pocket, and all the stuff I have hidden in there.

The EM lance is my best option right now. A bad idea is still better than no idea, that's what I always say.

The saying has yet to catch on with any of my peers within the agency.

I wait until we descend out of the mountains—I'll say one thing for my pursuers, they are persistent—and start driving through the sand. I want to make it as difficult as possible for them to repair their vehicle. I find a flat stretch of desert and let them pull up right behind me.

Even with the heads-up display in my left eye showing me precise angles—calculated off the side mirror reflection, no less—it's very difficult to aim a projectile weapon over my shoulder while driving in a straight line across ground that disappears as soon as the hover effect touches it. It's like piloting a boat through gravel. It doesn't help that the Kazakhs are shooting at me again. How much ammunition did they bring?

I spend precious seconds testing the best place to balance the EM lance, finally settling on the crook of my left arm, which is holding the steering wheel. I put my right index finger on the trigger and tilt the lance up, watching my HUD overlay to see when the projected trajectory lines up with the guard skimmer in the mirror. This is not easy.

A spray of bullets takes out my driver's-side mirror, and now I can't see behind me.

"Fuck it," I mutter, and whip my head around. They're not trying to kill me. They just want my car to stop moving. I hope.

My HUD blinks, red crosshairs paint the hood of the skimmer, and I pull the trigger.

The launcher kicks back against my palm. The lance flies in a parabola and hits the other vehicle with a loud crack. I don't wait to watch what happens next. I won't be able to see the EMP anyway. Or the expressions on the guards' faces, as much as I might want to.

I turn back, toss the launcher onto the floor, grab the steering wheel with both hands, and stomp the accelerator.

Something rattles behind me, and then I hear a pop, a crunch, and lots of shouting. What I don't hear anymore is the rumble of the skimmer's main thrusters. *Holy shit, that actually worked!*

I brace myself for the shooting to start again, but I get all the way up the next sand dune without incident. When the hovercar thumps over the top, I can't resist sticking my head out the window to look back.

The skimmer's half buried in the sand, nose first, and four guards are kneeling on the ground around a fifth who's lying on his back. One of the kneeling guards is struggling to open a red satchel with a white cross on it.

I have enough time, before my hovercar starts sliding down the far slope of the dune, to blink my eye into telescope mode and get a better look at the injured guard. It's Whiskey-Breath, the one I bribed with cash and chocolate. What happened? I don't see any blood . . .

It's not important. I should just go. *GTFO, Kangaroo.*

Never let it be said I'm not an equal opportunity insubordinate: I ignore my own advice just as often as I ignore anyone else's.

I turn the hovercar's steering wheel, still moving but staying on top of the dune to keep the downed skimmer in view. The guard with the med-kit rips it open and yanks out a bright orange box. He lifts the lid and extends two spiraling wires leading to round white pads. I recognize the device from my first aid training. It's an automated external defibrillator, used to shock a human heart back to its normal rhythm. But why would they need—

Oh, you gotta be kidding me.

I switch my left eye display over to playback and rewind the live mission recording back to my border crossing. I pause on my body scan of Whiskey-Breath. This time, instead of studying his hand, I look at his torso. And there it is. I thought that glowing outline in his chest was a shoulder-phone, but a phone wouldn't have wires going directly into his heart.

Whiskey-Breath has an artificial cardiac pacemaker. And I just fried it with an EMP.

Also fried? The AED his friends are trying to use now to revive him.

This is an accident. But nobody's going to care about that. The headlines won't read "Elderly Alcoholic Succumbs to Heart Disease"; they'll say "Ugly American Criminal Murders Husband and Father." Not to mention all the blowback at home will be on me and me alone.

Goddammit. One minute. One minute, then I'm gone.

I picture a grizzly bear in a white lab coat and open the pocket again. I pull out my own emergency AED and dangle it out the window, then turn the hovercar around and steer it back down the dune, toward the skimmer.

The shooting resumes before I get within fifty meters. In hindsight, yelling at the guards to announce my approach probably wasn't the best idea, since I don't speak Kazakh and the insulated therm-pack holding my AED looks an awful lot like an ammo pouch.

I retract my arm inside the hovercar and continue driving closer until a burst of gunfire cracks my windshield. Okay, apparently that's the operational limit of this spray-on poly shield. I pull the steering wheel over hard and toss the AED out the window toward the guards. Two of them dive for cover behind the skimmer.

"It's not a bomb!" I shout over my shoulder while driving away. "Help your friend! Aide! Medico! Medicina! Dottore!" I'm pretty sure those are all real words.

Well, these guys speak the international language of firefight, and they have plenty to say, if not an extensive vocabulary. It's only another minute before I scale the sand dune again and drop out of range, but it's a very unpleasant and stressful sixty seconds.

CHAPTER TWO

Earth—United States—Washington, D.C.
Several hours before I would prefer to be awake

Whenever I come home, I'm afraid it's going to be for the last time.

I walk into the building wearing a new suit. It's not my usual attire, but I want to surprise Paul. He always says I should take more care with my appearance—which is ironic, considering all the disguises and aliases we use. But of course he's talking about my appearance and behavior here at home, around the office, in the building.

There are only three people in my department of the agency—on the public budget sheets, we're listed as "Administrative Assistance for Director of Operations, Non-Territorial"—and we report directly to D.Ops. For the last ten years, that title has belonged to Paul Tarkington, code name LASHER, the man who acts as my handler. He's also the closest thing to a father I've had for most of my life.

I don't remember much about my biological parents. They were media historians who died in a vehicle accident on the Nimitz Freeway when I was five years old. The only thing they left me was an extensive archive of two-hundred-year-old entertainment vids, and I watched every one of those shows over and over, hoping to learn something about my mother and father from the annotations that popped up onscreen every once in a while.

Meanwhile, I had no other living relatives, so the great state of California bounced me around orphanages and foster homes for over a decade, until Paul found me on the worst night of my life and rescued me from what I thought was the deepest trouble I could possibly get into.

Now I know better. It takes top secret security clearance to *really* make a mess of things.

The front desk guards give me a funny look as I go through the security gate. They recognize my face, but I know they're thinking, this guy never wears a suit. Is today a special occasion? Are we retaking ID holos for our access badges? Am I doing a very well dressed walk of shame?

I smile to myself after I'm out of sight. I get a kick out of tweaking people's expectations. I walk around the corner to the freight elevator, which I ride down to the basement. Then it's just a short walk to the maze.

One of the two other people in my department is Oliver Graves. His job title is "Equipment Research, Development, and Obtention Specialist," and the maze was his idea.

I enter a dark room, lit only by fluorescent tubes overhead and crammed full of steel cabinets, cardboard boxes, and plastic crates. Inside these containers are actual paper files. The sign on the door outside says "Archival Document Storage." It's not a lie. It just doesn't tell the whole story.

I blink my left eye into spectrum analysis mode. The fluorescent lights here flicker at a very high frequency, imperceptible to unaided human vision, and the variation between individual lighting panels indicates a path through the maze. The maze has many exits, all of them blank walls, but one of them hides a doorway. There are many possible paths to that door, but only one path is ever valid, and that path changes daily. Pressure plates in the floor and motion sensors in the ceiling detect whether you're following the correct path, and if you're not, bad things happen.

I walk in circles until I reach the exit, then press my hand against the wall. Hidden sensors in what looks like concrete read my fingerprints, pulse, and subdermal agency transponder, and then the wall parts like the Red Sea, nanobots flexing their molecule-thin shells and scurrying out of the way to reveal a manual door—the kind with a handle you have to turn. I push it open, step into the stairwell, and close the door behind me.

Down one flight of stairs, out another manual door, and I'm back in time.

Our department's current office space used to be some kind of military bunker, built near the beginning of the Space Age to hide VIPs and shield them from any surface bombardments up to and including thermonuclear warheads. It's been retrofitted with automatic doors, a modern power system, and better toilets, but it's still cold and gray and heavy and linear.

I'm glad I don't have to stay down here all the time. But I think Paul actually likes being isolated from the modern world. He's always been fascinated with the end of the twentieth century—what he calls "the turn of the millennium"—and it tends to rub off if you spend any amount of time around him.

"Profligate," Oliver says as I walk into his workshop. He's tinkering with some kind of disk-shaped gadget, probably a flying thing—I see four exposed rotors. He doesn't even look at me. His dark eyes stay focused on the machine he's either building or taking apart.

"Them's fightin' words, cowboy," I retort. Oliver always throws around a lot of technical jargon, but when he pulls out the vocabulary words, I know he's looking for an argument.

"An electromagnetic lance is an expensive piece of equipment," he says. "More importantly, it is a very specialized instrument, only constructed by a few manufacturers, only available to a small number of people."

"Private security firms have them," I say. I've had a few hours to fashion rebuttals to his most obvious criticisms of my operational performance.

"And how many private security firms take contracts in Kazakhstan?"

I shrug. I didn't research that. Probably should have.

"The EM lance is a weapon of last resort," Oliver says. "It's too sophisticated for private security. Anyone who gets hit with an EM lance is going to know that it came from a first-world government agency."

"Didn't you tell me that the pulse charge also fries the casing? Burns away serial numbers, fingerprints, all that good stuff?"

Oliver sighs, rubs the bridge of his nose, and casts a baleful gaze from under his shaggy mop of dark hair. "It doesn't matter if they can trace the weapon, Kay. They don't need to know exactly where it came from. Their *suspicions* about its origin are enough to cause trouble."

Now I'm getting a little annoyed. "It's the only weapon I discharged on this op," I say. "I'd hardly call that 'profligate.'" He doesn't need to know about the AED; that's Jessica's inventory.

"We'll see about that," says Oliver. "Let's go check you in."

I follow him out of the workshop and down the corridor to the armory. He puts the flying disk thing on a flat, empty table and taps at a wall screen, bringing up the inventory of equipment I signed out last week. I put on a pair of insulated gloves. Grabbing one object out of the pocket's deep freeze is not a problem, but I'm going to be unpacking a lot of stuff here.

"One EM lance discharged," Oliver says, looking over my inventory list with a sour expression. "Which one was it?"

"Blackbird."

He manipulates the screen, updating that list entry. "Right. Robin Red-Breast, then."

I visualize the reference object—a small brown bird with an orange chest—and open the pocket.

My code name, the only name I have within the agency, is KAN-GAROO. Not because I'm originally from Australia, or because I can jump supernaturally high, or because I'm a genetically engineered human-marsupial hybrid. None of those things is true, and come on, that last one is pretty ridiculous.

I'm Kangaroo because I have a universe-sized secret pouch.

I call it "the pocket." Yeah, boring name, but give me a break; I was ten years old when the ability first manifested. Nobody knows how it works—not yet, anyway. Science Division keeps testing me every chance they get. They say I have the ability to open a "hyperspace shunt": a variable-size portal into a "pocket universe," an empty, apparently endless void that looks like deep space. It's very useful for smuggling things into places where they don't belong, or out of places where we don't want them to stay.

The reference objects—Science Division calls them "pointers"—help me keep track of where everything is inside the pocket. Having a different image in my mind when I open the pocket will put the portal in a different part of the empty universe on the other side. But imagining a pistol, or a clip of ammunition, doesn't help me if there's more than one in the pocket. I need a unique pointer to each location.

Opening and closing the pocket is a purely mental exertion. I have to be awake, and I have to concentrate, but it doesn't feel any different from moving a part of my body. It's like making my hand into a fist or sticking out my tongue. My brain just knows how to do it. Science Division hates that answer, but it's the only one I can give them.

Oliver watches as I pull the unused EM lance out of the pocket, followed by the rest of the special equipment I was issued for this operation. We weren't sure how deep underground the item was buried, so there's a lot: shovels, pickaxes, chisels, electric and hand drills, deep radar and lidar scanners, subsonic resonators, laser cutters, a portable plasma torch, maser cannons, lots and lots of battery packs, several bricks of malleable explosives with matching remote detonators, bundles of Kazakhstani banknotes, and three field ration bars.

This accounting is one of our post-op rituals. I always keep a lot of stuff in the pocket—it's the size of an entire universe, so why not?—but the agency demands that certain equipment be accounted for periodically. Other things, like perishables or delicate machinery, wouldn't survive floating in deep space for more than a few days.

Most equipment that goes into the pocket has to be stored in therm-packs to prevent freezing. It takes Oliver a few minutes to unpack everything and lay it all out on the table. I tried to help him once, and he nearly ripped my head off for lining up a set of seemingly identical power cells in the wrong order. So now I just wait while he does the count.

"I see you got hungry in the desert," he says, putting the ration bars in what appears to be alphabetical order by flavor name. "Where's the canteen?"

"Sorry," I say. "Forgot it in the hovercar when the Rangers burned it."

The soldiers who airlifted me out of the desert also used pyro charges to destroy any trace of our having been there. I could have put the hovercar in the pocket, but it was a bit large for a souvenir.

Oliver gives me an exasperated look. "That was a thermal canteen. State of the art. Do you know how much trouble it was for us to develop that? Not even astronauts need special containers to keep their water liquid!"

"Give me a break, will you?" I say. "I drove through the desert for three days straight. I'd already melted out all the ice I had. I needed to rehydrate after using the pocket. I was taking stimulants to stay awake. It was an emergency situation."

Oliver glares at me. This is another familiar post-op ritual. "I'll look forward to reading your full report."

"Are we done here?" I ask. "I can come back later if you want to yell at me some more."

"Much later," he says, turning back to his flying disk. Is that a smirk on his normally languid face? "By the way, Science Division would like you to stop by and run some new scenarios for Project Backdoor."

"I just got home," I groan. "By the way, can we change that project name to something else? Anything else?"

Oliver shrugs. "It's descriptive. Quite elegant, really." He holds up his hand with the palm facing flat toward me. "Front door." He rotates his hand 180 degrees, so the palm faces him. "Back door. And it was *your* idea, as I recall."

He returns to tinkering with his flying disk. I imagine using my own palm to slap that grin off his face. The bastard knew letting me choose that ridiculous code name when I was a teenager would come back to haunt me later in life. Nobody at Science Division ever says "Project Backdoor"— they say "the rotation problem" to avoid snickering. And they say it a lot, because pocket rotation is kind of a big deal.

After I put something in the pocket, when I want to pull it out again, I can open the portal on the far side of the item, rotated 180 degrees around it. Because the portal is locked to the item in the pocket universe and my location in our universe, Newton's laws of motion dictate that if I threw the item into the "front door," it'll come flying out the "back door" at the same speed. I just have to make sure I associated the item with a reference object that has two distinct sides—like a room with two entrances.

The problem is, I can only reposition the portal in that specific way, on the far side of the item directly opposite its original placement. If I could arbitrarily adjust the angle of the portal with respect to the item, I could add a whole new set of party tricks to my repertoire. I wouldn't even need to carry a gun. We could just shoot a few bullets into the pocket, and I could later open it back up, rotated and pointed at my target. Wham, bam, thank you, physics.

Unfortunately, I'm the only one who can train myself to do that. And I have no idea how the pocket actually works. It's simply a thing I can do, like bending my fingers—and just like I can't bend my fingers backward, I can't arbitrarily rotate the pocket. It's one-eighty or nothing.

However, Science Division believes they can help me overcome this limitation, and they love thinking up increasingly outrageous methods to expand my mind.

"Are these new 'scenarios' going to involve psychotropic compounds or invasive electrodes?" I ask.

Oliver doesn't look up. "We can only hope."

"Boy, it's great to be home."

I run into Jessica on my way from Oliver's workshop to Paul's office. We stop in the corridor, facing each other, and she looks me up and down.

Jessica Chu, M.D., Ph.D., is the third person in my three-person department, and very scary. Well, she scares me, anyway. She doesn't actually frown or grimace all the time, but the sum of her thin, angular features is a permanent disapproving look. And her long, slender fingers give the appearance of claws, especially when she's holding some sharp medical instrument. Her job title is "Surgical and Medical Intervention Practitioner," which also doesn't help. I don't like the idea of anyone "intervening" with my bodily functions.

"What's with the suit?" she asks.

"Job interview," I say.

Her face is a mask. "I need to download your med logs."

"Nothing about the tie?" I ask, following her into the exam room. "It depicts an ancient Russian folk tale. Very cultural."

"Take off your shirt."

"Why, do you mean my button-front, Oxford-weave dress garment?" I didn't spend two hours with a clingy personal shopper to *not* have someone notice these threads.

"Or I can just use the scissors." She holds up a pair of trauma shears.

"Okay, okay."

I hang my jacket on a wall hook, then sit down on the plastic-covered bench and remove my necktie. I carefully pull the thin end back through the loop holding it together, not wanting to undo the knot. It took me fifteen minutes and an instruction manual to tie the damn thing this morning, and I want to keep it until after I see Paul.

I've barely gotten my shirt unbuttoned when Jessica yanks my left arm up and jams an electrode into my armpit.

"Are we in a hurry? Hey, careful with the merchandise!" She jabs another electrode up under my chin and slaps an interface patch over my left eye. Half my vision disappears as the computer starts downloading sensor logs from my various implants.

"You're dehydrated," she says, studying a display screen.

"Had to use the pocket." Physiologically, opening the pocket acts like a night of heavy drinking, sucking water out of my body and suppressing certain neurotransmitters. I basically get a hangover afterward. "And I wasn't sleeping."

"You had a water surplus. What happened to the ice?"

"Spilled most of it," I reply. "You try pulling a frozen brick through a hyperspace shunt while driving a hovercar through the desert."

I stare at the side of her head. Jessica hasn't looked at me once since she started the exam. That's not normal. Usually, when I get back from a mission, she's all over me like Martian dust on . . . well, everything on Mars. There's a reason they call it "the red planet." Those fine-grained ferrous particles get into every nook and cranny.

Similarly, when I report in, Jessica usually examines me from head to toe, checking everything from my back teeth to my bowel movements. I'm the only person we know of who's ever manifested any persistent superhuman ability, and the agency doesn't want their prize Kangaroo getting sick. It's Surgical's job to make sure I keep laying golden eggs. So to speak.

She's definitely distracted today. Is something else happening in the office? Something she doesn't want to tell me about? Am I in trouble?

Of course you're in trouble, Kangaroo. When are you not *in trouble?*

"Stay away from caffeine for the next few days," Jessica says, turning away from her screen to yank off my electrodes and eyepatch.

"Are you trying to kill me?" I say, slumping forward theatrically.

"Drink plenty of water. And don't skip the gym."

"I'm not," I lie.

"Don't lie," she says. How does she do that? "You always slack off after an operation."

I don't feel like it's a good time to debate her on this point. "Fine. I'll get all sweaty on the treadmill and catch up on my soap operas. Are we done?" I can ask her for a new emergency AED later.

"For now," she says. "Science wants to test you on the rotation problem again."

"Yeah, EQ told me. Can't you write me a note or something, Surge?"

"I'm not your mother," she says. "Also, stop making up stupid nicknames."

"No, see, 'Surge' is short for 'Surgical,' which is your actual job title—"

"Drink more water," Jessica says, emphasizing each syllable as if I'm hard of hearing. "We're done here."

She picks up her tablet and taps at it while walking out of the room. I get dressed in silence, wondering if I'm going to have bruises later.

Paul is on a vid call when I walk into his office. I probably should have knocked first, but I'm here now, and staying will be marginally less awkward than leaving. I quietly sit down in one of the two chairs in front of his desk.

The wrinkles around Paul's eyes and mouth make him look dignified rather than old. His gray hair reflects more light than you'd expect, looking almost silver. If he put on some weight and grew a beard, he might look like Santa Claus. With a beard and pointy hat, Merlin. With muttonchop sideburns, an eighteenth-century robber baron. Or was that the nineteenth century? Whenever people were still building railroads.

He looks the same as that first night I met him. For better or worse, he's been the one constant thing in my life for almost a decade now. Different assignments, different partners, different objectives. But it's always been Paul calling the shots.

I glance at the reversed vid image being projected onto the clear plexi screen rising out of his desktop. It looks like the Secretary of State.

"This is on you, Paul," the Secretary of State says. There's no mistaking that voice. "You said your boy could handle it."

Paul keeps his eyes on the screen, where the camera is mounted, and gestures with his right hand, pointing at the tray on the bookshelf against the wall. I get up and pour myself a glass of water. Of course he's already gotten the medical report from Jessica.

"He did handle it," Paul says. "We successfully retrieved the item."

"You and I seem to have different standards for 'success.'"

"We needed Kangaroo on this operation," Paul says. "The item was larger than our sources indicated. Nobody else could have gotten it out of Kazakhstan as efficiently as he did."

"We also seem to disagree on the definition of 'efficient.' He left an American body back there. And he put a Kazakh citizen in the goddamn hospital."

Hospital. So Ol' Whiskey-Breath didn't die. That's a relief.

"I've got three different ambassadors yelling at my staff," State says. "Once the President hears—"

"Let me deal with the President," Paul says.

"Oh, you will." State glares out of the screen. "But this audit is happening, Paul. Kazakhstan was the straw that broke the camel's back. NSC is taking a fine-toothed comb to anything tagged OUTBACK."

"I don't have time for this."

"Then you'll make time," State snaps. "Really, Paul, how long did you think we were going to let you run your own private little op center without any oversight?"

"I thought the subcommittee was more interested in overlooking."

"Not today, Paul. I'm not in the mood," State says. "You're going to get some visitors from Langley, and you're going to cooperate fully. Do you understand?"

"I understand." Paul's voice is cold.

State sighs. "Get your house in order. That's my advice. As a friend."

The screen image ripples and disappears, and the plexi sheet melts back into the flat, shiny desktop. Paul looks at me. He's not smiling. I gulp down the rest of my water and put my glass on the desk.

"Do you know why there was a group of Hungarian operators monitoring Russia–Kazakhstan border crossings?" he asks.

I purse my lips. "Because they were following the chicken?"

"Because the *actual* State Department asked them to watch for black market arms smugglers," Paul says.

"Kazakhstan needs more nukes? That seems unlikely."

"This is serious," he snaps. "Just in case your debriefing didn't make that clear."

I stare at my empty water glass. "It did."

"It's going to take a lot of diplomacy to smooth this one over. You'll have to stay benched for a while."

I nod. "I brought you a present."

Paul stares at me for a moment, then says, "All right."

I open the pocket above the surface of his desk, with the barrier in place. Paul should just see a wavy, partially reflective surface from his side of the phenomenon—that's what Science Division found under laboratory conditions. From my side, the portal looks like a cloudy white disk suspended in midair, a filmy portal into darkness.

I reach in, pull out the canteen, close the pocket, and start unlatching the canteen lid.

"Didn't you tell Oliver you lost that?" Paul asks.

"I'm easily confused." The airtight seal opens with a soft pop, and I pull out the glass jar. It's cool, but not frozen. I set it down on the desk with the label facing Paul.

I see his face light up for a split second. Of course he can't approve of this. "Where did you get this?"

"Atyrau, on the Caspian Sea."

"You know what I mean."

"Why do people peel the price tags off gifts before giving them?" I ask.

Paul frowns, puts the caviar in a desk drawer, stares at it for a moment, then slides the drawer shut.

Something's going on. It can't be a coincidence that Jessica seems so distracted today.

"Thank you," Paul says.

"You're welcome."

He opens another drawer. "You're going on vacation for a few weeks."

I nod. "I figured. Any research I can do while I'm at home?"

He pulls out a small folder. "You're going off-world."

I reach for the folder. "What's the job?"

Paul doesn't give me the folder. He lays it flat on his desk, puts a hand over it, and waits for me to look at him again.

"This is not an operation," he says. "You're going on vacation."

I don't think I've ever heard him say that word in my life. "I'm going where?"

He pushes the canteen across the desk, toward me. "I want you to return this to Oliver and apologize to him."

I pick up the canteen. "This, uh, 'vacation' isn't at a nice farm upstate, is it?"

He hands me the folder. I open it cautiously. Inside, there's a transport ticket, a set of legend identity papers, and a brochure for a pleasure cruise to Mars.

The planet Mars. Several hundred million kilometers away. Which I haven't been allowed to visit since before the war. I'm not sure I actually want to go back. But I'm pretty sure Paul isn't giving me a choice here.

"This department is being audited," Paul says. "State and CIA were developing a relationship with KNB, and your exfil raised several red flags in management."

KNB is Kazakh National Security. If CIA was also involved—and the Hungarian Special Service—my stomach starts turning.

"I've just been ordered to open up our files for internal review," Paul continues. "The brass are not going to like what they find, and I don't want you here for the fire drill."

It shouldn't bother me so much. Paul's sent me all the way to Pluto on missions before. But this is different. He doesn't need me to go do something crucial to national or planetary security. He just wants to get me out of his hair. Like a parent banishing a noisy child who's preventing the adults from getting their work done.

Maybe I'm still just a kid who can't stay out of trouble.

"What about EQ and Surge?" I ask. I don't like calling Oliver and Jessica by their names when I'm talking to Paul. And I don't like feeling helpless.

"We'll be fine. Your elevator leaves tonight. You'd better start packing." His look tells me I shouldn't argue any more. I stand up.

"Thanks for the ticket." It's a dumb thing to say, but I don't have anything else. My mind is a fog.

"You're welcome," Paul says. "Don't forget Oliver on your way out. He'll be happy to see his canteen again."

The door to Paul's office closes behind me, and I realize he didn't say anything about my suit. Not a word asking why I'm all dressed up, when I usually show up at the office in a short-sleeved shirt, jeans, and sneakers. I look down at my pointy-toed dress shoes. Man, I even paid to get these polished.

I can't decide whether Paul's inattention is more annoying than the fact that I have to apologize to Oliver about the canteen. At least the former distracts me from the latter.

Oliver and the flying disk are both gone when I return to the workshop. I place the canteen on the corner of the table, find a tablet that doesn't appear to be running any special software, open a blank note, and scrawl FOUND IT SORRY BYE on the touchscreen.

I place the tablet next to the canteen, then walk out of the workshop feeling strangely empty. Usually, when I leave that room, I've loaded up the pocket with gadgets and weapons, ready to take on the world. It occurs to me that even though I admire Oliver, I've never tried to make friends with him. Never asked him out for a drink, never asked about his family. I always thought I was keeping my work and personal lives separate, but now I realize I don't actually *have* much of a personal life.

What the hell am I going to do with an entire month off duty, and off-world?

I nearly walk into Jessica as she enters the corridor. I instinctively raise my hands, palms up, to show that I'm not touching anything inappropriate.

"Sorry," I say.

"No harm done," she says, resuming her walk toward the stairwell. "Enjoy your cruise."

I stare at the back of her white lab coat for a moment, then run after her, overtake her, and spin on my heel, blocking her path. She looks up with an annoyed expression.

"What's going on?" I ask.

She squints at me. "I *thought* you were leaving."

"You were distracted all through my exam," I say. "You didn't even take any blood or tissue samples."

"Do you *want* me to stick a needle in you?"

"No," I say, "that's not the point."

"So to speak."

Now she's scaring me. "I thought you were distracted by prepping whatever my next job was going to be, but now Paul's putting me on leave, so it can't be that." I narrow my eyes. "Did he finally agree to loan you out to another division? Is that it? You're moonlighting or something?"

She stares at me for a second. The corner of her mouth twitches, as if it might curl up into a smile, but it doesn't.

"Kangaroo, it's a good thing you're a field operative," she says, "because you'd make a lousy interrogator."

I raise my hand and point a finger at her mouth, accusingly. "See? You're almost smiling. This isn't normal. Tell me what's going on."

"It's nothing big," she says.

"Just tell me!"

"It's nothing big," she repeats, and actually smiles.

I have to deal with the cognitive dissonance of a genuine human emotion on Jessica's face before I can process the joke she's making.

"The nanobots?" I ask.

She nods. "Science Division approved my proposal."

The nanobots are the latest biotechnology to be added to my permanently implanted arsenal of espionage tools. They're the same microscopic machines that hide the doorways in the maze and reshape Paul's plexi desktop display, but retooled for medical use. Right now, several billion of them are flowing through my bloodstream and camped out in my soft tissues, maintaining a body-wide wireless mesh network for my other tech implants.

This is the first time the agency has actually put the nanobots into a human—thanks, guys, that's not worrisome at all!—and they want to make sure nothing catastrophically bad happens before doing anything more complicated with them. Everyone remembers what happened the last time somebody released swarms of untested biotech into Earth's atmosphere. No one wants another agricultural disaster followed by a decade of environmental cleanup.

Enough nanobots working together can assemble and disassemble just about anything at the atomic level. That's great if you can control them and potentially apocalyptic if you can't. Because of what happened during the Fruitless Year, no government is willing to openly support nanotech development—but in secret, every military wants their own tiny tin soldiers.

Fortunately, I have one of the best doctors on the planet watching out for me. And my agency-built nanotech is nothing like the hybrid swarms that killed apple trees all over the world. My nanobots are purely technological, with no biological factors that could mutate out of control. They do interact with my body, but these nanobots are only using some blood sugars as fuel to power very basic radio functions. Fewer wires connecting my implants means fewer ways for the network to break.

Jessica has been champing at the bit to write her own nanobot software ever since our superiors approved them for field use last year, and she's been frustrated by how slowly the bureaucracy moves. We may work in an above-top-secret black ops intelligence agency, but we still work for the government.

"I tested the remote-programming setup yesterday," Jessica says. "There are some version control issues, but nothing insurmountable. I can already flash small batches of nanobots in the lab."

"Wait, it's working already?" Now I'm excited. "When do I get my hollow leg?"

Her frown returns. "I don't know what that means."

"We talked about this. The ethanol-eating program? I drink all I want, but don't get intoxicated, and the nanobots use the alcohol for fuel?"

Jessica shakes her head. "I just got the system set up. We're nowhere near ready for live testing yet."

"Come on, this is the perfect opportunity," I say. "I'm going on a cruise. It's the ideal environment for evaluating—"

"This isn't just another implant," she says. "This is a very complex combination of individual moving parts and cluster control algorithms."

"You mean a swarm?"

"Don't use that word," she snaps. "We never use that word. Understand? It's going to be tough enough to get future nanotech projects approved without reminding people of what went wrong in the past."

"Fine," I say. I was too young to understand the Fruitless Year when it happened, but I remember how spooked all the adults around me were. And the sudden lack of delicious apple pies. "I won't say the S-word. But I'm being serious here. I'll be gone for weeks, and I plan to drink a *lot* of—"

"Stop talking." Jessica points toward the elevator. "Go away."

"I can't believe you of all people are passing up the opportunity to achieve a potentially paradigm-shifting scientific breakthrough!"

"One of us has two advanced medical degrees. The other one has been ordered to leave the planet." She pulls open the door to the stairwell. "I'll have a better idea of what's possible after you get back. Good-bye."

The door closes. I stare at it. Nanobots. Who knew?

If my department survives this audit, things are going to be very interesting when I get back from Mars.

CHAPTER THREE

Pearson's Beanstalk is a commercial space elevator anchored off the east coast of Florida. Its carbon nanotube cable rises forty thousand kilometers to geosynchronous orbit and beyond, counterweighted by a small asteroid. Construction of the Beanstalk was cofinanced by the Ellis-Baker Global Amusement Partnership, which had the resources to build a suitable anchor platform and then drag it from its most efficient equatorial position to a more profitable offshore position—less than an hour's drive from Orlando, where their Legendary Lands of Lore theme park is located.

Two habitat-sized "PeoplePods" climb the Beanstalk every week, one going up and one coming down. Their exteriors have been molded to resemble enormous green vines and leaves. The interior of my climber lives up to Ellis-Baker's reputation for magical presentation, re-creating mythical settings from ancient folk tales and fairy stories.

It's going to take a full week to get from sea level to the Sky Five orbital station, where I'll board my cruise ship to Mars. Ellis-Baker has built a variety of attractions inside the climber to delight and distract children, and others to mollify their parents during the ascent. Some of the Ellis-Baker theme parks used to be "dry" establishments, serving no alcohol, but you can't pack that many families into an enclosed space for seven days and not expect the adults to need some liquid happiness of their own.

There are faster ways than a space elevator to get into geosync orbit, but not for a civilian. Especially not for a civilian whose boss wants him to be very difficult to reach for the next month. Nobody's going to attempt to intercept a vehicle moving up the cable at two hundred kilometers per hour. The cruise ship will be even more isolated. Just talking to someone on Earth will be prohibitively expensive, and the lightspeed transmission delay will make live conversations impractical.

Yeah, I'm going to need quite a bit of liquor to get through this trip.

As soon as I board the climber, I go looking for the nearest bar. That turns out to be the Hope and Anchor, a full-sized replica of an English pub tucked in the Haunted Woods behind the Unicorn Clearing and just past the Gingerbread House. There's limited space in the climber, but Ellis-Baker knows how to make the most of their available construction volume.

I belly up to the fake wooden bar and order a real Imperial pint. The noise around me is comfortable. It's adult noise, low-pitched and rolling—not like the startled shrieks erupting from the fantasy forest outside at unpredictable intervals. Vid walls show replays of recent cricket and rugby matches. I could almost believe I'm in Ol' Blighty.

The bar's pretty crowded with sports fans, so I move toward one of the cleverly hidden staircases. The pub has four levels, each themed to a different historical era of the British Empire. I make a beeline for an empty Elizabethan booth and almost run into another man who's headed to the same place.

"Oh, I'm sorry," he says.

"No problem," I say.

"I really need to rest my legs," he says. "Do you mind sharing?"

"Fine by me."

We sit down across from each other. The man is elderly—retired, I'd guess. His skin is a few shades of brown darker than my own. Curly, short-cropped hair clings to his scalp in gray and white clumps, thinning at the top. His hands circle a glass of whiskey on the table.

"Well, this is nice, isn't it?" he says. I'm still trying to place his accent. Definitely somewhere on the eastern seaboard. He raises his glass. "Here's to some time spent away from children."

I lift my mug and clink it against his glass. "I couldn't agree more. Cheers."

He sips his drink. I wonder if he's just taking it slow, or if he doesn't usually indulge. I gulp down a good quarter of my pint.

"You traveling with your family?" the man asks.

"Oh no," I say. "No kids. I've just never ridden a space elevator before. Or been to the Big 'L.'" The Legendary Lands of Lore is a tourist mecca, and the largest of Ellis-Baker's many massive resort properties. "Figured I'd kill two birds with one stone."

It feels strange, actually telling the truth about myself, not using a cover story. It feels good. Or maybe that's just the beer talking. I take another swig.

"Recapturing your childhood," the man laughs. "I like that."

"And you?" I ask. I'm still in spy mode, trying to extract information without appearing to try too hard at it. Finding turns in the flow of conversation when it feels natural to insert a question, guiding the other person with well-placed acknowledgments or comments. It's like dancing, except you can end up with much worse than your foot getting stepped on.

"I'm here with my wife, and our grandkids," the man says. "They're probably still running around that 'haunted forest,' scaring themselves silly. I just needed a break. Not as young as I used to be."

I can't think of an appropriate follow-up, so I just sip my beer.

"My name's Donald," the man says, extending a hand.

I shake his hand. "Evan." Low security on this trip, but I still have to use an alias.

It strikes me that I'm actually looking forward to having some fun. I wasn't happy about Paul shoving me out the door, but now that I've resigned myself to my fate, I'm beginning to see the possibilities. No job to do. No exfil to worry about messing up.

I wonder how many days off the agency actually owes me, as a federal employer. My accrued vacation time must be at least three or four months by now. Maybe I could extend this trip beyond Mars. It's not like Paul could send someone after me, if I decided to up and disappear into the asteroid belt.

He might even be impressed by my tradecraft. There's a thought.

"So I'm guessing this trip wasn't your idea," I say.

Donald laughs. "Now why would you think that?"

I shrug. "Seems like you and your wife could find better things to do with your time than two solid weeks of babysitting."

"Oh, I love my grandkids," Donald says. "You're still young, but believe me, you'll understand when you get older. When you can't do certain things any more, it's nice to be around people who can."

"Interesting," I say. I don't quite believe him, and something about his phrasing strikes me as odd. I drink more beer, trying to turn off the overly analytical part of my brain. All work and no play makes Kangaroo a dull boy.

"My daughter and her husband were supposed to bring the kids on this trip," Donald continues. "Big family thing. But you know how it is: urgent project at work, last-minute meetings, and suddenly they're stuck with nonrefundable tickets they can't use."

"Lucky for you."

Donald laughs again. The sound triggers a tiny alarm bell in the back of my head.

One of the first things I learned at the agency was how to play poker. Not because Paul expected I'd have to go undercover into a lot of casinos, or because he wanted me to socialize and make friends—nobody at the agency actually plays cards for fun. Too many damn cheaters.

Poker and other bluffing games are a structured way to learn how to spot a lie. And that's the first step toward developing an instinct for when a situation's not quite right. Even if you're not aware of the specific microexpression that belies someone's facade or the one incongruous detail that throws off the layout of a room, your subconscious is already yelling *Danger, Will Robinson!* And that's what I'm feeling right now.

But I've learned the hard way that falsehoods don't always mean danger. Everyone's got secrets. Donald probably has family issues, unresolved father-daughter stuff that he's not telling me about but which is at the top of his mind right now. It's not important. I drink more beer.

"I hear they got nine holes of golf in here," Donald says. "You play golf?"

The thing at the back of my head goes to Red Alert. *Too friendly,* it says. *Too forward, too much, too soon. Not right.*

I smile and shake my head. "Never quite got the hang of it." I decide to lay a trap. "I prefer swimming."

"Yeah? I hear there's a low-gravity pool on the top floor."

He's trying to get me to talk. Who the hell is this guy? Who even knows I'm here?

Okay, Donnie, let's see what you're hiding.

I make some inane comment about swimming being good exercise while I bring my left ring finger up to the side of my mug. I do it on the side closest to me, so the remaining brown ale will hide my movements from Donald. I press my pinky inward, squeezing the sides of my ring finger together. I squeeze, hold, release, and repeat three times, feeling the subdermal contacts tingle. My left eye HUD lights up, filling my vision with a false color overlay.

Donald's got a variety of implants, but just about everyone does these days. Mobile phone in his right shoulder, vision correctors in both eyes, personal data recorder in his left armpit. Nothing unusual there. I twitch a finger on my left hand, and my eye zooms in on the data pod in his armpit and switches imaging modes. Lines of magnetic force leak from the sides of the pod. That tells me how much power it's using, how much shielding it has—

I try not to act too surprised or hurried as I gulp down the rest of my beer.

"Get you another?" I ask. Donald shakes his head. "Be right back."

I stand up with my empty mug and make my way back to the bar. I leave the mug and walk out of the pub without looking back.

If "Donald" is who I think he is, there's trouble brewing back at the office.

The Ellis-Baker Adventurers' League Golden Society membership card that came with my travel documents has proven very useful. It got me past all sorts of lines inside the Legendary Lands of Lore and at the Beanstalk's boarding platform. Now it grants me access to a private office in the climber's business center.

The receptionist's eyes widened when she ran the card—probably seeing my outrageous credit limit—but the pleasant expression on her face remained otherwise unmarred. These people are well trained. Ellis-Baker theme park cast members would probably make pretty good spies, if it weren't for all the killing.

The office I'm renting has a transparent plexi door. A desk extends from one wall, with a chair on the far side. A screen faces the back wall. The receptionist, Wendy, pulls out the control console and leaves me to do my business.

I sit down at the desk and slide my gold card into the reader slot. The screen lights up with an animated character and a block of instructions. I look around the office. No obvious cameras, but I've already seen two other people walk past this room.

I take off my jacket and drape it over the screen and my head. I'm sure it looks ludicrous, but if anyone asks, I can claim there was glare on the display and I couldn't read the text. What are they going to think I was doing?

I open the pocket directly in front of the screen, just large enough to get my hand through. The barrier glows with a soft white light. Nobody's sure what causes that, since there shouldn't be any energy bleeding through from the pocket universe. Science Division has a whole truckload of theories about how it works, and every now and then, Oliver will try to explain something about virtual particles or quantum foam until I get tired of listening and wander off to find a snack. When the white coats aren't investigating the pocket itself, they're trying to reverse-engineer the barrier. So far, no luck on either project.

The pocket universe is hard vacuum. Without the barrier in place, the air in our universe will rush through the opening, and won't stop until I close the portal. The first time I ever opened the pocket, I accidentally sucked a bag of peanuts into the void and almost spaced the squirrel I was feeding. Kind of freaked out my best friend, too. He wouldn't talk to me for a week, until I realized the pocket was a perfect tool for shoplifting ice cream. Then we had to figure out how to get the frozen treats back out.

I was able to rotate the pocket before I first manifested the barrier. Priorities, you know. The barrier didn't help us retrieve our ice cream. But rotating the pocket 180 degrees around whatever item fell in will make the same item fall back out. Later on, I realized that being able to *put* things in the pocket, instead of just using the vacuum to suck them in, was much more versatile.

It took months of practice to figure out how to make the barrier semipermeable: thin enough to move items through, but not so thin that too much atmosphere leaks into the pocket. I need to concentrate harder than usual to get the field strength just right.

My mouth feels dry, and I struggle to pull my notebook through the barrier. Really shouldn't have downed that beer so quickly. Alcohol plus pocket use equals prizewinning pocket hangover later.

The screen casts barely enough light for me to make out the carrier code for the agency comsat relay. I mouth the numbers to myself silently, repeating them until I'm sure I can remember them for a few minutes, then put the notebook back in the pocket.

Revealing agency access codes would be bad, so I continue hiding under the jacket as I route my call through a military communications satellite. The last mile from the comsat to the Beanstalk will still be transmitted in the clear, but it's a short enough distance that the risk is minimal.

The screen flickers, and Paul's face appears. He's not in his office. The view behind him looks like Oliver's workshop.

"Kangaroo to Lasher," I say, using our respective code names. I don't want him to think this is a personal call.

Paul interjects before I can continue. "You're not walking the dog."

He means I'm transmitting in the clear. Reminding me that our conversation may not be private. It's a fair point, but I'm not planning to discuss any state secrets.

"Fido's taking a nap," I say. "But another mutt is following me."

Paul leans forward. "Did you take him to the vet?"

"Just got him X-rayed." I describe Donald's physical appearance and implants. "The data pod's new; surgery scars are recent. Commercial unit, available to civilians, but it's been modded with a military-grade hard crypto unit. I verified the—why are you looking at me like that?"

Paul's frown has shifted from concern to consternation. "Did you learn his name?"

"Donald," I say. "Wait, do you know this guy?"

"I do."

"Then you can find out who else is on his team." I'm getting excited now. "These auditors are playing dirty pool. They're probably setting up 'off-site meetings' for you and Surge and EQ too. But if you can identify the actors—"

"Stand down, Kangaroo," Paul says, his face once again a stoic mask. "We're not being targeted. *I* sent Donald to talk to you."

My excitement vanishes. "What?"

"I apologize for the subterfuge," he says. "Our friends at the office wanted a current psychological profile. You've never enjoyed those evaluations."

"So you decided to *trick* me into getting psychoanalyzed?"

"I was hoping you wouldn't notice."

Now I'm insulted. "And you couldn't find anyone better than Donald, the second-rate con man? Or do you just think I'm a moron?"

"We should talk about this later. After your vacation."

I feel anger heating my face, but the professional part of me knows raising my voice would attract unwanted attention. And I look silly enough already, hiding under my jacket to make a vid call.

"You really want me to sit on this for four more weeks?" I say. "Maybe I'll go back to the bar and get really drunk and start telling all sorts of people about my horrible boss."

His face doesn't change. Of course not. Paul's been playing this game a lot longer than I have. He's not going to lose his cool just because I am.

"I shouldn't have rushed this. I apologize. We'll have you sit down for a normal evaluation when you get back. Donald will not follow you onto the cruise ship. Nobody else will bother you on your way to Mars."

It's hard to be angry at someone when he's already addressed all your concerns with reasonable solutions. I try to summon some sort of indignation, but can only come up with a general platitude.

"People lie to me all the time," I say. "I don't want you to be one of them."

"I made a mistake. I hope you can forgive me."

And there it is. I should feel better about the tables being turned like this: it's Paul who screwed up, not me. But I just feel deflated. He's not supposed to screw up. He's supposed to protect me. He's supposed to protect all of us.

The silence is more than awkward; it's oppressive. I give up and change the subject.

"How's everything at the office?" I ask.

"Fabulous," Paul says, his lip curling. "You'll notice I'm hiding in Equipment's workshop."

"I thought you'd just redecorated."

Paul's eyes flick up for an instant. "I'm afraid I have to go answer more uncomfortable questions," he says. "If you call again, I expect there to be blood and interplanetary armageddon at stake."

"So you're saying don't call."

"Please try to enjoy your vacation."

The screen goes dark. I sit there for a moment, until the animated—dog? cat? weasel? what the heck *is* that thing?—bounces back into view and tells me how much my little chat just cost. I am so glad I'm not paying for this vacation myself.

CHAPTER FOUR

Earth orbit—Sky Five docking station
1 hour before the food court stops serving brunch

The Princess of Mars Cruises' flagship passenger liner *Dejah Thoris* is even larger than the Beanstalk climber, but a smaller portion of its interior volume is used to house passengers. The rest is the fuel supply, power plant, main engines, and cargo bays. It's one of the largest civilian spacecraft ever built, and that says a lot about human civilization: we have slipped the surly bonds of Earth, now let's party hearty.

I watch from Sky Five's main observation lounge as small tugs and spacesuited workers load supplies and freight onto *Dejah Thoris*. The ship is shaped like an egg, with a rectangular section cut out of its midsection on one side. Cargo containers are secured in that niche with scaffolding and latches and cables. At the small end of the egg is command and control. The large end hides the main drive reactor, which reveals itself in a honeycomb of engine bells.

This is going to be my home for the next week. I don't think I've ever spent that long on a civilian ship. *Vacation.* What do people actually *do* on vacation?

I suppose I'll start with heavy drinking and take it from there. Maybe I'll consider this a research trip: practicing how to camouflage myself within a civilian population.

My boarding group is called just after lunchtime. A bellhop in a ridiculous outfit, apparently intended to look like a nonspecific navy uniform, leads me to my stateroom. We weave past other passengers adrift in zerogravity and service robots trundling luggage up and down the corridors. I do not laugh out loud at the lopsided beret attached to the bellhop's head.

I do not sneer at the faux-luxurious decorations that cover every square centimeter of the vessel's interior: Rubenesque cherubs, brushed-metal abstract sculptures, oversaturated astronomy photos. I am playing the part of a clueless tourist who *wants* to be here.

I do tip my attendant generously, in cash, because I feel sorry for anyone who has to look like he does all day, especially floating through these garish hallways in zero-gee. We won't have gravity until the ship starts moving, just before dinnertime.

My stateroom is far too spacious for one person. I imagine that's why all the crew members kept raising their eyebrows when they saw that I was in an executive suite. It's four fully furnished rooms, each with a vid wall masquerading as a window. The walls show views of Sky Five that are all wrong for my current location, ten decks below the bridge and halfway to the centerline of the ship.

I find the wall controls and change them to display the Las Vegas Strip at night. If my view's going to be unreal, it might as well be fabulously unreal.

In the front room, next to the doorway leading to the bedroom, are a work desk and a wet bar. Velcroed to the top of the bar is a large basket filled with fresh fruit, candy, and liquor. I pluck the card from the basket and open it.

> Kanga:
> Welcome to your home away from home. Enjoy the trip. Don't forget to exercise.
>
> —Christopher Robin
> P.S. I've arranged a dinner seating for you at the Captain's Table. Please do your best not to embarrass your country.

Paul's sense of humor is more like a humor singularity, from which nothing funny can escape. But the booze in the gift basket is pretty good.

I take a mini-bottle of rum over to the computer built into the work desk. Now that I know where I'm going tonight, I can't resist doing some reconnaissance.

Edward Gabriel Santamaria, the captain of *Dejah Thoris,* stands nearly two meters tall. He towers over everyone else in the dining room as he strides toward the table where I'm seated for dinner with eight complete strangers. Even in this huge, multilevel space filled with people and noise, he stands out. Also because of the cam-bot hovering at his shoulder for passenger photo-ops.

I've read up on the captain. Not in depth—without a secure communications link, I don't have access to the agency's full data warehouse—but the promotional materials provided in my room were a start. An omnipedia search on the public Internet provided additional background.

It might seem silly for me to do all this, when I'll just have to pretend I don't know these things later. I'm sitting at the Captain's Table every night at dinner. Wouldn't it be easier, and less confusing, to ask about his life instead of investigating him in secret? Especially when I'm not even on the job, and there's no need for me to do the extra legwork?

I mean, it's not like I have anything to prove here. It's not like I want to demonstrate to Paul and Donald and the Secretary of State and anyone else who might be watching—now or later—that I can fly solo, that I can complete a mission without a babysitter. It's not like I'm going out of my way to show off my operational skills so everyone can see that I am, in fact, *not* the weakest link in the chain.

And I'm certainly not doing this because it's easier to think of "Kangaroo on vacation" as a cover identity than to figure out what I would actually enjoy doing as myself, without orders or instructions, without any kind of direction.

Boy, whichever agency shrink draws the short straw when I get back is going to have a whale of a time. At least they won't be able to grill me about my mother. I suppose that's one of the few benefits of being an orphan.

"Good evening, everyone," the captain says as he arrives at the large circular table. Up close, his white dress uniform isn't quite as ridiculous as the bellhop's was, but the huge shoulderboards and thick gold braids dangling under his arms look like they could lead a parade all by themselves.

We go around the table and introduce ourselves once again. I was the first one here, and I've heard some of these spiels three or four times now. It's interesting to watch how people puff up in the captain's presence. The man sitting directly across from me, Jerry Bartelt, said he was a salesman when he first sat down, but now he's a "regional sales director." Whoa there, slow down, big man. I won't be surprised if Jerry pulls out a cosmetics sample case or a set of steak knives for a demonstration at some point.

The captain politely gives everyone their fifteen seconds in the spotlight, including a handshake or hug for the cam-bot to record as a souvenir holo. He's got a pretty good mask on, smiling and nodding with great sincerity, but I can see in his eyes that he's done this a lot, and it's a bit too soon since the last time for him to really enjoy it. But he's not distracted, not preoccupied or thinking about something else. He is actually listening to each person, quietly validating their claim that they're important or interesting enough to be sitting at the Captain's Table. I wonder how much my seat here is costing the department.

I'm sitting to the captain's right, on purpose, so I'm the last to introduce myself.

"Evan Rogers," I say, extending my hand. I'm normally not much for excessive touching, but this is part of the role I'm playing.

The captain shakes my hand. I feel calluses on his palm and thumb. "A pleasure to meet you, Mr. Rogers. How are you enjoying your journey so far?"

"Oh, it's fantastic," I say, gushing just a little, not wanting to sell it too hard. "This is my first time on a cruise spaceship. I can't wait to try out all the different activities."

"And what do you do for a living?" he asks.

"Oh, I work for the U.S. State Department," I say, waving a hand, drawing attention to myself while pretending to be dismissive. "I'm a trade inspector."

"What kind of trade?" asks the captain. The question comes a fraction of a second too quickly. He's not just being polite; he's actually interested in the answer.

"Interplanetary," I say. "Imports, exports, tariffs, duties, taxes. Most people don't realize how much commerce there is between all the inner planets and our asteroid belt colonies. And of course, trade regulations have changed quite a bit since the war."

I don't have to name the conflict. Everyone knows I'm talking about the Independence War. A lot of things changed after Mars graduated from being a colony world to a full-blown planetary rival, and most of them don't make anybody happy.

All eight of the other passengers at the table are from Earth, six of them are American, and four are especially patriotic and talkative. The captain's eyes are livelier now, watching with genuine interest. He no longer needs to drive the conversation. I wonder how many of his dinner guests expect him to be the master of ceremonies throughout the entire meal.

The background music in the dining room fades for a moment, and a male announcer's voice tells us that *Dejah Thoris* has passed Lunar orbit and is now in interplanetary space. A smattering of applause follows, and then the music resumes.

One of the women at my table asks the captain how fast we're traveling. He consults his wristband display and answers her precisely, in kilometers per hour, then adds that the ship is still accelerating—that's why it feels like we have gravity.

"Just under nine meters per second squared," Santamaria says. "That's about ninety percent of Earth normal."

Dejah Thoris will continue accelerating, he explains, until we reach "midway"—the middle waypoint of our trip, halfway between Earth and Mars—on the fourth day. Then the engines will throttle down until the ship's at zero acceleration again, propelled forward only by inertia, and we'll be in freefall. That will last for one full day, during which several sections will be converted into weightless open spaces. Passengers can register for sessions of various zero-gee activities, aided by crew chaperones and recorded by flying cam-bots like the one following the captain around now.

Everyone else at the table looks excited—"Weightless Day" is one of the big selling points of this cruise—and I feign enthusiasm. These people haven't suffered through hundreds of hours of military spacewalk training. Well, maybe Captain Santamaria. His beard hides most of his face, but his skin is aged and mottled from exposure. I wonder if he was in the Outer Space Service before retiring to this cushy job.

Santamaria continues his breakdown of our voyage. During midway, *Dejah Thoris* will slowly rotate until the ship is facing backward, with the engines pointing in our direction of travel. Then everyone will go to sleep, and wake up again under point nine gravity, only this time we'll be decelerating until we reach Mars orbit.

The purpose of all this, he explains, is to shorten the time it takes to make the trip. We build up a lot of speed during the first half, and we need to burn it off during the second half, otherwise we'd completely overshoot our target at several thousand kilometers per hour. Once we get to Mars, we'll dock with the space elevator there, and the passengers will disembark to continue our holiday on the red planet.

That includes me. I'll ride the Mars elevator down and meet my contact in Capital City, who will tell me whether it's safe for me to go back to

Earth. If so, I'll board a high-gee military transport and endure a fast return trip—hours instead of days. If not, I've got a date with the tourist traps around the Martian polar ice caps.

The last time I saw those ice caps was the day the Independence War started. I saw them out the window of a private spaceplane, one of the last vessels to break Mars orbit before Earth warships established a blockade. Paul recalled me as soon as the shooting started. I was ready to evacuate— as the most junior agent at Galle Crater station, I routinely got stuck with the least interesting surveillance and maintenance tasks—but I didn't expect to be the only passenger on that flight home.

I never asked Paul how difficult or expensive it was to get me off Mars that day. I don't really want to know.

Our Captain's Table dinner arrives. It is an extravagant, multicourse indulgence of red meat, seafood, more meat, hot cheese fondue, meat stuffed inside another kind of meat, and perfunctory helpings of bread and vegetables. I'm not complaining—I like animal protein as much as the next red-blooded omnivore—but I do watch the reactions of my dinner companions carefully, noticing who goes for which dishes and how they attack each course.

The captain takes a small portion of every one of the seemingly endless varieties of meat offered by the servers—but only a small portion. He doesn't dip into the cheese, but dumps a lot of salt on his vegetables. I wonder if he's had any heart attacks or stern warnings from his cardiologist yet.

I resist the urge to turn on my eye and look inside his chest. The implant is for work. My own, biological, limited eyes are for play. And I'm having fun guessing at who people are from just their appearance and manner.

My seat at the Captain's Table came with a bottle of fancy wine, and I drink half of it before I realize how much it's affecting me. I'm talking loudly, possibly even flirting with the woman to my right who keeps touching my elbow. I can't remember her name. That seems bad. My medical sensors say my body temperature is several degrees above normal. I switch to water, not wanting to regret anything in the morning.

After dinner, there's a live band and dancing in the ballroom below, but I escape and find my way up to the Promenade.

The shops and tables here offer items ranging from the extravagant to the mundane, all easily charged to a passenger's account with one swipe of the thumb. Jewelry, liquor, clothing, toys, reader tablets, sewing kits, and "personal items," as a discreet sign proclaims. Makes sense. There's no getting off this ship for the next six days, so everything a passenger might want or need has to be available on board.

This section is just inside the outer hull, with a long stripe of transparent window running overhead. There's not much to see outside, just blackness and the occasional glint of a distant asteroid or spaceship. Normally space vehicles wouldn't have many windows, if any—the radiation danger is too severe. But most of the ionizing radiation in this part of the Solar System comes from the Sun, and the entire bulk of the ship and all those cargo containers are shielding the passenger sections.

I walk down the length of the Promenade, stretching my arms and legs and looking up at the void, but really I'm here to watch the people. Most of them are drunk to some degree. The sober ones are more interesting. I surreptitiously study a family of four and guess, based on the younger child's hair color and earlobe shape, that Mom did some fooling around. But Dad's attitude toward both children—eye contact, tone of voice, touching behavior—implies that he knows, and he's okay with it. Interesting.

I suddenly realize I'm completely lost. Should have studied those deck plans more closely. I stop at an information kiosk, my mildly inebriated brain momentarily mesmerized by its vid loop of a woman in a slinky dress holding up a dessert tray, advertising a nearby late-night buffet. As if the nine different kinds of cake at dinner weren't enough.

Someone walks up and stops beside me. I'm surprised to see that it's Captain Santamaria, sans cam-bot. I guess the show's over for tonight.

"Captain," I say, nodding.

"Mr. Rogers," he says.

We both stare at the dessert lady for a moment.

"That's not your real name," Captain Santamaria says, "is it?"

"I'm adopted," I say.

He smiles, then looks me in the eye. "Fair enough."

We stare at each other. I feel like he's gotten some sort of advantage on me, and I furiously try to make some further deduction by studying his face. Can I tell anything more about his personal history from his complexion? Those acne scars covering his cheeks? I'm severely tempted to turn on my eye scanners and see what kind of tech implants he's got.

"Not a lot of kids around now," Santamaria says.

I nod. "It's pretty late."

"And this is not a cultural playground."

It takes my wine-addled brain a couple of seconds to recognize what he's saying. And then I still can't believe it. But before I know what I'm doing, my training—the often-absurd behavior that's been drilled into me by the agency—takes over.

"Children's fitness is of much interest to me," I say.

"A grandfather never exhibits such things."

He looks away. The code phrases are a few months out of date, but they're agency protocol. Those three lines of strange dialogue are how our field agents identify themselves to each other when they can't use other means, or when there's a chance they'll be overheard by hostile forces.

Santamaria works for the agency. And he wanted me to know that.

"Enjoy the rest of your night," he says, looking back at the kiosk. "And if you go here"—he gestures at the restaurant advertisement—"try the strawberry cheesecake. It's excellent."

Paul picked this ship. He picked *this* ship. He must have known who the captain was.

"Thanks," I say. "Maybe I will."

What does this mean? Why did Paul put me at the Captain's Table for dinner? What did he want me to notice? What does he want me to do?

"Goodnight, Mr. Rogers," Santamaria says.

I watch him walk away, hands folded behind his back. He moves with the slightest hint of a limp—chronic condition? Combat injury? Did he captain a warship before *Dejah Thoris*? Did the agency recruit him before or after he got this civilian command? How well does Edward Santamaria know Paul Tarkington?

What the hell are you trying to tell me, Lasher?

I don't know about the cheesecake, but I definitely need another drink.

CHAPTER FIVE

Dejah Thoris—Deck 10, Promenade
At least 2 hours past my bedtime

"Is this your first time?"

Jerry Bartelt, the salesman from dinner, is standing next to me. I've wandered into a little alcove off the main Promenade, a semicircular area with colorful interactive displays about Mars. You know, for kids. I'm having some trouble with the controls, which consist of four gigantic red buttons.

"Nah. Just had a little too much to drink," I say. The "strawberry cheesecake" turned out to be a fancy cocktail, and the bartender at the late-night buffet was very liberal with his pours. I half expected him to be another agent, leading me on some kind of covert scavenger hunt, and it took me several drinks to figure out that nope, he's just working for tips.

You seriously need to get out more, Kangaroo.

I stab at another button and miss again. "I'll get it sooner or later."

Jerry smiles. "I meant going to Mars."

"Oh, that." I finally manage to hit one of the buttons, and the big screen in the center of the alcove lights up with a rotating image of the red planet. "Yeah, first time off-world. You?"

"I've been there a few times. On business. This time it's personal."

"Vacation," I say.

Jerry nods. He's watching the display very closely. Too closely? His eyes dart back and forth as place markers fade in and out on the surface, showing us where the cities and major geological features are. Is he looking for something?

"No wife and kids?" I ask.

"Divorced," he says. "No children. She kept the dog. I had him cloned, but it just wasn't the same."

It takes me a moment to process this information. "You cloned your dog?"

"Well, technically, by that point, it was my ex-wife's dog," Jerry says. "But it was in the pre-nup. If we ever got a pet, and then got divorced, if the pet was still alive at the time of the divorce, one of us would get to clone it."

"That's a little unusual," I say.

"It was her idea," Jerry says. "She could be a little, you know, clingy sometimes."

"So how did you decide who got the clone?"

"Flipped a coin."

"I suppose that was in the pre-nup, too."

Jerry smiles and exhales a puff of proto-laughter, as if he's not sure whether he should be amused at this. "You know lawyers. They want you to specify everything."

I nod and manage to push another button. A large title tells us the image of Mars is switching to an elevation view, and the rusty orange globe fades into oversaturated blues, yellows, greens, and reds. The bands of color shimmer as the animated image rotates. Some parts of the map are just a little blurrier than the others. A civilian observer might not notice the difference, but I recognize those areas as battlefields from the Independence War.

At first, the fighting was limited to the area around Hellas Planitia. Earth Coalition didn't want to confront the Martian Irregulars on their home turf, especially not in the mountains or near the poles. But Mars is a small planet without a breathable atmosphere. The only possible hiding places were underground, and those were susceptible to orbital bombardment.

All the dark circles spinning past on the globe are craters. Most of them are manmade. Some of those places will be uninhabitable due to radiation for another decade or more.

I see a blue smudge across a green crater near the east edge of Argyre Planitia, just below two yellow dots, and I feel a pang of recognition. Galle Crater. We used to call it "Happy Face Crater"—that's what the dune formations looked like from orbit, before Earth Coalition shot down a Martian flyer there. Now it's just a faceless crash site.

The Martian Irregulars had been attempting reconnaissance of the EC troops landing at Argyre, not anticipating they'd land with effective anti-aircraft weapons. But before crashing, the Martian pilot set the flyer's auto-destruct to trigger on impact. The blast obliterated the curved "smile" dune and everything within a fifty-meter radius—around, above, and below.

The agency's Galle Crater station was barely thirty meters underground. It was my first assignment after getting my field agent certification, and the post I vacated on the first day of what turned out to be the Independence War. I didn't want to stay, but I still felt bad abandoning my fellow station officers in the middle of a crisis.

I never saw any of them again.

"Are you staying in Capital City?" Jerry asks.

I shake my head. "Polar ice cap tour. One of those package deals. You?"

"I . . . haven't decided yet," Jerry says.

His expression is thoughtful as he studies the thermal view of Mars, and it suddenly occurs to me to be suspicious. What kind of divorced, middle-aged salesman takes a multiweek vacation on impulse, without planning, and without any traveling companions? No girlfriend, no drinking buddy, not even a destination he's been dying to see since childhood?

Just as suddenly, it occurs to me that I could easily be describing myself—at least, my cover story. But I'm playing a tourist. I *have* somewhere to go and something to do. Jerry seems to have neither in mind.

"What are you running from, Jerry?" I ask.

He hangs his head. "Is it that obvious?"

"I should also add that I'm not looking to hook up," I say.

We stare at each other, then both burst out laughing.

"Sorry," Jerry says after catching his breath. "I didn't mean to give you the wrong idea."

"'Sokay," I say. "Comes with the territory when you look as good as I do."

I have trouble finishing the sentence. Jerry doubles over with laughter, and I clutch the railing next to the control panel to keep from falling over. It feels good to laugh. Even if it did take two or three liters of alcohol to get here.

An elderly couple walks past and looks at us as if we're crazy. I point at the display and call out to them. "Mars! It's hilarious!"

I feel something at my elbow and turn to see a uniformed crew member giving me the stink-eye. He's young, early twenties maybe, and his slim build belies his strength. He gets a firm grip on my arm and stands me upright.

"Can I help you gentlemen find your way back to your berths?" he says.

At first I think he's saying "births" and I wonder why he's being so philosophical and metaphorical. My alcohol-soaked brain rolls the first coherent words it finds down to and out of my mouth.

"I never knew my mother," I say. "Not really. I mean, maybe I was an orphan and maybe I wasn't. Who's to say? You don't know. Who are you again?"

The crewman stares at me impassively, and some small, quiet part of my brain wonders how often he has to do this. He taps his glowing blue earpiece with one hand and says, "Guest assistance in Promenade section four, please."

Two more crewmen appear behind him. One is a taller, bulkier fellow, and the other is a woman, about the same height as Blue-Ear but more muscular. The new arrivals are wearing the same blue earpieces, so I decide I need to make up different nicknames for them.

"I'll call you 'Chunk,'" I say to the bulky fellow, pointing a finger past him down the corridor. I turn and smile at the woman. "And you're 'Daisy.'"

Daisy frowns at Blue-Ear. "Didn't I see these two at the Captain's Table tonight?"

Blue-Ear nods. "Yeah. Captain must have been feeling generous with the vino."

Something clatters behind me. I turn my head to look at the same time that Blue-Ear spins us both around, and the effect is more than a little dizzying. *Have I really drank that much? Drunk that much? Is it "drank" or "drunk"? Shit.*

Suddenly I'm staring at the high ceiling of the Promenade and I have a very strong sense of vertigo. There's no up or down in space, right? But I'm feeling gravity. That ceiling is very far away. This is all very confusing.

My free arm, the one not being held by Blue-Ear, swings out, searching for something solid to brace against. My hand clutches at a shoulder. I pull myself upward and see that it's Daisy, not looking very happy about this interaction.

"Sorry," I say. "Seem to be having trouble with my balance—"

She pushes my hand away, but it swings back toward her—that arm appears to be even more confused than the rest of my unsteady body. Daisy deflects it again, this time grabbing my forearm and using my momentum to spin me back around to face Blue-Ear. He grabs my collar and yanks me forward, away from Daisy.

"That's great," she says. "I was wondering if I'd get groped tonight."

"On the bright side," Blue-Ear says, "just two more and you'll get your self-defense stripes."

"Funny."

"Was an accident," I say over my shoulder. The dizzy feeling intensifies, and my face smacks into Chunk's palm. He pushes me back up and grabs my disobedient arm. "Oh, hey, thanks."

"Let's move out of the thruway, sir," Blue-Ear says.

Daisy eyes me as I struggle in his and Chunk's grip. "You want any help there, Mac?"

"We got this one," Chunk says. "You might want to grab that other guy before he puts his head through the screen. Or worse."

"Frozen crap on a stick," Daisy mutters, then goes after Jerry, who's crawling over the railing and into the display alcove.

My uninhibited male brain can't help but admire Daisy's backside as she leans forward and pulls Jerry back from the edge, and I'm momentarily envious of him. Why aren't I the one being manhandled by the athletic Valkyrie?

"Hey," I say to Chunk and Blue-Ear as they drag me away. My legs don't seem to be working, and my feet drag along the deck, making occasional squeaking noises. "I'm not drunk, you know."

"Whatever you say, sir," Blue-Ear says.

"I've got a hollow leg!" I think I'm singing now. Jerry appears to be dancing with Daisy, or possibly wrestling. Hard to tell from here.

"Just another Sunday night, huh, Greg?" Chunk says to Blue-Ear.

Blue-Ear shakes his head. "Glad I joined the navy."

There are no clocks anywhere on this ship. Well, not literally, but there are no time-telling devices in most places where they would actually be useful to passengers. No clocks in my stateroom, no clocks in the elevators, no clocks in the dining areas. It's somewhat counterintuitive, considering how tightly scheduled all shipboard activities are. For example, breakfast service ends at 11:00 a.m. precisely—and I mean *precisely*; there's actually a metal shutter that closes over the buffet area—and lunch doesn't start until 11:30, so there's a whole half-hour when the only food option available appears to be vegetation from the cocktail bars.

Okay, it's probably not quite that bad, but that's how it feels when I stagger out of bed at 11:05, wondering just how much alcohol I consumed last night. I shamble from one dining area to another, watching other passengers finish off their meals and gazing forlornly at the closed-off serving sections where, mere minutes ago, heaping piles of hot, salty, possibly deep-fried foods were just waiting to be shoved into my face.

I spend probably a full minute staring at a half-eaten strip of bacon on someone's discarded plate, at war with myself over whether to stoop that low, until a boxy cleaning robot comes along and clears the table. My stomach rumbles. My head hurts. A lot.

I have many important questions to consider. Why Paul put me on this ship. What it means that the captain is also in the loop. But most important, where the hell I'm going to find some goddamn food right now.

If this were a planned mission, I'd have emergency rations in the pocket. But it's not, so I don't. And those analgesics I pulled earlier expired and froze solid two years ago. I took them anyway. They didn't help.

The word HEADACHE pops into my head, followed by the word REMEDIES. Not just the words as abstract concepts—those specific letters, rendered in a very specific font. And this is in my memory, not in my HUD. Why am I remembering this? Where did I see this?

Then the full image blossoms in my consciousness, and it might as well be accompanied by a heavenly chorus singing *Hallelujah*: it's Sola's Sundries, the always-open gift shop on the Promenade. I remember the animated picture window advertising all kinds of personal items, including HEADACHE REMEDIES. Hell, they might even have some snacks for sale. Delicious, sodium-laden snacks.

Now I just have to find my way out of the buffet and down to the Promenade.

One might think that a pleasure cruiser designed to ferry mostly elderly passengers between planets would be easily navigable on the inside. One would, in the case of *Dejah Thoris,* be as wrong as the day is long. Because passengers are trapped inside this technological marvel for a week or more at a time, and if they get lost, well, there's always a helpful crew member nearby prepared to guide them back to the nearest bar.

I'm not sure how many times I circle the buffet, dodging cleaning robots, before I finally find a human crew member who's willing to stop and show me to an elevator. Maybe they thought I was running laps or something. The elevator buttons are helpfully marked with symbols as well as letters and numbers, and I stab at the one that looks most like a shopping bag.

A moment later, the elevator dings, and the doors open to reveal a lanky young man holding a computer tablet.

"Good morning!" I'm sure he's not actually shouting, but my eardrums feel like they're about to burst. The bright lights of the Promenade flood around him, causing my eyes to tear up, and I can barely read his name tag: WARD. "How are you doing today, sir? Do you have exciting plans for the afternoon?"

My throat makes a weird grumbling noise before I can convince it to speak. "I'm actually looking for a little less excitement right now."

"I understand, sir. Have you heard about our wide variety of onboard excursions?" Ward asks, shoving the tablet in my face. It's showing an animated brochure. The motion makes me queasy. "We offer astronomy shows and spacewalks, if you want to see the stars—"

"I think I'd rather stay inside, thanks." I stagger out of the elevator and past Ward. He follows me down the Promenade.

"Not a problem." Ward taps at his tablet and holds it up again. It's still moving too much. I look away. "We offer several behind-the-scenes tours of *Dejah Thoris*. Did you know this is the largest civilian spacecraft ever built?"

"By Earth," I say without thinking.

"Sorry, sir?"

I stop myself before spewing a whole dossier of intel: *Mars Orbital Authority has a four-million-cubic-meter drydock in high orbit. LiuWuJiang has a mining collar roaming the asteroid belt that can expand to a diameter of one thousand kilometers. Porta Collina InterPlanetary is assembling a solar sail the size of the friggin' Moon—and they would have finished it a year ago, if the agency hadn't sent a team to sabotage it.*

Instead, I say, "Other planets have built bigger spaceships."

"Very true, sir. Do you work in the industry?" Ward asks. His plastic smile remains in place, though I can see his eyes losing it a little. It must be tough getting rebuffed all day by grumpy passengers who just want another damn drink.

"I just do research."

"Desk jockey, eh?" Ward sneaks the tablet under my nose again. "Have you ever seen an actual, working ionwell drive up close?"

The tablet shows an animated image of a uniformed crew member standing on a catwalk above a large circular thing with lights chasing around its circumference. I start to feel nauseated and push the tablet aside. "I'm not really interested—"

"For just a nominal fee," Ward says, "you'll get a full hour in our engineering section with one of our crew specialists, who will explain how *Dejah Thoris*'s ionwell reactor produces the electroplasma energy that powers—"

"Look, friend." I point to the gift shop, which may conceal within its depths a magical cure for this pounding inside my skull. "I'm just trying to get something to kill this hangover."

He raises the tablet toward me again. Now it's showing a payment page with a blinking signature box. "For just a nominal fee, sir."

I squint at him. "You work on commission, don't you?"

Ward shrugs. "You might be seeing a lot of me this week, sir."

Fuck it. Paul stuck me here, he can damn well pay to ease my suffering. I press my thumb down on the signature box until it flashes green.

"Thank you, sir!" Ward grins and yanks the tablet away. "One of our crew guides will come by your stateroom at two o'clock to take you to where the tour starts. If you're not in your room, just look for any crew member and tell them you're on the 2:00 p.m. engine room tour. They'll direct you to the right place."

"Great." I push myself off the wall and am able to stand upright on my own. "I'm going to leave you now."

"Have you tried some 'hair of the dog'?" Ward keeps talking even after I turn my back to him. "I hear that a Bloody Mary is an excellent hangover cure. You can get one at the Red Sky Bar, at the far end of the Promenade!"

"So helpful," I mutter, and resume my pilgrimage to Sola's Sundries.

CHAPTER SIX

Dejah Thoris—Deck 6, Stateroom 6573
How the hell is it mid-afternoon already

My headache has abated slightly by the time someone pounds on my stateroom door at five minutes to two. Unfortunately, my recuperative nap coincided with lunchtime, and I still haven't eaten anything aside from that packet of salted cashews I found at the gift shop. I open the door to yet another smiling crew member, name-tagged PARVAT.

"Aren't cruise ships supposed to have ridiculous amounts of food available for consumption at all times?" I ask.

Parvat's smile flickers for an instant. "I'm here to escort you to your two o'clock engine room tour, sir."

"Right. I'll just fill out a complaint card later."

"I'm sorry, sir, I don't—"

"That's fine." I step into the hallway and pull my stateroom door closed. "Lead on, MacDuff."

"My name is Parvat, sir."

I refrain from joking for the rest of our walk down to engineering. Parvat makes small talk, asking me how my cruise is going so far, and I do my best to answer him without being too condescending. Like Ward said earlier, I'm going to be running into the same crew members a lot over the next week. Probably best not to irritate the people who are preparing my food and cleaning my bathroom every day.

Wait a minute. Is it possible Ward's hard-sell routine wasn't an accident? I mean, obviously it wasn't an accident, but could he also be in the loop—an agency operator—like Captain Santamaria?

It wouldn't be the first time Paul's secretly planted helpers along my path. He's always telling us how important it is to compartmentalize information, for security purposes. I think he just enjoys being the only one who knows everything—the spider in the center of the web. But he also hates deploying personnel without good reason.

More people in the field means more chances for others to compromise our operational security. Paul wouldn't throw extra agents at a situation unless he saw a specific need, and I can't imagine what that might be in this situation. There's only so much trouble I can get into while trapped on this cruise. Paul's got more important things to worry about right now—like saving our department from being audited out of existence.

Am I just being paranoid? Am I incapable of relaxing and being on vacation?

"Here we are, sir," Parvat says. I snap out of my reverie and look around.

We've reached deck fifteen, where the boarding and excursion airlocks are located. Three other passengers are already waiting here: two middle-aged men and a white-haired woman who looks like she should be someone's grandmother. We introduce ourselves. The taller, skinnier man, Arnold, has a pencil-thin gray mustache. The other man, who's balding and wearing a short-sleeved shirt printed with colors that should not exist in nature, is Jason. The woman, Gemma, has a surprisingly strong grip. Must be all that knitting and crocheting.

"Are we all ready for the tour?" Parvat asks cheerfully. I mutter an affirmative noise, which is drowned out by Arnold and Jason's shouts. Gemma nods. "Excellent! This way, please."

We pass through two different security gates, the first while moving from the passenger area into the crew-only lower decks, the second when entering the engineering section. There's a distinct change in the environment when we pass into the crew sections. Nothing here is decorated, just bare walls with occasional scuff marks, probably from service robots dragging supplies and luggage around out of view of the passengers. There's no constant, faint background music. Even the smell is different: no subtle food odors added to entice passengers to buy snacks or drinks, just the antiseptic fragrance of recycled air.

Being in the crew section feels strangely soothing. The plain gray surfaces remind me of our basement offices back in D.C. *Home.* Whatever Lasher and Equipment and Surgical are doing right now, they can't possibly be having as much so-called fun as I am.

After the second security gate, Parvat leads us down a stairwell into a very narrow corridor. I allow my fellow tourists to go through first. Jason and Arnold shove each other the whole way. Gemma slides through delicately, arms raised as if she's afraid of touching anything. I follow without any problems. Compared to a military spacecraft, this is downright luxurious.

I hear gasps, then murmurs as the three civilians exit the narrow corridor into a wide, open area. I'm sure Parvat took us through that passage on purpose, for the dramatic reveal; I can see a much larger service corridor leading here from an elevator on the left. We're standing in the middle of a large chamber, right at the edge of a black-and-yellow safety line on the floor. The edges of a thick door protrude from the far walls on either side.

Directly in front of us is a circular railing overlooking a transparent plexi disk set into the center of the deck. On either side of that opening, and along the three surrounding walls, uniformed crew stand at various control stations while service robots scurry about. I wonder if this much activity is normal, or if this is just for show during the tour.

"Welcome to Main Engineering," Parvat says, spreading his arms in a grand gesture. "If you will step forward to the railing, my friends, you can look down and see the ionwell that powers this entire ship."

He leads us up to the round viewing window in the floor. There's not much to see—the exterior of the reactor is just a big metal sphere with occasional protrusions—but it's very big.

"Boy, that's big," Arnold says.

"You said it," Jason agrees. "Bigger than we had on the *Maitland,* even."

"I didn't know you served," Gemma says. She sounds surprised, but I'm not. These two act just like a lot of the overeager space cadets I've had to deal with. Even though they look old enough to know better.

"Oh, yeah," Jason says. "Two tours patrolling this side of Red Alley for 'stray rocks.' And Arnie got even closer. Right, Arn?"

"Close enough to spit at 'em," Arnold says.

"Damn right. You guys could have won the war, if not for—"

I'm surprised when Gemma interrupts him. "Gentlemen, if it's all the same to you, I'd like to continue *this* tour."

"Same here," I say, and point at a random display. "What's that do?"

"Well," Parvat says, waving us to one side, "if you'll follow me, stay together, and please do not touch anything, I'll point out some of the major components of our ionwell engine . . ."

"You okay, ma'am?" I ask Gemma quietly.

She nods. "I've heard more than enough about the war."

The way she says it makes me think she lost a family member. Her spouse? A child? I don't want to pry, but I'm still curious. I'm trying to figure out how I can coax the information from her when Parvat stops us.

"Unfortunately, we're not allowed to get any closer to the controls, but you can see the primary reaction sphere, where over three quarters of the ship's power is generated." Something clanks on the far side of the console next to him. "And here's *Dejah Thoris*'s chief engineer to tell us more about how the ionwell works!"

I know it's a show. This whole ship is one big put-on, a gaudy curtain drawn over the vast, bleak emptiness of outer space, a choreographed diversion from the boredom that generally defines space travel. It takes a long time to get from one planet to another, and there's not much of anything in between. So hey, look at these shiny objects instead!

But as much as I knew our entrance into the engine room was staged, I was still impressed by the presentation. And even though I know the officer coming around the corner must make this appearance repeatedly, as a routine duty, I can't help but feel a little thrill after Parvat's enthusiastic introduction.

The chief engineer of the whole ship! And . . . she's a pretty lady?

I never thought anyone could make a blue work jumpsuit and black insulated boots look sexy, but this woman does. Her long, straight brown hair is tied back in a ponytail that reaches down to her shoulders. Her big, bright eyes and wide smile express nothing but genuine delight at meeting yet another bunch of tourists gawking at her engine.

"Hello, folks," she says. "I'm Eleanor Gavilán, chief engineer of *Dejah Thoris*. You can call me Ellie."

She shakes our hands as we introduce ourselves. I'm last in line, and I make a monumental effort to keep my eyes on her face and not her body as she grips my hand for the briefest of moments.

"Evan," I say.

"Nice to meet you, Evan," she says, and steps back. "So, who here has seen an ionwell up close before?"

Jason's hand shoots up. "Right here, miss."

"Okay, Jason," Ellie says. "You can call me Ellie, or Chief, or sir. Do you work in astronautics?"

Oh, I like her. Ex-military? She's old enough to have been in the war. Or to have known better.

"Uh, no," Jason replies. "I'm in the Outer Space Reserve. Did a tour on the *Maitland* during the war. Electronics Technician, Power Systems—"

A loud noise blaring from above us drowns out Jason before he can tell us his full name, rank, and serial number. The alarm is accompanied by orange lights that illuminate all around the compartment, flashing above every control console.

"Sorry, folks," Ellie says in a calm and even voice. "Please stay where you are. Nothing to worry about. Just give us a moment to sort this out."

Parvat steps forward and offers his own reassurances while Ellie turns to talk to one of the other engineers. I'm not familiar with *Dejah Thoris*'s alert protocols, but I would guess that an Orange indicator—somewhere between you-might-want-to-pay-attention Yellow and we're-all-going-to-die Red—is fairly serious.

I look over my fellow tourists to see if one of them might have stepped over a safety line or something. Gemma's eyes dart around nervously, both arms wrapped across her midsection. Arnold and Jason watch the engineers. They don't seem overly concerned. Arnold's scratching his arm, and he even seems a little excited. Is he just rubbernecking, or did he come on this tour to cause trouble?

I blink to activate my eye scanners, cycling through the medical view—Arnold's skin temperature is on the warm side, but he doesn't appear otherwise agitated—and going to the electromagnetic spectrum. A false-color overlay appears over the entire compartment, showing me ambient radio waves and energy fields. That's when I see it.

"It's not the ionwell," I say, raising my voice over the alarm and projecting toward Ellie.

She stops working at a console and turns to frown at me. "Excuse me?"

"You're reading a power spike, right? Possible containment breach? It's not the ionwell." I point at Arnold. "It's him."

Arnold's skin temperature shoots up a few degrees. "What? I didn't do anything."

Ellie calls to another engineer, who hands over a portable scanner. She moves back toward the ionwell railing and aims the device at Arnold.

"Son of a bitch," she says, then looks embarrassed. "Sorry. Arnold, you've got an electromotive battery implant."

"Oh. Yeah." Arnold rubs his left shoulder sheepishly. "Brachial nerve damage from the war. The docs had to rewire some stuff. Is that a problem?"

Ellie points toward the black-and-yellow stripes in front of the main doors. "I need you folks to move to the other side of that safety line, please."

Parvat herds us back while Ellie consults with her crew. After a moment, the alarm goes silent, and the lighting returns to normal. Ellie hands off the scanner and walks back to the tour group. Her face is neutral, but her vitals indicate severe annoyance. I suddenly feel like I'm invading her privacy. I turn off my eye.

"Sorry about that, folks," she says. Arnold looks away to avoid her stare. "We do ask when you sign up for the tour whether you have any implants."

Jason grunts. "A lot of fine print on that registration form."

"Shoulder-phone signals can interfere with our equipment," Ellie continues. "And military power cells tend to trip the safety monitors here in Main Engineering." She glares at Jason, then turns to me. "You gentlemen know each other?"

"We've never met," I say, a little too quickly. *Dammit.* Now I have to come up with a cover story for why I knew Arnold had a battery in his arm. "I just heard those two fellows talking about being in the war, and I took an educated guess."

"Were you in the service?"

"Oh, no. I work for the State Department. Interplanetary trade inspector. I know a little bit about spaceships. Just enough to be dangerous." I flash her my best innocent smile.

She nods. "Okay, folks. I won't be able to walk you around the compartment, but you've already seen the ionwell, and you can still see everything else pretty well from back here."

"Not much of a tour," Jason mutters.

"You're welcome to leave any time," Ellie says. "We'll give you a full refund."

Arnold elbows Jason in the ribs, and he shakes his head. "Nah, it's cool."

Ellie turns to Gemma and me. "Most of Earth's warships utilize second-generation ionwell propulsion systems. *Dejah Thoris* is the newest Princess of Mars Cruises spaceliner, and she was built with state-of-the-art technology." She waves at the center of the floor. "This is a fourth-generation ionwell, which incorporates design improvements and safety features originally copied from the Martian frigate *Valor,* which was detained by Earth Coalition forces during the first days of the Independence War."

"Hell, yeah," Jason says. "We spanked those Reds at hide-and-seek."

"What kind of safety features?" Gemma asks.

"Well, you can see how much physical shielding there is around the engine," Ellie says. "There's no radiation danger from the ionwell itself, but the superheated plasma produced by the reactor is highly volatile. Shielded conduits direct that plasma out through our main drive rockets and also into generators that supply power to the whole ship."

"That does sound dangerous." Gemma seems genuinely concerned. I wonder if this is her first space voyage.

"All the power generation systems are located in the engineering sections," Ellie says. "And as you've seen, we monitor everything down here very closely. We don't send anything except electricity up to the passenger decks."

"Not even the kitchens?" I ask, attempting to make a joke.

Ellie raises an eyebrow. "You wouldn't want to cook with this stuff. Not unless you like your meat fused into charcoal."

"It ain't pretty," Jason adds. "We had a plasma conduit rupture on the *Maitland*. Vaporized two spacemen—"

"What happens if there's a rupture here?" Gemma asks Ellie.

"The whole system is designed for safe shutdown in the event of failure," Ellie says. "If the exterior of any conduit overheats by even a single degree, it's shut off and flagged for inspection. If the ionwell is damaged— even if the shielding goes out of alignment by as little as one centimeter— the reactor will scram automatically.

"The ionwell reaction itself requires a delicately balanced environment. We have personnel on duty twenty-four hours a day, monitoring to make sure nothing goes wrong. In the unlikely event of an emergency, our backup batteries and solar panels can provide full power to the whole ship for thirty-six hours."

Jason and Arnold have been muttering to each other this whole time. I don't really care to know what they're saying.

"If this is just the top part of the ionwell," Gemma says, pointing at the metal sphere in the floor, "and it's a ball shape . . . How large is it, exactly?"

"Including shielding, the reactor sphere has the same circumference as the ship's beam, or width," Ellie says. "If you look at a diagram of *Dejah Thoris*, all of deck twenty-five is the full diameter of the ionwell."

"That seems awfully exposed," Gemma says, frowning. "If one tiny dent can shut down the reactor, shouldn't it be more protected? More inside?"

She is truly worried about this. I can see it in her face. So what's important enough to get this nice old lady onto a ship that she thinks might kill her?

Ellie nods. "Very true, Gemma, that is a concern. Though outer space is mostly empty, we do sometimes encounter debris in our flight path. And because we travel at such high velocity, even a small object striking the hull can cause serious damage."

"Like birds hitting aircraft," I say, hoping a familiar analogy will help put Gemma at ease. Her face tells me that probably wasn't the right analogy to make.

"Right." Ellie smiles at me. *Just part of the show,* I remind myself. "Although out here, it's more likely to be frozen human waste that's been dumped out by other spacecraft."

Everyone laughs, including Gemma. *Nice save, Chief.*

"Fortunately," Ellie continues, "*Dejah Thoris*'s navigational deflector system mitigates any potential impacts. Radar sensors detect any approaching objects of a size and speed likely to cause more than cosmetic damage to the ship, and then flash-lasers blast those objects until they're no longer a threat."

"You worked on NAVDEF, didn't you, Arnie?" Jason bellows.

"Yeah, I have," Arnold says. "Um, Chief, is the *Thoris* using EP to drive those lasers?"

"*Dejah Thoris,*" Ellie corrects, with a smile and a hard stare. "And yes, we do route electroplasma directly to the exterior laser pods. But those lasers are all mounted in the nose of the ship, or around the lower, engineering decks." She nods at Gemma. "Nowhere near the passenger sections."

"But you gotta get the plasma from down here all the way up to the nose," Jason says. "You can't do that without moving it through the passenger decks."

Ellie turns to me. "Those power conduits run through the cargo section. If you saw *Dejah Thoris* from Sky Five, before you boarded, you may have noticed a large number of cargo containers on one side of the ship."

"Yeah," I say. "Like a block carved out of a hard-boiled egg."

"That's a good analogy. I'll have to remember that one." She taps the

side of her head and winks at me, then turns back to Gemma. "In addition to passengers, *Dejah Thoris* transports several thousand metric tons of
cargo on every sailing. Some of that is supplies for the cruise—food,
drink, and other consumables—but a large portion of it is commercial
freight. After loading the cargo, the 'cut-out' section is covered with solar
panels, and we fly with that side of the ship always facing the Sun to collect additional power."

"Wouldn't it be more cost-efficient to move cargo by other means?"
Gemma asks.

"Not necessarily," Ellie says. "I won't bore you with the math, but the
nature of the ionwell reaction dictates how large the reactor sphere has to
be in order to move a ship of this size. And though we don't have to worry
about aerodynamics in the vacuum of space, we do want a symmetric hull
structure for the engine to push against. The accountants at Princess of
Mars Cruises have also done the math, and they've determined that carrying both cargo and passengers is cost-efficient."

"That's one word for it," Jason scoffs. Arnold elbows him. "What? I'm
just saying. The Reds wouldn't hesitate to blow a cargo drone out of the
sky. They'll think twice about shooting at a few thousand civilians."

"Cool it, man," Arnold says, giving the rest of us an apologetic shrug.
"The war's over."

"Yeah, you keep telling yourself that, pal," Jason says.

Gemma whirls to stare down the two men. "Why the hell are you even
going to Mars, if you hate them so much?"

The two men blink at her for a moment. Then Jason says, "It was my
wife's idea."

"Me too," Arnold says. "Our anniversary is next week."

"Happy anniversary," Gemma says, her voice shaking. She turns back
to Ellie and a somewhat ashen-faced Parvat. "I'm sorry. I have family on
Mars. I was very happy when the war ended. I didn't really care who won
by that point." She looks at me. "You're probably too young to remember
any of this."

"No, I remember." *I'm sure I know more about it than you do.* The agency
refused to put me in the field when I first joined, and while Paul wrestled
that red tape, he put me to work sanitizing military footage from the inva-
sion. I saw a lot of things that no teenager—no human being, really—should
ever have to see. "I'm very sorry for your loss, Gemma."

Her hasty smile threatens to twist her face into something else. "I didn't say anyone had died."

"You didn't have to."

She blinks wetness from her eyes and takes a deep breath. "Oh, I'm so sorry. I didn't mean to completely derail the tour like this."

"It's okay," Ellie says. "The war was difficult for all of us. But that's why Princess of Mars Cruises built *Dejah Thoris* so soon after the conflict." I can tell she's reciting this bit. "We feel it's important to maintain commerce between our two worlds, to share the best of our cultures with each other and remember what we all have in common."

"The desire to get really, really drunk right after this?" I say. That gets at least a chuckle from everyone. Parvat seizes the opportunity to retake control of his tour.

"Okay, thank you, Chief Engineer Gavilán!" he says, clapping his hands. We follow his lead in giving her a short but at least fifty percent enthusiastic round of applause. "Now if you'll follow me, please, our next stop is one of the ship's power generators, where plasma energy is converted into electricity . . ."

I let Jason and Arnold lead the way, then wave Gemma ahead of me and bring up the rear again. I don't like it when strangers walk behind me. As we start exiting down the main hallway toward the elevator, I feel a hand on my shoulder.

I turn around. It's Ellie.

"Hey, thanks for doing that, Evan," she says. "I'm pretty good with machinery, but not so much with people."

"No, you were great," I say. "Thanks for the tour. Sir."

She smiles. "How did you know about Gemma, by the way?"

"Lucky guess," I say. "Like you said. The war was tough on everyone."

Ellie nods. "You're a pretty good guesser."

I put on my innocent face again. "Thanks. I deal with some difficult people in my line of work." It's not a lie. "I've learned to 'read the room,' as they say."

"Well, thanks for your help," she says. "Enjoy the rest of your tour. And the rest of the cruise."

She shakes my hand and walks away. I don't move for another second, mesmerized by the sight of her ponytail swaying back and forth.

I'm not complaining about the attention, but there's no reason she should be personally interested in me. Is there? Why else would a spaceliner's chief engineer be curious about a guy who claims to be a deskbound researcher, but seems to know quite a bit about interplanetary spacecraft drive systems and military power implants?

She turns and waves at me over her shoulder, still smiling.

Goddammit. I really hope she's not in the loop.

CHAPTER SEVEN

Dejah Thoris—Deck 6, Stateroom 6573
7 hours before I start causing trouble

My job is to gather information. When I'm not in the field actively collecting it, I'm sitting at a computer, trawling the electronic communications that connect nations and planets and distilling meaning and intent from the noise. Even when there are no specific questions to answer—like hey, why is that satellite seeing heavy neutrino emissions characteristic of nuclear fission inside a three-thousand-year-old structure deep in a Mesoamerican jungle?—the agency's always on the lookout for things that break normal patterns.

Unusual isn't always bad, but *interesting* is always worth a second look. And I've definitely discovered two persons of interest on this ship.

First of all, there's Captain Santamaria. Obviously he's ex-military, probably OSS, maybe even intelligence. How did he end up working for the agency? What is he doing for the agency while captaining a civilian cruise ship? And why did Paul put *me* here, on Santamaria's ship?

Then there's Ellie Gavilán. Also possibly ex-military; where else would she have worked on ionwells before *Dejah Thoris*? The technology was only declassified on Earth after the war. And there's no way an Earth corporation would make a Martian citizen chief engineer on their newest flagship.

My interest in both of these people is purely professional. Absolutely professional. I am clearly in the middle of something here, even if it only turns out to be Paul pulling a prank on one of his old drinking buddies, and I will get to the bottom of it. It has nothing at all to do with Ellie's shapely body inside her form-fitting jumpsuit. Or her sparkling personality. Or the way she squeezed my shoulder.

This is business. I'm a spy. This is what I do. Curiosity may have killed the cat, but the Kangaroo loves legwork.

The most efficient way I know to get the best information is to plug into the agency's data warehouse. If you've ever passed through the sight line of a security camera in a public place anywhere in the Solar System, we know about it, and I can look it up and tell you to the millisecond when you were there.

Unfortunately, I didn't board *Dejah Thoris* with most of the special equipment I would carry on a live op. I don't have the long-range antenna relay I need for my shoulder-phone to bounce a secure signal off military navigation relays. And hacking into the cruise ship's telecom system is sure to attract unwanted attention.

Fortunately, I do have a few items in the pocket that I always carry for emergencies.

I spend the next few hours planning my own little operation. I need the time because I don't have my usual tactical support team of Equipment and Surgical in my ear, telling me what to do and how to do it. I don't want to screw this up.

After I've figured out the shift changes for ship's security and found the blind spots in their camera coverage, I sign up for one of the scheduled after-dinner spacewalk excursions. I pretend to be nervous and flustered as a crew member helps me into my spacesuit. I ask about all the different parts of the suit and all the "funny-looking equipment" so I can surreptitiously scan everything, find the locator beacon that's hidden in the radio, and measure its broadcast frequency. I also note the length of my tether cable when I'm outside, and go as far as I can around the circumference of the ship without arousing our chaperone's suspicions.

Theoretically, *Dejah Thoris* could do passenger spacewalks all the time. There isn't day or night when you're hurtling through the void. But the human body evolved in a diurnal cycle, and it gets first confused, then sick, if you disrupt its natural rhythms for too long. So all passenger vessels operate on a twenty-four hour day, and *Dejah Thoris*'s meal times and activity schedules reflect that.

The last spacewalk of the night ends at 2100 hours. It's two hours later when I sidle up to the excursion area, bypass the door lock, and step inside.

It's dark. I leave the lights off and blink once, then look right, left, right, and blink three times. The night vision implants in my left eye come to life, magnifying the dim light sneaking in through cracks in the doors and walls and showing me the spacesuit storage locker.

I set my shoulder-phone to jam the suit's locator beacon. I know from my earlier scans that it won't start transmitting until I power up the suit, so I don't need to worry about interfering with other, expected radio traffic. If any crew are outside, they're on an entirely different frequency.

It takes me almost fifteen minutes to put on the suit by myself. While I'm doing that, I scan the airlock again, to confirm that it's not connected to any external monitoring system.

I can feel my heart beating faster. I'm scared, but also excited. I feel like a kid riding his bicycle without training wheels for the first time—and preparing to ride the bike off a ski jump ramp, over a cliff, and into the ocean. Maybe not a great idea, but it's sure going to be *fun*.

The airlock cycles open. I hope nobody's passing by the corridor outside, but the locker room, lounge, and office should provide decent sound insulation. I step inside the airlock and close the inner door. It seems to take an eternity for the atmosphere to vent and the status light to turn green. The outer door opens onto a black infinity. I step out onto the excursion platform, walk to the railing on the Sunward side, and start looking for handholds on the hull. A big ship like this needs plenty of maintenance grips and niches to allow in-flight repairs.

Dejah Thoris's constant acceleration simulates gravity. Ascending fifteen decks until I'm past the cargo section is going to be like climbing up the side of a skyscraper. Except if I fall, there won't even be ground to hit—either my tether will hold, and I'll get yanked back into the side of the ship, or the tether will break, and I'll float through interplanetary space until I get close enough to a relay buoy to send a distress signal with my puny shoulder-phone. That's if I don't get fried by the main engines as I tumble past the bottom of the ship.

Did I mention this is going to be fun? *Yeah. Fun.*

I've connected several tether cables together to make a run long enough to get me past the cargo section. I attach the carabiner at one end of my mega-cable to the bank of rings above the airlock, wrapping the cable around twice just to be safe. Then I engage the magnets in my boots and start climbing.

It's slow going only because I have to avoid windows. Walking up the side of a building turns out to be surprisingly easy. This *is* fun. I try a few experimental hops, just to see how far off the hull I can get. The gravity makes things tricky; once I'm not attached to the ship, it accelerates past me and I fall backward. But maybe if I rig the cable . . .

My helmet's faceplate dims automatically as I come over the horizon into sunlight. I'm at the edge of the cargo section, where the rectilinear containers have been lashed together on the outside of the ship and covered with solar panels. Just like Ellie described. I take a moment to admire the structure, multicolored bricks beneath a gleaming blue mirror.

Then I switch my left eye into telescope mode and find the Earth: azimuth negative forty degrees, elevation plus five. This side of the ship always faces Sunward. That allows *Dejah Thoris* to maintain communications with Earth, and it'll do the same for my equipment.

I think of a fish-covered pizza and open the pocket—without the barrier, since I'm already in a vacuum. That makes it much easier to pull out the Echo Delta.

The full name is "emergency communications dish," but I guess "Echo Delta" sounds snappier. The bulky military case falls out of the pocket and nearly yanks my arm out of its socket. I clamp the twenty-kilo weight to a maintenance shelf before I open it and start assembling the unit. Fold out the parabolic dish, screw it onto the tripod, bolt that to the hull after scanning for wires. Attach power pack, scrambler module, microcell transceiver.

I test the dish by tuning to a public broadcast news feed and smile at the tiny vid image in my left eye HUD. Now I can use my shoulder-phone to talk to the dish, and the dish can connect me to Earth.

After I drop the empty case back in the pocket, I take a moment to admire my handiwork. It's not the most circumspect assembly job ever, but it works. And I did it all by myself, using only my emergency field equipment and my own wits. Paul would be proud, if I ever told him. Not that I plan to.

I celebrate by doing a few stunts on the way back. I rig my tether cable to a handhold, kick myself off the hull, and freefall until the cable goes taut. Like jumping off a cliff! But safer. In some ways. I wonder how far away from the ship I can get before swinging back.

I stop after my third tumble, when my glove slips and I fly ten meters farther than I intended. The ship suddenly looks very small in a vast sea of nothing. I slowly crawl along the hull back to the airlock.

I'm pretty pleased with myself, whistling as I peel off the spacesuit and run down my checklist: suit power off, check. Stop location beacon jamming, check. Replace suit in locker, check. Continue basking in your own triumph, check.

It's just after 0200 when I walk out of the locker room. Plenty of time before the next shift change. Maybe I'll stop by the arcade. After what I just did, that Lunar Lander vid game doesn't look so tough.

I step into the lounge and go blind.

I think I make a noise as I close my eyes, and then I notice the overload indicator in the corner of my HUD. I move my eyes around until the night vision enhancement switches off. All this I do instinctively, so I don't even feel nervous until I open my eyes and see three security guards standing in front of me, stunners raised.

The one in the middle and closest to me is a woman—tall, dark, short brown hair, pale eyes that look like ice. I wonder if her stare is always that cold, or if it's only when she catches a trespasser. The two burly men flanking her look just as unhappy to see me.

"Hands where I can see them," the woman says, her finger just touching the trigger. She really wants an excuse to shoot me.

I raise my arms slowly, never taking my eyes off her. She's clearly the leader. I suddenly realize that they're much too concerned about a mere trespasser. They were looking for someone. Someone dangerous. The woman is holding her stunner too firmly, and her arms are braced against a nonexistent recoil. She's wishing she had an actual firearm, so she can drop me if I make a move.

"Mike, pat him down," she says.

The man to her right holsters his weapon and walks over to me, staring me down all the way. He gives me a very thorough frisking.

"He's clean," Mike says. He takes a step back, standing behind me, and pulls out his stunner again. I decide it's time to say something.

"Look, I'm sorry," I say, using my best pathetic-civilian voice. "I—I didn't think anybody would—"

"Shut up," the woman says.

I shut up.

She's actually thinking about whether she should shoot first and ask questions later. I can see her sizing me up. I relax my body and hunch my shoulders. I want to appear to be as slight a physical threat as possible.

"Danny," she says to the other guard, "check his ID."

Danny grabs my right hand and presses the thumb against a handheld scanpad. After a second, his wristband—a gauntlet of touchscreen controls for his duty equipment—lights up with my passenger record. "Evan Rogers. Stateroom 6573."

The woman seems disappointed, but she doesn't lower her stunner.

"What were you doing outside the ship, Mr. Rogers?" she asks.

"I just wanted to do another excursion. By myself," I say. "I did a space-walk right after dinner, and it was so amazing, I just wanted to enjoy that—that freedom without a bunch of noisy people all around me. I'm sorry if I caused any trouble."

She mulls this over for a moment, probably trying to decide if I'm lying or not. I'm pretty sure she can't tell. I'm good at my job.

Then she takes a step toward me and jams the tip of the stunner up under my chin.

Apparently I'm not that good.

"What the hell were you doing outside the ship, Mr. Rogers?" the woman repeats. This time, she says it like she doesn't believe that's my real name.

I make a choking noise for effect. She's not actually hurting me, but I want her to get some satisfaction here. I'm still assessing whether I can take down all three of them at once, and if I do go for it, I need them to be as overconfident as possible.

My heart is pounding. I didn't expect to get caught here, and I didn't expect security on a damn cruise ship to be so hardcore. If this were a real op, I would have three layers of cover stories and remote support through my implanted comms. Or I could just plead the Fifth and wait for Paul to bail me out.

But this isn't an actual operation. I don't have backup, and there's no guarantee the agency will come to my rescue.

I don't have a lot of options here. However, I do want to stop the choking.

I grab the woman's wrist with my left hand and push it away, aiming the stunner at the ceiling. At the same time, I kick backward, catching Mike in the stomach and putting him on the floor. I launch myself forward, pushing the woman into Danny and slamming him against the wall, and simultaneously open the pocket behind me, thinking of a small woolly mammoth.

I reach back through the barrier for my pistol and pull it out. I close the pocket before anyone can see it—I hope—and put my back to the wall with my arm wrapped around the woman. I place the barrel of my pistol under her chin. Now her body is shielding me from Mike and Danny's stunners, and they all know I mean business.

"I thought you searched this guy!" the woman hisses at Mike. He has no response.

I speak in a loud, clear voice. "I am not the person you're looking for. I am not working with the person you're looking for. Do you understand?"

"Oh, yeah," the woman says. "I'm totally convinced now. You can go about your business."

I sigh and say to Danny and Mike, "I need you to get Captain Santamaria down here."

"Fat chance!" the woman snaps. At least she's not struggling or biting. I hate it when people bite me.

"I need you to call Captain Santamaria," I say, "and tell him that I'm a friend to lumber but not columns."

The woman twitches and does her best to turn her head toward me. "You know Paul Tarkington?"

Now I don't have a response.

"What do you want us to do, Chief?" Danny asks.

"Do what he says," the woman orders. "Call the captain."

CHAPTER EIGHT

Dejah Thoris—Deck 15, excursion lounge
20 minutes after security decided not to shoot me

Danny and Mike leave the room when Captain Santamaria arrives in the excursion lounge. It's just me, the female security officer, and the captain. I'm sitting on one of the couches. The woman stands with her back against a wall, stunner still in her hand but dangling at her side instead of pointed at me. I've handed my pistol over to her, as a gesture of trust. Her unspoken promise to take a half-second longer to drop me if I move is, I guess, her way of reciprocating.

The captain stands in the doorway for a moment. He seems more curious than annoyed. The look he exchanges with the woman is priceless. He actually appears to be amused at her exasperation. It's too familiar to be the relationship between mere coworkers, but too casual for lovers. Relatives? Father and daughter? But they look nothing alike.

"He was carrying this sidearm," the woman says, handing over my pistol. "We don't know where he was hiding it. Mike gave him a full pat-down. And the piece was cold as ice."

The captain turns the pistol over in his hands. He ejects the magazine and examines the ammunition. He replaces the clip, checks the safety, and hands the weapon back to the woman.

"That's practically an antique," he says. I'm not sure if he's talking to me or her.

"We didn't find anything in the pressure suit he used," the woman says. "He must have been jamming the locator beacon."

The captain nods. He sits down in a chair across from me and asks, "Mr. Rogers, which department do you work for?"

I flick my eyes over to the woman, then address the captain. "Your chief of security has me at a disadvantage."

"You don't get your weapon back until you're off this ship," the woman snaps.

"Chief," the captain says, "he means he doesn't know your name."

The woman frowns. "Who the hell talks like that?"

I can see the barest hint of a smile underneath the captain's beard. There's definitely something between these two. It feels like family, but I can't quite make the connection.

"This is Chief Petty Officer Andrea Jemison," the captain says. "Head of security aboard *Dejah Thoris,* as you've correctly surmised. She served six years at Olympus Base, through the end of the war. You can look up her full record yourself, can't you?"

I've been moving my jaw muscles as soon as he said her name, constructing a query to send over my secure connection to the agency. Anyone might notice that, but it would look like nervous teeth-grinding to a civilian who didn't know about my control implants.

"And I'm sure you can look up my record as well," the captain continues. I tap my molars together, transmitting my search parameters, and my left eye HUD blinks while waiting for the response. Back on Earth, the data would have come back instantly, but out here there's a lightspeed delay.

The woman—Jemison—has tensed up. A lot. "Captain, what the hell is going on?"

Without looking at her, Santamaria says, "Mr. Rogers snuck outside the ship to set up a secure communication link with Earth. Right now he's using his shoulder-phone to search for our military service records. Once he knows how much security clearance we have, he'll decide which cover story to feed us."

"He's a field operative?" Jemison says, as if it's hard for her to believe.

"Well, they can't all be as handsome as I was," Santamaria says.

Jemison makes a dismissive noise. "I don't see an interface and he hasn't been talking to himself. How is he working the phone?"

"I would guess there's a heads-up display in one of his eyes," Santamaria says. "And biometric sensors implanted throughout his body. A few eye movements or twitches of specific muscles will control the phone and whatever other devices are hidden under his skin."

The search results light up in my vision. I don't bother trying to hide my eye or finger movements as I read the information. There isn't much. A lot of the relevant records are still sealed. But I see that Jemison and Santamaria served together for eight months at Olympus during the war. Before that, Jemison was quartermaster of the Earth Coalition corvette *Cincinnati*. And Santamaria's prior command was . . . First Mars Battalion? *Jesus, he fought in the vanguard?*

And now they both work for Paul Tarkington.

Ellie Gavilán, on the other hand, seems to have made a clean break after her prewar military service. She's barely even visited a VA hospital since then. Definitely not in the loop. Is that good news? Does that mean she's actually interested in "Evan Rogers"?

Not now, Kangaroo. You're still in a situation. Focus!

I blink away my HUD and retrain my eyes on Santamaria. I study his face for a second, then look over at Jemison. Each of them has earned a stack of war commendations they can never wear. Their service records will only be declassified long after they're dead, and they'll both have ships of the line named after them.

I feel really bad about holding a gun to Jemison's head.

"Captain, Chief," I say, "I'm sorry for any trouble I've caused you. I'm not here on assignment. I'm on vacation. I just—got a little bored, and wanted to be able to communicate securely with my department back on Earth. I'm not used to being isolated like this. I hope you understand." It sounds a lot dumber coming out of my mouth than it did in my head.

"Apology accepted," Santamaria says. "Isn't that right, Chief?"

"Yeah," Jemison says. "Now answer the captain's question. What department do you work for?"

I have nothing to hide from these people. "I report directly to Director Tarkington. My code name is Kangaroo."

Jemison sucks in a breath. "So that's where you hid the gun."

Even Santamaria seems impressed. "I can understand why Lasher sent you on a vacation. Sounds like a real shitshow back home right now."

My head is spinning. My whole world has just been turned inside out— instead of the big, bad spy strutting around a ship full of civilians, I've been reduced to a schoolboy in the presence of giants. Santamaria even knows what's going on in the office right now. He apparently knows things that Paul flat-out refused to tell me.

So what else is new, Kangaroo?

Even if I could get a status from D.C., there's nothing I can do to help. Is there?

"I have to ask, Captain. How connected are you to the agency these days? Not many people know about me and—what I can do."

Jemison actually laughs out loud before covering her mouth. "Sorry," she says. "You didn't look up our *current* service records?"

I feel my face growing hot. I need to work on not always appearing to be a bumbling idiot.

Santamaria says, "Those would be under higher security. Probably not accessible off-world, or at least filed under a different section."

"I've powered down the dish for now," I say. "Why don't you just tell me, Captain?"

He smiles. "Your abilities notwithstanding, the agency still does plenty of traditional smuggling. We have a regular supply route through the inner planets. About five percent of our cargo containers, usually."

I sit down on the couch. Now I know why I'm on this particular cruise. This is a milk run for Santamaria and Jemison, but Paul can trust them to get me out of any trouble I might get into.

They're my babysitters.

"Captain," Jemison says, "maybe Mr. Rogers can help with our current situation."

Wait. What situation?

Santamaria pauses before asking me, "Rogers, what kind of scanners do you have in that eye?" He points to the left side of my face.

"The full kit," I say. "Passive sensors through the entire EM spectrum. Now that I've got the comms link, I can also download any analysis software I need. I see through walls better if there's a baseline particle emitter on the other side, but I can pick up a lot just by zeroing out ambient sources."

"That's better than what we've got now," Santamaria says.

"Which is nothing," says Jemison.

"What do you need to scan for?" I ask. What kind of problems could cruise ship passengers cause that would require high-tech scanners to resolve?

Santamaria stands. "It's probably easier if we just show you."

I notice that Jemison is holding my pistol out, grip facing me. Her stunner is in its holster.

"Your sidearm, Mr. Rogers," she says.

I can't quite make the word *sorry* come out of my mouth. I'll try again later. I'll have to apologize to Danny and Mike, too. That will almost certainly be harder. I can see in Jemison's eyes that she doesn't hold a grudge—when you put enough secrets into play, they're going to start colliding with each other.

Besides, I'm sure she could take me down at any time if she really wanted to.

"Thanks," I say, standing and taking the pistol.

I decide to show off. I turn to my right—facing away from the captain and the chief—then think of a small woolly mammoth, and open the pocket without the barrier. It appears as a black disk hovering in space, surrounded by a ragged, sparkling white halo. Air rushes noisily into the portal. I let go of the pistol, and it flies into the pocket. I close it, and the room is still again.

"Wow," Jemison says.

I'm sure I have a huge grin on my face. It's not often that I get to impress people with my superpower.

CHAPTER NINE

Dejah Thoris—Deck 5, passenger section
The middle of the night, when I should be asleep, but this seems more interesting

Santamaria and Jemison accompany me into a service elevator, and Jemison fills me in on the situation.

"We're keeping this quiet so we don't cause a huge panic aboard the ship," she says. "While you were having fun outside the ship, a fire alarm sounded in one of the passenger staterooms. Crew responded and found two bodies."

"Bodies?" I repeat. "People died in the fire?"

"It's not clear what happened," Santamaria says. "Nobody in the adjoining areas heard anything unusual before the alarm went off. But we do have decent soundproofing between staterooms."

"Two bodies," Jemison continues. "But there were three people booked into the stateroom. One passenger is missing. That's who we were looking for when we found you."

"How *did* you find me, by the way?" I ask. "I thought I was pretty careful about covering my tracks."

"You're a lousy acrobat."

I always do my victory dance too early. "Somebody saw that, huh?"

"You tripped one of our exterior proximity sensors," she says. "You're lucky you weren't moving any faster. Our navigational deflectors almost fried you."

My mouth suddenly feels very dry. "Hmm." *Note to self: ask more questions during engine room tours.*

We stop in front of stateroom 5028. Jemison hands out plastic covers for our shoes and nitrile gloves, then opens the door with her thumbprint.

I walk inside and immediately put a hand over my nose and mouth. The odor of burnt flesh is overpowering. I look for the bathroom in case I need to throw up.

"Sorry about the smell," Jemison says. "We're running the ventilators, but this is still a crime scene, and we can't clean it up until a real forensics team goes through here."

This suite must be four times the size of my stateroom. The bedrooms are smaller, but there are three of them leading off the central area, one on the left, two on the right. The largest bedroom, on the left, has its own bathroom, and there's a second bathroom next to the kitchen area.

The living room is a shambles. Lamps have been shattered, the coffee table is smashed, and there are pieces of glass and plastic all over the couch and floor. Anything flammable has been charred to some degree. Everything is also soaked, I presume from the automatic sprinklers that put out the fire.

"Who was staying here?" I ask through my hand.

"The Wachlin family," Santamaria says. "They won a sweepstakes. Random drawing for a free cruise."

"Lucky family."

"Good and bad luck."

Jemison leads me into the master bedroom. There's a body on the bed, and blood everywhere. The body is a woman, pale-skinned, gray-haired, probably in her eighties. It looks like she was sleeping when somebody slit her throat. She must have woken up and struggled while being held down. There are dark red smears across both her wrists.

"This is Emily Wachlin," Jemison says. "She was traveling with her two adult sons, Alan and David. David is currently missing. Alan's in the other bedroom."

We walk through the living room, to the bedroom directly across from the kitchen. It's a blackened mess. The remains of a burnt human body lie on the bed.

I gag and turn away, doing my best to keep down the gourmet dinner I enjoyed a few hours ago. I'm not successful. I run to the bathroom and throw up in the sink. I wasn't expecting anything quite this gruesome on my first cruise.

"Take your time," Santamaria says while I rinse out my mouth. "David isn't going anywhere. He can't leave the ship, and we're broadcasting his face now. Everyone on board will know he's dangerous."

"I thought you were trying to keep this quiet."

"Come into the other bedroom when you're ready."

Jemison is waiting for us in the last bedroom, next to the open closet. There's a plastic tub on the floor.

"We bagged some objects after imaging everything," she says. She reaches into the tub and hands me a clear plastic bag with several orange cylinders inside.

"Stelomane," I read off a label. "And Dalazine."

"An antipsychotic and a sedative," Jemison says.

"These belonged to David Wachlin?"

"And this." Jemison holds up a larger bag, containing a metal doughnut with a wedge cut out of one side and a control panel attached to the top. "Our ship's doctor identified this as an alpha wave generator. It's supposed to stabilize the user's brain wave patterns, help him relax."

"So you've got a schizophrenic on the loose," I say. I've received enough medical briefings from Jessica to know the basics. "Probably having a prolonged psychotic episode. You can tell people he's dangerous without telling them what he's actually done."

"I don't want a panic on my ship," Santamaria says.

"How long has he been missing?" I ask.

"Three hours at most," Jemison says. "Doc estimates that Emily and Alan were killed around midnight."

"Mind if I take a look around?"

Jemison nods. "That's why you're here, Rogers."

I activate my left eye. "Anything in particular I should be looking for? My eye isn't too good at distinguishing organic compounds, but I should be able to spot metal, ceramic, most thermosetting polymers—"

"Start with metal," she says. "We still haven't found the murder weapon."

"I don't suppose you have a composite fermion emitter on board," I say.

Jemison blows a puff of air through her lips. "Not today. You don't have one in that pocket of yours?"

I shake my head. "I just need something that radiates a steady and known frequency in EM. Shorter wavelengths are better. A radio transmitter should work."

Jemison and I stare at each other for a moment. Then her eyes light up, and she says, "Kitchen."

I don't understand the word at first. She walks out of the bedroom, and I follow her into the kitchen area.

"Maintenance, this is Security Chief Jemison," she says into a radio button on the collar of her uniform. "I need an electrics toolkit and two pairs of insulated gloves in suite 5028."

I stop behind her in the entryway. Santamaria stands on the other side of the kitchen counter, watching us with muted interest. I wonder why he's still here. Probably to make sure I don't annoy Jemison so much that she decides to beat me up after all.

She taps the glass door of the box hanging below one of the kitchen cabinets, and I understand what she's thinking.

I smile. "Now we're cooking with gas."

She frowns. "What? This is a microwave oven."

"Never mind."

While we wait for the maintenance delivery, I run the microwave oven and tune my eye to its specific frequency. I can see the metal parts inside glowing a brilliant blue-green as they're bombarded with radiation. The wavelength is just over a millimeter.

The doorbell rings. Jemison opens the door for a cube-shaped service robot. The top of the cube flips open, revealing a cargo compartment. Jemison crouches down to grab the supplies from inside, then taps the robot's front-facing control panel with her wristband. Cube-bot rolls away as Jemison stands and closes the door.

She returns to the kitchen, dismantles the oven like she does this sort of thing every day, and removes a squat gray cylinder with a small protrusion on top and two terminals toward the bottom—the magnetron, a compact microwave emitter. I put on the insulated gloves and hold the magnetron while she connects its terminals to a portable battery. The entire room lights up when she attaches the wires.

I'm breathless for a moment as I look around, seeing every metal object glittering blue and green as electromagnetic waves bounce off its surface. A yellow-orange aurora ripples around Jemison's forearm as the microwaves meet the radio waves emitted by her control wristband. I almost forget where I am and what I'm doing.

"It's working," I say. "Want me to tell you how many fillings you've got in your teeth, Chief?"

"Maybe later," she says. I make a mental note: Jemison doesn't like jokes when she's working.

Jemison disconnects the power, and we move the rig into the late Emily Wachlin's bedroom. I hold the magnetron in front of me with both arms outstretched and slowly walk around the room. Jemison follows, making sure I don't pull the cable out of the battery. Santamaria watches from the doorway.

It takes a long time to go through the entire bedroom. We have to check each individual metal signature to make sure it belongs. I look at every railing, every strut, every furniture rod. It's a little easier to be here when the corpse is obscured by my eye's HUD overlay.

We don't find anything. Jemison and I search the two other bedrooms as well, but there's nothing unusual, either added or missing.

At 0600 hours ship time, Santamaria tells us to take a break.

"We have a staff meeting in three hours," he says to Jemison. "Chief, can you prepare a briefing?"

"Yeah. Not much to say, though." Jemison looks at me. "Rogers, would you mind joining us for the meeting?"

I wait for the captain to say something, but he doesn't. Of course not. The chief wouldn't have suggested it if she didn't know he would approve. These two have known each other long enough to make accidental disagreements unlikely.

"What do you want me to say?" I ask.

"Just tell them what you saw in here," she says. "Don't worry about blowing your cover. What's the standard story these days? State Department researcher?"

"Interplanetary trade inspector. It's a classic." Obscure enough to explain my implants, boring enough that nobody asks.

She nods. "The eye's unusual, but not implausible. If anyone asks about where you hide your gun, we can hand-wave that."

"Sure. I'll tell them I'm a ninja."

"Don't quit your day job," Jemison says without missing a beat. "Go take a nap or get breakfast or something. I'll send a security escort for you at 0900."

CHAPTER TEN

Dejah Thoris—Deck B, officers' briefing room
30 minutes after room service delivered an unsatisfying omelet

I'm glad it's not Danny and Mike who show up to escort me to the staff meeting. No awkward conversation required. The security guards lead me into a crew elevator, which takes us to a conference room near the top of the ship.

The elliptical chamber is located directly behind the ship's main command and control center, commonly called the bridge. There's one door leading to the bridge, and one door leading to a hallway connecting to the service elevator. A large circular table occupies most of the floor space. Monitors and control panels cover the walls. There are no chairs.

Santamaria and Jemison are already in the briefing room, standing next to a slim woman with red hair and freckled skin. On the other side of the redhead is a square-jawed man tapping at a computer tablet.

Santamaria introduces the woman as Commander Erica Galbraith, the ship's executive officer. Her smile is friendly and open as she shakes my hand, and I'm pretty sure the stripes on her uniform shirt are purely decorative. A cruise ship doesn't need to have all ex-military personnel as officers, but passengers probably enjoy the illusion of rank and implied authority.

The man with the tablet is Jefferson Logan, the ship's cruise director. I've heard his cheery voice making announcements several times a day over loudspeakers. I notice something precise, but not military, about the way Logan moves. Acrobat, maybe? Definitely some zero-gee movement training there. According to the cruise brochures, he's in charge of all midway activities and excursions.

The door from the hallway opens, and a bald, dark-skinned man enters. He's wearing a white lab coat, and his pockets are bulging with equipment. The captain introduces him as Dr. Rahul Sawhney. I shake the doctor's hand and wait patiently, trying to look nonchalant, as Santamaria explains who I am and why I'm joining their briefing.

"We've been broadcasting David Wachlin's face on all the information kiosks throughout the ship," Santamaria says. "Jeff, has anybody come forward with information yet?"

"Nothing that we can confirm," Logan says. "Twenty people reported to security that they saw someone who might have been David Wachlin, but we couldn't verify using cameras or internal sensor logs."

"Doctor," Santamaria says, "were you able to contact the Wachlins' physician back on Earth?"

"Yes," says Sawhney. "Dr. George LaMori. He said that David has experienced episodes of confusion before, but nothing that ever suggested he was capable of violence, much less murder. Doctor LaMori prescribed the Stelomane and Dalazine—and, more recently, also the alpha wave generator, at the family's request."

"Could the alpha wave generator have triggered the psychosis?" Galbraith asks.

"It's unlikely," Sawhney says, almost sighing. "Alpha wave generators have never been conclusively shown to produce the calming effects that their manufacturers claim. They're a homeopathic remedy, a placebo. It's more likely this trip into space is confusing David's body, and the unfamiliar discomfort is aggravating his mental state."

"It's a long way from spacesick to double homicide," Jemison says.

Sawhney raises his hands and shoulders in a shrug. "Schizophrenia is still poorly understood. We can treat certain symptoms, but it's impossible to know what's going on inside David's head."

Santamaria nods. "Chief, why don't you tell everyone what you and Mr. Rogers found in the stateroom."

Jemison describes the scene in the Wachlins' suite. I watch the reactions around the table. Logan hasn't heard any of this before, and he's horrified. Galbraith is hearing some of the details for the first time. The doctor seems preoccupied.

"Still no sign of the murder weapon," Jemison concludes. "Doc estimates it was about fifteen centimeters long, a smooth, sharp blade. Probably some kind of knife."

"That's right," Sawhney says. "Both Emily and Alan were killed with the same weapon."

My head jerks upward. "Wait. You didn't tell me that." I look over at Jemison, then Santamaria.

Jemison says, "Sorry. There was a lot going on last night."

She's lying. They were testing me, seeing if I would notice on my own, ascertaining just how useful I might be overall. I can tell from the apologetic expression in Santamaria's eyes. But even he's not that sorry.

I'm not angry at them. I just have something to prove now.

"Alan Wachlin's body also had third-degree burns all over," Sawhney continues. "Post-mortem damage. He was killed before the fire started."

"So why burn one body, but not the other? David killed both of them with the same knife. Why not finish the job the same way?" I ask.

"Maybe the fire scared him," Galbraith says.

"It was pretty severe," Jemison says. "Fire suppression was in progress when Ellie and I arrived—"

"Our chief engineer responded to a fire alarm in a passenger stateroom?" Santamaria says.

"We were in the neighborhood," Jemison says. "Long story. Anyway, we grabbed handheld extinguishers and ran in to assist."

Something's bothering me about this scenario. Something doesn't add up.

"Doctor." I turn to Sawhney. "How long does it take for third-degree burns to develop?"

"It could be less than a second, if the temperature is high enough," he says.

Temperature.

"The sprinklers would have triggered immediately," Galbraith says. "The sensors respond to heat."

I remember my trip outside the ship, the sight of the cargo containers, and the disassembled microwave oven. I also recall what my left eye was originally designed to do.

"What if he wasn't burned by the fire?" I ask. "What if something else caused that tissue damage?"

Jemison glares at me. "What the hell are you talking about, Rogers?"

"Did you determine what started the fire in the first place? Was there a lighter, a book of matches, a nearby source of open flame? A plasma leak?"

"That's not possible," Galbraith says. "The EP conduits don't pass anywhere near any passenger staterooms or crew quarters."

Santamaria and Jemison exchange a glance. "Mr. Rogers, what are you suggesting?" the captain asks.

"Something started that fire," I say. "Something hot enough to give a human body third-degree burns in the short time before the sprinklers could activate. Something that internal sensors didn't register as fire before then."

There's a moment of silence while everyone stares at me.

"Ionizing radiation," Santamaria says.

"What?" Jemison shakes her head. "All the passenger decks are shielded. We sail with the cargo sections turned toward the Sun. And even that's not anywhere near enough exposure to cause visible burns."

"It didn't come from outside the ship," I say. "Captain, with your permission, I'd like to take a closer look at the body."

Dr. Sawhney takes a detour to Sickbay, then meets Santamaria, Jemison, Galbraith, Logan, and me in the hallway outside suite 5028, carrying a radiation detector. The rest of us watch as the doctor switches on the device and points it at the door. Security already cleared the hallway, so there are no gawking passersby to be alarmed by the high-pitched, staccato beeping that bursts forth from the detector.

"Good Lord," Sawhney says, "that's nearly ten curies! What could be producing that much radiation?"

"Jeff, evacuate all passengers in this section, and one deck above and below," Santamaria says. "Move them to empty staterooms in other sections. Chief, we'll need crew in hazmat gear to collect the Wachlins' belongings and decontaminate what we can."

A thought twitches in my head as Logan leaves and Jemison steps away to issue orders by radio. The crew only has civilian hazmat gear. They'll be shielded from biochemical contaminants, but what about radiation? A ship like this doesn't normally have any heavy emission sources on board, not even in engineering. Ionwells burn clean.

"Mr. Rogers," Santamaria says to me, "would you mind looking up Alan Wachlin's military service record?"

"Already on it," I say. I powered up the dish and began inputting my query as soon as the detector started making noise.

"He wasn't active military," the doctor mutters, almost to himself. He's taking readings from either side of the door. "And all passengers and luggage are screened before boarding. How could he smuggle any radioactive material on board? Why would he?"

"You're searching through classified military records?" Galbraith asks me.

"They're not all classified," I say. "Just looking for more detail on exactly what he did in the service."

"Doctor," Santamaria says, "did Alan's medical records say which branch of service he was in?"

"United States Army. Special Forces."

Santamaria nods and says to Galbraith, "Special Forces are often involved in unconventional warfare operations. They may be outfitted with special equipment to help them deal with extraordinary situations."

"But what equipment would he still have with him? Wouldn't he—" Galbraith stops, then stares at me. "You're talking about surgical implants."

"Yes," Santamaria says. "Many soldiers are implanted with battery packs to power their in-body equipment. Communication gear is the most common. A few decades ago, the army experimented with more powerful technologies. Atomic energy cores, for example."

Galbraith frowns. "Isn't that, uh, insanely dangerous?"

"To say the least," Sawhney says. He shakes his head and turns off the detector.

"Which is why they stopped doing it after the Independence War," Santamaria says. "But it turned out to be impossible to remove some of the atomics without killing their owners."

A declassified military service record flashes into my eye. "Alan Wachlin was deployed on Mars," I say. "Olympus Base, eight years ago. Prewar peacekeeping unit. He received a field implant package with a particle emission capture core."

Nobody speaks for a moment.

"Is it still burning?" Santamaria asks.

"Still burning?" Galbraith's voice comes out as a squeak.

I switch my eye to sensing mode and peer into the stateroom. I wasn't looking for this type of radiation before, but now I can see it everywhere, splashed all over the walls where the visible char marks are. There's a fizzing sphere in the center of the bed, right around where Alan's heart would be.

"Yes," I say. Everyone starts talking at once.

"Nobody goes into that stateroom until we reach Mars orbit," Santamaria says.

"We all need to start radiation treatment right away," Sawhney says. "Everyone who was in that room. My God!"

"We have some extra baffle shielding in storage. I'll send serv-bots to seal off the contaminated areas," Galbraith says.

Jemison finishes her radio call and walks back into the babble of voices. "I'm guessing this isn't good news," she says.

"Alan Wachlin had a PECC in his chest. It's still burning," I say.

Jemison blinks. "Shit."

While everyone else runs around, doing their jobs, I play back my data recording of the crime scene from my earlier inspection. There's definitely blood on Alan's bed, so he was still alive when his power core went critical. I can't tell from the vid whether he had any knife wounds other than the one across his throat.

It's hard to trace the microcables implanted in his body through all the damaged tissue, but it doesn't look like any of the major lines have been cut. And that wouldn't have caused a meltdown anyway. Either his attacker—his brother, David—stabbed him in the chest and cut into the circuitry of the power plant, or David's weight on Alan's chest pressed the core against his spine, and the fifteen-year-old outer casing cracked.

I report my findings to Santamaria as we stand in Sickbay, waiting for Jemison to finish her radiation treatment. We've all changed out of our clothes and showered, scrubbing our skin to remove as many irradiated cells as we can.

"David's probably scared out of his mind," I say. "He's been off his medication for, what, twelve hours now? I can't believe nobody's run into him yet. Where's he hiding?"

"We don't have complete internal sensor coverage," Santamaria says. He sounds more thoughtful than annoyed. What does it take to make this guy lose his cool? His service records say he fought at Elysium Planitia, in one of the most brutal battles of the Independence War. I wonder if he grew the beard to hide his scars.

"All we have are cameras in public areas, and door lock sensors," Santamaria continues. "I'd like you to go with Chief Jemison and scan for heat signatures, but first we'll need to narrow down the range of likely hiding places."

Jemison walks out of the exam room, grimacing. "I forgot how horrible that medicine tastes. Yuck." She gets a paper cup and fills it with water from the cooler while the captain asks her about a search plan. I make a mental note to look up the effectiveness of civilian anti-radiation meds.

Jemison gulps down her water and says, "Security's been on alert since last night. He had maybe a two-hour window to find a hiding place. It can't be any of the restaurants or activity areas. Staff would have found him when they opened."

"Where does a schizophrenic suffering a psychotic episode want to go?" I wonder aloud.

"We don't have any sensors in the service stairwells," Jemison says. "That's as good a place to start as any. We'll see what we can think of as we go along."

Santamaria nods. "Proceed, Chief. I'll be on the bridge."

We leave Sickbay. Santamaria walks to the passenger elevator. Jemison leads me the other way, to the service elevator.

"So, after we don't find anything in the stairwells, where do we look next?" I ask.

Jemison's radio beeps before she can answer. "Security to Chief Jemison," says a tinny male voice.

Jemison squeezes the radio button on her collar. "Jemison here, go ahead."

"Chief, this is Blevins. I've got a search detail on deck eight and we've found something."

CHAPTER ELEVEN

Dejah Thoris—Deck 8, restricted area
Hopefully not minutes before somebody else gets killed

Jemison and I step out of the crew elevator to find four security guards clustered around a large access door marked LIFEBOAT. We're at the perimeter of the ship, one circular hallway out from the nearest state-rooms, next to a vending machine alcove. Two of the security guards have their stunners drawn. Another one is holding a hand scanner. Out of habit, I read their name tags as soon as I get close enough. More information is never a bad thing.

The guard named Blevins walks out to meet Jemison and me as we approach. His face looks awfully familiar, and after a second, I remember. He was one of the guards who interrupted my inebriated stroll that first night—the one I nicknamed Blue-Ear. He doesn't appear to recognize me, fortunately.

"Friend of ours?" he asks Jemison, nodding at me.

"Name's Rogers. He's cool," Jemison says. Apparently that's enough for Blevins. "What did you find?"

"This section is vacant," Blevins explains. "We were sweeping it just in case the missing person managed to sneak into a crew area, like your friend here did last night."

Okay, so he did recognize me. I suspect Danny and Mike have been spreading vicious lies about me through the ranks of ship's security.

"What did you find?" Jemison repeats, not even acknowledging Blevins's attitude.

Blevins stops giving me the eye and straightens up. "That." He points to the controls next to the lifeboat door. A mess of red streaks covers the not-quite-closed plastic panel.

I know blood when I see it, and so does Jemison—her hand moves to the stunner on her hip. "Someone's inside?"

"Heat signature matches one adult male. He's not moving."

"Rogers," Jemison says to me, "is that David Wachlin in the lifeboat?"

"How is he going to know?" Blevins asks.

"I'm a U.S. State Department trade inspector," I say. "I have a cargo scanning implant. It might not work in this situation, but it's worth a try."

"Go ahead, Rogers," Jemison says.

I switch on my HUD and activate my eye's radiation sensors. I see the heat signature as I cycle through scanner modes. The size, shape, and temperature are consistent with an adult human, sitting on the floor at the far end of the lifeboat.

But that could be anyone. I change the detection spectrum, and the image becomes a splotchy pink outline of a torso, head, and arms. David Wachlin might have cleaned himself up, but he can't get rid of the radiation damage from his brother's broken PECC.

"It's him," I say.

"Does he have a weapon?" Jemison asks.

"I need a radio source."

Jemison taps her radio button. "All security personnel, this is Chief Jemison. I'm going to transmit a long squawk as a test signal. Turn down your speaker volume and stay off this channel for the next thirty seconds.

"Repeat, I am squawking a long and loud test signal, starting in three, two, one, *now*."

She taps her wristband while talking. The four guards nearby do the same. After Jemison says "now," I hear a soft, rhythmic beeping from her radio button.

All sorts of metal objects and magnetic fields light up in my HUD. It takes me a few seconds to locate the knife. I'm confused by the shape at first, because I was imagining a kitchen knife, like a chef's knife, which would be long and roughly triangular. But why would someone bring a kitchen knife onto a cruise? That might seem suspicious during a luggage search.

On the other hand, Alan Wachlin was in the army, and it wouldn't be unusual for him to keep souvenirs from his military service.

"I see the knife," I say. "It's on the first bench against the wall, on the left, near the entry hatch. He's sitting on the floor, all the way in the back on the right."

"Thank you, Mr. Rogers," Jemison says. I step back to let her put my intelligence into operational action.

She silences her radio and motions for the two closest guards, Scotton and Beseda, to stand back and cover the door with their stunners. The one with the heat sensor, Yang, puts his equipment down and draws his own stunner. He and Blevins follow Jemison and position themselves on either side of the hatch. Blevins puts one hand on the handle and looks at Jemison, who's aiming her stunner directly at the lifeboat hatch. She nods.

I'm looking at an infrared view when Blevins yanks open the hatch. Jemison stays where she is while Yang snaps his body into the open doorway, brandishing his stunner. Blevins mirrors him on the other side of the hatchway, barely a second behind. The man inside the lifeboat doesn't react at all.

I switch off my HUD to get a better, stereoscopic view. The sensors are useful, but it can be tiring, not to mention disorienting, to see a different image in each eye for too long.

The lower part of the man's face is wet, as if he's been drooling. His head is tipped back against the wall, and his eyes are unfocused. His knees are bent up to his chest. His arms are wrapped loosely around his legs. His hands are shaking.

I couldn't see the blood through my scanner view. It's all over his chest, soaked through his shirt, covering most of his neck and the lower part of his face. I'm surprised he didn't track more of it through the ship on his way here.

"David Wachlin," Jemison calls into the lifeboat. "Can you hear me?"

The man says nothing.

"Mr. Wachlin, I'm Security Chief Jemison. We're here to take you to Sickbay. Can you understand me?"

No answer. Would disorientation from space travel really affect a schizophrenic this badly?

"We're coming into the lifeboat now," Jemison says. "We're going to help you.

"Yang, get the knife," she says in a quieter voice. Yang pulls himself out of the doorway, retrieves a plastic pouch from the equipment kit lying on the floor of the corridor, and steps into the lifeboat just far enough to bag the knife. It's an army survival knife, standard issue for infantry. The blade is nearly thirteen centimeters long and coated with dried blood.

Jemison enters the lifeboat, followed by Blevins. It's a long, narrow space, with benches along either wall. Yang covers them from the hatchway. Blevins stands over David Wachlin, stunner at the ready, while Jemison rolls him onto the floor and binds his wrists together. She tries to be gentle, but he's a heavyset guy, and it doesn't help that his body is completely limp. He'll probably have bruises tomorrow.

"Okay," Jemison says. "Let's get a nurse down here with a stretcher."

Scotton calls Sickbay. Inside the lifeboat, Blevins and Yang sit down on the benches on either side of Wachlin, watching him. Outside in the corridor, Beseda and Scotton holster their stunners. Jemison walks back to me.

"Any idea how he got inside without tripping the alarm?" I ask.

She shakes her head. "No. The seal was definitely broken, so the circuit must have been opened."

I look back down the empty corridor. "Is this section powered down? To conserve energy when you don't need full life support, something like that?"

"The lifeboat alarms are on a different system," Jemison says. "They're always on."

"And it's pretty unlikely that Wachlin could have bypassed it," I say.

"Not in his current state," Jemison says, looking back at the glassy-eyed, catatonic man lying on the floor of the lifeboat. "Even if he had, we'd be able to tell. The locking mechanism is purely mechanical, so there's no electrical . . ."

She trails off and walks past me, heading back toward the elevator. I follow her. She stops in the middle of the corridor, kneels in front of an access panel, and pulls it open.

"Shouldn't that be locked?" I ask.

"Yes," she says. "But it's a mechanical lock. No alarm."

She pulls a small flashlight from her belt and shines it into the recessed area. I can see switches and wires and little yellow tags. She traces her fingers along one bundle of wires, finds a tag, and leans in to read it.

"Goddammit," she says. "Bad cable. Tagged for maintenance six months ago, never repaired. I am going to have somebody's job for this."

She slams the panel shut and stands back up.

"So, no tampering, then," I say.

"Power was on, but the comm line was out. The alarm tripped, but the signal didn't go anywhere. I swear to God, heads are going to roll."

She doesn't raise her voice, but her eyes are on fire. I try to imagine how she feels. Probably something like how Paul feels when I screw up. It's not his mistake, but it's his responsibility.

While Blevins and company take David Wachlin to Sickbay, Jemison and I check more lifeboats, then report back to the captain in the briefing room. Commander Galbraith and Dr. Sawhney are also at the conference table when we arrive.

"Three other access points in that section," Jemison says. She taps her wristband against the conference table. The surface lights up with data. "Same inspection date, no later service date. The cable tags don't agree with the maintenance logs, which say they were fixed a week later. But we checked the cables themselves, and they're definitely worn."

Santamaria looks over the table display. "We need to review all our maintenance logs and work schedules for the last six months. Erica, sorry, but that's yours."

Galbraith shrugs. "You know how much I love paperwork, Captain."

Santamaria smiles, but it fades quickly. "Doctor, how's our patient doing?"

"Stable, and in restraints," Sawhney says. "We put him on a sedative drip for now. We don't want to risk any of his current medications, in case they trigger another episode. Unfortunately, we can't do a full blood panel here. We don't have the right equipment. We're running a tox screen, but it won't be finished until tomorrow."

"Very well." Santamaria turns to me. "Mr. Rogers, thank you for the assistance."

I nod. "I'd say it was my pleasure, but that seems a little inappropriate."

"Chief Jemison will escort you back to the passenger sections. Enjoy the rest of your cruise," he says.

Santamaria and Galbraith return to the bridge. Sawhney disappears down the hallway. Jemison leads me back to the elevator.

We ride down to deck six in silence. When we arrive, I step out into the corridor, then notice she's not following. I turn around and look back into the elevator.

"Good working with you, Rogers," she says, extending her hand.

We shake hands, and I suddenly don't want her to go.

No—it's not *Jemison* I want to stay. It's this feeling of having something to do. I actually enjoyed that meeting just now, and I hate meetings.

Being in the meeting meant I was on the job. I don't want to be a civilian again.

Jemison releases my hand, and I raise my arm to hold the elevator door open.

"Can I ask you for a favor?" I say.

She hesitates for the briefest of moments. "Sure. You want an extra mint on your pillow? We get that a lot."

She's not smiling, but I am. No matter how much she might deny it, working with me today wasn't a complete pain in her ass. I can tell.

"I have a dinner seating at the Captain's Table," I say. Her expression tells me that she sympathizes. "But I don't really feel comfortable there. I'm not a tourist. Is there any chance I could eat in the crew mess instead?"

"You don't appreciate the wide selection of fine dining options available on the lido deck?"

"The small talk is killing me," I say. "I'm not antisocial, I'm just—not a tourist."

"You could do a better job of pretending," she says, smiling.

"I'm on vacation," I say. *And apparently I suck at being on vacation.*

"I'll talk to the captain," she says. "Now, if there's nothing else?"

I drop my arm and step backward. The elevator doors close. Something else is bothering me, but I can't quite put my finger on it. I go back to my room and dig into my gift basket. It takes several miniature bottles of whiskey and a few hours of sleep for me to suss out the bother.

CHAPTER TWELVE

Dejah Thoris—Deck 17, crew mess hall
4 hours after the unsatisfying omelet

Captain Santamaria agrees to let me eat in the crew mess, and Chief Jemison leads me there for lunch. She's on her radio when she knocks on my stateroom door, sorting out something to do with children polluting swimming pools, and all my attempts at interrupting her during our walk are met with increasingly hostile glares. I decide to wait until we sit down to talk to her about David Wachlin.

That tiny alarm bell in the back of my head has been jangling all morning. It's an awfully big coincidence that out of all the places someone could hide on this enormous ship, the guy suffering a violent schizophrenic episode just happened to stumble into a lifeboat with its alarms disabled. Too many unlikely occurrences piled into one incident.

Maybe it's nothing. But what if it's not nothing?

I don't imagine the *Dejah Thoris* security staff normally conducts many criminal investigations. And I'm undoubtedly better trained in analysis than any of the crew; that's what I did for the duration of the war, when the agency wouldn't let me travel off-world. They didn't want to risk their only access to the pocket getting captured or killed. I learned a lot sitting behind that desk.

Jemison can use my help, whether she wants it or not. Especially if she also has to deal with the normal passenger shenanigans all week. How *did* those kids sneak so much soup out of the buffet and all the way over to the hot tub?

The crew mess hall is utilitarian and sparse, all bright, flat, off-white surfaces—nothing like the ornate and gilded main dining room. I imagine

Santamaria up there, making small talk with a new group of folks who feel special just because they get to sit next to a guy in a costume. I look around the slightly dingy but entirely functional mess hall and take a deep breath, inhaling the smells of steamed rice, curried meats, and stewed vegetables. Nothing fancy or gourmet. Just good, basic, square meals.

Jemison leads me through the food service line and then the moderately crowded seating area—it's dense enough that I have to maneuver to avoid people, but not so bad that collisions are inevitable. We wind our way to a table against the back wall while I consider the best way to start this conversation.

Hey, Chief, that looks like a tasty sandwich. Speaking of sandwiches, are you familiar with the term "suspicion sandwich"? What Intel calls a PBJ: Possible But Janky?

"That's going to be a laugh and a half," Jemison grumbles, turning off her radio and dropping her tray on the table. "Hey, stranger."

"Hey yourself," says a familiar voice. I step out from behind Jemison, toward one of the other chairs at the table.

I don't recognize the woman sitting in front of me for a few seconds, until she lowers her reading tablet and looks up. Her hair is down, and it frames her face and just touches the shoulderboards on her dress uniform. She looks like she's ready for a parade.

It's Ellie Gavilán.

Jemison waves a hand at me. "Ellie, this is Mr. Rogers, an observer from the State Department. Rogers—"

"We've met," I say.

Jemison frowns. "Where?"

"Oh, Evan took the engine room tour yesterday," Ellie says. "I didn't know his last name, though. Rajah?"

"Evan's fine," I say. "Just call me Evan."

We shake hands. Her palm feels soft and warm. I don't want to let go.

I must have a stupid grin on my face, because Jemison kicks me in the shin. She's already taken her seat and started eating. I release Ellie's hand and sit down. Ellie puts her tablet aside. I also start eating, so my sudden inability to make small talk will be less obvious.

"What's with the whites?" Jemison asks, nodding at Ellie's outfit.

"VIPs," Ellie says, raising one hand and twirling her index finger. "I have to give a full power plant tour, then choke down a formal dinner in the main dining room at five."

"A fate worse than death," Jemison agrees.

Ellie turns to me. "So Evan, you're with the State Department? Trade inspector, I think you said?"

Of course my mouth is full. I nod. "Mm-hmm."

"I hope we're not in any trouble," Ellie says, and winks at me. I can feel my heart melting.

"Rogers is on vacation," Jemison says. "Captain asked me to show him around. As a professional courtesy."

"Hmm." Ellie seems dubious. "Why is a trade inspector so interested in spacecraft engines?"

"Always wanted to be an astronaut. Couldn't tough out the higher math, but I turned out to be okay at bean-counting." All this fake disclosure is starting to make me uncomfortable. "What about you? How did you get into space?"

She shrugs. "The usual way. Joined the navy."

"Ellie served six years in US-OSS," Jemison says. She pronounces the acronym "you-sauce," like a proper spaceman, and I nearly choke on my food.

If Ellie served in OSS, she was in the same branch of service as my standard off-world cover identity. She almost certainly knows more than I do about actually being in the military.

My heartbeat races before I remember that I'm not using that legend right now. I'm a different person, on vacation, not on mission. I hope my smile doesn't look too fake. I didn't prepare at all for this outing, and I feel like I'm sinking in the deep end of the pool.

"Well," my lizard brain says, "thank you for serving."

"Oh, that reminds me." Ellie taps at her wristband controls. "Andie, we need to reschedule the maintenance in 5028." She glances at me. "Can we talk about this now?"

"We can talk," Jemison says. "Rogers knows all about it. But we can't reschedule. Tomorrow's midway."

"And you don't know how many sections we still need to secure before zero-gee," Ellie says. "Our last turnaround was way too short."

"The passengers can do without a few extra activity spaces," Jemison says. "5028 is a crime scene. That takes precedence."

"Okay, law-and-order, but do you really want me to pull an entire sanitation crew for one stateroom?"

Jemison leans forward and lowers her voice. "Your guys will be in full hazmat gear. It's going to take them twice as long to do anything. And we've got less than twelve hours."

"Security already imaged every square centimeter of that stateroom," Ellie says. "We're going to make more of a mess packing everything away than zero-gee will."

"Fine." Jemison jabs at her own wristband. "I can give you four people at 1600."

Ellie cocks her head. "I'm guessing these aren't going to be volunteers."

"Nope, so you'd better have some leave vouchers handy."

"I can live with that. Are you coming to join us in the soup?"

Jemison shakes her head. "Other duties."

I remember what Jemison said in the briefing room: that she and Ellie first responded to the fire in 5028. How long did they spend in there? How long were they exposed to the radiation they didn't know was leaking from Wachlin's damaged PECC?

I blink my eye into sensing mode. Both women are silhouetted in pink, just like David Wachlin was. That can't be good. The less time anybody spends in that stateroom, the better. I turn off my eye.

"Can't the maintenance robots handle the cleanup?" I ask.

"Not without supervision," Ellie says. "Robots are good at repetitive, predictable tasks. This is going to require human initiative."

"So how long do you reckon it'll take?"

Jemison squints at me. "Why do you care, cowboy?"

"I could help," I say.

The squinting continues. "We wouldn't want to waste your talents."

"It's not a problem."

"Let's keep it that way."

Ellie chuckles. "So. Evan. How long have you and Andie known each other?"

"What?" Jemison and I say in unison. We exchange puzzled glances, then look back to see if Ellie's joking. She's not.

"We don't," Jemison says.

"We just met," I say, overlapping her.

"Yesterday," Jemison adds.

"Oh," Ellie says. She seems disappointed.

"Why would you think—I mean, no offense, Chief, but why would you think that?" I ask Ellie.

She shrugs, and she makes even that tiny motion look cute. "It's just the way you two talk to each other. It feels like you've, I don't know, been through something together."

Normally, I would be panicking now. She's just made me, seen through my cover to something real underneath, and that usually means I've been compromised and need to get the hell out of the situation.

But instead of panic, I feel . . . unburdened. Ellie just gave me permission to relax my disguise.

"You know what it is," I say. "It's because we were both stationed on Mars for a while. Before the war."

We weren't there at the same time or anywhere near the same place, but I hope Jemison plays along. Out of the corner of my eye, I see her hand curling into a fist under the table.

"Stationed?" Ellie raises an eyebrow. "As what, a street urchin? Were you even out of school before the war?"

"Absolutely." It's not a lie. "I'm older than I look."

"And I didn't know you were on Mars, Andie," Ellie says to Jemison.

"I don't like to talk about it," Jemison says. There's an edge in her voice.

Ellie nods and turns back to me. "So what were *you* doing on the red planet, Mr. State Department Trade Inspector?"

There's a lilt in her voice. She expects me to be evasive, too.

"Spying," I say.

Ellie bursts out laughing. "No, seriously."

"I am serious," I say. "What, you don't think I could be a spy?"

Ellie shakes her head, smiling. "Evan, I think you would be the worst spy in the entire Solar System."

I force my own smile to remain in place. Does this mean I'm doing my job really well or really badly?

I turn to Jemison and ask, "And what do you think?"

She's been frowning and pursing her lips this whole time, but now she loses it, doubling over with laughter. Ellie starts laughing again too.

"Okay, yeah, that's hilarious," I grumble. "Thanks for the vote of confidence."

"Sorry, Rogers," Jemison says, recovering her composure. "It's just such a ridiculous thought, you know?"

She wipes some post-guffaw tears from her eyes and grins at me. I chew my food and give her a blank stare.

"I'm sorry," Ellie says. "I didn't mean to destroy one of your childhood dreams."

"Don't worry about it." I turn toward Jemison. "People underestimate me."

"I can believe that," she says, chuckling.

Ellie reaches across the table and puts her hand over mine. I do my best not to stare, but my heart rate shoots up, and the display in my left eye pops up a medical warning, just in case I didn't notice my pulse skyrocketing. I twitch my other fingers—the ones not being held by Ellie—and turn off the display.

"She does this with everyone," Ellie says, patting my hand. "It's nothing personal."

I feel lightheaded. "Thanks," I manage to say through my happy haze.

"Have you been to Mars recently?" Ellie asks. "Since the war, I mean?"

I shake my head. "I've been pretty busy elsewhere."

"Sometimes," Ellie says, and stops. She lowers her voice. "Sometimes I feel very glad that US-OSS discharged me before the shooting started. Is that wrong? Is that selfish?"

"No," Jemison says. "You should never feel bad about staying out of a war."

I don't know what to say.

Ellie's wristband beeps. "Oh, boy. Are you seeing this, Andie?"

Jemison raises her wrist and frowns. "Seriously? Where are the parents?"

Ellie stands up. I reflexively do the same. "Sorry to eat and run, Evan, but I need to go take care of this." She smiles. "It was nice to see you again."

"Likewise," I say, hoping she'll offer to shake my hand. She doesn't.

"We should go, too," Jemison says. "Get a box for that, Rogers."

"Where are we going?" I watch Ellie walk out of the mess hall, admiring how the uniform flatters her figure.

"I'm going back to work. You're doing whatever you want."

I turn back to Jemison. "I thought you wanted my help."

She shakes her head. "You're on vacation, Rogers. Enjoy it."

I lean close to her and lower my voice. "We need to talk about David Wachlin."

"Don't worry about him. We're dealing with it."

"I can help."

"I'll tell you if we need your help."

"I have tools that nobody else on this ship has."

"And we don't need any of them right now. Go. Have fun."

I don't know how. "Okay, well, how about the radiation thing? I can use my eye—"

"What part of 'go away' do you not understand? We actually do know what we're doing around here, Rogers. I appreciate the offer, but it's going to be more trouble adding you to the mix than just letting the crew do their jobs. Now come on."

She picks up both our trays and heads for the exit. I follow her reluctantly.

It's pretty clear I'm not going talk Jemison into deputizing me to help with anything. But there is someone else I can talk to. Someone who can get me back into Jemison's good graces after I demonstrate my usefulness on another task. Someone who ought to care a lot more about radiation hazards.

Someone who's having dinner with some VIPs tonight.

CHAPTER THIRTEEN

Dejah Thoris—Deck 10, Promenade
4 hours before Ellie's VIP dinner

I say good-bye to Jemison at the elevator, go to the excursions booking desk on the Promenade, and flip through the offerings on the automated kiosk. I don't see any listings for a VIP dinner with the chief engineer. Maybe it's a private group.

I step away from the kiosk and into the actual booking area, a small niche with a wraparound vid wall and a single work desk. The wall shows an undersea reef scene with various colorful aquatic creatures. I walk up to the desk and sit down in one of the two cushy chairs in front of it. The crewman behind the desk stops working on his computer and turns to greet me. I don't recognize him until it's too late.

"How may I help you today, sir?" Ward says. "Oh. Hello, sir." His grin only falters for a split second. I have to admit, the kid's a professional. "Good to see you again. Did you enjoy your tour of the engine room?"

"Absolutely," I say. "Will the booking agent be back soon?"

"I am the booking agent, sir."

"I thought you—never mind." I lean forward. "I have kind of a strange request."

"I will do my best to assist you, sir." He makes it sound like I'm seeking psychiatric help.

"I was talking to someone at the bar," I say, "and he mentioned there's some kind of VIP table at dinner tonight? Like the Captain's Table, but with some of the engineering officers?"

"We offer several types of hosted dining sessions," Ward says. "Would you like me to check?"

"If you don't mind."

He turns to his computer and taps at the keyboard. "Ah, yes. Our chief engineer will be dining at the five o'clock formal dinner tonight."

"That's right," I say. "Are there any more seats available at that table?"

"I'm sorry, sir," Ward says, allowing his smile to evaporate, "but this particular table has been reserved by a private group."

"Oh, I know." I am totally making this up as I go along. "My friend from the bar? He's one of them. He invited me to join them."

"I see." Ward nods. "And what is your friend's name?"

"Shit. I knew I forgot something." I force a laugh. "Didn't get his name. Listen, maybe you could just switch me to that table for tonight's dinner? I'm usually at the Captain's Table, but you know. I've already heard all his space stories. Could do with some new company."

Ward doesn't answer right away. He appears to be savoring this moment of power. If I were drunk, I'd be thinking about smacking that smug expression off his face.

"I'm so sorry, sir," he says. "Only the guest who made the original booking is allowed to change the reservation. Perhaps you could ask your friend to make the request."

"Right. Sure." I stand up. "Thank you. I'll just go see if he's still at the bar."

"Of course, sir. Have a wonderful day!" Ward smiles and waves as I retreat.

I walk around the corner and halfway down the Promenade before doing a brief frustration dance, punching the air with both fists and jumping up and down.

You have years of training with a first-world intelligence agency, Kangaroo. Did you really just get outmaneuvered by a fucking travel agent?

No. No, I didn't. I have options. There are always options.

It's too bad I can't solve this problem with my fists. People say violence is never the answer, but learning how to beat down kids twice my size sure helped me out when I was younger.

That was before I met Paul. Before he showed me that people can be manipulated without physical contact, as long as you have access to the right resources. You just have to figure out what your target wants.

Well, I've got some stuff in the pocket. So what does Ward want?

Ward works on commission.

I find the nearest restroom, hide in a vacant stall, open the pocket, and retrieve a small bundle from my emergency equipment reserve. Then I walk back to the excursions desk.

"Hello again, sir," Ward says. "Is there something else I can help you with?"

"I remembered my friend's name," I say, sitting down. "It's Jameter Maitland."

I lay a crisp hundred-dollar bill on the desk and slide it forward. A holographic bust of the late President Maitland shimmers from the surface of the banknote.

Ward, to his credit, doesn't react visibly to my bribe attempt. He looks past me to the Promenade, his eyes scanning left and right, then fixes me with a stare.

"I think he had a twin brother," he says, "didn't he?"

I was prepared for this. I peel another hundred from the roll in my other hand and slide it across the table.

"Actually," Ward says, "I'm pretty sure there were *three* brothers."

I frown. "Really?"

He nods. "Really."

I pulled that second bill too soon. This is what happens when you don't rehearse the play. But hey, it's not my money. I drop a third Maitland on the desk. Ward reaches for the bills, but I don't let go.

"So you can help me with this request?" I ask.

He nods, retracts his hand, and turns back to the computer. After a moment of typing, he says, "I can't seat you with the VIPs, but I can place you at a table right next to them. You'll have a clear view. Good enough?"

I was hoping to talk to Ellie during dinner, but I can at least catch her before she goes back into the crew sections. Still better than breaking in and risking Jemison's ire. "That'll do."

I lift my hand. Ward sweeps the cash away in one smooth motion. "Are you all set for formalwear, sir?"

"You guys aren't *that* strict about the dress code, are you?"

I really don't like Ward's smile.

I didn't read all of the Princess of Mars Cruises introductory documents before boarding this jolly vessel. I was in a hurry. So I failed to pack appropriate attire for the formal dinners. And the agency does not consider a tuxedo important enough to qualify as always-in-pocket emergency equipment.

The good news is, there's a tailor shop on the Promenade, which Ward is all too happy to direct me toward. And I'm not paying for this holiday.

The tailor takes my measurements and tells me to come back in an hour. After pausing in front of the barbershop next door and deciding I don't want to mess with my hair right now, I go back to my room to shower and shave.

The mirror in my bathroom must have some kind of high-tech defogging mechanism, because it's not even clouded when I step out of the shower. I have a very clear view of my average body and nondescript face as I approach the sink.

Paul really lucked out, finding a brown kid with a superpower who would do his bidding. In additional to implanting my bionic left eye, the agency re-cut my face before I went into the field, to make me look as unremarkable as possible. Shallow chin, flat nose; not too handsome, not too ugly. I can blend into most any crowd, and as long as I don't open my mouth, people can mistake me for a local pretty easily.

The agency gave me a new identity, a new life, and all I had to give up was my face. I was okay with that. I didn't want to be a scared kid anymore. I wanted to leave everything behind. I wanted to be somebody else.

So who are you going to be tonight, Kangaroo?

This self-cleaning mirror is so clear, it's a little disturbing.

I finish up in the bathroom, throw on some clothes, and return to the Promenade to try on my tuxedo. I stupidly insisted on getting an actual bow tie, which takes several minutes to attach to my neck without choking me. After a quick trip back to my room to drop off my street clothes—during which I get several appreciative nods from other passengers—I head down to the main dining room.

It's 1710 hours when I get there, and people have already started eating. The dining room staff stationed every couple of meters ask for my table number and point me toward the large staircase at the rear. Ellie's table is directly in front of the stairs, working on their appetizers.

The VIPs in question are a group of teenage girls and two adult women. When I get closer, I notice they're all wearing matching blue-and-gold logo pins. I don't recognize the design. I snap a picture with my eye and then power up my comms dish to start an image search.

My table—right next to Ellie's, just as Ward promised—is half full when I sit down. The small talk isn't quite as scintillating as my first night at the Captain's Table. I'm seated with two couples, both on vacation. One of the couples are regular cruisers and trying to convince the other couple to try longer sailings to other planets. I let them guide the conversation, happy that I don't have to participate much. It gives me more time to observe Ellie.

If she's noticed me sitting over here, she hasn't shown it. Her attention is focused on the teenagers at her table, who seem to be asking a lot of questions. The dining room's noisy enough to prevent eavesdropping. I could turn on my long-range microphone, but that feels like cheating.

As if on cue, my image search returns a match on the logo pins: National Science and Technology Council. Federal education program. I thought it looked familiar. Maybe I can use that to start a conversation later. When I accidentally-on-purpose bump into Ellie in the hallway.

I wave off all offers of alcohol from the servers. I want to stay clear-headed tonight.

The VIP table finishes eating before mine does. I don't feel too bad about abandoning my dining companions to catch Ellie just as she walks out the front doors of the dining room.

"Well, hello there, Chief," I say, waving.

She looks up from her wristband. "Oh, hello, Evan." Her startled expression relaxes into a smile. "That's a nice look for you. Did you enjoy your dinner?"

"Yes. Thanks." I debate for a moment recounting the story of my last-minute tailor shop expedition, but decide I don't want to be that guy tonight. "Are you headed back to work?"

Ellie gives her wristband one more tap and lowers her arm. "Not until midnight. Plenty of time to change." She shrugs. "I was going to check on the cleanup crew, but it sounds like they're almost done. No need for me to suit up and go in again."

I couldn't have manufactured a better segue. "So how did that go? The cleanup, I mean?"

She looks around at the passengers strolling past us. "We probably shouldn't talk about it here. What's your interest anyway?"

"Oh, you know, professional curiosity. I'm an interplanetary trade inspector."

"Yeah. You did mention that." She seems dubious.

"Radiation's a big issue for outer space commerce. I'd love to hear more about *Dejah Thoris*'s radhaz procedures. In a more private setting. When you have some free time." She's grinning at me. "Did I say something funny?"

"Evan, if you want to ask me on a date, you should just ask me on a date."

"That's not," I say. "I wasn't." My brain seems to be vapor-locked all of a sudden.

"Liar." Ellie hooks her arm through mine, and I swear a tingle literally goes down my spine. "Let's take a walk. You know how to get to the arboretum?"

CHAPTER FOURTEEN

Dejah Thoris—Passenger elevator
3 minutes after Ellie changed my plans

It's a long elevator ride up to the arboretum. I have plenty of time to contemplate how I'm going to deal with this new scenario. I was prepared to talk engineering and radiation and space stuff, to lure Ellie into a conversation; I didn't expect her to *want* to come with me. So what's my play now? How do I regain control of the situation?

Or do I maybe just enjoy her company for a while?

David Wachlin's in custody. The radiation danger is contained. I'm just doing follow-up now, and honestly, my hunch about something more sinister going on here could simply be me itching to work because it's the only thing I know. Maybe I'm more scared of being a genuine human being than fighting bad guys.

Ellie's been oddly silent this whole time. What is she thinking about? Should I ask? What would a normal person do?

"So how were your VIPs?" I ask.

"Oh, not too bad. It was a school group. I always get nervous when I have to talk to kids," Ellie says. "The pressure of being a role model, you know."

"I wouldn't."

She laughs and pats my arm. My heartbeat flutters. Should I talk more about kids? I don't know anything about children. And is that really what a woman wants to talk about on a first date? Does she think this is a date?

The elevator doors open to bright yellow light shining through a stand of leafy trees. I make some kind of gurgling noise and put up a hand to shield my eyes. "Is that actual sunlight?"

"What are you, a vampire? Come on." Ellie takes my hand—causing my heart rate to shoot up—and leads me out of the elevator and down a paved path through the trees. "Yes, it's real sunlight. Plants need it to perform photosynthesis."

It smells like nature in here—dirt, grass, wood bark. I could almost imagine we're strolling through the countryside. "We must be above the cargo sections, then."

"Very good, Evan." She pokes my arm. "You get a gold star."

"I had a good tour guide yesterday. I didn't realize you were a teacher, too."

"I'm not," she says. "I volunteered for chaperone duty once back in US-OSS, showing some grade school kids around base. The guy from the Department of Education liked me, and he's been haunting me ever since."

"Did he like you, or did he *like* you?" She's not wearing a ring, but does she have a boyfriend back home? A girlfriend? More than one?

Ellie rolls her eyes. "I think you have me confused with the teenagers."

I refrain from complimenting her youthful appearance. That's back-fired on me too often. What else can I talk about? I'm drawing a blank.

"So this arboretum is nice." *That's brilliant, Kangaroo. At least you didn't mention the weather.*

"Trees from all over the world," Ellie says. "Six different sections, each one representing a different Earth climate."

"Do you spend a lot of time here?" I ask. I might know even less about plants than I do about children.

She gives me an exasperated expression. "Come on, Evan. I expected something better than 'do you come here often.'"

I smile like an idiot because she's smiling and I don't know what else to do. "Maybe you could share some of these expectations with me, so I can make sure to live up to them." *Please help me, I'm dying here.*

"Attention arboretum visitors!" Cruise Director Logan says. I just about jump out of my skin before I realize his voice is coming from a loudspeaker hidden in the floor. "Please stand clear of the flashing yellow lights . . ."

"Something you forgot to tell me?" I ask Ellie as the announcement continues.

"I wouldn't say 'forgot,'" she replies, smiling.

Streaks of yellow flash along the edges of the walking path. A second later, the deck below us shudders and starts moving. I don't realize I'm clutching Ellie's shoulder until she pries my fingers away and elbows me in the side.

"Surprised?"

"One of us probably thinks this is hilarious."

She chuckles. "It gets better."

"Is 'better' the right word?"

"Come on, landlubber." She tugs me forward down the path.

My inner ear finally decodes what I'm feeling: the entire, disk-shaped deck surface is rotating around the central elevator shaft. Ellie leads us in the direction of the rotation, toward one of the walls that divide the arboretum into wedge-shaped regions. The translucent panel—looking for all the world like a less glowy version of the pocket's air barrier—pops open a circular opening as we approach, puffing forth warm, dry air.

We step through into another world: a desert oasis, surrounded by sand dunes as far as the eye can see, all the way to a flat horizon below a clear blue sky. The air is definitely drier here, and even the sunlight feels warmer on my back. Or is that just my imagination?

Hey, funny story about the last time I was in a desert . . .

The divider closes behind us. A moment later, the deck rotation stops. I'm still racking my brain for a new, nonclassified conversation topic when Ellie guides me to a tall palm tree.

"Here we go." She points at our shadows on the sand. "Watch."

It actually looks like a sunset, albeit in fast-forward. Our shadows lengthen in front of us and stretch up to the nearest sand dune in less than a minute. But turning the ship just to change its angle toward the Sun for this effect would push *Dejah Thoris* off course. What's the trick?

"Okay, that must be a vid wall out there," I say, "but how—"

"You tell me," Ellie says. "And no peeking behind you. That's cheating."

"I didn't realize there was going to be a quiz."

"Did I mention there's a time limit, too?"

I know she's joking. But I'm also relieved, because this is a task I know how to perform. I know how to beat a test. I know how to backsolve a system to figure out the fastest way to defeat it without setting off an alarm.

I can do this without pretending to be somebody else.

"All right," I say. "That's actual sunlight behind us. It's coming in from the far side of this deck, and through the divider behind us. The ship itself isn't turning, so there must be something else redirecting the light. Something *inside* the ship. Mirrors?"

Ellie makes a loud buzzing noise. "Nope. Try again."

I frown at our shadows, which continue to expand across the ground. "Right. The deck rotates, so each section faces the Sun at some point— simulating day and night. Clever. Something just needs to *block* the light. Am I on the right track?"

She responds with a noncommittal humming noise and a shrug.

This isn't an *actual* test, is it? That would be way too weird. Even for an engineer. I imagine Ellie bringing all her potential suitors up here, shoving them into the desert and shouting math questions at them to separate the worthy from—

"The dividers," I say. "The panel that irised open to let us in here. It's some kind of programmable material. It was translucent before. It can be fully opaqued in specific, timed patterns to mimic environmental effects— like sunsets." I give Ellie a sideways glance. "Can I turn around now?"

She grins. "Absolutely."

I turn and see that I was right. Most of the divider panel has darkened to blackness, shutting out all but a single stripe of sunlight, and that stripe is moving downward. It's an illusion, but then, so is this whole ship. *Dejah Thoris* was designed to evoke the romance of a luxurious past that never existed.

Everything around me is a lie. I should feel right at home.

"Nice deduction, Sherlock," Ellie says.

"Thanks," I say. "And the walls and ceiling here are vid screens too?"

"Transductile display crystal," Ellie says. "The latest in materials science. Filters cosmic radiation, projects holographic images, resists fatigue. Every window on *Dejah Thoris* is a TDC panel. They do require constant power, but we don't have to worry about passive radhaz."

The desert section is completely dark now. Slowly pulsing red lines trace the edges of the walking path. As my eyesight adjusts, I notice something about the night sky.

I point at the horizon. "Those are real stars in front of us, aren't they?"

"Yeah," Ellie says, sounding surprised. "The sunset program depolarizes the hologram, and then you can see through the crystal into outer space. How did you—"

"The stars above us are twinkling," I say, "because that image was recorded on Earth. But the ones straight ahead aren't. No atmosphere."

"Good eye." I feel her take a breath, her side pressed against my arm. This tuxedo wasn't designed for a desert environment, and I'm sweating like crazy. My shirt is plastered to my torso. I hope Ellie can't smell it.

"So tell me." She nudges me forward down the path. "How did Evan Rogers come to work for the State Department?"

I got my best friend killed and almost started a war. You know, the usual.

I have to lie to her. I have to lie about this.

"I wanted to know why coffee was so expensive," I say.

This speech, I've rehearsed. I've recited this legend so many times I'm starting to improvise embellishments just to keep it interesting for myself. Sometimes I find strange coins inside a bag of whole beans; sometimes it's a hand-carved wooden toy. But I never touch the core story, which was carefully crafted by a team of agency specialists to be unverifiable. And the more I use their words, the more I can believe that it's not really me lying to Ellie.

"Wow," she says when I'm finished. "That may be the nerdiest reason I've ever heard for wanting to travel abroad."

"You think that's nerdy? I know this woman who goes to the arboretum to watch a hologram show."

That gets me a playful punch on the arm. That's good, right? I'm sure that's good. Should I punch her back? No, probably not.

We walk through the next divider, into a cooler and more humid section of the arboretum. This portion has also converted to nighttime, so I can't see the foliage very clearly, but it looks like ferns.

"So why are you *really* going to Mars, Evan?" she asks.

"I'm on vacation." It's not a lie.

Ellie shakes her head. "You're not on vacation. Or you're the worst tourist ever."

"I'm a pretty bad tourist."

She stops walking and fixes me with a stare. Did I say something offensive? Does she have strong feelings about tourists?

"Okay, Evan," she says. "Seriously. If you don't start putting the moves on me soon, I'm going to have to seduce you."

I wasn't expecting anything that direct, so it takes a moment for me to comprehend her meaning, and a longer, sweatier moment for me to figure out a response.

"I'm going to kiss you now," I say.

"Good."

My eyes close before our lips make contact. It's been a long time since I kissed anyone, and even longer since I kissed anyone without an ulterior motive. Maybe never.

At first I'm just glad I can find the target. Then a strange sensation sizzles through my entire body, and I'm falling, floating, flying.

I can't breathe, and I don't want to. I want to stay here forever.

After the longest and shortest four seconds of my life, Ellie pulls away. "Now that wasn't so bad, was it?"

"I can't complain," I say, inhaling deeply. I smell something that reminds me of ice cream. "Are there vanilla plants in here? Or is it your fragrance?"

She wrinkles her nose, and it's so adorable I could die. "I don't do perfume. You've been using that fancy shampoo in your bathroom."

I shake my head. "I didn't smell it before now."

She smiles. "I guess you weren't sweating much before now. It reacts to perspiration."

I should really pay more attention to product labels. "Or maybe it's just humid in here."

"If you don't believe me," she says, leaning forward again, "we can go back to your room and I'll show you."

I may be stupid, but I'm not that stupid. I take her hand and practically run back to the elevator.

It's only after we're in my stateroom and half-naked on the bed that I think about contraception. Ellie shows me there's a stockpile of condoms in my mini-bar. I guess this particular late-night situation isn't too uncommon on cruise ships.

Ellie knows what she wants. Fortunately, I want pretty much the same thing.

She's amazing. I hope I'm adequate.

We both fall asleep afterward. The beeping of her wristband wakes me. I sit up in bed and see her closing up her uniform jacket in front of the mirror. She silences the alarm, then notices me and turns back to lean over the bed.

"Duty calls," she says, and kisses me. "I'll see you later?"

I don't see why she thinks that should be a question. "You won't be able to keep me away, Chief."

Her smile lights up the whole room. "We're civilians. Call me Ellie."

"Ellie," I say.

"Evan."

That's not my name.

Another kiss, and then she's gone.

CHAPTER FIFTEEN

Here's a terrible thing: I always have nightmares after I have sex. Always. It doesn't matter if I stay awake for days afterward; the next time I sleep long enough to dream, I'll have a bad night. The first few times I chalked it up to anxiety, because those were not good experiences, but after that— after Paul put me to work—I couldn't ignore the pattern.

It's never about the person I just slept with, and it's never explicitly sexual. Some kind of baked good usually makes an appearance. I try not to analyze it too deeply. And I certainly don't tell Surgical about it.

This time, the horrific nightmare that wakes me involves being trapped inside a microwave oven and being cooked to death while a group of robots watches. It also reminds me that I was going to research the effectiveness of civilian anti-radiation meds.

After an unproductive half-hour of omnipedia lookups, I realize that I have no idea what I'm searching for, and I wouldn't know how to interpret the results anyway. I know who I need to ask about this. I need to ask for Chief Jemison's sake, for Captain Santamaria's sake, for anyone else who's set foot in stateroom 5028 since the fire.

I need to ask for Ellie.

The comms dish on the hull outside will let me interface with the agency's internal phone system, but I'm a little apprehensive about calling Jessica. Then again, she's several hundred thousand kilometers away. What's the worst she can do? Yell at me? Must be Tuesday.

I sit down at the work desk in my room and wave my hand to bring the computer out of standby. The twenty-four-hour clock reads 0058 hours.

Until we reach Mars, *Dejah Thoris* operates on the time zone of our departure port, so it's the same time here as back in D.C.

I'm not sure what is actually involved in an internal agency audit. Whoever is investigating our department doesn't have to physically visit our office. Someone who can call heat down on D.Ops surely has a high enough security clearance to remotely access any data he wants. If I can do it from interplanetary space, they can do it from within the same city.

The only reason I can imagine for auditors to visit in person is to conduct interviews. Interrogations. The hairs on the back of my neck prickle. Paul, Jessica, and Oliver are being threatened right now, and I'm not there to help them. Why would Paul send me away? Why wouldn't he want me there?

I know the answer. Paul doesn't want me there because I'm the weakest link in the chain. I am his ace in the hole, the secret weapon that gives him leverage over more powerful people. But I'm also the least experienced and most likely to go off-script. He doesn't want me audited because he doesn't think I can protect myself, much less any of them.

Well, I'm all alone on this cruise ship—no support, no prep—and I've already helped apprehend a murder suspect. I can handle flying solo. This is my chance to demonstrate that I'm not dependent on Lasher and Surge and EQ.

Right after I make one phone call.

It takes me a few minutes to figure out how to securely connect my shoulder-phone to the desktop computer. There's no disputing the miraculous efficiency and total-concealment advantage of having a complete display built into your body, but my eyes get tired after too long focusing on things that aren't there. And if this isn't a very short conversation, it's going to be a very long one.

The transmission delay will be an issue. We're almost halfway to Mars now, which means it'll take over one hundred seconds for a radio signal from *Dejah Thoris* to reach Earth. That's more than three minutes between each of my messages and Jessica's responses.

On the bright side, she won't be able to interrupt me like she usually does.

First I login to our department's shared workspace to see if I can find out how the audit's going. Not surprisingly, nobody's been posting status updates. I wonder if that's by choice.

I start recording a vid message to Jessica, don't like how I sound, and stop and start over. I do this at least six times before deciding that the less I say, the better.

"Kangaroo to Surgical. I am transmitting and receiving via Echo Delta. I need to know about the effectiveness of civilian anti-radiation meds. Please respond soonest. Over."

Three to four minutes is a hell of a long time when you're waiting to get yelled at. I was half hoping Jessica wouldn't still be in the office, but I'm not surprised that she is. I've never actually seen her arrive in the morning or leave at the end of the day. Sometimes I wonder if she sleeps on that bed in the exam room.

I am, however, surprised to see her with her hair piled up high and wearing flawless makeup and a strapless evening gown. She looks like a fashion model. I'm so distracted, her words don't register at first, and I have to replay the message.

"Kangaroo, Surgical. I don't know what the hell you're doing, but since you're calling *me* and not Lasher, I'm going to assume that this is *not* an actual emergency. And I'm not going to ask—no, actually, I *am* going to ask why you're using your emergency comms dish. Because someone is going to notice the signal, and more likely than not—" She shakes her head and takes a breath. "No. That's fine. I'm going to let Equipment give you that lecture."

"That'll be fun," I mutter. *Later.*

"To answer your somewhat disturbing question," she continues, "the effectiveness will depend on which medication we're talking about and exactly what radiation the patients were exposed to. The cruise ship should have given you a general radioprotective inoculation when you boarded. They'll probably have Genisalin or Tribetaine on hand, but those are not effective against all types of radiation. If you can get close to the emission source, send me a scan. And if *you* were exposed, I want your somatic sensor logs, too. As soon as possible! Over."

I pack up the files and send them to her with a brief message.

"Surge, Kangaroo. I'm sending my scans and body logs. We were exposed to a damaged particle emission capture core. Not for very long. The ship's doctor has already treated us with Genisalin. By the way, what are you wearing? Did you lose a bet or something? Over."

It's nearly five minutes before her reply arrives. I'm in the bathroom when my eye lights up, and I watch the vid while still on the toilet. I've done worse.

"Kangaroo, Surgical. Stop calling me 'Surge.' I'm not a Russian hockey player." Jessica taps at her computer console while talking, barely looking at the camera. "And I am wearing this ridiculous outfit because I was at the opera, which—why am I telling you this? It's not important. The auditors are trying to distract me while they interview Lasher and Equipment. They think they can divide and conquer—" She shakes her head. "No. Not important. I need you to tell me how many other people were exposed to the PECC. I will assume the ship's doctor is not a complete idiot, and that he made you all shower and scrub and incinerated your clothes in addition to administering Genisalin. That will protect you in the short term, but your somatic sensors show signs of bone marrow damage. I should be able to contain it. Wait one. Don't go anywhere. Over."

I finish up in the bathroom and, since I have nothing better to do, record another message while I'm waiting.

"Surge, Kangaroo. Look, you don't need to worry about this too much. I'm not feeling nauseous or losing hair or anything, and it's been a full day since the exposure. It looked like the PECC was mostly burned out by the time we got there, right? I don't think this ship has any facilities to synthesize pharmaceuticals, so there's probably not much more I can do about this—I mean, it'll be tricky to set up a chemistry lab in my stateroom. Sounds like you have other things to deal with anyway. So just let me know whether I should, I don't know, avoid greasy foods for the next few days and I'll stop bothering you.

"And thanks for not telling Paul. He doesn't need to worry about a minor thing like this. Over."

I'm pretty sure Jessica doesn't actually listen to my whole message, because her next burst arrives in barely three minutes and twenty seconds.

"Kangaroo, *Surgical*. I need to know how many people besides yourself were exposed to that PECC, I need to know if any of them were children under ten or adults over sixty, and I need to know exactly who issued that power core. Eight years ago we were using three different kinds of combination alpha-beta PECCs in military implants, and your eye can't resolve that kind of detail. Go back and find the serial number if you need to, don't worry about the added exposure, the nanobots can fix it. Over."

I'm not sure I heard that last part correctly, so I play the message again, then send a reply with Alan Wachlin's service record attached.

"Surge, Kangaroo. I'm sending you the army personnel file on the deceased owner of the PECC. That should tell you when he was implanted.

Also, did you say 'nanobots'? It sounded like you said 'nanobots.' But that can't be right, because not only are they highly classified experimental bio-tech, you also only started being able to program them the day before I left. A week and a half ago. Please clarify. Over."

She can't be planning what I think she's planning. Can she? There's no way Paul would authorize it. And how would it even be possible? She can't have made that much progress on the nanobot software in ten days. Manipulating organic matter is completely different from wireless net-working, and if anything goes wrong—well, it might not be the end of the world, but it would definitely be the end of our agency.

Three to four minutes passes very quickly when your mind is boggling.

"Kangaroo, Surgical. I have the personnel file, I'll need to do some more research, but I should be able to find what I need from that. And yes, I said nanobots. I'm reprogramming them to repair your radiation-damaged tis-sue and chromosomes, and to kill any precancerous cells before they start spreading. The code is almost ready to upload. Do not go anywhere. Wait for my all-clear. Over."

Okay, this is getting ridiculous.

"Surge, Kay. Let me get this straight. I've been on vacation for ten days, and you've cured cancer? Over."

"Kangaroo, Surgical! I am trying to work here, and this is not a cure, this is triage. It will take the bots a few weeks to locate and break down all the affected areas. You've got time, but another day and the damage could be too extensive for them to deal with, so I need to figure out how you're going to help the civilians who were also exposed. You should have called me as soon as this happened. Now just wait."

She doesn't even bother saying "over," just smacks the controls to end her transmission.

"Surge, Kay. I apologize for all these questions, but I wasn't expecting you to be able to use the *tiny robots* in my *blood* to fix *cancer*." Sometimes I wonder if Jessica is actually human. "Are there going to be any side effects while they're doing this? Am I going to feel anything? Is there any chance they'll modify the wrong things and, I don't know, take apart my kidney or something? Over."

Nearly six minutes pass before I get her reply. She's staring straight into the camera.

"Kangaroo. Surgical. You will not feel anything. The nanobots are ma-nipulating individual molecules inside your cells. These are microscopic changes. Most of the work is preventing further damage. And this is not new science. Medical doctors have been working on oncological detection and prevention for over a century." Her eyes unfocus slightly. "I had a life before the agency. I developed molecular change agents for twenty years. This type of tissue repair was the core of my proposal to Science Division. I could have deployed the technology months ago if they hadn't questioned every little detail—" She stops, takes a deep breath, then holds up her palm and exhales. "No. I'm over it. We're moving on.

"This transmission includes the new nanobot program. Your shoulder-phone should be unpacking it and flashing the bots right now. Leave this channel open in case it needs to re-fetch some data. I will contact you in a few hours about the civilian issue. Over and out."

CHAPTER SIXTEEN

Dejah Thoris—Deck 3, Barsoom Buffet
6½ hours after my delightful conversation with Surgical

Dejah Thoris reaches midway just after breakfast time, following repeated loudspeaker warnings from Cruise Director Logan to make sure all loose items and children are safely secured. The announcements also help wake me up in time to make it to the buffet before breakfast service ends.

Chaperoning four thousand civilians in zero-gravity is no small undertaking. Letting them float around an entire cruise ship for a whole day is just asking for trouble. That's why certain areas have been sealed off, and every single one of *Dejah Thoris*'s roughly two thousand crew members appears to be on duty, stationed anywhere a passenger might want to go and ready to assist with moving around while weightless. It appears to be impossible to get away from them, but that's part of the cruise contract: during midway, safety trumps privacy.

I'm finishing my morning coffee—which has been served in an enclosed drink bulb, in anticipation of our loss of gravity—when Logan makes the final announcement. Three different crew members walk by to offer complimentary pairs of zero-gee slipper-socks, in case we've forgotten them in our staterooms. I smile back at them and show off my red-and-white footwear with grippy soles. Then they offer to rent me a cam-bot to follow me and record my weightless adventures. I politely decline. Nobody needs to see me flailing around all day.

A trilling alarm sounds continuously for the last minute before we lose gravity, and red lights pulse gently all around us, drawing attention to the floor, which will very soon be just another wall. Half the passengers around me look apprehensive, and the other half look excited, as the crew lead us in a countdown chant.

"Three . . . Two . . . One . . . *Zero-gee!*"

At first, it's a bit anticlimactic. Some children near me jump up and down and are disappointed when they don't go flying away. It takes about a minute for the main engines to fully shut down. Then the dining area fills with screams and whoops and hollers as several hundred people experience prolonged zero-gravity for the first time in their lives. *Dejah Thoris* passengers only had a few hours on Sky Five during the transfer from the Beanstalk; this is going to be a whole day of being disoriented and possibly terrified.

Crew members move through the crowd, keeping people from drifting away. The maroon stripes on the floor, which I thought were decorative, are actually stick-strips: high-friction material that clings to shoes and socks, keeping people anchored.

I survey the noise and commotion for a few minutes, then turn my thoughts back to the chore I've been postponing since last night.

I don't know how long it will take for Jessica to figure out a radiation treatment for me to sneak to the crew, but I know I won't be able to administer it on my own. Just tracking down the specific crew members will require access to personnel records.

No, the only way this happens is if I con one of the officers into backing my play. I don't know how I'm going to do it, but Jemison is the mark. The buck stops with her, and if I can get her to swallow my fish story, I'm golden.

All I have to do is convince an OSS war veteran and experienced intelligence operative that she should get several of her crewmates to submit to what is likely to be an experimental medical procedure performed by yours truly.

Right. Piece of cake.

Hmm. I wonder if there's any cake in the buffet—

"Mr. Rogers?"

I jerk at the sound of Jemison's voice, and the motion sends me out of my seat. I manage to catch the edge of the table with my fingertips and bob there for a moment until I get my bearings and pull my feet down to a stick-strip. My left hand slips off the corner of my food tray and almost sends it flying. I manage to stop it with my other hand. I re-attach the tray to the friction-grip tabletop.

Jemison is in front of me, her feet anchored to a stick-strip on the other side of my table, wearing the impatient scowl I've become so familiar with. Two security guards I don't recognize float behind her, gripping hand-holds molded into the planters surrounding the dining area. Like the rest of the crew, they've traded their normal uniforms for zero-gee jumpsuits.

"What are you doing here?" I say without thinking.

"Evan Rogers?" Jemison says, more forcefully, glaring at me even harder.

Okay, Chief, I'll play along. "Yes, that's me. Uh, is there a problem?"

She waves the two guards forward. "If you'll come with us, Mr. Rogers, we'd like to speak to you in private, please."

The guards don't look like they're in on this joke. I lean forward and lower my voice. "Should I be causing a scene here?"

"No, sir," Jemison says loudly. "Just come with us and we'll sort this out."

They lead me out of the dining area—Jemison in front, me and one guard in the middle, and the other guard taking up the rear. Other passengers mutter as we move down the corridor toward a service door. I try to remember if I've done something since yesterday to get myself into more trouble.

As soon as we're in a crew-only section and the door shuts behind us, I ask, "Okay, what's going on here?"

Jemison waves off the two guards, who seem happy to be rid of us, and points toward the elevator. "This way."

I resist the urge to reply with "If I could walk *that* way . . ." and attempt to follow her, with limited success.

The floor and wall surfaces here aren't covered in red stick-strips like the passenger sections. Instead, there are handholds built into the panel-ing every meter or so. For some reason, I literally can't get the hang of moving down this hallway in zero-gee.

I miss half a dozen handholds and managed to crash into all four walls before Jemison stops and turns around. She grabs my collar and drags me into the elevator.

"Thanks," I say. "It's been a while."

"It's not acrobatics." She pushes a button. The elevator doors close. "Keep it simple. Small moves."

"Right. Can we talk now? What was all that with the guards back there?" I ask.

"Sorry about the theatrics," she says. "I had to get you out of the passenger sections without anybody thinking you're someone special."

That seems bad. "What's going on?"

"David Wachlin's awake," Jemison says, "and he says he doesn't remember anything."

"Schizophrenic episode?"

"No. Doc Sawhney says Wachlin went to sleep after our first day in space and didn't wake up until this morning."

I frown. "He's been asleep for two days?"

"That's what Sawhney says," Jemison says. "He ran blood tests and a basic brain scan, didn't find anything unusual. Not an episode. He also says Wachlin's blood sugar levels and other body chemistry are consistent with his last meal being two days ago, followed by a long sleep."

"You're not convinced."

"Which is more likely?" Jemison snaps. "That he sleepwalked his way through a double homicide and into that lifeboat, or that he's lying?"

The elevator dings, and the door slides open. "So why are you telling me this? And where are we going?"

"Sickbay," Jemison says. "Doc refuses to give Wachlin any more drugs, so I need your eye to play lie detector."

I smile at her. "You need my help."

Jemison pushes me into the elevator. "Not if you're going to be insufferable."

"I guarantee plenty of suffering."

"Already regretting this," she mutters as the doors close.

It's not much of an interrogation. David Wachlin is confused and belligerent at first, but he cracks in less than a minute under Jemison's barrage of questions. My left eye can detect basic vital signs—skin temperature, heart rate, respiration—and run software to analyze those involuntary responses for possible deception. This guy doesn't trip any of the thresholds.

As far as David knows, he went to sleep in his stateroom and then woke up in Sickbay, secured to an exam bed with restraining straps. He breaks down completely when Jemison tells him that the rest of his family is dead. She tops it off by showing him the bloody knife from the lifeboat, and he starts bawling like a baby.

My eye confirms he's not faking. My heart sinks. We still have a murderer on board the ship, and now we have no idea who it could be.

"What's going on there, Chief?" I hear Dr. Sawhney calling.

He flies around the corner, summoned by David Wachlin's miserable wailing, and nearly slams into the wall beside me, managing to stop himself on a handhold. I jerk away only to thump into Jemison. The evidence bag holding the knife slips out of her hand.

My arm collides with hers as we both grab for the loose pointy object tumbling away into Sickbay. She elbows me in the side and grabs the knife.

"What the hell!" she says.

"Sorry," I say. "Zero-gee. But you see this?"

David didn't even look up. His body convulses with loud sobs.

"Yeah." Jemison doesn't look happy, and I'm sure it's not because she feels any sympathy.

"What happened?" Sawhney asks, glaring at Jemison.

"Just had to ask him a few questions," Jemison says.

"Are you done now?"

"We're done," Jemison sighs. "He didn't kill them. Right, Rogers?"

"Right," I say. "I guess that's the good news."

"Unfortunately, I may have some bad news," Sawhney says.

Jemison frowns. "What?"

"I will report to the briefing room in ten minutes," Sawhney says. "The captain will want to see as well."

"Fine."

I follow Jemison out to the elevator. She doesn't have to drag me this time, but I still lag a good fifteen seconds behind. Are these handholds just small, or are my hands really that huge?

Jemison pushes the elevator button once I'm inside, then pulls a small canister off her belt and hands it to me. "You know how to use one of these?"

I turn the object over in my hand. It looks like a flimsy set of brass knuckles, molded from aluminum and with a narrow cylinder as the palm grip. A nozzle protrudes from the knuckle-guard between my index and middle fingers.

"Hand thruster, right?" I say.

Jemison nods. "The thumb switch is semi-automatic. One short burst of compressed nitrogen, whether you hold it down or not; recoil pushes you backward. Don't point it at anyone. That's two hundred atmospheres in there. The gas kicks out at fifty meters per second."

"Right. And why do I need this?"

"For moving around the ship. I'm tired of watching you flounder in zero-gee."

"I don't work in outer space that much."

"Thank God."

CHAPTER SEVENTEEN

I feel underdressed. Everyone else in the briefing room is wearing sleek jumpsuits with colorful rank insignias and department emblems. Captain Santamaria, Commander Galbraith, and Chief Jemison wear PMC's standard navy blue and gold; Cruise Director Logan stands out in bright orange and yellow; and Dr. Sawhney broadcasts his profession in white and red. I'm wearing denim jeans and a faded T-shirt.

Jemison updates everyone on the situation. "Dr. Sawhney, Mr. Rogers, and I all examined David Wachlin, and we concur that he's not lying."

"How is that possible?" Galbraith asks.

"That's the sixty-four-thousand-dollar question," Santamaria says.

"I never know what you're talking about," Jemison mutters.

"It's a game show," I say. "You know. Like *Twenty-One.* Or *Jeopardy!*"

Jemison squints at me. "You are not helping."

"I believe I have an answer," Sawhney says. He touches the conference table to clear the display, then holds up a plastic bag containing two pill bottles. "These are David Wachlin's prescribed medications: Stelomane and Dalazine, standard schizophrenia treatments."

He opens the bag, pulls out a bottle, and hands it to Logan. "Mr. Logan, please remove one of the tablets from that vial."

Logan unscrews the cap and gives the bottle a gentle tap. Three round yellow pills float up out of the container. He catches one between his thumb and forefinger, then scoops the rest back into the bottle and replaces the lid.

"That vial is labeled 'Stelomane,'" Sawhney says. "An antipsychotic. Here is the pharmacy reference."

He taps the table. A rectangle of text, a spinning molecule, and a photograph appear. He touches the image to make it larger: two pills with numbers embossed front and back.

The pills in the picture are oval, not round.

"These aren't the right pills," Logan says. "The shape's wrong. And the code numbers don't match."

"Could they be generics?" Galbraith asks.

"That is what I thought as well," Sawhney says. "But the labels on these vials claim differently. And when I looked up these actual tablets by their appearance, I was faced with disturbing results."

He brings up a second pharmaceutical record, showing the round pill Logan's holding. A few keywords in the text jump out at me. Sawhney's right. This is bad news.

"Phencyclidine," he says. "Originally an intravenous anesthetic, abused recreationally during the twentieth century. High doses can cause catatonia in schizophrenics."

Jemison says what I'm thinking: "Fuck!"

Santamaria snaps his fingers. "Erica, I need passenger background checks. Find out who had connections to the Wachlin family."

"Yessir," Galbraith says, and kicks herself back from the briefing table. She does a twist in midair to end up sailing head-first toward the door.

"How does a schizophrenic not know he's taking the wrong pills?" I ask.

"As Commander Galbraith said. Generics often look different than brand-name drugs," Sawhney says. "But I fear this was an intentional deception. These vials were not pharmacy printed. The bar codes are fakes; they don't scan properly. Somebody wanted David Wachlin to take the wrong medication."

"Doctor, I want you to run another tox screen on David Wachlin," Santamaria says. "Verify that these drugs were in his system."

"It's been over two days," Sawhney protests. Then he sees Santamaria's glare. "We'll do our best, Captain."

"Thank you, Doctor." Santamaria drums his fingers on the edge of the table as Sawhney collects the bag of pills and heads for the elevator.

"Jeff," Santamaria says after a moment. "How do we handle this?"

"We can't tell the passengers," Logan says. "Especially not now. A panic in zero-gravity would be impossible to control."

"Agreed," says Santamaria.

"We don't know what the killer wants," Logan continues. "It may be that he's already accomplished his goal of killing Emily and Alan Wachlin and framing David. But if that was all, he could have waited until the end of the cruise, when we'd have less time to catch him."

"So he's not done," Santamaria says. "We need to find out who his next target is."

"I should go help Erica," Logan says. "Cross-reference onboard activities. We'll start with passengers who haven't been doing much, haven't been eating in public areas. The killer would need time to cover his tracks."

"Go," Santamaria says. Logan spins himself and flies off toward the bridge.

Now it's just the captain, Jemison, and me in the briefing room.

"Rogers," Santamaria says. "I need you to contact our mutual friend and authorize the release of Alan Wachlin's complete military service record."

I see a message waiting for me as soon as I power up the comms dish. I blink away the notification. I'll have to deal with that later.

After coding a text message directly to Paul with my records request and very vague explanations for why I want the information, I turn back to Jemison, who's huddled over the tabletop display by herself. I guess the captain returned to his other duties.

"I'll check for a response in half an hour," I say. "What are we doing now?"

Jemison frowns. "You go do whatever you want. Pick up a phone and dial security when you get the file."

"I can help with whatever analysis you're doing there."

The frown becomes a scowl. "I don't have time to explain this to you."

"I'm a pretty quick study. I can just watch over your shoulder—"

"Let me put it another way," Jemison says. "This will go a lot faster without you annoying me the whole time. Come back when you have the file."

The agency has never been shy about stating that the pocket is the reason they keep me around. But it still peeves me to hear someone say it out loud.

"Fine," I say. "I'll try not to get too drunk because I have nothing better to do."

She doesn't even look up when I leave the room.

I'm getting tired of being treated as less than human. *Special* doesn't always mean *better*; I've known that since I became an orphan. Discovering the pocket made things interesting for a while, but now I seem to be in a rut.

As strange as it sounds, I think I was actually happier during the war, when I couldn't go out on pocket missions and had to develop other skills to earn my keep at the agency. Well, now I'm on vacation. I should stop trying to work and start having fun.

Just as soon as I figure out what "fun" is.

An alert pops up in my eye again, reminding me that the comms dish still has a buffered message waiting. Might as well deal with this now. I move into an empty crew stairwell to watch the vid.

It's Jessica. "Kangaroo, Surgical. Respond soonest. Out."

Her words seem even more clipped than usual. I ping her to request a live connection. She responds in just under five minutes, wearing her usual white lab coat over a plain blue shirt. Steam rises in translucent gray spirals from a large mug on her desk.

"I found out which radioactive isotope was used in Alan Wachlin's PECC," she says without any preamble. "I have a solution for the radiation treatment problem, but it's going to require some work on your part. And you can't tell anyone about it."

"If I can't tell the crew, how am I supposed to treat them?" I say to myself.

"I know that makes things harder, but you'll figure it out." Jessica looks into the camera. It feels like she's staring straight at me. "You need to do this. We are talking about saving lives here. Please acknowledge, over."

"Surgical, Kangaroo," I say. "I'm going to have to tell these people something. I can't give them pills or shots or whatever without explaining it, right? I just need a cover story. Over."

"Kangaroo, Surgical. *No.*" She snaps the word like a curse. "We are operating off the books, fully in the black. If this goes sideways, you can tell them it was all my idea. Save this vid for evidence at my court-martial, I don't care.

"Now listen carefully. There's a blood sampler in your emergency medkit, in the pocket. Get that out, then find a centrifuge and some very expensive liquor. Do this within the next twenty-four hours. We wait too long, and the tissue damage will be too extensive to repair. Please acknowledge. Over."

I have an inkling of what she's asking me to do. Except that can't possibly be right; it's completely insane.

"Surgical, Kangaroo. Please tell me you're not asking me to do what I think you're asking me to do," I say. "Over."

"How the hell do I know what you're thinking?" Jessica replies, scowling at me across time and space. "And I'm not asking, Kangaroo. I'm telling you, if you don't do this, everyone who was exposed to that PECC radiation will develop some form of somatic cancer within the next decade. Acknowledge. Over."

There's a murderer on the loose, and she wants me to go on a scavenger hunt? And then deploy experimental biotech into a civilian population? This is worse than any idea I've ever had. And that's saying a lot.

"Okay. I'm not going to say the N-word, but is that what we're talking about here, Surge? And how the hell is it okay in any way to dose *civilians* with that tech? Over."

"Yes. I am talking about the nanobots. You're going to separate a batch of them, then I'm going to reprogram them to function outside your body for thirty days. That, along with the standard meds, should be long enough to heal any major radiation damage. After a month, the nanobots' hardware failsafes will shut them down, and they'll get metabolized by the liver. Even if someone's looking for them, there will be no evidence they were ever there.

"I can't order you to take this action," Jessica says, her expression softening. "But this is why we created nanobots in the first place, why we didn't abandon the research after the Fruitless Year. The potential rewards are tremendous. We can use this tech to repair any living tissue precisely and reliably. We can use it to save lives.

"You are the only person who can do this, Kangaroo. Nobody else can help those people resist radiation poisoning. This is the only chance they have. And in twenty-four hours, not even you will be able to save them."

I shake my head, trying to dismiss the names and faces running through my head: Captain Santamaria. Chief Jemison. The firefighting crew. Anyone else who went into that burned stateroom.

Ellie.

"I'll contact you with a full procedure soon. Get the equipment. Over and out."

Goddammit.

Special doesn't always mean better. Being unique means having responsibilities that other people don't. I'm the only one who can possibly do this. And I can't ignore the one thing I can do to help right now.

I hover in the stairwell, first wondering how I'm going to get access to a centrifuge, then racking my brain for another way. After fifteen minutes, I give up. Anything else will take too long to execute.

I have to go tell more lies to the woman I slept with last night.

CHAPTER EIGHTEEN

Dejah Thoris—Deck B, crew stairwell
23½ hours before my nanobots can't help these civilians anymore

Unlike the passenger areas, the crew sections of *Dejah Thoris* don't have large directional signs or maps displayed prominently every few meters, and there are no large touchscreen kiosks to help guide a person to the nearest bar or other desired attraction. PMC must train their crew members to know what these alphanumeric codes painted on the bulkheads mean. Deck number is easy to figure out, but the rest is tougher to decipher. I remember the code I saw displayed in main engineering, but it takes me a few trips up and down the stairwell and peeking in other sections to figure out the pattern.

Before leaving the stairwell, I pull my State Department legend out of the pocket. Most of my fake papers are just simple cards or badges that look plausible when flashed in front of a guard or receptionist. I use this one quite a bit, so it's actually tied to a full cover identity that will pass even the most rigorous background check. Just in case.

A jumpsuited crewman accosts me as soon as I enter main engineering, the large chamber overlooking the ionwell I toured earlier. His name tag says XIAO. "Sir! I'm sorry, sir, you can't be in here right now."

I hold up my phony identification. "I need to speak to Chief Engineer Gavilán."

Xiao's eyes widen. He looks from my ID to my face and back again. "Is there a problem, Mr. Rogers? Perhaps I can assist you?"

I briefly consider bluffing this guy instead of Ellie. He looks young, certainly not older than I am, probably just out of the military or trade school. The way he responded to my show of authority implies the former. If I can get what I need from him, then I won't have to lie to Ellie.

But I want to see her again. And what's one more little white lie on top of the mountain I've already built?

"Thank you . . . Xiao?" I'm not quite sure how to pronounce that name.

"Xiao," he says.

"Xiao," I do my best to repeat.

"Xiao."

"Xiao?"

"Close enough, sir." His expression tells me I should just drop it. "How may I help you?"

I tuck my ID into the back pocket of my jeans. "I just need to talk to the chief."

Xiao nods. "Very well, sir. What should I say is the issue?"

"Tell her it's about photosynthesis."

Xiao's face lights up with a grin. "Right! I thought your name sounded familiar. Chief Gavilán said she had a very nice walk through the arboretum with a young man last night."

I blink at him while processing this information. "Is that, uh, common knowledge, then?"

"Only among supervisors. She mentioned it during our morning briefing."

"Ah."

"I love the arboretum. So romantic." Xiao holds up his left hand, showing me the silver band around his ring finger. "I proposed to my husband there."

"Mazel tov," I say reflexively. "By the way, just curious, what else did Chief Gavilán say about last night?"

Xiao winks at me. "Don't worry, Mr. Rogers. She's not one to kiss and tell. Wait here, please." He caroms off the floor and spins toward one of the consoles.

I notice he didn't actually answer my question. I do my best to appear nonchalant as I look around the compartment to see if anyone else is eyeing me now.

Most of the engineering personnel are wearing small jetpacks. The shoulder straps and belt blend in well with their uniform jumpsuits, but I can see and hear the tiny blue-white plumes pushing them around the open space. Probably some kind of compressed gas, like the hand thruster

Jemison gave me. I've seen astronauts who can perform entire acrobatic routines in spacesuits. These engineers aren't quite that graceful, but they're good at holding position, which is most of the trick. All the little twitches and shifts that don't matter in gravity push you all over the place when you're weightless.

A hissing sound catches my attention, and I grab a handhold on the wall and turn to see Ellie, parking herself in front of me by manipulating a control paddle in her left palm.

"Hello, stranger," she says, smiling. "You know you're not supposed to be down here, right?"

"I just couldn't stay away." I return the smile but make no move to touch her. If I start, I won't want to stop. "So I hear we're the talk of the town."

"Sorry about that. My colleagues like to gossip." She shrugs. "They don't get out much."

"Right. Listen, I need to ask you for a tiny little engineering-related favor."

Her eyes twinkle. She uses her jetpack to move down to my eye level. "This sounds interesting."

"Yeah, you don't know the half of it." *And I can't tell you.* "I need to borrow a centrifuge."

Her smile falters for a split second. "A centrifuge."

"Just for, like, an hour or so."

"There are so many issues with that request," she says, "I'm not even sure where to start. Why do you want a centrifuge?"

"It's kind of a long story. I don't suppose you could just trust me?"

We stare at each other for a long moment. She does trust me—I can see that—but only up to a certain point. That's fair. She's only known me for one day, and the most personal thing I've told her is about my abiding love of coffee. Not exactly a deep dark secret.

"Are you actually going to use it?" Ellie asks.

I consider lying, but decide against it. "Yes."

"What are you spinning down?"

Well, now I have to lie. "I don't know."

She frowns. "Okay, I'm going to need a little more here, Evan."

I thought up a ridiculous story on my way down here. I was hoping I wouldn't have to use it. I don't usually devise my own legends, and this one is pretty over the top. But that's what the agency teaches us: the more outlandish the lie, the better. Make the target laugh if you can. Elicit her sympathy without explicitly asking for it. Encourage her to underestimate you.

"I made a bet," I say. "At the bar. With a chemist."

Ellie folds her arms. "You bet him you could get a centrifuge from engineering?"

I make a show of sighing, as if I'm preparing to reveal some particularly embarrassing details. "You know the drink of the day? The 'Zero-Gravity Football'?"

"I'm not really much of a drinker."

"Well, it's today's mystery drink. The bars advertise a different one every day, because booze has the highest profit margins—"

"I know how cruise ships work," Ellie says. "So you enjoyed a few too many of these drinks and made a stupid bet?"

"No," I say, "I made a stupid bet about the drink."

She's smiling again. That's a good sign. "Do tell."

I give her the most pathetic expression I can summon. "Because it's a mystery drink, the servers and bartenders won't tell us exactly what the ingredients are. The chemist thought he could distinguish at least two different types of liquor. But I think the crew are going to keep it simple, because they're making a lot of these drinks all day. I'm thinking there must be some kind of premixed flavor packet—to make it taste more complicated than it actually is, right? That would be cheaper than using more booze."

"I'm still waiting for the part where you need a centrifuge."

"Well, the guy at the bar—the chemist—said he could analyze the ingredients if we separated them by—I think 'specific gravity' is what he said—"

"Hold on," Ellie says. "You're talking about an alcoholic solution. You'd have to boil off most of the water to do any useful analysis." She narrows her eyes. "Please do not tell me one of our passengers has built a still in his stateroom."

"I didn't ask a whole lot of questions," I say. "To be honest, there was a lot of yelling. I think some of those guys were pretty drunk."

"Let me smell your breath."

I clutch my free hand to my chest. "You wound me, sir! I am of sound mind and body."

"This is a sobriety test, not a cute test." She taps her jetpack controls to nudge herself closer to me. I can't find another nearby handhold to escape, and honestly, I don't want to. "I want to know how drunk *you* are."

"Well—"

Before another lame excuse can escape my mouth, Ellie kisses me.

Her eyes are shut, and I look around frantically to see if anybody's watching. Fortunately, Ellie's smart: she maneuvered me into a niche between the control console and one of the side access doors. We're completely hidden from view of the rest of main engineering.

Might as well enjoy it, Kangaroo.

I let my eyelids close. Her lips are incredibly soft. Her tongue dances over mine. She pulls away long before I'm ready to stop. "Yeah, you're good," she says, smiling.

"Are you sure you don't want to check again?" I ask.

She pats my chest, pushing herself backward. "I'll have someone deliver a portable spinner to your room."

"Oh, I can move it myself," I say. "I know everybody's pretty busy today. Wouldn't want to interrupt anyone's work."

Ellie frowns. "It's a large piece of machinery."

"We're in zero-gravity. It'll be fun."

She shakes her head and taps at her wristband. "If you say so. But you break it, you buy it, mister."

"I'll be careful. I'm very good with my hands, as you know."

She actually blushes. "All right, you need to leave now, Casanova. You know where ship's stores are?"

I don't. She gives me directions to one of the upper crew decks and a requisition number to repeat to the chandler.

"Also," she says, "I'm off duty at 1800 hours today. That's six o'clock to you. And I'm free from then until midnight."

I do my best to keep my grin merely stupid and not entirely shit-eating. "Do you already have plans for dinner?"

"Why, no, I do not, Evan."

I try to recall the name of the fanciest restaurant on the ship. "Have you tried the food at that Silk place yet? I hear it's new."

Ellie's eyebrows threaten to lift her entire face. "Are you talking about Fête Silk Road?"

"That's the one. Say seven o'clock?"

"I'm not sure you can get a reservation this late."

"Let me worry about that." I'm confident President Maitland and his brothers can get us in.

"If you say so." She taps her jetpack controls, spinning away from me slowly. "Make it seven-thirty. That'll give me more time to get ready."

She gives me one more dazzling smile over her shoulder before she flies away.

I float, literally and figuratively, up to ship's stores. The chandler gives me a funny look, but the chief engineer's signature on a requisition isn't something he's prepared to argue with. He brings out the centrifuge in a bulky, padded bundle, a cube roughly one meter across on each side. I wrestle it down the corridor until I'm sure nobody's watching, then think of a fuzzy blanket with a colorful zigzag pattern and push the centrifuge into the pocket with a nudge.

Zero-gravity! Fun. I start thinking about what I'm going to wear to my fancy dinner tonight. I can't possibly be seen in the same tuxedo two nights in a row. And Ellie's going to be out of uniform, I'm sure.

I nearly have a heart attack when I run into Jemison coming out of the elevator.

"What the hell are you doing?" she asks.

"Going to Mars?"

"What are you still doing in the crew section," she says, enunciating every word.

"Where else am I going to go?"

"You're on a goddamn cruise ship, Rogers," Jemison says. "There are fifteen decks of amenities to keep our passengers entertained at all hours."

"I told you, I'm not a tourist."

"So you're just creeping around here watching people work?"

That probably wasn't the best explanation I could have come up with. "Are you saying I'm not welcome here, Chief?"

Jemison stares at me. "She's on duty right now. That's why you can't find her."

"Who's on duty?"

Jemison folds her arms. "You do understand what a 'vacation romance' is, right?"

I don't like what she's insinuating. "Sure. As a matter of fact, I just picked up *Scotsmen Prefer Blondes* from the bookshop on the Promenade. Want to borrow it after I'm done?"

Jemison rolls her eyes. "Forget it. Did you get Wachlin's file?"

I blink my eye over to comms. "Not yet." Paul must be busy; a routine request like that wouldn't take very long to clear. "How's your investigation going?"

"We can talk about it over lunch. Come on."

"Does this mean you want my help?"

"Lunch first," she says. "I can't deal with you on an empty stomach."

CHAPTER NINETEEN

Dejah Thoris—Deck 17, crew mess hall
8 hours before I start dosing civilians with experimental biotech

The crew mess hall seems more crowded than yesterday, but I quickly realize that's because people are standing on every available surface, including walls and ceilings. In zero-gravity, every room has six possible floors.

Lunch here is similar to what was available in the passenger buffet. Everyone has a choice of meal types today: "Apollo," which re-creates the rehydratable food-in-a-tube menu options available to the very first space travelers; or "Discovery," which offers more conventional preparations served in sealed plastic trays. Thirty seconds in a wide-spectrum light oven, and that chunky yellow brick turns into a serving of shrimp and grits you can actually eat with a spoon like a civilized human being.

Jemison grabs two trays of food and an empty drink bulb. She heats both trays in an oven while filling the bulb from a coffee dispenser. I choose a chicken quesadilla, then look around the room while waiting for it to cook.

The crew must know about the murders by now. Santamaria couldn't keep that quiet, not with so many people involved in the radiation cleanup detail. That's got to be pretty unnerving.

Jemison leads me to an empty table, and we "sit" across from each other. In zero-gravity, human bodies at rest naturally relax into a sort of half-crouch. I unwrap my food carefully, blowing away the steam that was sealed inside the plastic.

"We need Alan Wachlin's file," Jemison says. "Logan's scrubbing through the ship's security footage, but if the killer was planning this before we sailed, they wouldn't want to be seen interacting with any of the Wachlins.

We need background information to cross-reference with our passenger records."

"You'll know as soon as I hear back from the office," I say. "Have you worked up any other leads? Do you want me to interview anyone else? I can use my eye—"

"It's not that we don't appreciate your help, Rogers," Jemison says. "But everyone on this ship, including you, is stuck here for the next four days. You're already risking exposure. If something else goes sideways, you don't have an escape route."

"I hear this ship has plenty of lifeboats."

"Not funny."

"Too soon? Or I could just hide out in the crew sections and keep you company."

Jemison replies through a mouthful of food, but my train of thought has just switched tracks. I look around the mess hall. Unlike the passenger areas, where people are dressed in all kinds of gaudy outfits, everyone here is wearing some kind of uniform. Nobody stands out.

It's the perfect place to hide.

"What if it's one of the crew?" I ask, interrupting whatever Jemison was saying.

She frowns at me. "What are you talking about?"

"The murderer," I say. "What if it's one of the crew? All the access doors *into* crew sections are locked. No one gets in without a thumbscan. But what about *within* the crew sections?"

"We have additional locks on sensitive areas," Jemison says. "Engineering, the bridge, the computer core, some of the supply areas. Also anything leading to an airlock. You need special authorization to open those doors."

"What about the elevators? Stairwells? I haven't seen a single security camera in either of those places. Crew members can move between decks without being observed."

"I get the idea," she says, biting off the words. "Shit."

"Logan's looking at the passengers," I say. "Nobody's looking at the crew."

"I can put some guys on that."

"Danny and Mike? Are you sure you can trust them?"

Jemison makes a face like I just asked if she wants to eat some Moon rocks. "My people are solid."

"Do you have a motive for these murders yet?" I ask. "Security would have the most access of anyone on this ship short of the senior officers. Are you one hundred percent certain that your people could never be turned?"

"Yes," she replies. "You're barking up the wrong tree."

"Kangaroos don't bark."

My best material is wasted. "Don't tell me how to do my job, Rogers."

Before I can provoke her any further, my eye lights up with a comms notification. It's from the office. There's a vid message and a data attachment. I ignore the former and check the latter.

"I've got the data," I say. "Alan Wachlin's complete service record."

"Good." Jemison opens a pouch on her belt and pulls out a data card. "Copy it onto this."

I take the small rectangle of translucent blue memory crystal. "You understand this is classified information."

"Air-gapped machine, burn after reading. I know the drill." Her eyes are cold. "I've been doing this a lot longer than you have."

I nod. "This'll just take a minute." I reach one hand under the table, think of a green pencil, and open the pocket with the barrier. I push my forearm through the portal to grab my field data inscriber.

"What are you—" Jemison ducks under the table for a second to see what I'm doing. "What the hell! Are you crazy?"

"Relax." I pull my arm back, close the pocket, and put the inscriber on the table. "All done. Nobody saw anything." I risk a smile. "*I've* been doing *this* a lot longer than you have."

"Just give me the file, Rogers."

"What's the magic word?"

I didn't think it was possible for Jemison to look angrier than she did just a minute ago. "*Now.*"

It takes a few seconds for the inscriber to start up, half a minute for me to transmit the data from my shoulder-phone to the inscriber, and maybe fifteen seconds for the inscriber to write everything to the data card. Jemison grabs the card out of my hand as soon as I pull it from the inscriber slot.

"You want to talk about security risks?" She stands up and leans over me. "In my professional opinion, you are our biggest liability at the moment. I get that you're special, Rogers. You can do things that nobody else on this ship can do. But that doesn't give you immunity from screw-ups. If anything, it makes you more vulnerable to exposure. Do you understand?"

I don't like being talked down to. "I'm not an idiot."

"We'll take care of analyzing this data. Consider yourself off duty until I call you again. Don't do anything operational. Go have some fun. Just stay out of trouble, okay?"

There appears to be no chance of that, ever. "I'll do my best."

"Enjoy your lunch."

Jemison takes her tray and pushes away from the table. I resume eating my quesadilla, which has now cooled and hardened into some kind of salty plastic substance.

Might as well watch the vid that came with the Wachlin file. Can't be any worse than getting chewed out in person.

I twitch my fingertips to start playback. It's Paul. Great.

"Kangaroo, Lasher," he says. His eyes are bloodshot, and he's not wearing a tie. I don't think I've ever seen Paul without a necktie. "I'm sending the data you requested. Since you didn't state the precise nature of your interest in this person, I can only assume you suspect him of some wrongdoing. I've reviewed the file, and I urge you to proceed with caution. Though I would prefer you to avoid contact altogether. Please advise soonest any escalation."

He reaches toward something offscreen, then stops. "If, for some reason, the situation worsens but you are unable to contact the office, I want you to reach out to *Dejah Thoris*'s captain and the ship's chief of security. They are both agency employees. Authenticate using live drop challenge. Whatever might happen out there, Captain Santamaria and his crew can handle it.

"Stay out of trouble, Kangaroo. Keep your head down. That is all."

The vid ends. I don't feel very hungry any more.

Everyone is so concerned about me screwing things up. It's true, I'm not as experienced or skilled as Jemison or Santamaria at certain things. That's fine. I'll stay out of their way. But there are other things that only I can do.

I open Alan Wachlin's service record in my eye and flip through it. Joined the army, Special Forces training, Mars deployment, dishonorable discharge, blah blah blah.

There it is. *Thoracic implant: particle emission capture core. Radiation hazard. Quarterly medical inspection recommended.*

Nobody else aboard this ship has radiation-treating nanobots in their blood. And it's always easier to beg forgiveness than to ask permission.

CHAPTER TWENTY

After returning to my stateroom and locking the door, I power up my comms dish and call Jessica. She doesn't answer. I wait fifteen minutes and try again. Still nothing.

I have no idea how the audit's going or when she'll be free again. And honestly, I'm not looking forward to getting yelled at by a third person in one hour. I know what I need to do.

I think of a fuzzy blanket and pull the centrifuge out of the pocket.

All the furniture in my stateroom is bolted down to prevent it from moving. I unpack the boxy centrifuge from its padding, place it in the center of the low coffee table, and retrieve some elastic straps from one of the many field equipment kits I always keep in the pocket.

After securing the centrifuge to the table, I open the pocket to a different location and find my emergency medkit. I haven't actually looked at this thing since my annual first aid refresher course, which was several months ago. It takes me a minute to remember which of the gadgets are the blood samplers. I feel like Jessica could have labeled these a little more clearly.

I try to convince myself that the queasiness I feel while poking the syringe into my arm is my lunch disagreeing with me. It's not the pain of the initial puncture that bothers me, or the soreness afterward, or even the sight of blood. I've seen plenty of blood—knife fights with artisanal hand-crafted shivs were a popular orphanage pastime. Also, a good hard punch in the nose will bust open some arteries and stop most arguments.

Bleeding doesn't bother me. It's knowing what *else* is in my blood now that disturbs me.

After I fill the test tube, I bandage up my arm. Then I realize I have no idea how to use this centrifuge.

I unstrap the metal box from the coffee table and find its make and model stamped into a plate on the bottom. I tie the centrifuge back down and use the desk computer to go online and find an operation manual. The medical section of my omnipedia says that spinning human blood at three thousand RPM for three minutes should be enough to separate plasma from heavier cells.

I call Jessica again. Still no response.

I find an eyedropper in my bathroom and siphon about a third of my blood out of the test tube and into a plastic vial from one of the roulette-wheel sections in the centrifuge rotor. I fill another vial with water for counterbalance, then close the lid and punch my settings into the control panel.

Before starting the spin, I put the half-full test tube of blood in the mini-bar refrigerator and try Jessica again. Still nothing.

Do I really need her to walk me through this? How difficult can it possibly be? College undergraduates run lab centrifuges all the time. I'm a smart guy. I read the manual.

I double-check the centrifuge settings and push the START button.

The metal box starts wobbling almost immediately, and I grab the straps and hold it. My arms vibrate as the whine of the motor rises in pitch, and I feel the urge to look away, as if the thing might explode right in front of me. I remind myself that's pretty unlikely, since the vials inside are made of a shatterproof polymer.

Regardless of my sound reasoning, the noise and vibration are nerve-wracking. I consider leaning forward and trying to press the ABORT button with my nose, but decide I don't want to get my face that close.

The three-minute run lasts for an eternity, and when I hear the centrifuge spinning down, I realize that I was holding my breath.

I open the lid of the centrifuge and pull out both vials. I take the blood—now separated into a thick red layer at the bottom and translucent yellow liquid at the top—into the bathroom. This next part might be tricky.

The nanobots in my blood have short-range wireless radio transceivers. They communicate with my other tech implants to form a mesh network. As long as I keep the nanobots within about half a meter of some part of my body, they'll remain connected. They're programmed to stay close to blood serum proteins, some of which they use as raw materials or fuel. That means they're all floating in the top layer of yellow liquid in this vial.

I work fast, because the blood won't stay separated for long in zero-gravity. First I use another eyedropper to suck up all the blood plasma. Then I squeeze the plasma into an empty vial and close it tightly.

The vial of plasma goes into the zipper pocket on the upper left arm of my souvenir zero-gee jumpsuit, just below the round *Dejah Thoris* logo patch. Everything else that's touched my blood goes into a biohazard bag. I start to unstrap the centrifuge, then decide to try Jessica one more time, just in case I've done something wrong.

Still no answer. I pack up the centrifuge and put it back into the pocket.

Now, where am I going to find some booze that absolutely everybody will want to drink?

There's some kind of a very loud parade going through the Promenade, complete with dancers in colorful outfits and performers in animal costumes with giant heads. Very unsettling. I ride the elevator past that deck, get out near the casino, and look for the nearest bar.

It must be happy hour or something right now, because the first five bars I visit are bustling with literal barflies. Passengers are hanging off every surface, herded by uniformed crew members, and apparently having a great time. I wonder if people get intoxicated more quickly in zero-gravity for some reason.

The sixth bar, a lonely outpost near the Barsoom Buffet—currently closed until dinner service opens, I mean what is even the point of having this here?—has attracted only a few patrons. I approach the bartender, who has his back turned.

"Excuse me. What's the most expensive bottle you've got?" I ask.

He turns around. It's Ward again. I cannot believe my luck.

"That is an excellent question," he says, smiling like I imagine Satan would. "Are you looking for liquor or wine, sir?"

I attach my feet to the stick-strip under the bar and extend a hand. "Call me Evan."

He shakes my hand. "Ward."

"Yeah, I know." I have to admit, he was right about me seeing a lot of him this week. "How many jobs do you actually have on this ship?"

Ward shrugs. "I'm paying off some student loans."

"Right," I say. "Anyway, I'm thinking wine. Something to enjoy with dinner tonight."

"I see." Ward turns to his bartop computer and taps at the screen. "Tonight, the dining room is offering a variety of pasta entrées—"

"Actually, we're eating at that Silk place tonight."

"Fête Silk Road?" Ward purses his lips. "I see."

"Table for two. Seven-thirty. You can make that happen, right, Ward?"

He smiles. "I'm sure I can work something out, Mr. President."

It's nice to know we're on the same wavelength. "Good. Now about the wine. I want the most expensive bottle you've got on board. Price is no object."

Ward taps his screen a little faster. "Our best wines would exceed the daily charge limit on your account. You'd have to make a separate purchase. Cash or credit."

I hold up my platinum credit card. It's the one that Paul issued from his personal accounts, the one that won't be declined by any merchant in the Solar System, the one I'm only supposed to use for emergencies. I've already decided to worry about my debriefing later. Much later. Or maybe I'll just run away from home. I'm honestly not sure which choice will be less excruciating.

Ward raises an eyebrow, then nods. "Just so you know, this is going to run into the low five figures."

"That's not a problem." I lean forward. "Here's the situation, Ward. I really want to impress a lady friend, and nothing but the absolute finest will do. I want the most interesting thing you've got. Something that is so rare, so unique, that it's guaranteed to impress anybody. Something that even a teetotaler can't resist taking a sip of, just for curiosity's sake."

"What's a 'teetotaler'?" he asks.

I frown. "Really?"

"Nah. I'm just pulling your leg. You want the Red Wine."

I can't tell if he's still joking. "What kind of red wine?"

"No. *The* Red Wine," he says. "From Meridiani Planum."

CHAPTER TWENTY-ONE

Dejah Thoris—Deck 3, Barsoom Buffet
6 hours before my outrageously fancy dinner with Ellie

Ward has to call his supervisor, one of the ship's sommeliers, for approval to sell me the bottle. Even after seeing my platinum card, the sommelier seems hesitant. He arches an eyebrow as I repeat my weaksauce cover story. I really should have come up with something better.

"I thought it would be a nice treat for dinner tonight," I say. "You know, fine wine, zero-gravity, doesn't that sound like a magical experience?"

"Certainly," the sommelier says drily.

"And the fact that this is wine from prewar Mars, well, that's just icing on the cake. So to speak. Sorry, I'm bad with metaphors." I appear to be bad at many things. "You know what I mean."

"I understand, sir," the sommelier says. "If I may, just to clarify: you wish to purchase our single bottle of Meridiani Planum Cabernet Mitos?"

"Yes."

"And you understand *this* is the price of that bottle?" He raises his display tablet.

"I do." Why do I feel like he's about to make me sign a contract in blood?

"And you wish to purchase just this one bottle."

"Is that a problem?"

"Of course not, sir," the sommelier says. "Perhaps you and your companion would like to enjoy the wine with a meal. I can arrange for you a table in the observation dome. Tonight we offer a special *prix fixe* menu—"

"We've already made dinner arrangements," I say, giving Ward a glance. He gives me a discreet nod. *Good man.* "At Fête Silk Road."

The sommelier only pauses for a second. "Very good, sir. But if I may, their cuisine may not be best suited to this particular vintage. I could recommend a cheese pairing. Or some seafood. We have a special today on raw oysters—"

"Just the wine, thanks." *Would you please shut up and take my money?*

The sommelier stares at me for a moment, then nods. "Very good, sir. If you'll just wait here, I need to verify your credit with the issuing bank. It will take a few minutes, due to lightspeed transmission delays. I apologize for the inconvenience."

"No worries," I say. "You can't change the laws of physics, right?"

"That is not my job, sir."

"You know, that wine's aging inside the bottle as we speak."

He turns and disappears through a service door. Ward and I look at each other.

"Is he always like that?" I ask.

"Only on days ending in -AY," Ward says. "Make you a drink? On the house."

"Sure." I look over his shoulder at the backlit wall of liquor bottles. "Surprise me."

Ward starts assembling a cocktail. "Anyway, don't take it personally. Abdi's just doing his job."

"I thought his job was to sell wine."

"It is," Ward says, squirting clear liquid from a squeeze bottle into a transparent shaker. "But he's selling to *everyone*. The drinks are as much for show as they are for personal enjoyment."

He adds another clear liquid to the shaker. In zero-gravity, the air bubbles stay suspended, making the mixture look like a gelatinous ooze. Ward rattles the shaker, and the gel swirls around. "Yeah, I can see that."

"And no offense, Evan," Ward says, "but you don't seem like the kind of guy who regularly drops five figures on liquid refreshments." I wonder how he's going to get that liquid out of the shaker. "There's been some crew chatter about you. Federal employees aren't exactly known for their deep pockets."

"I've actually been saving up for a long time. You only live twice, right?"

Ward frowns at me. "I think the saying is 'You only live *once*.'"

"No, I'm pretty sure it's twice. One for sorrow, two for joy?" Or am I thinking of something else? I've never been good with poetry.

"Well, in any case. I hope you're enjoying the cruise."

"Best vacation of my life." It's not a lie.

Ward stops agitating the shaker and holds it up between us, one hand at each end. He twirls it on its long axis. The liquid inside becomes a cylindrical vortex. Ward plucks off the shaker lid, and the liquid spirals out of the container. He puts down the lid and picks up half of a drink bulb, placing it opposite the open end of the shaker to catch the liquid as it crawls sideways. With his other hand, he pulls away the shaker and picks up the other half of the drink bulb. He lines up both halves of the bulb with the ends of the floating liquid, then brings them together, sealing the cocktail inside the transparent sphere.

"Nice trick," I say as he pokes an olive and then a straw through a valve in the bulb.

"It's all for show," Ward says, handing me the drink. "The company wants you to see other passengers enjoying the various amenities aboard and then wanting those things for yourself. If you order a fancy drink, we make sure everyone around you knows about it. Cheers."

"I get it. That's why Sour Grapes wanted me to take the wine up to the observation dome." So I could advertise the existence of ridiculously expensive fermented grape juice, and hopefully entice others to shell out for their own bottles. I sip my mystery beverage. "What am I drinking here?"

"Vodka martini."

I've never had one before. "It's good. Thank you."

Ward nods. "It's about advertising luxury. Do you know the history of the Red Wine?"

Probably better than you do. "Yeah. One of the first viable vineyards on Mars."

"*The* first," Ward corrects me. "The Yarrow family built their habitat dome in Airy Crater specifically to grow wine grapes. The soil was already rich in iron oxides and volcanic basalt, but the vines also needed the right atmosphere and bacteria to thrive. It took them years to get the environment just right, but when they finally produced, it wasn't just drinkable. It was revolutionary. The Yarrows pioneered techniques that influenced not only vintners back on Earth, but also farmers and gardeners everywhere."

"Don't tell me," I say. "You have a degree in botany."

"Molecular biology, actually," Ward says. "I minored in botany."

If that was a joke, it's terrible. "And you're working odd jobs on a cruise ship because . . . ?"

"I told you. Student loans."

Oh no you don't. "Green Sky has been hiring botanists like crazy for the last decade. You could pay off an Ivy League education after two years with any of their asteroid belt subsidiaries. And you wouldn't have to sell things to drunk people."

Ward shrugs, not looking at me. "I like selling things."

That's when it hits me. "It's Mars. You wanted to go to Mars. That's it, isn't it? And working a cruise liner is the easiest way to get there, if you have more time than money."

He picks up another drink bulb and wipes it with a rag. "I wouldn't call it *easy*. But it's at least possible to get through customs to the surface with the cruise line vouching for us."

I realize I don't know Ward's full name. "Your last name wouldn't happen to be Yarrow, would it?"

"No," he says, splitting the empty drink bulb open. "My cousin's was."

"Your cousin."

"Matthew Yarrow."

Well, this just became really awkward. "I'm very sorry for your loss."

"What happened during the war was horrible," Ward says. "The loss of life alone would have been bad enough, but to also lose all those cultivars, and all that research—that was the real tragedy."

If he tells himself that enough times, he might even start to believe it.

My martini is very strong and very dry.

I know who the Yarrows were. I know because I researched them during the war. The agency assigned me to write up threat analyses and tactical assessments for Arabia Terra and bordering settlements. Paul kept me on Earth as long as he could, but he needed me to be useful. And I've always been a good spotter.

Probably less than twenty people ever saw the raw footage from the final battle in Airy Crater. I'm one of those people. I was assigned to review the vid from Earth troops' helmet cameras and summarize it for the agency's report to the Joint Chiefs. I wanted to erase the worst of those recordings, so nobody would ever have to see or hear any of it again.

Meridiani Planum is where the NASA rover *Opportunity* landed in the early twenty-first century to collect rock and soil samples. The Yarrows staked a claim there during the second wave of Martian settlement, when living in a dome was no longer life-threatening on a daily basis. The new colonial government wanted businesses to exploit the unique opportunities available on Mars. They wanted to show that Mars could be a better home than Earth.

Some people say they succeeded too well. Some people say that's what started the war. Some people are idiots.

In the fourteenth month of the war, an Earth troop transport went off-course and landed in Arabia Terra, just north of Airy Crater. Martian infantry boiled out of the Chaos regions to the west and overran the invaders. The battle turned into a siege that lasted for weeks.

Airy Crater is larger now. The ground is irradiated to a depth of fifty meters, and nothing will grow there for several hundred years. The popular myth is that the Yarrow vineyard workers welcomed the first wave of Earth soldiers into the dome, then killed them with poison gas. It's a good story, but it's not true. I know how those soldiers died. I saw their helmet vids.

I also know exactly when and how Matthew Yarrow died. I wish I could tell Ward, but he doesn't really want to know. Knowing doesn't make it any better.

It's a mystery how many bottles of Meridiani Planum wine still exist. Most of the Yarrows' records were destroyed during the war. Rumors still circulate about the family having a secret underground cellar somewhere in the polar regions, but nobody's been able to find it, of course. The only thing we know for sure is how to identify a genuine bottle of Meridiani Planum Red Wine—by verifying the integrity of the seal over the cork and confirming the cryptographic hash in the holo code on the label.

It's not just a bottle of wine. It's a piece of history. Nobody would refuse to at least taste it, and that's all I'll need to deliver the nanobots and save their lives.

"So," I ask Ward, "have you ever tasted this Red Wine, yourself?"

"No," he says. "I prefer whites."

I can't tell if he's joking.

CHAPTER TWENTY-TWO

Dejah Thoris—Deck 6, stateroom 6573
5 hours before my nanobot-flavored dinner with Ellie

As soon as I get back to my stateroom with the Red Wine, I lock the door, activate the comms dish, and call Jessica again.

This time she answers. She's wearing an olive-green, ribbed, wool pullover with patches on the elbows and shoulders. The room around her is dark except for a couple of computer displays and a few blinking lights on her medical instruments.

"Where the hell have you been?" she asks. "I've been trying to contact you for—" She shakes her head. "Never mind. Please confirm that you've secured all the equipment. Over."

"Affirmative." I pull the vial of plasma out of my jumpsuit and hold it up, transmitting vid from my eye. "I spun down a sample of my blood and separated out the plasma to extract the nanobots. By the way, why are you wearing an SAS commando sweater? Over."

"We can discuss my fashion choices later. Give me a wideband radio spectrum view of that vial. I need to make sure the nanobots precipitated correctly. And please verify that you've kept the vial within half a meter of your body at all times. Over."

I wiggle my fingers to adjust my eye's sensors, and a series of glowing outlines appears over my arm and hand. Tiny bright circles blink at the bottom of the vial. I pull it closer so Jessica will get a good picture. "Let me know when you've got enough. Over." I leave the channel open, streaming data back to Earth.

Jessica nods at her display. "Serum nanobots look good. I'm uploading their new firmware now. Do not disconnect, repeat, *do not* disconnect your receiver until I say so. Over."

I tuck the vial back into my jumpsuit and wait. After a couple of minutes of staring at the side of Jessica's head, I open the box containing the Red Wine, pull the bottle out of its tissue paper wrapping, and turn the label so we can both see it. "So will this do for the expensive booze? Over."

She turns her head back to face me and says something in Mandarin. "Please tell me you did not steal that! Over."

"Of course not," I say. "I'm on a cruise ship. Everything's for sale. I paid with the platinum card."

Jessica makes a fist, raises it as if she's going to slam it down on her desk, then slowly opens and lowers her hand. "Just in case you've forgotten. Let me remind you that we are trying to *hide* what we're doing. Is there some reason you think Lasher will *not* notice a ten *thousand* dollar purchase and demand an explanation? Over!"

"Relax," I say. "He's got bigger fish to fry. If he does ask, I'll say I felt like having some fun on my vacation. That's what he told me to do, right? I'll tell him I was trying to impress a girl." It's not a lie. I sure hope Ellie appreciates this outrageous wine.

"And how will you explain all these long-distance comms with me? Because he's going to notice that, too. And *I* am the one who gets court-martialed for running illegal medical experiments! Over."

"You know about fancy wines, right? And . . . women . . . things? Yeah? I wanted to ask you for some guidance before my big date. There we go."

Jessica glares at me. "Nobody is going to believe that."

"Trust me, I can sell Lasher. Asking you for relationship advice wouldn't be the dumbest thing I've ever done."

"I suppose that's true."

She turns and looks offscreen. After a few minutes of her silent treatment, I put the bottle away and decide it might be good to change the subject while we wait.

"So tell me again why you're wearing a commando pullover in the dark?" I ask. "Because it's a very flattering look, and I wonder why you don't go with this particular ensemble more often. Over."

"It's a funny story. I'll tell you later," she says. "Upload complete. Your nanobots are now programmed to seek out and destroy cancerous and pre-cancerous cells, and repair chromosome damage. Get them inside each of the affected people before noon tomorrow, and they should be all right. But first you'll need to let them multiply for a while."

The nanobots replicate themselves using compounds found in my bloodstream—they have to, since multitudes of them need replacing every day as they wear out from normal operation or are destroyed by my body's natural defenses. I try not to think too hard about the fact that billions of tiny robots are cannibalizing each other's parts all the time inside my body.

Jessica walks me through the procedure. My vial only contains five cc's of nanobot serum, which is less than one percent of the volume of the wine bottle. In order to make sure that a single sip will deliver at least one nanobot into the drinker's bloodstream, I need more nanobots. And they need more fuel.

I pull a candy bar out of the mini-bar, break it into pieces inside a plastic bag, and grind the pieces into as fine a paste as I can between a metal spoon and the desktop. Then I scrape the candy paste into five empty plastic vials, use an eyedropper to transfer one cc of nanobot serum into each vial, fill it the rest of the way with water, close the lid, and shake to mix everything up before stowing the vials in another of my jumpsuit's many zippered storage compartments.

"Replication confirmed," Jessica says after I scan the bottle. "Leave that for an hour and you're good to go."

"Look, I know this is a stupid question," I say, "but I have to ask. Are you sure I can't tell anyone about this? I could probably work the ship's doctor with a cover story. This will go a lot easier if I have some help." *And I'm afraid I'll screw it up.* "Over."

"No, no, *no,* and once again, NO." Jessica leans forward. The fact that she's not yelling is even scarier than when she raises her voice. "Let me remind you that the very existence of these nanobots is classified Above Top Secret. Nobody finds out about this. *Nobody.* Best case, it causes a shipwide panic; worst case, Lasher is indicted before Congress and we all go to federal prison. Do you understand? Over."

"Yes," I say, "I understand. But if this is such a terrible risk—" I can't think of an elegant way to ask her what I want to know, so I just blurt it out. "You've never even met these people, Surge. Why do you care so much? Over."

Jessica stares into the camera for what feels like a lifetime. "I'm a doctor," she says, finally. "I took an oath." She looks over her shoulder. "Dammit. I have to go. I probably won't be able to contact you again today, so it's very important that you get this right. Don't screw it up, Kangaroo. Those people are depending on you." She pauses. "Good luck."

"Thanks," I mutter. I wonder what the hell is going on back home.

The image of Jessica in my HUD reaches forward, then pauses. "One more thing. Stop calling me 'Surge'! Over and out."

My doorbell rings.

I float over and look through the peephole to see Jemison. She raps the door with her knuckles. "Rogers! Open up."

The centrifuge is still strapped to the coffee table. If Jemison sees it, she's going to ask a lot of questions I don't want to answer.

"Just a minute!" I shout through the door. "I'm not decent! Let me get dressed first!"

I push back from the door, stuff the Red Wine back into its box, and shove the box into the bottom drawer of my desk. Then I launch myself to the coffee table, unstrap the centrifuge, and suck it back into the pocket, hoping the rush of air into vacuum isn't audible through the stateroom door.

I strip off my jumpsuit—with my luck, Jemison will have a reason to search me at some point—then yank open my closet and retrieve the first outfit I see: a pair of plaid pants and a short-sleeved, Hawaiian-print shirt. I pull on the clothes and open the door.

Jemison scowls at my wardrobe. "What the hell are you wearing?"

"You don't like it?" I say. "I'm trying to blend in."

"Forget it," Jemison says. "I need to show you something."

That sounds ominous. "Is this murder-related?"

I can't decipher her expression. "It's easier if I just show you."

CHAPTER TWENTY-THREE

Dejah Thoris—Deck D, security office
3 hours after I voiced my suspicions about the crew

Jemison leads me to the ship's main security office. I hope we can wrap up whatever this is in time for me to get a new outfit tailored for tonight. I'm thinking about that so hard, I don't even notice Mike and Danny flanking me as I float through the doorway.

They slam the door shut behind me and grab my arms. My reflex is to throw them off and get the hell out of there, but I suppress that and settle for glaring at Jemison. "Something you forgot to tell me, Chief?"

"Funny." Jemison taps a control panel. "I was going to ask you the same thing."

The display screen in the center of the vid bank behind her lights up with what appears to be security footage. It takes me a few seconds to recognize one of the thruways on the Promenade, right next to—

"Oh," I say.

It's a recording from the first night of the cruise, showing my drunken tirade in front of the Mars projection globe.

"You want to tell us about your friend?" Jemison asks.

"My what now?"

She freezes the image and points at the man standing next to me. "I don't know if you're actually drunk here, Rogers, but that is the worst goddamn brush pass I have ever seen."

"What? No. No!" I shake my head, causing my whole body to move, and Mike and Danny grip me tighter. "I don't know who that is. I met him at dinner that night."

"Right." Jemison folds her arms. "And he just happened to follow you out of the dining room to have an extended conversation about a children's educational exhibit."

"I was drunk! He was drunk! And the entire ship is designed to funnel passengers through the Promenade, because that's where all the retail shops are!"

"That's the best you've got?" Jemison says. "Did you not even bother to work up a cover story? Did you think we were just going to let you do whatever the hell you wanted on this ship?" She looks over my shoulder at Mike. "Check his fingers."

Mike and Danny each grab one of my hands by the wrist and pry my fists apart. I resist the instinct to fight back. I can probably get some leverage by pushing off the floor, but I don't quite have my zero-gee sea legs yet.

The two security guards rub the tips of all my fingers—not very gently, either. What are they looking for? Chemical residue? What do they think I touched?

"Nothing here, Chief," Mike says.

"Times two," Danny says.

They release my wrists and clamp their hands on my shoulders again. I raise both hands as much as I can, palms forward, in a gesture of surrender. "Look, Chief—"

I'm suddenly staring at the business end of her stunner. *Damn, that's a fast draw.* "Don't even think about it."

"I have no idea what you're talking about!" Now I'm getting angry. "I don't know who that guy on the vid is. And I don't know why you're pointing a gun at me!"

"Mike, Danny, cuff him," Jemison says.

I will myself to keep quiet and stay still while Mike and Danny grab my wrists, yank them behind my back, and secure them together with something cold and metallic. I lose my cool again when they also bind my ankles.

"Oh, come on!" I say. "What the hell do you think I'm going to do?"

Jemison's lips have pressed themselves into a thin smile, but her eyes are still glowering. "You know, I didn't give you enough credit, Rogers. You really had us fooled. Even the captain. But you got sloppy with your computer hacking, or maybe just lazy. I don't know. I don't care. Whatever deal you were running on the side here, it's over."

My stomach is churning almost as much as my mind. Why am I so anxious, when I know I didn't do what she's accusing me of? The computer thing is a problem, but all I did was set up an encrypted comms channel to the office—there's no way Jemison could tell who I was talking to, or about what.

I feel my arm and leg muscles tensing up, instinctively testing my restraints. I have to pull myself out of operations mode. If I fight back, Jemison will take that as further proof of guilt. Of course, pretty much anything I do right now is likely to aggravate her. I can't give her what she wants. How do I convince her of that?

"What did the other guy tell you?" I nod at the screen behind her. "The guy in that security vid."

Jemison scoffs. "I'm not going to waste time interrogating a cutout. You're the goddamn operator."

"Wait." I study her face. "You didn't even talk to him?"

"I want the op-tech," Jemison says through clenched teeth. She thinks I'm using some kind of agency equipment to do . . . whatever she thinks I did. "Where is it?"

"Now hold on," I say. "Both of us were right there when Security showed up. We were both forcibly escorted out of that area. You've got a security breach, fine. Why would you assume I'm to blame? The other guy had just as much opportunity."

"We didn't catch the other guy doing an unauthorized spacewalk," Jemison says. "The other guy didn't trick our chief engineer into giving him a centrifuge out of ship's stores."

My stomach knots up as I realize what I have to do—what I have to tell her to clear my name.

"And the other guy hasn't been acting squirrelly ever since the captain and I learned who he really is," Jemison continues.

"Whoa," I say. "Chief. I don't think Danny and Mike are *dog people,* are they?"

I stare hard at Jemison. *These civilians are not cleared for what we need to discuss.*

She stares back, then says, "Mike. Danny. Wait outside."

"I'm not sure that's a good idea, Chief," Mike says.

"He's tied up. I've got a stunner." Nobody moves. "Now! That's an order!"

"All right, we're going." Danny opens the door. Mike pulls himself through, shaking his head. "But if we hear any screaming, we're busting right back in here."

"You hear screaming, it's going to be him," Jemison says.

"We don't want *you* killing anybody, either, Chief," Danny says. "Too much damn paperwork."

He closes the door, and it's just Jemison, her stunner, and me.

"That was a joke, right?" I ask. "About the screaming and the paperwork?"

"You try using your 'pocket' and I will crack your skull open," Jemison says. "Tell me what the hell is going on."

"Chief, I know it's not what you want to hear, but I honestly do not know—"

I don't even see her hand move. The butt end of the stunner's handgrip hits my cheek, snapping my head to the right. Pain shoots through my jaw.

"Ow!" Did she just fracture a tooth?

"Was it a graph-glove?" Jemison asks. "Mimic film? What did you use?"

Those are both devices used to fool biometric sensors. She thinks I copied someone's fingerprints. Why would I want to do that? "I didn't—"

Jemison smacks me again, with her open palm this time, which brings an entirely different type of stinging pain to the other side of my face. "Who are you working with?"

"Nobody!" I say. "I'm on vacation!"

The third impact knocks my head back to the right. "Why the fuck do you need a centrifuge? And don't give me any of that bullshit you fed Ellie."

"I'll tell you!" I say. "But can we stop with the hitting and talk like civilized people?"

Jemison is still as a statue except for her right index finger, which moves off the trigger guard of the stunner and onto the trigger. "Talk."

Cards on the table, Kangaroo.

I take a deep breath and say, "I have nanobots in my blood."

She blinks. "What?"

"Nanobots," I say. "They're microscopic machines that—"

"I know what the fuck nanobots are," she says. "You've got a *swarm* in your *blood*?"

"It's not like that," I say. "They're tech only. No biologics. Software driven, very limited functionality. I hacked into my stateroom computer to set up encrypted comms so I could talk to my Surgical officer, and I *borrowed* the centrifuge so I could spin down a blood sample and extract some nanobots for Surgical to reprogram." Jemison's not hitting me, so that's good. "I couldn't tell Ellie because she's not in the loop."

"And what exactly are you going to do with this classified, experimental, military biotech on my ship?" Jemison asks. Her finger is still on the trigger.

"We're using the nanobots to detect and eliminate precancerous cells."

Jemison sighs. "I don't know how your Surgical talked you into this, and I don't care how noble your cause is. You're not running unauthorized medical experiments on civilians. How do we stop these crazy robots?"

"This isn't an experiment," I say. "This is *triage*. To fix the radiation damage from Alan Wachlin's PECC. Surge tested the new program on me first, and now I need to administer the same treatment to you, and Captain Santamaria, and Ellie, and any other crew members who spent more than five minutes in the Wachlins' stateroom after the fire."

Jemison stares at me, then shakes her head. "No. I'm not an idiot, Rogers. This is an interplanetary spacecraft. We have safety protocols. Everybody who went into 5028 followed procedure to limit their exposure."

"Only *after* you knew Alan had a PECC implant! How much time did you spend in there before then, checking the crime scene? How long were you and I and the captain in there looking for the murder weapon? How long were you and Ellie in there that first night?" I pause to let that sink in. "Nothing else on the ship can treat this type of radiation damage. I don't do this, and you all die of cancer."

Jemison's finger slowly moves off the stunner's trigger and back onto the trigger guard.

"I want to check these robots before you deploy them," she says.

I nod. "I'll tell you how to scan for—"

"No," Jemison says. "I'm going to draw your blood and run my own damn tests."

"You can't tell the doctor. You can't tell anyone," I say. "I told you because I need you to believe that I'm telling the truth. I did not copy anyone's fingerprints!"

Jemison frowns. "How the hell does telling me about your nanobots—"

"Because why the hell would I tell you something that could end my career," I say, "and *not* admit to picking a damn lock?"

She stares at me for a second, then slides her stunner back into its holster.

"Does this mean we're friends again?" I ask.

"Jesus fucking Christ, Rogers," she says. "Do you have a lot of practice rolling over and showing your belly, or is it just dumb luck that I got the big show today?"

I glare at her. "Maybe you should visit the casino later."

"Yeah." She opens a cabinet. "Right after I test your blood for swarming robots."

"*Nano*bots."

"Shut the fuck up."

CHAPTER TWENTY-FOUR

Dejah Thoris—Deck D, security office
3½ hours after I opened my big suspicious mouth

Jemison brings Danny and Mike back into the room, but leaves me tied up while she does the blood draw, which means after she's done, I can't apply pressure to the hole she's poked in the crook of my elbow. When Jemison leaves to test my blood, Danny holds a gauze pad against my arm. Mike watches me suspiciously.

"You're probably wondering how a blood test is going to prove my innocence," I say.

"Not really," Mike says. "Chief's going to do what she does, and we'll take it from there."

I study his face, then look at Danny. "You two really trust her that much?"

"She's the chief," Danny says, as if that explains everything.

"How long have you worked on this ship?"

Danny narrows his eyes. "I think we should all just wait quietly."

"Come on, guys—"

"There might be some duct tape in one of these storage compartments," Mike says.

"Okay, okay! I can take a hint." I turn my head and look straight ahead, at the image still frozen on the main display.

The security camera must be mounted on a wall opposite the Mars display, about three meters up. Jemison froze the image just as I was leaning over to talk to the other guy. I don't remember the conversation very clearly. The vid shows our faces in profile, and I struggle to recall what the other man looks like. I do have some practice recognizing faces, even though my eye can automatically tag and record any suspicious characters in my vicinity. You never know if poor lighting will confuse the face-reco software, or whether you might lose the data link with the office.

This guy, though—I'd be hard pressed to describe his features in any sort of detail. Brown hair, yes, and maybe brown eyes? The face I see in my memory is hazy, as if nothing about him was remarkable or unusual enough for me to notice and remember. How is it possible for a person to look so bland, so—average?

The door opens. Jemison pulls herself inside, her face neutral. That's an improvement.

"Untie him," she says to Mike and Danny, then continues over to the control console under the vid screen.

"Aye, Chief." Danny undoes my wrist restraints, and Mike rotates in midair to do the same to the ties around my ankles.

"Just like that?" I ask as I float free of the wall. "You're not even going to ask what she did with my blood?"

Jemison shoots me a look over her shoulder. "We don't have time for this."

"Chief'll tell us if it's important," Mike says. "I'm guessing some kind of DNA test to confirm your identity."

"Nah, those take days to run," Danny says. "I'm going to say testing for a viral or bacterial infection, to corroborate your alibi or previous whereabouts."

Jemison turns and glares at all three of us. "Am I the only one here concerned about the security of this vessel and the safety of our passengers?"

"Am I staying here?" I ask. "Or am I staying out of trouble?"

Jemison grumbles and points at the far end of the console. "Foothold."

I float over and hook my feet into an indentation in the floor, hoping my expression isn't too smug. Mike and Danny push off the wall and join Jemison in front of the screen.

I'll talk to her about distributing the nanobots later. Right now, we've got a possible murder suspect. And I'm part of the team. I'm confident we can wrap this up before dinner, and then I'll really have something to celebrate with Ellie.

"We log all crew accesses through locked doors," Jemison says, pointing at the screen. "Janice Long, one of the officers on the Promenade that night, started appearing in two places at once later in her shift."

"Wow," I say, "it's a good thing somebody suggested investigating the crew, huh?"

She ignores my remark. "This was the first time during that shift when she encountered any passengers. We're going to finish checking this footage, then go on to the next segment."

Jemison taps a button, and the vid begins playing again. "Rogers. Do you recall your friend doing anything suspicious here?"

"Nothing comes to mind," I say. "Also, not my friend."

"It's too bad we don't record audio," Jemison says, watching me mouth off to the security guards onscreen.

"I can read lips," Mike says.

"Of course you can," I say.

"'I'm . . . not . . . drunk?'" Mike says. "And Blevins says, 'Whatever you say, sir.'"

"You know," I say, "we can't even see our person of interest from this angle."

"Just tracking everyone's position," Jemison says. "It doesn't hurt to be thorough."

"It might be better to work faster, considering we still have a murderer on the loose."

Jemison nods. "Do you have the footage from the other camera, Danny?"

"Just scrubbing through now," Danny says. "Here we go."

The screen changes to show a view from farther down the thruway, next to the Mars exhibit. Danny touches another control, and the still image goes into motion.

Long breaks away from me and the two other security guards. She pulls my so-called friend back from the globe. He stumbles as she hauls him over the railing, then falls down on top of her. She does a quick roll to get out from under him and drags him up by one arm. He grabs her hand and waist and twirls her as if they're waltzing. It takes Long a few seconds to extricate herself and get behind the man to push him toward the elevators.

"Spin that back," Jemison says. "Go to where he falls down, freeze, then step forward frame by frame."

Danny turns a dial, rewinding the vid and then advancing it slowly.

"There." Jemison stabs a finger at the screen. "Back one frame and zoom in."

The picture shifts. The security camera's shutter speed is low enough that Long's and the passenger's arms are blurred as they spin around, but the man's hand is clearly visible when she pulls away from him.

"Hold that zoom and advance to the next frame," Jemison says.

The man's palm streaks across the screen.

"One more," Jemison says. "Show me that hand."

His hand flickers to the left and sharpens. Danny taps some controls, and the man's palm expands to fill the screen. There's a faint but distinctive grid pattern covering his skin. It would be invisible to the naked eye, but the security cameras also see infrared and ultraviolet.

"There's something on his palm," Danny says.

"A tattoo?" Mike says.

"Mimic film," I say. "He pressed her fingertips against his palm. Copied her prints." I've done similar lifts before, but never that smoothly. Whoever this guy is, he's a professional.

"Pull up his account," Jemison says.

"Running facial recognition." Danny punches some keys, and the display above us changes, shrinking the security vid and adding a grid of more than a dozen unremarkable male faces on the right side of the screen. "That's odd. More hits than usual."

"A lot more," Mike says.

"He's got one of those faces," I say. "Average features. Unremarkable."

Jemison turns to me. "You saw him up close, Rogers. Which one is he?"

"Give me a second." I scan the grid of faces. "Are these recent images?"

"They're the ID holos we took during boarding," Danny says. "Controlled lighting conditions, no aging or facial hair issues."

It takes me a few seconds to find my so-called friend. "There. That guy. Jerry Bartelt."

"Get his passenger record," Jemison says. "And start a face scan on all our other security footage."

"On it." Danny taps at his keyboard.

"Did he know the Wachlins?" Jemison asks Mike. "Did he board the ship with them, meet them for meals or activities, anything?"

Mike studies the console, then shakes his head. "No intersections yet. Still collating data."

"Face scans will take a while too," Danny says. "I'll need to do multiple passes to zero in on Mr. Average here."

"Jerry Bartelt," Jemison says. "Who the hell are you, and why would you want to kill those nice people?" She looks at me. "Mike, Danny, forget those searches. I have a better idea."

CHAPTER TWENTY-FIVE

Dejah Thoris—Deck D, crew section
4½ hours after I suggested I might assist Security in some way

Jemison leads us out of the security office while explaining her plan. I like how it's an opportunity for me to show that I'm not a liability, but I don't like how it puts me and Jerry Bartelt in a room alone together. Chances are there's going to be a scuffle, and I'd rather not show up for my dinner with Ellie missing any body parts.

"Wouldn't it be better just to get a security team together and bust in unannounced?" I ask. "Why the whole masquerade?"

"Bartelt thinks you're just a good ol' boy who likes to drink," she says. "You're going to get friendly with him and find out what he's up to." We've reached the elevator at the end of the hallway, and she's punching the call button repeatedly. "Danny, find out where Janice Long is right now and get two goons to detain her."

"You call your security people 'goons'?" I say.

"It's a term of endearment," Mike says. Danny taps his wristband. The elevator car arrives, and we all squeeze in.

Jemison turns to me. "Rogers, do you remember what Bartelt was drinking at the Captain's Table?"

"Same as the rest of us," I say. "Red wine—a Sangiovese, I think—and champagne. They also offered a Chardonnay, but he didn't have any of that."

"No cocktails? A martini? Maybe an after-dinner whiskey?" she asks.

I shake my head. "I wasn't really paying attention. Why are you so interested in his drinking habits?"

"I'm trying to find you a plausible excuse for showing up at his stateroom.

171

If you're drunk and carrying half a bottle of his favorite booze, he might be inclined to invite you in."

I decide not to mention the Red Wine in my stateroom. "Right. So it only *looks* like I'm trying to proposition him. Is this a murder investigation or are we acting out one of your private fantasies here?"

"That would be a different kind of sting," Mike says, snickering.

Jemison raises a finger and points it at Mike. He goes quiet.

Danny looks up and says, "Blevins and Yang just picked up Janice Long. They've confiscated her security gear and are escorting her to the drunk tank now."

"Did she put up a fight?" I ask, leaning around her.

"Sure sounded like it," Danny says, tapping his earpiece.

I give Jemison a significant look. "The innocent never sleep in a holding cell."

"She knows the book as well as we do," Jemison says. "It's not going to be that easy."

"What's the motive?" Mike asks. "Why would Janice Long or Jerry Bartelt want to kill Emily and Alan Wachlin?"

"He's not going to just tell us," I say. "Even if we ask him nicely."

"No shit," Jemison says. "I figured some liquor would help loosen his tongue."

"It's the wrong approach." I drum my fingers on the wall of the elevator car. "Getting that friendly with him will take too long. I can put him on the defensive much more quickly and try to shake something loose. He has no reason to suspect that I'm looking at him for murder. I can play dumb better than any of you."

"I guess some things just come naturally," Jemison says.

"Thanks for the vote of confidence."

"I thought you were a State Department researcher," Mike says. "How is it you seem to know so much about interrogation techniques?"

"Trade negotiations can get tricky."

Mike narrows his eyes. "Right."

The numbers on Jerry Bartelt's stateroom door glow a soft red color, and the display panel on his door below the stateroom number says DO NOT DISTURB. I can see the reflection of the red numbers in the gray camera dome on the ceiling, right at the T-junction where the hallway from the elevator intersects a longer, curved corridor.

I could sneak through the cameras' blind spots, just like I did when I broke into the excursion room to set up my comms dish, but if Jerry is watching, I need him to see me playing drunken idiot. I zigzag down the corridor, bouncing from one wall to another, letting my body flip and rotate freely, not even trying to keep myself oriented.

At one point, I pretend to get jammed upside-down in a corner, until I use my arms to roll around so I'm facing away from the wall again. For a moment, I'm concerned that I've been throwing myself around too vigorously. I press my back against the wall to make sure the hand thruster Jemison gave me earlier is still clipped to my belt at the base of my spine, hidden underneath my floppy Hawaiian shirt.

After one final collision with the wall directly opposite room 7681, I grab the door handle and bang my fist against the DO NOT DISTURB sign until my hand starts to hurt.

"Gerald fucking Bartlett!" I yell, mangling his name on purpose. "Open up, you pear-shaped sonuvabitch! I know you're in there! Come out here and face me like a man!"

I've nearly run out of insults by the time he opens the door. Jerry looks the same as he did the last time I saw him: totally ordinary, completely unremarkable. The only unusual thing right now is how angry he seems to be.

"You?" he says. "What the hell are you doing here?"

"Who were you expecting? The Spanish Inquisition?" I lean forward and shout right into his face. He instinctively draws back from me. I lever around the door frame and push myself into the room, slamming my left shoulder into his chest.

"Hey!" he says, spinning back and out of my way. He wasn't expecting that move, so he wasn't braced against it. I wonder if he's had even less experience moving in zero-gee than I have. I need to use every advantage I can against this guy.

The passenger staterooms on *Dejah Thoris* are designed so that an average-sized adult is never more than an arm's length from a wall or a piece of furniture. I'm sure this is to prevent people in zero-gee from getting stranded in the middle of an empty space. A lot of people think they can "fly" in a weightless environment by flapping their arms and legs, as if they're swimming, but that doesn't work. Air will just move out of your way, and you'll be stuck hanging there. This is why the crew uses hand thrusters and jetpacks.

Jerry's stateroom is a single-occupancy studio. I let momentum carry me forward until my legs hit the side of his bed, then bend my knees and flail my arms, turning my body until I'm facing the door again, upside-down, and plant my feet on the ceiling.

I catch a glimpse of Jerry closing the lid on his laptop computer. I hope Jemison and Danny and Mike noticed it too, through the vid link we set up from my eye to Danny's wristband. If Jerry was using the laptop to monitor the security camera feeds, he's now blind. That's their opening.

"You're drunk," Jerry says, holding on to the desk.

I kick off the ceiling and lunge at him. He doesn't even try to get out of the way, which confirms he's protecting the laptop. I grab his shirt collar and land both my knees in his stomach. He coughs and looks even an-grier. *Good.*

"You oughta be ashamed of yourself," I say, slurring my words just a little. I want to appear coordinated enough to be dangerous. "I saw what you did to that poor woman! It makes me sick, just looking at you."

Jerry grabs my wrists and tries to pull my hands away. I yank myself toward him once, hard, and tilt my head down at the same time. I score a lucky shot, banging my forehead against the bridge of his nose. Pain shoots through my head, but judging from the noise Jerry makes, it hurts him even more.

"Yeah, how does it feel, big man?" I yell in Jerry's face. "How does that feel? Doesn't feel good, does it?"

"I don't know what you're talking about!" he says.

I jerk my head to the side, stealing a glance into the empty bathroom and at the closet, then linger on the inside of the stateroom door before turning back to Jerry. I hope Jemison can see that the room is clear, and that she gets my hint about the front door. *What the hell is taking them so long?*

"Don't lie to me, you sick, perverted, lousy sack of—"

Jerry slams the heel of his right hand against the side of my head and uses his left hand to punch me in the side. I do my best to hold on, but after a couple more kidney-punches, he closes his right hand around my throat. I can feel his fingers pressing on my arteries.

This guy's definitely a professional, and I've got about five seconds be-fore I pass out.

I let go of his collar and do my best to make *I-surrender* noises, but Jerry doesn't care. I can see it in his eyes. He's not going to let me go until I'm unconscious, and I really don't want to imagine what he might do to me between then and whenever Jemison and Danny and Mike finally come charging through the door.

Jerry only has one hand free, and I make him use that one, too. I slap my right palm against his face, weak and limp. I'm not really faking that part. He closes his eyes reflexively, and I sneak my left hand around my back and grab the hand thruster. By the time he gets his left hand around my right wrist to restrain it, I've got my left arm up again.

I aim the thruster nozzle directly into his ear and press the button.

Momentum is the product of the mass and velocity of an object. In order for a small object, like a collection of gas molecules, to move a large object, like a human being, their velocity has to be correspondingly higher. That also makes them forceful enough to break an eardrum at close range. *Science!*

Jerry screams. His grip on my throat weakens, but he still doesn't let go. I shove the nozzle into one of his nostrils and thumb the trigger again. He makes a noise like a startled cat and releases me, his hand going to his nose. I close my fist around the gas canister and deliver a swift jab under his chin. I hear his teeth click together as the punch lands.

He's dazed now, but he's still got a death grip on my right arm, and I can't give him any time to recover. I extend my left leg, putting my shoe on the edge of his desk, and twist my body to that side until I can kick down. I slam my right foot into his side and stomach repeatedly, with as much force as I can manage from this angle, until he releases my hand. One more kick and he spirals away from me toward the opposite wall.

I scramble over to the stateroom door and yank it open. Jemison and Danny and Mike rush in. Mike is in front, with his stunner in both hands, and he zaps Jerry as soon as he has a clear shot.

Jerry goes limp. Danny and Mike gather him up while Jemison checks me for injuries.

"Where the hell were you guys?" I croak.

"He locked us out," Jemison says.

"Can't you override that?"

"He reprogrammed the lockpad," she says. "Bastard's got a lot of tricks."

"We need to search the room," I say. "He closed the laptop as soon as I came in."

Jemison nods, looking over the desk. "Yeah. Be careful. He's had three days to set up booby traps in here."

I take another look around, using my eye to scan for any possible dangers. If Jerry Bartelt was well prepared for this trip, he could have smuggled in any number of deadly devices, or the components to make them. But I see nothing out of the ordinary. I tell Jemison it's safe.

Jemison gestures toward Danny and Mike. "You two, secure the prisoner here."

"Not in the brig?" Mike asks.

"Absolutely not," Jemison says. "This guy's a professional. Chances are he's rigged that laptop to self-destruct if he leaves the room without issuing the proper command. Just tie him down to something solid and get more security in here to sweep for electronics. Gag him, too. I don't want him talking to anyone or anything." Voice controls for shoulder-phones are pretty common, and an easy way to disguise more sinister interfaces. No need to touch anything if the bomb responds to your voiceprint.

"Will do," Mike says. "Where are you going, Chief?"

"Rogers and I are going to talk to the captain."

CHAPTER TWENTY-SIX

Dejah Thoris—Deck C, officers' quarters
1½ hours before Ellie starts wondering where I am

We pass a large advertisement for onboard dining experiences on our way back to the crew section, reminding me that I have a dinner date.

"Listen, Chief," I say once we're inside the crew elevator, "about the nanobots—"

"How much time do we have?" she asks.

I blink a countdown clock into my eye. "Sixteen hours. But sooner would be—"

"We'll deal with it later," she says.

"Maybe you can have someone start compiling a list of affected personnel?"

Jemison glares at me. "I just took one of my security officers into custody. Let's not assign any new projects until we know who we can trust."

I can't wait for Jemison to help me with this. I'm the one responsible for dispensing these nanobots. And I already have an appointment with my first patient.

We continue in silence. I don't know what Jemison's thinking, but I'm working on how to exfil myself from her mission and get back to my own. Maybe our chat with the captain will give me an opportunity.

When we reach Santamaria's quarters, she presses her hand against the lockpad to announce herself. The door swings open, and he looks at us through red-rimmed eyes.

He's wearing his uniform pants and a gray, short-sleeved undershirt. I can see four tattoos on his arms, but I only recognize three of them. One of those is the same one Paul Tarkington has burned into the skin of his right forearm.

"Chief," Santamaria says. "Mr. Rogers. Is there a problem?"

Jemison pushes me through the doorway, follows me in, and closes the door behind herself. I'm not sure what I expected Santamaria's quarters to look like. Maybe I thought it would be more naval, or nautical, or— I don't know, but decorated with pictures of seascapes and ancient sailing vessels. Maybe a tiny ship in a bottle that he built with painstaking precision over a period of months. As usual, I was wrong.

If it weren't for the clothing visible in the open closet and the computer tablets clinging to stick-strips above the small desk, I might have thought these quarters were unoccupied. There are no family holos or diplomas or the display case of rank insignia and service medals one might expect a decorated military veteran to have. But more unnerving than the lack of personality is the complete lack of clutter.

Even Oliver, the most fastidious neat freak I know, leaves stuff lying around his workshop all the time. Sure, it's all perfectly lined up at right angles, but it's still lying around. Santamaria's quarters are completely devoid of anything that could be construed as mess or disorganization— that would imply some kind of organization to begin with, and there's simply nothing here. I wonder if he's just OCD about zero-gee stowage protocols, or if there's some deeper psychological reason for the spartan décor.

"We may have found the real murderer, Captain," Jemison says, and gives a quick rundown of how we identified and apprehended Jerry Bartelt. "Guy's got professional written all over him. Danny and Mike are sitting on him in his stateroom. He was using a laptop, but we don't want to mess with it yet. Thought you'd want to talk to him first."

Santamaria nods. "If Jerry Bartelt is a known operator, his file will be in the high-value section. We won't be able to access that over an insecure connection."

"I'm end-to-end encrypted," I say. I blink my network feed into view and start powering up the comms dish on the hull. "I can run a face-reco search through the warehouse. Just give me a few seconds to—"

Santamaria grabs my face and jams his thumb under my left eyelid, pushing it up into my brow.

"Ow," I say, predictably.

"Do not send that signal," he says. There's no special emphasis or threat in his voice, but, as with his stateroom, it's the lack of ornamentation that unsettles me.

"I'm just running a records search," I say. "Even if it comes back with a restricted-access marker—"

"That's not the point," Santamaria says.

"You might tip off Bartelt or his bosses," Jemison says.

"What?" I ask. "We've got Bartelt in custody. He didn't have any chance to alert his superiors. They don't even know we're looking—"

"He'll have regular check-in times," Jemison says. "Once or twice a day, I'm guessing. Whatever time that is, he's going to miss it. We've got a few hours at most before his handlers know something's up."

"At that point," Santamaria says, "our advantage will be keeping them in the dark about the fact that Bartelt's been captured. They won't know if he's simply been injured, or taken ill, or missed his check-in for some other, mundane reason. We don't want to do anything to make them suspect he's been apprehended."

"How would they—can you please let go of my face, Captain?"

"Do not send that signal."

"I won't."

"And power down the dish."

"I will."

He releases me, and I deactivate the comms dish. "Okay, the dish is offline. But how would these hypothetical bosses know what kind of signal they were seeing anyway? This ship must be transmitting dozens of different radio beacons at any given time."

"Your Echo Delta uses US-OSS frequencies," Santamaria says. "We don't want to advertise that there is a military presence aboard this ship."

My stomach tightens as I remember all the calls I've made to Jessica, but I can't worry about that now.

"Did you notice anything about Bartelt's behavior?" Santamaria asks. "Anything that might indicate a country of origin or specific training?"

"Oh." I think back to my encounters with Jerry Bartelt: first at dinner, then in the thruway, and finally in his stateroom. "No, nothing stands out. American accent—sounded like a native English speaker. Very smooth body work with the security guards. You don't get that good without training, but that could be any national program."

"I didn't see anything distinctive in his fighting style," Jemison says. "But he was tussling with Rogers in a small stateroom. Not a lot of space to maneuver, not many moves you can use to begin with. So that doesn't tell us much."

"He did say something odd," I say, "that first night, after dinner. About how he'd been to Mars before, on business, but this time it was personal."

Santamaria scratches his beard. "Hmm."

"He also mentioned something about cloning his dog." I retell the anecdote as well as I can remember it. "Seemed like a weird thing to offer up as a cover story. All I asked was if he had a wife and kids, and he went into this whole spiel about going through a messy divorce. Maybe he was drunk, but it still seems sloppy for a professional."

"Maybe he really is on vacation," Jemison says, "and murdering innocent people is just a hobby."

"I bet you're tons of fun at parties," I say.

"If we're going to continue speculating," Santamaria says, "I'm going to need some coffee."

Jemison nods. "Sorry, sir. We'll wait outside while you get dressed."

She drags me into the corridor. Santamaria closes the door behind us. After a moment, he emerges wearing his full uniform.

"We're going to the radio room," he says, pulling himself down the corridor. Jemison follows alongside him, and I bounce from one wall to the other behind both of them. "I'll code a personal message to Director Tarkington with Bartelt's face. There's a dead drop on the State Department's public web site. Mr. Rogers, you'll upload my package in the same burst as whatever reports you're submitting as cover."

"Right," I say. "What reports are those?"

Jemison turns to frown at me. "Didn't the agency set you up with a cover story?"

"I'm on vacation!" I don't like being blamed for things that aren't my fault. "Lasher handed me a ticket and told me to go away. I've got some legend papers, but that's all. I don't think he expected me to have to run with this."

Santamaria looks at Jemison. "Chief?"

"We've got some docs on file," Jemison says. She doesn't look happy about it. "I'll send them up to the radio room. But after that, I think we should interrogate Bartelt."

"And by 'we,' you mean me," Santamaria says.

"Yes, sir."

He exhales. It's not quite a sigh—he's not that effusive—but it has a similar effect, pausing the conversation and underscoring his reluctance. "We're not authorized for that kind of action."

"We'll get authorization," Jemison says. "Include the request in your package to Lasher. You know he'll approve whatever you ask for."

"That's not guaranteed," Santamaria says.

Jemison scoffs. "This is the guy who personally pinned a medal to your chest after the war. The guy who gave you the nickname—"

"We're not authorized." Santamaria's voice is tighter now. "You said yourself we don't know anything about Bartelt. Suppose he really is just a garden-variety psychopath? What happens after we rough him up, when we find out he's a civilian?"

"Fat chance," Jemison says. "He's an expert pickpocket, a computer hacker, and he nearly killed Rogers in hand-to-hand combat."

"Hey now," I protest. They ignore me.

"Every minute we waste arguing about this, he's got more time to plan an escape, and his bosses have more time to suspect something's gone wrong," Jemison says. "We need to crack this guy."

"Torture is an unreliable method of information gathering," Santamaria says.

"Didn't seem that way on Mars," Jemison says.

Santamaria glares at her. My entire body is tense. I'm afraid he's going to take a swing at her, and I want to be ready to get out of the way.

Finally, he repeats, "We are not authorized for that type of action."

"Okay," Jemison says. "We're not authorized to do anything, agency-wise. But you are still the captain of *Dejah Thoris,* and you have the authority to question a passenger who is the prime suspect in a double homicide. Just talk to him. Maybe you'll notice something we missed."

Santamaria unclenches his fist. "Very well."

CHAPTER TWENTY-SEVEN

Our errand in the radio room takes only a few minutes. I've decided to delay slipping away to get ready for my fancy dinner. I've still got time. And I can't pass up the chance to see the captain in action. Watching Jemison dismantle a clueless civilian during questioning was one thing; Santamaria interrogating an actual secret agent is sure to be a real prize-fight.

Danny is standing guard outside Bartelt's stateroom when Santamaria, Jemison, and I float up to the door. Jemison's not happy about this.

"You left Mike *alone* with him?" she shouts, jabbing at the lockpad.

"I was watching the hallway," Danny says, "in case he had other accomplices—"

"Later!" Jemison smacks the last number into the keypad, and the door swings open. She kicks herself off the floor of the hallway, spinning to land upside-down on the ceiling with her stunner drawn.

I am not ashamed to admit that I flatten myself against the outside wall as soon as Jemison opens the door. I hear Mike's voice: "Chief! What's going on?"

"What the hell are you doing in the closet?" Jemison says.

I poke my head into the doorway. Mike is crouched inside the narrow closet between the bed and the bathroom. The closet is empty except for him and a large, clear plastic bag containing a bundle of clothes wedged in the far corner.

Mike has positioned himself under the top shelf of the closet, where a small metal safe is bolted to the wall. The safe door is open, and the safe itself appears to be empty. A square access panel has been removed from the wall beneath the safe. Mike is holding a portable scanner against the exposed circuitry.

"I was checking his personal belongings, then the safe," Mike said. "Nothing in there—it wasn't even locked—but there were some scratch marks on this access panel. Looks like he put some sort of device in here. Not sure yet what it does."

Jemison holsters her stunner and moves over to the closet. Mike hands her something. I follow Santamaria into the room.

"Which systems are routed through there?" Jemison asks.

"Nothing critical," Mike says. "Power taps for this stateroom and the one next door, climate control sensors, and PCI."

"PCI?" I ask, looking over Jemison's shoulder.

"Public computing infrastructure," Jemison says. "Same as he could get over wireless. He wouldn't need to hack that."

The device in her hands is a small, flat, gray rectangle, with no visible markings or instrumentation. If Mike had found it in the trash, it might have looked like a flange that broke off another piece of equipment. Easy to hide, easy to explain away, easy for people to forget ever seeing.

Just like the devices Oliver fabricates for me.

Jerry Bartelt is tied to the tiny stool that swings away from the wall underneath the desk surface to make a seat. Plastic zip-ties bind his wrists, elbows, knees, and ankles. His forearms are secured to his thighs with duct tape, which also appears to be wrapped around the stool. Mike and Danny seems to be experts at improvising restraints. Our prisoner is bent forward, maximizing discomfort and preventing him from getting any leverage against his bonds.

I look at his face, expecting an angry glare. But his expression is completely blank, his face slack above the duct tape covering his mouth. His nondescript brown eyes are staring off into space, unfocused, and—

"He's blinking!" I call out, and kick off the side of the closet, head-first toward Bartelt.

I stretch out my hands to grab his head. He tilts out of the way. My knuckles smash into the wall behind him. I curse and extend my legs to the floor, attaching my feet to the stick-strip next to the desk. I manage to put my hands on either side of his head and jam my thumbs into both his eyeballs. I'm not nearly as careful as Santamaria was with me, and Bartelt cries out through his duct-tape gag. I ignore him and swipe my thumbs up, lifting his eyelids and holding them open.

Both the captain and Jemison have floated over to the desk. Santamaria's behind my left shoulder, and Jemison's on my right.

"Son of a bitch," Jemison says, leaning forward. "I can't believe I didn't see that before."

"They make the overlays hard to spot on purpose," I say, examining both eyeballs until I find the telltale grid of a corneal display implant. "Here. In his right eye."

Santamaria taps my shoulder, and I lean to one side, allowing him a more direct view of Bartelt. I've moved my right hand away from his head. My left hand is still holding his right eye open and keeping him from completing whatever control sequence he was inputting. I hope he wasn't blinking the whole time we were gone, doing who knows what through a wireless interface with his laptop or that device in the closet. We might be completely screwed already.

"Mr. Bartelt," Santamaria says, "I'm Edward Santamaria, captain of *Dejah Thoris*. I'd like to know why you killed two of our passengers."

Santamaria's trying to get a reaction. I watch Bartelt's face with my eye scanners enabled, but I don't see anything. He's definitely a professional. A civilian who's been accused of murder is going to react in some way; even if he doesn't twitch, his pulse and skin temperature will vary.

His eyes jump back and forth, looking at each of the people in the room in turn. He gives a single, short, sharp nod.

Santamaria grabs the duct tape and rips it off in one quick motion. The sound makes me cringe, but Bartelt shows no sign of feeling any pain. In fact, he's smiling and looking straight at the captain.

"Nice to meet you, Hades."

I don't even see Santamaria move. The only thing I'm aware of is a dull *thock* sound, and then Bartelt's head snapping back. I jerk my arm away instinctively. His head hits the wall, bounces forward, and waggles back and forth a few times. A dribble of blood bubbles out of his right nostril.

"What the hell was that?" I ask, in a much higher voice than I intended to use.

Jemison puts two fingers on the side of Bartelt's neck. "He's alive."

"Good." Santamaria massages the heel of his left palm with his right hand. "It's been a long time since I did anything like that."

"Yeah, well, you've still got the touch," Jemison says. "Danny! Mike! Help me move this guy to the brig."

"I thought you didn't want him in the brig!" I say. "What about booby-traps?"

Jemison looks over to the bed. "How long was he awake, Mike?"

"He came to about five minutes after you left," Mike says.

Jemison turns back to me. "He's had enough time to activate anything he set up in here. We need to keep him from doing anything else now."

"You can't interrogate him if you keep him sedated," I say.

"He's not going to tell us anything," Santamaria says.

"Also not the point," Jemison says. "Sedating him means getting someone close enough to administer the drugs every few hours. We can't risk that much contact."

"So you're just going to leave him tied up like this?" I ask. "You'll have to post a twenty-four guard anyway. Why not put him on IV sedation—"

"We're going to put him in a Faraday cage!" Jemison yells into my face. Danny and Mike, who have just finished separating Bartelt from the stool, look up in surprise.

"What's a Faraday cage?" asks Mike.

"We have a Faraday cage?" asks Danny.

"Shit," Jemison says.

Santamaria puts a hand on Jemison's shoulder and pulls her back before she can say anything else—or, maybe, take a swing at me. She sure looks like she wants to hurt me. I'm getting used to it.

"Mr. Egnor, Mr. Brown, we need your help," Santamaria says. "We're dealing with some very sensitive matters now—matters of planetary security—and we need to know that we can trust you with this information."

Danny and Mike exchange a look that appears to be half shock and half barely concealed delight. I wonder how long they've both been waiting for a promotion.

"One hundred percent, Captain," Mike says.

"Hell, yes. Sir," Danny says.

"Good." Santamaria nods toward me. "You've probably guessed that Mr. Rogers is not exactly what he appears to be."

"Yeah, that's pretty obvious," Mike says.

"Is 'Rogers' even your real name?" Danny asks.

"Mr. Rogers is on board to oversee the transportation of certain cargo from Earth to Mars," Santamaria says. "One of the containers is electro-magnetically shielded to prevent its contents from being scanned."

"You're smuggling for the State Department?" Mike asks.

I wait for Santamaria to run interference. He doesn't.

"It's not smuggling," I say. "Think of it as an unusually large diplomatic pouch."

"So that's what you were doing outside," Danny says. "Checking the cargo."

I put on my best fake smile of contrition. "Can't be too careful."

"He's going to pack up the Faraday cage and bring it down to the brig," Jemison says. "We'll install it in one of the holding compartments and secure Bartelt inside. The cage will prevent him from transmitting or receiving anything."

She releases me, and Santamaria grabs my arm and spins me to face the door.

"Come on, Mr. Rogers," he says, "I'll help you get suited up."

CHAPTER TWENTY-EIGHT

Dejah Thoris—Exterior, cargo section
I'm probably going to be late for dinner

The agency regularly smuggles things all around the Solar System—I've done more than a few delivery runs myself—but I was never interested enough to inquire about the logistical details of how they concealed and transported all that cargo.

Data is easy to move around. Encrypt something well enough and you don't even have to hide it, because the math guarantees that nobody will be able to crack the code before the heat-death of the universe. Physical objects are a little trickier.

Many things can be broken down into their component parts, which are either innocuous or can be made to appear so; chemicals and certain electronics fall into that category. But some items, like weapons-grade nuclear material or the firing coil of a particle beam cannon, can't be disassembled or disguised. I am currently the agency's preferred method of transporting those items, but I'm a scarce resource.

Santamaria helps me into my spacesuit and gives me a quick rundown of the cargo attached to the niche in *Dejah Thoris*'s hull. I download a map of the numbered containers, and then he sends me on my way.

I'm running radio silent because Santamaria is still concerned about some hostile party monitoring our communications, and there's no easy way to encrypt the spacesuit comms. I think he's being paranoid, but I'm not about to disagree with his orders.

The container I'm looking for is in the innermost layer of the cargo mass, with one end pressed up against the hull. All the containers are oriented "gravity-wise," like a multicolored brick wall stacked against the cut-out side of *Dejah Thoris*'s egg-shaped hull.

I pull myself into the interstitial scaffolding between containers carefully, not wanting to tangle my lifeline. Once I've attached my magnetic boots to one of the scaffold rails, I unclip my long tether and secure a shorter line from the waist of my spacesuit to the top of my target container, right above the seam where the double doors meet.

These containers aren't designed to be opened in vacuum, but they're not completely airtight, either. All of them were evacuated of atmosphere before being loaded, and if any of them contain perishable items, those are in their own airtight packaging inside the large metal boxes. I enter the captain's access code into the security panel, then work my gloves around the door handles, brace myself, and turn them downward until the long metal bars holding the container closed creak out of their fittings.

The doors only swing out so far before clanging against the scaffolding. I have to turn my body sideways and slowly wiggle myself through the opening into the container, all the while hoping there aren't any sharp metal parts poking out to tear a hole in my spacesuit.

Once inside the container, I tap my suit's wrist controls and switch on my helmet lamps. The interior is just as Santamaria described it: one stack of cellulose crates forms a wall just inside the doors, obscuring everything but a narrow passage on the far left side of the container. Whatever cargo the agency is smuggling will be hidden behind these innocent-looking crates marked as various dry goods.

I lumber forward, still not used to the way these magnetic boots stick, and make my way around the decoy crates. This opening isn't quite as tight as the outer doors, and I walk through facing forward and see a giant hole in the far end of the container.

It takes me a moment to make sense of this unexpected sight. There's a large metal-mesh cube to my right—the Faraday cage—and farther down the long container are more unlabeled containers; some look like chemicals, and others might be weapons or ammunition. I sweep my helmet lights over everything, and finally come back to the thing that shouldn't be here: the giant hole.

The exterior of the cargo container is a thick, lead-lined steel alloy, designed to protect the contents of the vessel from cosmic radiation and dust impacts. There's not a lot of solid matter in interplanetary space, but when you hit anything traveling at several million meters per second, it's going to leave a mark. It takes serious hardware to cut through that material. I study the edges of the roughly circular hole. They definitely look like they were melted with a high-temperature cutter.

And on the other side of the hole, according to these hull markings, is a service airlock leading into the ship.

Man, I could have taken a shortcut.

"What do you mean, a hole in the container?"

Santamaria, Jemison, and I are alone in the briefing room. After I brought the Faraday cage inside, Security set it up in a holding cell in the brig and confined the still-unconscious Jerry Bartelt inside. Now I'm describing the other things I saw in the cargo container.

"Hold on." I finish transferring the vid from my left eye to the conference table and play it back, freezing the image on a clean view of the breach. "Now that's right up against the ship's hull, and it's way too circular and large to be accidental."

Jemison pulls her face closer to the tabletop and squints at the image. "Son of a bitch."

"Is there anything on board that can cut through steel alloy like that?" I ask. "If there's missing equipment, maybe we can track Bartelt through the crew sections and see what else he's been up to."

"I'll ask Eng," Jemison says, tapping at her wristband. "But we have limited camera coverage in the crew sections. If this guy knew exactly where to cut through to extract the cargo, he also knows where our blind spots are."

"What else did you see in there?" Santamaria is looking down, but his eyes seem like they're staring right through the tabletop.

I spin the vid forward. "Everything else was still secured, except for this set of straps." I point to the ends of four yellow tie-downs, hanging in zero-gee like seaweed, the metal buckles unlocked and open. "The Faraday cage hadn't been touched."

"We need to determine exactly what's missing from that container," Santamaria says.

"You don't know?" I say.

"Compartmentalization," Jemison says. "If we don't know what we're transporting, we can't blow the operation."

Something else occurs to me. "Did you have any control over the loading procedure? Whoever cut into that container knew exactly where it was, and which section inside the ship would lead there."

"The agency takes care of the paperwork," Santamaria says. "Our transport containers are always loaded near the center of the cargo mass. That position gives them better protection from radiation and accidental discovery."

"Well, are they always up against the ship's hull? And right next to an airlock?"

"Yes. To allow for emergency extraction, if necessary."

"Even if there are hazardous materials inside?"

Santamaria's dark eyes are hollow, and I see the flicker of something sharp and angry back there. "We don't transport hazardous materials."

"It's got to be someone inside the agency," Jemison says. "Someone who knows about this run."

"A mole," Santamaria says.

"We need to contact Lasher," Jemison says.

Santamaria nods. "Yes."

"What happened to avoiding detection?" I ask.

"Have you not been paying attention?" Jemison snaps. "We're way beyond that. Bartelt and whoever his bosses are, they know more than any civilians should about our operations on this ship. The device that Bartelt hid in his closet was tapped into our internal comms. Bartelt was monitoring crew chatter, probably to make sure he could sneak around the ship without running into anyone."

"But we still don't know *why* he was sneaking around the ship," I say. "Have you interviewed Janice Long yet?"

"Yeah, she's clean. Innocent victim of a professional thief. And I'm guessing Bartelt was sneaking around to kill Emily and Alan Wachlin and pin their murders on David, the brother."

"It still doesn't make sense," I say. "Even if Bartelt wanted just Alan Wachlin dead, why not kill all three of them? No witnesses—"

"To give us a plausible suspect, and deter further investigation!" Jemison says. "But our speculation will get a lot better after we obtain some more goddamn facts from the office!"

"Okay, okay!" I start blinking my eye into communication mode. "Give me a minute to warm up the Echo Delta."

Santamaria presses his fingers to the tabletop and taps out a series of letters and numbers. "You're going to use this relay port to get a direct line to Director Tarkington's office." He scrolls down and taps out a different sequence of gibberish. "Then use this encryption key and route the call to my quarters."

I frown at him. "Wait a minute. You want to use my shoulder-phone, but you don't want me on the call?"

"I'm sorry, Rogers, Chief," Santamaria says. "Neither of you has the security clearance for this discussion."

Before Jemison and I leave, we work out how to securely tie my shoulder-phone into *Dejah Thoris*'s internal wireless network. Now I can go about my business anywhere on the ship, and it won't interfere with the captain's communications link to Paul.

Jemison says good-bye to me in the corridor outside the briefing room. "Don't stay up too late. We're going to have some more fun with the prisoner tomorrow."

"Can we talk about the nanobots?" I ask. "I just need a list of names. That's all. I can take care of the rest myself."

Jemison grabs a handrail and stops her motion down the corridor. "Fine. I'll get you the damn names. Tomorrow morning. And you're going to walk me through your crazy medical procedure before you do anything to anyone."

Sure, I'm going to let you believe that. "Can I ask you one more thing?"

"What?"

Jemison doesn't like talking about the war. She's made that abundantly clear. She also doesn't like chatting with me. I'm hoping the combination of the two will repel her long enough for me to get my nano-business squared away without interference.

"Why did Bartelt call the captain 'Hades'?" I ask.

We're floating at least three meters apart, but I swear the temperature drops by a good five degrees in the moment before she responds. "We're not going to talk about that right now."

"Are we ever going to talk about it? Sounds like a great war story."

I flinch as Jemison snaps up her left arm, hand clenched in a fist. She bends her elbow and uses her other hand to work her wrist controls for a few seconds.

"You now have thumbscan access to the crew sections," she says. "Captain might need to see you again later. I don't want to. Stay out of trouble."

I watch until the elevator doors close, then rush back to my stateroom, pull the centrifuge out of the pocket, spin down the newly multiplied nanobots into the Red Wine, and fill two drink bulbs with the dosed alcohol. I hope I haven't made Ellie wait too long. My tuxedo takes forever to put on. Why didn't I ask for the clip-on bow tie?

CHAPTER TWENTY-NINE

Dejah Thoris—Deck 10, Promenade
20 minutes late for dinner, dammit

Not every place name on this ship is a terrible pun, but most of them are pretty bad. I suppose that's to be expected aboard the Princess of Mars Cruises flagship *Dejah Thoris*.

The fake-jade dragon's-head gateway into the Fête Silk Road restaurant glows green on the upper level of the Promenade, between the Joy of Specs and Hats in the Belfry shops, both of which sell exactly the accessories you'd imagine. I arrive at 1950 hours, breathless after my bumpy flight down the crew stairwell, and give my name to the maître d', an excessively glamorous woman wearing a red qipao and iridescent chopsticks in her hair.

"Ah, yes, welcome, Mr. Rogers," she says. "Your dining companion arrived a few minutes ago. She's waiting for you at the bar. If you would care to join her, we'll come fetch you both as soon as your table is ready."

I thank her and float past the green dragon's teeth and into the bar area. There's quite a crowd here, and it takes me a minute to locate Ellie. Mostly because she looks so stunningly different in a glittering black-and-white ball gown. She's still wearing her duty wristband, and a pair of flat black zero-gee slipper-socks, but she makes the whole ensemble work.

I haven't had any time to think about how I'm going to excuse my lateness. I can't tell Ellie the truth, obviously; I can never tell her about the nanobots or my security errands. I've made my peace with that. But who do I need to be to accomplish my current objective? How is "Evan Rogers" going to get her to drink this fancy Red Wine without appearing to be a creeper?

How about don't be an idiot, Kangaroo. Let's start there.

It doesn't matter what this woman thinks of me. In less than four days I'm off this ship, and then I'll probably never see her again. Hell, depending on how tonight goes, I may not see her again for the rest of this cruise. And that doesn't matter, as long as I get her to drink this nanobot potion.

It's all about the mission. It's always about the mission.

Not tonight.

Ellie doesn't notice me until I'm floating right next to her at the bar, holding out the two bulbs of wine.

"Buy you a drink, lady?" I say, sticking my feet to the floor.

She looks at me with those brilliant eyes and smiles. "Hey, stranger. About time you showed up."

"Sorry. I had a longer than expected talk with the sommelier. I wanted to select the perfect wine for tonight."

"And I'm sure he or she encouraged you to spare no expense."

I hand her one of the bulbs. "Judge for yourself, mademoiselle."

It occurs to me that *I* haven't tasted this wine. Ellie puts a hand on my arm to stop me before I can bring my drink bulb to my lips.

"Hold on there," she says. "You can't drink fancy wine without making a toast first."

"Okay. What are we toasting?"

She raises her bulb. "To meeting new people."

I tap my bulb against hers. "To new friends."

Ellie takes a sip of her wine. I blink my eye into scanning mode and watch as a fuzzy column of false-color green descends into her torso and diffuses outward, like branches of lightning crawling through her dark blue figure. I suddenly realize it probably looks like I'm staring at her chest, and quickly turn my head away.

Mission accomplished. Now what?

I don't know.

She sticks her drink bulb to the bar and grimaces. "Well, that's different."

I quickly take a swig of the Red Wine and wonder if it might have gone bad. The airtight seal was definitely intact—I watched the sommelier verify the holo code, and I also checked it with my eye—but maybe it was a bad batch to start with? Maybe the radiation in Airy Crater did something to it?

The liquid washes across my tongue and seems to evaporate, just a little, before I register the mixture of fruity and bitter flavors and familiar tang of ethanol. It tastes like wine, and I have to admit, I've never actually tried anything this expensive. How do I know what it's supposed to taste like? The agency doesn't train us to be food critics.

"It's not that bad, is it?" I ask.

This doesn't matter. The nanobots are in her system now. They'll start repairing her radiation-damaged cells within the next few minutes. They'll replicate themselves until they finish the job, and then they'll self-destruct. I've finished the job. I could leave right now and get back to work, tracking down murderers and hunting spies.

But I don't want to.

"Tell you what," Ellie says, "the next drink's on me."

"Fine," I say. "I'll let you order it, but I'm paying."

"Evan—"

"I have an expense account." It's not a lie.

She narrows her eyes. "Okay. You can pay for dinner tonight. But next time, I'm buying."

I can't keep the smile off my face. "So what's good here?"

Ellie launches into an in-depth critique of the new menu at Fête Silk Road, which debuted on this sailing and has apparently been the subject of some discussion among the crew. I'm only half-listening as she describes the exotic ingredients, some of which are actually grown on board the ship in hydroponic gardens.

She said "next time."

Dinner with Ellie is the longest single meal I've ever had, and it's still over too soon. We close down Fête Silk Road at eleven o'clock, after taking our time ordering and then consuming each spectacular course. I can tell it's closing time because our server, who has been a paragon of courtesy all night, brings our check without even asking if we're ready, and with the barest hint of a smile.

I sign the check to my room without looking at or caring about the amount. As we leave our table, I grab both of our half-empty Red Wine bulbs. Ellie gives me a funny look.

"Hey, *I* like it," I say. *Who doesn't like experimental nanotech?*

She shakes her head, smiling. "There's no accounting for taste."

We float to the crew elevator together, holding hands. I can tell from Ellie's body language that she thinks our evening is over—she's becoming less relaxed, stealing glances at her wristband more often—but I still have to make one last attempt.

"I don't think I mentioned it earlier," I say, "but you look beautiful tonight."

"Thanks." She gives my hand a gentle squeeze. "I was worried you'd gone blind or something."

"I suppose you'll need to change back into uniform now."

"Yeah. A mermaid gown doesn't exactly command respect in Main Eng."

I give her what I hope is a sly smile. "Want any help getting out of that dress?"

She laughs, puts her mouth right next to my ear, and whispers, "Having sex in zero-gee is very difficult."

"I'm a fast learner."

"Oh, I don't doubt that. But I'm on duty in less than forty minutes."

"Can't the boss be a few minutes late?"

"First of all, no. We need to do a full systems check before turning up the reactor for our deceleration burn. Timing is pretty important if we want to remain on course. And second"—now she's whispering again—"forty minutes isn't nearly long enough for what I want to do to you."

"You are a terrible person."

"Yeah, I know." The elevator arrives. "I think you're terrible too."

She releases my hand and drifts forward. Time slows to a crawl while I stare, wanting to remember every detail of this moment: the shimmering curve of the dress covering her hips, her shoulder-length brown hair sailing past her face as she turns around, her teeth showing in a smile and her eyes twinkling as they catch the light.

"See you tomorrow," she says.

"Tomorrow."

The elevator doors close, and the entire world seems dimmer.

I stare straight ahead for a moment, then look down at the drink bulbs in my hand. Time to get back to work. There are several more people who need to try this lousy Red Wine.

First, I go back to my room and change out of the tuxedo. I've only ever worn it when I'm with Ellie, and that's the way I want to keep it. Maybe it's a silly sentiment. I'm allowing myself to be silly this week. I'm on vacation.

I head up to the crew sections carrying the bottle of nanobot-laden Red Wine in a complimentary Princess of Mars Cruises duffel bag. All the senior officers need to have a drink. Maybe if I can get one of them tipsy, I'll have an easier time tracking down the other crew who were exposed.

One thing at a time, Kangaroo.

I arrive at the briefing room behind the bridge just before midnight. Galbraith and Logan are the only ones there, bobbing at opposite ends of the conference table. They've divided the tabletop display into two halves, and each of them is tapping and dragging data boxes and occasionally sliding them across the table to the other person.

"Hello, Mr. Rogers," Galbraith says. "Couldn't sleep?"

"Something like that," I say. I'm still giddy from my dinner with Ellie.

"We're going to start decelerating soon," Logan says. "You might be more comfortable in bed."

Depends on the company. "I'll be fine. Thanks for the warning."

"Something we can help you with?" Galbraith asks.

Yes. I need you to drink some wine so you don't die of cancer. Long story. Just trust me?

I open my mouth to speak and hear a *bong* noise. I start to look around, then hear it echoing—an acoustic effect that wouldn't happen in this room—and realize it's prerecorded. It repeats, sounding like an old analog timepiece striking its hour chimes.

"Is that a grandfather clock?" I ask.

"Audio recording," Galbraith says. "The captain likes antiques."

Just as the clock strikes twelve, a band of red lights up all around the room where the walls meet the ceiling. The red lights begin pulsing. A shrill sound erupts from hidden loudspeakers, blasting five times in quick succession.

"Something's wrong," Galbraith says. I imagine that's for my benefit.

The door to the bridge slides open, and Santamaria flies into the room. He catches himself against the edge of the table.

"Rogers," he says. "You stay. Erica, Jeff, we've got a situation."

He slaps his hand against the table, and Jemison's face appears. She looks like she's ready to go to war.

CHAPTER THIRTY

Dejah Thoris—Deck B, officers' briefing room
Just past midnight and more than halfway to Mars

Jemison feeds us a vid from the security camera in main engineering. It shows Ellie Gavilán floating into the room at the start of her graveyard shift, wearing her work jumpsuit, waving to greet her crew. I see half a dozen people and at least as many robots working the control stations surrounding the ionwell. Apparently that wasn't just for show during the tour. Xiao, the self-appointed bouncer and arboretum enthusiast from this morning, pulls himself around the ionwell railing to meet Ellie and hands her a tablet.

Then a man dressed in black from head to toe—including gloves, a mask that covers everything but his eyes, and a small backpack—slams into Ellie from behind, and all three of them crash into the railing and bounce upward. The attacker throws his arm around Ellie and kicks Xiao away, pushing himself and Ellie off the bottom edge of the screen. Xiao crashes into another crewperson before he can reach his jetpack controls and stabilize himself.

Alarm lights start flashing everywhere. Someone must have hit the panic button. There's no sound on the recording. The engineering crew stare offscreen with horrified looks on their faces. Then, one by one, they move out of the room, crossing the yellow-and-black safety line and going through the main doors.

Xiao lingers, and I see his mouth flapping as he waves the others on. The attacker pushes himself forward into frame again and touches his feet against the floor—probably wearing stick-shoes to keep himself anchored.

He has one arm around Ellie, pinning her arms to her sides. His other arm holds a knife to her throat. She's no longer wearing her jetpack.

I'm doing my best to analyze the situation tactically. I tell myself it's just like reviewing battle source vids during the war. It was my job to witness, not to judge or intervene. I clinically recorded the details of each awful event so nobody else would need to suffer the horror of seeing it firsthand.

But this is different. It's not an anonymous soldier whose carotid artery is in danger of being severed onscreen. That's Ellie. We were having dinner together barely an hour ago, and now—

"How old is this recording?" I ask.

Erica points at the timestamp in the corner of the vid, then checks her wristband. "Three minutes."

Three minutes. If he opens that artery, she's dead in sixty seconds. Come on, Ellie, fight!

But I know this doesn't end well.

The attacker's face mask ripples and moves. Xiao's mouth flaps as he lands and anchors his own feet. He unstraps his jetpack, flings it aside, pats his chest.

I can guess what Xiao's saying—*let her go, take me instead*—and I know it won't happen. Xiao's about the same size as the attacker. Ellie's smaller, easier to subdue with physical force. And she's the ship's chief engineer. More valuable hostage.

I wouldn't make the trade.

More silent arguing. The attacker tightens his arm around Ellie, shakes her body. I can tell she's doing her best to stay still, to avoid provoking him. I hope she's doing that on purpose. I hope she's planning something.

Xiao's expression becomes sullen. He turns to the nearest control station and taps the console. The doors to main engineering slide shut.

"Goddammit!" I hear myself saying.

The attacker says something else. Xiao shakes his head. The attacker jostles Ellie again and presses the knife under her jaw. Her skin tightens around the blade.

Xiao turns to the console and slowly works the controls. The attacker steps forward. Then, almost casually, he moves the knife away from Ellie and plunges it into Xiao's back.

I hear Galbraith gasp. I think the captain's saying something in another language. I'm not sure. *Blade went in flat. Between the ribs, into a lung. That's training. Trained killer.*

On the vid, Ellie struggles to break free of the attacker's grip. He pivots at the waist and slams her head into the station next to Xiao, hard. Ellie goes limp, and the attacker shoves her to the ground.

A dark stain is spreading across Xiao's back. The attacker grabs Xiao's head, pulls the knife from between his ribs, and draws it across his throat. A spray of red covers the display in front of them.

The attacker jerks Xiao's body back from the console and lets it tumble away. Blood escapes from his neck in a slow ribbon that separates into dark, quivering, wine-colored blobs. The attacker bends down and grabs Ellie again. He turns her to face the camera—*fuck, he knows where the cameras are, what else does he know?*—and presses the bloodstained knife against her unconscious face. The message is pretty clear.

Then he stabs the knife into the control console, and the recording ends.

The feed switches back to Jemison. She's outside the door to main engineering. I see security and engineering crews behind her, jamming tools into open access panels.

"The other engineers say he threatened to kill her if they didn't clear the room," Jemison says. Her voice is steady and cold.

"What does he want?" Galbraith says.

"We don't negotiate with terrorists," Jemison says.

"But Ellie—"

"Ellie's gone." Jemison's glare could cut glass. "If she's not dead already, she will be soon."

My hands are fists, and my fingernails are digging into my palms.

"You don't know that!" Galbraith says. "She could be—"

"We do not negotiate!" Jemison says. "Not for hostages, not for any-thing! We do not give this bastard *any* leverage over us."

Galbraith turns to Santamaria. "Captain."

"Chief Jemison is right," he says, not looking at her.

Galbraith's eyes widen. "Captain!"

Santamaria holds up a hand. "We proceed as if Chief Gavilán is still alive. We do our best to minimize any potential danger to her from our actions. But we cannot disregard the safety of four thousand civilians while attempting to rescue a single crewperson.

"Our priority is regaining control of the ship. And we do not negotiate with terrorists. Is that clear?" He looks around the table at all his officers. Most of them nod silently.

Galbraith smacks her palm against the table and clenches it into a fist. "Yes, Captain."

I know he and Jemison are right. It's everything the agency's ever taught me: no single asset is worth blowing the mission.

Well, I don't seem to be very good at following orders this week.

Why does my brain feel like it's on fire? I've seen people die before. Thousands, if you count the war vids I had to analyze. I've even killed people myself. Why does this feel different? Why am I taking this personally?

Because you've never been this close before.

It's true. I've never been close to those who died, either physically or emotionally. They were either hostiles or associates. Nobody I actually had a personal conversation with.

Nobody who got engaged in the same arboretum where I first kissed Ellie.

And when I had to eliminate a target, it was always at a remove. Drop them in the pocket, push them off a tall building, shoot them from a distance. I never had to watch a human being bleed out right in front of me. I never had to end someone with my bare hands.

I bet I could, though. I would have absolutely no qualms about squeezing the life out of that hijacker's—

"Rogers!"

It's Captain Santamaria. How long has he been trying to get my attention?

"Yes, sir," I say. "Sorry, sir."

"Get down there and scan Main Eng," Santamaria says. "We need to know what he's doing in there."

Jemison is standing back from main engineering when I arrive. There's a rough semicircle of security guards around the main doors, which have closed on the yellow-and-black safety line. Three engineers in welding gear are huddled right in front of the doors, attempting to cut through. Their torches shoot sparks and cast flickering shadows against the walls.

I pull myself up next to Jemison, gripping a handhold. "Chief."

"Rogers." She doesn't look at me. "Give me something."

"Wait one."

I've already adjusted my left eye sensors to see through the bulkhead.

The lines of electrical force coming off the ionwell are pretty obvious and easy to zero out, leaving three human-shaped interference patterns, dark blots against a glittering golden background.

There's Xiao's body, tumbling free and a slightly different shade because it's cooling from loss of blood. Below him, I see another shape, motionless, stuck to the circular railing around the ionwell.

Ellie. Probably restrained. Still unconscious. I should be seeing interference patterns around her wrist, from her control band's radio, but there's nothing. The hijacker must have smashed it.

And the third shape. The hijacker. "He's on the left side of the room," I say. "Just standing there. His arms might be moving. Which console is that?"

"Emergency lockout panel," Jemison says. "Dammit. He knows this ship. He knew where the security camera was. He knows how to move in zero-gee."

I can hear what she's not saying. Jerry Bartelt was the decoy, and we missed the real threat. Just like we were supposed to.

And now Xiao's dead, and who knows what this hijacker is going to do to the ship. *And Ellie.*

"How long before they cut through the door?" I ask.

"Best case, fifteen minutes," she says.

The hijacker's shape changes, and it takes me a second to interpret what I'm seeing. "He's turning. I can't tell if he's looking in this direction or away from us, but—"

I hear some kind of siren, far away, muffled. Then a grating noise, metal against metal. A dark rectangle moves down, filling my field of view and erasing yellow field lines as it goes.

"Something's happening," I say. I'm not sure what I'm seeing.

"Goddammit," Jemison mutters.

Something clangs behind the doors to main engineering, and my left eye goes dark. I blink it a few times, switching modes, to make sure the sensors are still working.

"GODDAMMIT!" Jemison screams, slamming her fist against the wall. She has enough presence of mind to hold herself in place with her other hand, so the force of the blow doesn't send her careening down the corridor. I have enough presence of mind to move out of her way and keep my mouth shut until she's ready to talk.

"He closed the containment bulkhead," she says. Her voice is hoarse. "They're thicker than the outer hull. No chance of cutting through with less than a pulse laser." She looks at me. "I don't suppose you keep one in your pocket."

"No." I don't feel like explaining right now.

The engineers at the other end of the corridor are cursing, many of them much more colorfully than Jemison. They bang their own fists against the door. Security pulls them back before they hurt themselves or damage their equipment. I wonder if the guards envy them that emotional release.

All I can think about is Xiao's body, drifting there in the room, lifeless and growing cold. The hijacker killed him without hesitation, like it was nothing to take a man's life. What will he do to Ellie when she wakes up? What kinds of threats will he make—and act on—if she doesn't cooperate?

Or will he just kill her, too, and save himself the trouble?

I caught another glimpse of Ellie's shape as I was cycling through the sensing modes in my eye. I don't know what else to do, so I play back the buffer to see her again.

As I'm stepping through the sensor images, one frame at a time, not wanting to miss what might be my last sight of Eleanor Gavilán, I see a flash of color.

"He's military," I say quietly. "I've got a reading here, a radiation signature. He's got a power implant."

Jemison says nothing for a moment. Then she whips her entire body around to face me. "What kind of power implant?"

I stare at the HUD floating in my eye, struggling to make sense of the readouts. "Looks like a particle emission capture—"

The last word stops in my throat. I feel my mouth hanging open. Jemison's mouth is closed, her lips pressed together.

"Sickbay," she says.

Dr. Sawhney is treating some of the engineering crew when we arrive. Jemison doesn't even say hello to him. She flies over to an equipment storage cabinet and flings it open, clattering metal and plastic as she digs through its contents.

"Chief!" Sawhney says, floating over to us. I'm doing my best to catch things as Jemison tosses them out of her way. "Are you injured? What are you looking for?"

Jemison stops for a moment. "The alpha wave generator. The one we found in the Wachlins' stateroom."

Sawhney gives her a disapproving look, then turns around and opens a different cabinet. He pulls out a clear plastic bag with a metal donut inside. Jemison grabs the bag, tears it open, and turns the device over in her hands.

"Please be careful with that," Sawhney says, half a second before Jemison rips off the top of the casing. Inside is a mass of wires, circuit boards, and round gray disks. Sawhney sighs.

"What does this look like, Doctor?" Jemison asks.

Sawhney glares at her, then takes the disassembled device and looks at it. After a moment, he frowns and starts poking at it, pushing aside wires to examine other components.

"This is not an alpha wave generator," he says. "It doesn't even have a power supply. There is a niche here, and connectors, but there's nothing in it."

"Just the right size for a PECC," I say.

Sawhney's head snaps up. "Atomic power? Why would this machine need so much energy?"

"It's not a machine," Jemison says. "It's a shell. They used it to hide the second power core. It looked like a medical device, so port security didn't think twice when it pegged the radiation scanners. David Wachlin had a goddamn prescription."

"I don't understand," Sawhney says. There's obvious concern on his face as he looks from Jemison to me and back again. "Why would someone wish to smuggle an atomic power core on board the ship? Is this related to the hijacking?" His face goes pale. "Does the hijacker plan to destroy the ship?"

Jemison's not listening to him. "Alan Wachlin wanted us to think he was dead. So we wouldn't be searching for him. He knew we'd be watching every passenger like a hawk during midway, and he wanted to hide until he was ready to break into Main Eng."

"He still has his PECC," I say. "That's what I saw in engineering. He smuggled the other one aboard in this casing, so he could plant it with the dead body we thought was him."

"Pardon me," Sawhney says. "If what you're saying is true, and Alan Wachlin is still alive—then who is the person we found in his bed?"

"That's an excellent fucking question," Jemison says.

A trilling noise fills the room, and a stripe of blue light outlining the floor begins pulsing. I feel like I should recognize this.

"Should we be worried about that?" I ask, pointing to the blue lights.

"That's the acceleration warning," Sawhney says. "Prepare for gravity."

"But aren't we still at midway?"

"He has navigation control," Jemison says. "The fucker's changing course."

CHAPTER THIRTY-ONE

Dejah Thoris—Deck B, officers' briefing room
19 minutes after the hijacking

Captain Santamaria, Commander Galbraith, Chief Jemison, Cruise Director Logan, and I are gathered around the conference table, looking at the images from suite 5028 and my eye scans of main engineering. I've stowed my duffel bag of Red Wine in one of the wall storage compartments. I'm pretty sure nobody's going to want any wine right now.

"Am I the only one who thinks this is completely insane?" Galbraith asks.

"Which part?" Logan asks. "The murder or the hijacking?"

"Let's go over this one more time," Santamaria says, looking at Jemison. "Chief?"

"Sir." She pulls up my radiation scan, taken from the hallway outside 5028. "This is the best image we have of the body we originally identified as Alan Wachlin. We thought the PECC was inside the chest, but after closer analysis, it looks like it's just about level with the spine. Probably burned through the body when it reached critical mass. Wachlin knew the fire and radiation would make identification nearly impossible."

"Can we test the DNA?" Santamaria asks.

"That will take time," Logan says. "Dr. Sawhney is collecting samples now. He says he can send the data back to Earth, but it'll have to go through PMC Legal and FBI for authorization and a privacy release before we can even search for a records match."

"That could take weeks," Jemison grumbles.

"Mr. Rogers," Santamaria says, "do you think the State Department might be able to speed things along?"

I nod. "More than likely."

"Thank you. Please work with Dr. Sawhney on that," Santamaria says. "Logan. Has anyone else on the ship been reported missing?"

Logan shakes his head. "I've asked all our cabin stewards to verify their passengers visually. We'll have a full count soon. Security is helping to get everyone secured in their staterooms."

"Good."

"Can I just get this straight?" Galbraith says, waving her hands over the tabletop. "You're saying that Alan Wachlin killed his own mother. He intentionally gave his brother David the wrong medication to drug him into a stupor, then killed their mother while she was sleeping.

"After that, he abducted another passenger, murdered him too, and then put the body in his own bed with a spare atomic power core he'd smuggled aboard earlier? Is that what we're saying?"

"Yes," Jemison says. "And then he dragged his catatonic brother to a lifeboat and planted the murder weapon on him. Alan Wachlin wanted us to think his brother was the killer. He was probably hoping we wouldn't find David until later, after he'd died from the drug overdose."

"And now this man has hijacked the ship?" Galbraith says, her voice almost cracking. "He killed his mother, framed his brother for the murder, hid himself from every housekeeping and security inspection for three days, and now he's locked himself in Main Eng with Chief Gavilán as a hostage? What is he, some kind of supervillain?"

Jemison and I exchange a look. I steal another glance at the captain, but he's staring down at the tabletop. We can't tell anybody else what we suspect: Alan Wachlin had help from Jerry Bartelt. Bartelt was Wachlin's handler.

And someone else is running both of them.

"He's ex-army," I say. "Special Forces. He probably did worse things during the war."

"Most of the ship's systems have primary control routed through Main Eng," Jemison says. "We still have life support, but he's cut us off from everything else, including external comms, navigation, and propulsion."

"He chose this ship and this sailing for a reason," Santamaria says. "Erica, have you been able to determine our new course yet?"

"Yes. We don't have engine control, but I still have read access to the nav computer," Galbraith says. "This new course doesn't make sense, though."

"Explain."

Galbraith moves her hands over the tabletop, touching control areas. The display changes to a black background and a collection of colored dots joined by curved lines. Alphanumeric labels float next to some of the dots and curves. I can understand the words EARTH and MARS, but that's about it.

"This was our original course." Galbraith traces a curved white line with her finger. "Earth to Mars, standard delta-vee plus-and-minus with mid-way turnaround. Seven-day travel time, orbital insertion at Earth perigee.

"We've been under constant thrust since the engines restarted. This is the new course he programmed." Galbraith points to a yellow line leaving the midway marker. "We're actually accelerating *toward* Mars. If he doesn't change course or speed, we'll arrive in just over a day."

"Why would a hijacker take us where we were going anyway?" Logan says.

"Erica," Santamaria says quietly, "would you expand that navigation view into Mars orbit, please."

Galbraith nods and manipulates the navigation chart. Mars grows from a red dot to a large disk in the center of the display. The white line showing our original course curls backward around the planet, putting *Dejah Thoris* into orbit around the planet. The end of the yellow line—our new course—stabs sideways into the edge of the red disk.

"He still wants to go to Mars," Santamaria says. "He just doesn't want to stop when we get there."

"Oh," Logan says.

"Bastard," Galbraith says. "That's why he chose this sailing. Dammit."

"How is that even possible?" I ask. "Don't interplanetary transfer orbits have to be very precisely calibrated?" That's what Oliver always yells at me when I ask if I can change my space travel plans.

"Yes," Galbraith says. "But our current voyage is the shortest Earth-to-Mars transit possible. It's timed to take advantage of when the two planets are closest to each other in their solar orbits."

"Perigee," Jemison says, making it sound like a curse.

"We always carry an emergency fuel reserve," Santamaria says. "Combined with our normal fuel load, it's more than enough for a full burn."

"And he won't even use all of it," Galbraith says, tapping on the table and making more numbers appear. "See? We're thrusting at point nine gee, same as we would have, and all he had to do was re-aim the ship and time the delta-vee properly. Our original course had us thrusting outward, and now we're heading one-six-seven degrees off that. We're actually precessing Mars orbit even more than—"

"Fantastic," Jemison says. "Where are we going to hit?"

Galbraith frowns. "Excuse me?"

"He doesn't just want to crash the ship," Jemison says. "He wants to scare people. It's going to be a populated area, or a landmark, or both. Check the planetary rotation."

"It's not going to matter," Galbraith says. "*Dejah Thoris* masses over ninety thousand metric tons. The impact will crater half the planet."

"So Mars needs to know which half to evacuate," Jemison says.

"Do the math, please, Erica," Santamaria says.

Galbraith stares at Jemison and says, "Aye, Captain."

"We need to evacuate the passengers," Logan says. "How much time do we have?"

"Twenty-five hours and eleven minutes," Galbraith says.

"Go, Jeff," Santamaria says.

"Going." Logan leaves the briefing room.

For a moment, the only sounds are the whir of the air conditioning and the tapping of Galbraith's fingers against the tabletop. Then I hear the captain chuckling. Jemison stares at him.

"Something funny, sir?" she asks.

"He's making a statement," Santamaria says.

It's clear from the captain's tone of voice that "he" is not Alan Wachlin. "He" is whoever's back on Earth, pulling the strings and masterminding this operation. Santamaria wants Jemison and me to think this through, help him figure out who's ultimately responsible—who we can tell Paul to take down.

"No warning shots," Santamaria continues. "The Martians drove asteroids into our oceans when the war started. You remember. Close enough to coastal cities so civilians could see pillars of steam rising from the sea for days. They wanted us to know the cause of the dead fish washing up on our beaches. It scared people, but in the end, Earth was more angry than scared."

"He's going to start another war," Jemison says.

"No." Santamaria shakes his head. "In his mind, the last one never ended."

That "he" is starting to sound less like a pronoun and more like a specific person.

"Captain," I say, searching for an excuse to talk to him alone, "can I ask you about that DNA—"

"Okay, I think I have the target site," Galbraith says. I'm amazed that she managed to tune out everything in the room except her trajectory calculations.

"I need to check something in my quarters," Santamaria says, and walks away from the table.

"Captain," Jemison says.

She moves to intercept him, but she's got the whole length of the table and Galbraith in the way. Santamaria goes out the door, and Jemison stops short as it slides shut again, her hand gripping the edge of the conference table.

What's in his quarters? And why aren't you following him, Chief?

"What just happened?" Galbraith asks.

"Never mind," Jemison grumbles. "Where's the target?"

"Well, the plot's kind of rough, and I had to estimate atmospheric drag—"

"Best guess."

Galbraith suddenly looks like she doesn't want to answer. "Hellas Planitia. Southern rim. Capital City."

I hear Jemison grinding her teeth. "Thank you. Rogers, get yourself to a lifeboat."

"What?" She can't be serious. "I'm not leaving. You need me." I lower my voice. "You need my *specific skills*."

Jemison clamps a hand around my left wrist. "Let's talk about this outside."

I wait until we're in the hallway and the briefing room door slides shut behind us before speaking again. "You're really going to send me packing? Now?"

"Are you or are you not the only person in the known universe with a goddamn superpower?" Jemison hisses, still gripping my arm. "You're a triple-A Diamond asset. We have standing orders to convey you out of harm's way."

"I'm an *agent*," I say, "not an asset." *I don't need your so-called protection.* "And we still don't know who we're fighting. It's not just Wachlin and Bartelt. What if there's a whole squadron of fighters shadowing us?"

"There's nobody out there," Jemison says. "As soon as Wachlin killed our external sensors, I put people on visual scanning. We'll know if anything bigger than a cantaloupe gets within a thousand kilometers."

"And then you'll fight them off with what, kitchen knives?"

"You have weapons in that pocket?"

"Maybe."

"Fine," Jemison says. "Take out all your equipment and supplies and leave them here. Then get yourself off this ship before we crash."

"I want to speak to the captain." *What is he doing in his quarters? What did he figure out when he saw our new course, and why is he not telling the rest of us?*

"The captain's busy."

What are you *not telling me, Chief?* "Doing what?"

"None of your business."

I look over at Jemison's face. She continues staring straight ahead, not meeting my gaze—and not saying anything. Not explaining why I'm wrong. Why not? Why isn't she giving me another detailed lecture about how off-base I am or how I'm not following protocol? There's no reason for her silent treatment right now, unless—

"You don't know what's going on," I say out loud. "You have no idea what Santamaria's doing in his quarters."

"That's *Captain* Santamaria," Jemison says, "and like I said, it's none of your business."

"But it *should* be *your* business." I use my free hand to point at her. "You're the captain's right hand. Not Galbraith, not Logan, not any of these *civilians*. You're *agency*. You fought a war with the man. The two of you stood shoulder to shoulder at Olympus, and now he's cutting you out of the loop? What could he possibly—"

I'm not exactly sure how Jemison manages it, but without releasing my wrist, she spins me around and slams my face into the wall. The tendons around my shoulder scream with pain as she applies pressure.

"I am only going to say this once, Rogers—"

Aw, fuck this.

I open the pocket right next to her face. I couldn't have done it unless we were both facing in the same direction, but now I can punch a hole into hard vacuum two centimeters in front of her nose. I open the pocket without the barrier, so Jemison's staring into a black circle while air rushes past her face and into the void.

She goes stiff and stops talking, as expected. I hold the pocket there for a few seconds to make sure she understands what she's seeing.

That's deep space in there, friend. I can never fall in, but I open this portal large enough, and you're gone. I close the portal and you're trapped in the pocket universe all alone. No air, no light, no heat, no rescue. Science Division says it's even money whether you'd freeze to death before you suffocate.

Do. Not. Fuck with me.

I let that sink in, then close the pocket.

It takes a remarkable effort, pushing against Jemison, to peel my face off the wall and turn my head to look at her when I speak. Her free hand moves to her hip, but I've already got my hand over her stunner holster. I'm not an idiot.

"The name's Kangaroo," I say. "And there must be something useful I can do with this pocket."

Jemison releases my arm and shoves me away. I steady myself against the wall and turn around to face her.

"Maybe," she says. "I don't know about the pocket, but we definitely need your Echo Delta."

Of course. Santamaria's going to want to get new orders, maybe even call in reinforcements. And he can only use the comms dish outside the ship—which neither Wachlin or Bartelt knows about, and which they can't disable remotely—if he goes through my shoulder-phone.

I probably could have just mentioned that, instead of threatening Jemison with asphyxiation.

"Come on." She nods her head back the way we came. "Let's go talk to the captain."

"Thank you," I say, heading for the elevator. "I'm glad you're finally seeing reason."

"Shut up," she says. "You didn't convince me, you just reminded me. We need the captain's access codes to bypass your shoulder-phone and access the Echo Delta directly from the radio room. *Then* I'm putting you off the ship."

"We'll see what the captain says about that."

I don't actually think Santamaria will be any more sympathetic than she is, but I do want to know what the hell he suddenly had to go do in private. We're staring down a crisis with a short timeline, and a commanding officer in this situation doesn't leave his post without a very good reason—or a very bad one.

The fact that Santamaria chose not to tell any of us why he left gives me a very bad feeling. I mentally prepare myself for another unpleasant confrontation.

CHAPTER THIRTY-TWO

Dejah Thoris—Deck C, officers' quarters
25 hours until we hit Mars

When Jemison and I reach the captain's quarters, she presses the annunciator pad by the door. We wait for ten seconds, but nothing happens. Jemison presses the pad again, then puts her ear to the door. I don't think she can actually hear anything, but I refrain from pointing this out. She curses and squeezes her radio button.

"Danny," she says. "Where's the prisoner?"

The radio crackles, and then Danny's voice says, "Still in his cage, Chief. What's up?"

"Just checking," Jemison says. "Over and out." She swipes her thumb across the door's lockpad. The pad blinks red.

"Captain!" she shouts at the door. We both wait for a few seconds, but there's no response. "Shit. Get that panel open."

I get my fingernails under the edge of the lockpad and pry it up. I'm surprised at how easy it is, but I guess nobody on a cruise ship expects the crew to be too insubordinate. Jemison pulls an electronic tool off her belt and shoves one end of it into the open access port. It emits a soft beep, and the lockpad glows green. The door pops open.

Jemison shoulders the door aside and leaps into the stateroom. By the time she hits the floor in a crouch, she's swapped the multi-tool for her stunner, which she sweeps around the room. I am happy to let her lead the way, and only poke my head in the doorway so I can see what's happening.

Santamaria is sitting at his desk, which is empty except for a single display tablet, wearing only his short-sleeved undershirt. His uniform jacket lies crumpled on the bed behind him. He's hunched over and his eyes are closed. I see a pair of white wires leading up the side of his face, and tiny white earbuds fitted into his ears.

His eyes pop open when Jemison enters the room. He swings his head around to look at the noise, then looks back at the door and sees me. I read panic in his eyes. That's new.

He yanks his earbuds out with one hand and reaches for the tablet with his other hand.

I rush into the room and kick the door shut behind me. Santamaria's fingers miss the tablet by a centimeter, and I grab it and look down at the display.

The tablet shows a headshot of Jerry Bartelt and a list of vital statistics. *Good. The records lookup came back from Paul. Now we know exactly who this guy is.*

My mild elation sours as soon as I read the text next to the photograph. I can't quite believe what I'm seeing, and I page down to read more. But there is no more, and my gesture flips the display over to a different document—an agency covert cargo transport authorization form, dated and signed with a familiar name: E. SANTAMARIA.

I look at the captain. "What the fuck!"

"What is it?" Jemison asks. She's put her stunner back into its holster and is standing up.

Santamaria has both his hands raised. I can hear tinny brass music coming out of the earbuds on the desk. "I can explain."

I don't care anymore. I'm tired of not knowing what's going on, tired of always being a step behind everyone else. I'm tired of feeling like a tool instead of a person. And I'm tired of not being able to trust anyone or anything. I'm exhausted, but I have enough indignation left for one more outburst.

My subconscious takes over as soon as I've made the decision. I'm younger than Santamaria by a good twenty years. I have faster reflexes. And he didn't grow up in an orphanage, which I know from personal experience is only slightly better than a men's prison in terms of getting beat down on a regular basis. I know how to fight, and I am willing to fight dirty.

I drop the tablet and launch myself forward at the same time. I raise my elbow as I crash into Santamaria, knocking him out of his chair and toward the back wall. We tumble across the small stateroom, and I use the momentum to pull both of us up as we hit the wall, standing behind him and jamming my forearm under his chin.

I'm not choking him. He can still make noise. That means I'm not choking him.

Something cold and hard touches the back of my neck. I'm pretty sure it's the business end of Jemison's stunner.

"Let him go, Rogers," she says.

"You pull that trigger, you'll knock out both of us," I say.

"Yeah," she says, "but I'm only going to break your jaw while you're unconscious."

I feel anger boiling inside of me, and then I have a sudden moment of clarity. I surprise myself by relaxing my chokehold on Santamaria. As soon as Jemison moves the stunner away, I reach my right arm behind me and yank the weapon out of her grasp. I put a foot in her stomach and kick her away, at the same time pressing the stunner up against Santamaria's right temple.

Jemison stops herself against the door and glares at me. "You're a dead man, Rogers."

I find the tablet on the floor and kick it over to her.

"Read that first," I say. "Then decide which one of us you want to kill."

She shakes her head. I see her muscles tensing. She can cross the room in a less than a second. I'm sure I'd be unconscious milliseconds after that, and I'll be lucky if a broken jaw is my only injury.

"You think you can get over here faster than I can pull this trigger?" I shout. "Fifty thousand volts, right into his skull! READ IT!"

We stare at each other for a moment. Then Jemison bends her knees and lowers herself slowly, eyeing me the whole time, and I'm not sure if she's going to pick up the tablet or if she's preparing to jump me.

She snatches the tablet off the floor and gives me another full second of her dagger-stare before looking down at the display.

Her eyes don't actually widen, but I can see the muscles in her face working to contain her expression of surprise. She blinks twice before she raises her head. She looks like she's about to cry.

"Captain," she says, in a shaky voice I never expected to hear from her, "you can explain this?"

She bites off the words, as if they're distasteful in her mouth. I relax my grip on Santamaria and lower the stunner. If he makes any trouble now, Jemison will take care of him.

"He lied to me," Santamaria says.

I let Jemison ask the question. "*Who* lied to you?"

Santamaria exhales, and it feels like he's deflating in my grip. "Terman Sakraida."

I can't believe I heard that right. "*Director of Intelligence* Terman Sakraida?"

"You *know* D.Int?" Jemison says. At least I'm in good company.

"He lied to me," Santamaria repeats.

And then he tells us a story.

Terman Sakraida and Edward Santamaria met while waiting in line at the Marine Corps Officer Candidate School, because their last names were called one right after the other alphabetically. They came from different backgrounds—Santamaria enlisted to get out of the ghetto, and Sakraida joined after college as an act of rebellion against his upper-middle-class family—but they shared a romance with the myth of military camaraderie.

When the first Martian attack asteroid vaporized one of the last Antarctic glaciers, Sakraida was on spaceport construction duty at Air Station Endurance. He talked his entire work crew into transferring to the front lines. He didn't know that his old friend Eddie, then a lieutenant colonel, had also volunteered to put on a spacesuit and go stomp some Reds.

The Outer Space Service's Expeditionary Forces didn't exist then, but those first troops deployed to Mars were the direct ancestors of today's X-4s. And Santamaria and Sakraida were among their best.

A lot of the military records from that time are still classified. The First Mars Battalion did a lot of things in secret. But I've spent a lot of time staring at the data, and I've learned to read between the redacted lines.

The Battle of Elysium Planitia is historic for many reasons. It was the first time any nuclear devices were detonated by Martian forces. It was the first use of an orbital satellite to bombard a planet with an energy weapon. And though Earth Coalition won the battle, both sides suffered terrible losses that crippled their capacity to wage war for weeks afterward.

Elysium Planitia is a wide, flat expanse of Martian plain dotted by ancient volcanoes. The tallest of those is Elysium Mons in the north, and when Earth Coalition drove the Martian Irregulars out of Hellas Planitia, they fled northeast. They established a base in Elysium Mons, including a broadcast tower for Mars Free Radio. Earth Coalition launched several assaults against the mountain, but were beaten back every time.

The First Mars Battalion—calling themselves "1MB"—landed in Hellas Planitia at the end of that week. Earth Coalition set up their camp on a ridge overlooking Elysium Planitia, in the no-man's-land between the Hellas Planitia habitat and the peak of Elysium Mons. The colonists in Hellas didn't want troops crowding their community, and the military didn't want civilians—including possible Martian collaborators—too close to their base of operations. It was the only feasible compromise, and it was the worst of both worlds.

The Battle of Elysium Planitia started on a Tuesday morning. It ended on a Thursday evening, just as the sun was setting, with a focused high-energy particle beam blasting down from orbit at the same time that a barrage of surface-to-air missiles launched from Elysium Mons and spiraled up to the attacking satellite. The top of the ancient volcano erupted again, and at roughly the same moment, a miniature star blossomed in Mars orbit.

In terms of hardware, the Martian Irregulars suffered far worse in that final exchange of fire than Earth Coalition did. EC lost their prototype death ray, but they got a successful test firing out of it. The MIs lost an entire mountain full of weapons and supplies, plus a lot of morale. They eventually recovered, of course, but the next few months were pretty harrowing.

Both sides suffered terrible casualties at Elysium Planitia. EC cleared everyone they could find out of the mountain before the satellite strike, but they had to fight their way across the plain and up to Elysium Mons first. Martian defenses made air support and heavy armor impractical, and Earth Coalition's commander-in-chief demanded a swift resolution.

This was back when they still thought the war would be over in a few weeks. Idiots.

Edward Santamaria commanded 1MB's ground deployment at Elysium Planitia, and he made countless impossible choices. He ordered thousands of men and women, including his old friend Terry, into one of the ugliest and deadliest battlefields in human history. He did that for two days straight, knowing most of them would never return.

I understood then why Bartelt called Santamaria "Hades." He sent his troops into hell. He sent them down to Elysium, where they would rest as heroes—but they would still be dead.

Sakraida was one of the few who did make it back up the ridge, bursting out of the ground just ahead of the MIs who used an old survival tunnel to bypass EC defenses and infiltrate the command post. A land mine had plunged Sakraida's squad into one of those tunnels. He and the other 1MBs who survived the blast fought their way through a surprised Martian scout team and burrowed out of the ground just meters away from Santamaria's position, warning them about the Martian attack minutes before it happened.

Sakraida may not have made the best tactical decision. He could have taken the remains of his squad and used their suit sensors to avoid MI patrols. They could have followed the tunnels straight into the underbelly of Elysium Mons. That is how EC finally did penetrate the mountain, hours later.

Some agency analysts argue that Sakraida and his three remaining squadmates didn't have enough firepower to take the stronghold. Others argue that Sakraida's squad could have provided valuable reconnaissance that would have saved lives in the later assault.

None of that matters. Terman Sakraida saved Edward Santamaria's life that day. What happened at Elysium bonded them. Their careers diverged after the war, but they've been brothers ever since that day on Mars, and they'll always help one another, no questions asked. Even if it means leaving others out in the cold.

"He lied to me," Santamaria says. "That son of a bitch came to my home and sat at my table and lied to my face. And I believed him."

He's sitting again and staring at the tablet, which Jemison has put down on the desk. I'm standing by the back wall, and Jemison is next to Santamaria's chair.

This isn't just a proverbial bombshell. This revelation is a ground-level nuclear detonation that changes the geography of the battlefield. We thought we were dealing with some national or planetary rival, someone trying to infiltrate and break down our defenses. We were wrong. This danger is in our own house, rooted in the highest levels of what we thought was our most secure stronghold.

These people already know all our secrets. So what are they trying to accomplish here?

I look at Jemison and am shocked by her expression. Her previous anger has evaporated, and she's watching Santamaria now with intense scrutiny—almost desperation. Her arms are folded across her chest, and her deep frown doesn't disguise the fact that tears have welled up in her eyes.

"So let me make sure I understand this correctly," I say slowly, evenly, not wanting to perturb either Santamaria or Jemison too much. Some days my life depends on me reading a room and playing along with other people's moods, and I am acutely aware of being in that situation right now. "Director Sakraida asked you to sign that transport order, authorizing a sealed piece of cargo onto your ship. No inspection, no questions asked."

"Not onto my ship," Santamaria says. "Into the cargo container."

"Sorry," I say. "But you knew that container was going to be loaded onto *Dejah Thoris*."

Santamaria nods. "That was the deal. I would make sure his cargo reached Mars. It would be unloaded and stored in lost and found, and he would send someone else to retrieve it."

"So you have no idea what was in there."

He looks at me with weary eyes. "I do not."

Jemison coughs. "I want to believe you, sir, but this whole thing is—" She shakes her head. "Why would you do something like this?"

He looks up at her. "I'd do the same for you, Andie."

"I would never ask."

"I know."

They stare at each other for a long moment. Then Jemison unfolds her arms and extends her right hand. Santamaria clasps his hand around her wrist, and she does the same to him. They grip each other for a long moment, exchanging some invisible communication through their touch.

"So who the hell is Jerry Bartelt?" I say. We don't have time for gratuitous camaraderie.

Santamaria releases Jemison's hand. She glares at me. He says, "Non-Territorial Intelligence. Bartelt reported directly to Director Sakraida."

"And why did your old war buddy put him on this ship?" I ask. "He already had a suicide bomber—Alan Wachlin. Why send a second agent when you've already got one on the job?"

"Because Wachlin wasn't a professional," Jemison says. "Sakraida didn't trust him with the details of our cargo arrangement."

"So Bartelt's the one who cut into the container?"

"And extracted something to hand off to Wachlin."

"Great. How do we find out what it was?" I ask.

"Security's already checking camera footage for suspicious activity." Jemison taps at her wristband. "Nothing yet."

"Wachlin was able to carry on a very large knife and a nuclear power supply," Santamaria says. "Bartelt already had his personal electronics. What would they need to smuggle aboard that neither man could hide in his luggage?"

I point at the tablet on his desk. "That manifest doesn't say anything at all about the nature of the cargo?"

Santamaria hands me the tablet. "Maybe you can read between the lines."

I scroll through the entire authorization document again, twice. There's very little information here, which is just how the agency likes it: the less data we record, the less there is for anybody to compromise. But the people on the ground do need to know certain things, and coded entries are an easy way to hide information in plain sight.

"Here." I highlight part of the cargo manifest. "'Approximate mass: 70.23 kilograms.' You don't use two decimal places for an approximation. That's got to be a coded reference number."

"Doesn't do us any good without knowing the code," Jemison says.

"And there are dimensions here," I say, highlighting another set of numbers. "2.1 meters long, 70 centimeters wide, 60 centimeters high. If that's accurate, the box was pretty big." I try to visualize it. "Big enough to hold a lot of things—"

"No." Jemison's staring at the wall. "Big enough for one thing."

Santamaria stands up, watching Jemison intently. "Chief?"

"Three hundred and forty linear centimeters," Jemison says. Her eyes are glistening. "That's a military casket."

I open and close my mouth. Jemison's file showed that she oversaw cargo operations for most of her time at Olympus Base. Her last three years there were during and immediately after the Independence War. And corpses count as cargo.

I can't imagine how many of those caskets she had to process for shipment back to Earth.

"I'm just going to sit down here for a minute," I say.

"They needed somewhere to put that fake power core implant," Jemison says as I sit, feeling lightheaded. "I'm going to bet that a DNA test will tell us we found Alan Wachlin's corpse in 5028. They cloned him—enough of him to look like a human body—so we would find the right number of corpses at the crime scene."

"Doesn't it take a lot of time to grow a human clone?" I ask. I seem to recall Jessica ranting at Science Division about this a few years ago.

"They didn't need a working brain," Santamaria says. "Just a body."

He flexes his left arm, and another tattoo shimmers into being on the inside of his elbow: a caduceus encircled by pixel patterns. Muscle-activated medical inventory tag. That's not the arm he was born with. I wonder if any of his internal organs are also cloned replacements.

"We had to stop searching for him," Santamaria continues, pacing in a tight circle. "They knew we'd be watching every single passenger closely during midway, to minimize zero-gee mishaps. Wachlin could only hide if we thought all souls on board were accounted for."

"But they didn't need to kill his whole family," I say, rubbing my temples. "Why didn't Alan Wachlin just fake his *own* death? Why would he need to burn the whole goddamn stateroom?"

"'Need' is a strong word," Santamaria says.

"You're saying he did it for fun?"

"Not exactly." Santamaria stops pacing. "But Bartelt was *running* Wachlin. He was giving orders."

My headache has abated slightly. I stand up. "That device we found in his closet. He was hiding comms inside the ship's existing network."

Santamaria nods. "And inexperienced operators don't always follow orders to the letter."

"So you're saying Wachlin went off-script, and Bartelt had to scramble to salvage the mission."

"It's a common problem within terrorist organizations," Santamaria says. "Zealots need to be micromanaged."

"Bartelt did look pretty annoyed when Rogers visited him," Jemison says. "Angry, even."

"Okay, but we're saying D.Int is behind this. The *head* of Non-Territorial Intelligence. The man who runs all of the agency's surveillance and recon assets throughout the entire Solar System." My headache's coming back. "If this *is* his op, he'll have contingency plans up the wazoo. He must have anticipated that either Bartelt or Wachlin would get captured." I should stop staring at the captain. "He knew *you* were on board. Would he really think he could hide all this from you? And *why*? We crash into Mars and it's war. There's no other possible outcome. Who benefits from that?"

"Well," Santamaria says, "I know someone we can ask."

CHAPTER THIRTY-THREE

Dejah Thoris—Crew elevator
24 hours until we hit Mars and start another war

Jemison gets a call on her radio as our elevator descends to the lower decks. Santamaria and I exit the elevator when it reaches the holding area, but Jemison stays inside.

"I need to go work security," she says. "Rumors are spreading. Passengers are panicking. Some don't want to get in the lifeboats. We need to break up the crowds before they turn into mobs."

"Go," Santamaria says. Jemison nods as the elevator doors close.

Danny and Mike are guarding Jerry Bartelt. Danny is in the corridor, just outside the door to the holding area, leaning against the wall. As soon as he notices Santamaria and me approaching, Danny steps forward and stands up straight.

"Captain," Danny says. "Mr. Rogers."

"At ease, Mr. Egnor," Santamaria says. "Any trouble from the prisoner?"

"No, sir," Danny says. "Mike's been checking in every five minutes. No problems."

"Is that standard procedure?" I ask. I can't imagine drunk and disorderly passengers would merit that kind of constant attention.

"No," Danny says, "but the chief told us to watch this guy real close. Said he's dangerous."

"He is," Santamaria says. "Open it up."

Danny nods and taps his radio button. "Got two coming in, Mike."

The door slides open with a pneumatic hiss—I note that it's not a simple hinged affair, which makes it that much harder to force open, and probably has an interlock to keep it closed even in case of power failure. It's almost as if Jemison expected she'd have to keep a dangerous prisoner in here at some point.

Bartelt's cell is at the far end of the compartment, the last of six small berths fitted with clear acrylic panels for doors. Mike is standing in front of that last cell, with his back up against the door and both hands clutching at his neck.

Santamaria mutters a curse and calls back to Danny. I rush forward and blink my eye into scanning mode. The Faraday cage disrupts active scan frequencies, but it doesn't stop the rest of the EM spectrum from showing through and registering on my passive sensors.

The transparent doors on these cells give a clear view of each holding cell, presumably to minimize the chances of prisoners getting up to too much mischief inside. Each clear panel has a series of breathing holes cut into it, making a dotted line across the midsection of each cell door. The holes aren't large enough to fit anything bigger than a writing stylus through— they're designed to be the only ventilation in the cell.

Despite all those safeguards, Jerry Bartelt was able to slip a loop of piezoelectric filament cord through one of the air holes and maneuver it around Mike's neck. I can see the glowing outline of the filament ending at Bartelt's right wrist. It must be a garrote implant, but I can't see the reel that should be under his skin.

That's when I realize: I can't see anything. On its current setting, my eye should be able to pick out most of the equipment that Bartelt must have surgically hidden in his body. There's got to be a computer core, a power source, and at least one comms package implanted somewhere, not to mention the garrote he's got around Mike's neck. But I can't see any of that.

It's not until I get closer that I notice it. There's a slight sensor shimmer all over Bartelt's body—an interference grid built into his skin itself, masking certain EM frequencies. I can see his biological heat map, but his implanted tech is camouflaged. I've heard Jessica and Oliver talk about Science Division working on ways to "cloak" a field agent's implants—it's one research area where their two normally disjoint areas of expertise overlap. There still isn't a way to do it without dangerous chemicals, unstable power sources, or both.

So either Jerry Bartelt's got toxic fibers surgically woven into his epidermis, or he's been given some exotic gene therapy that alters his body chemistry and will probably kill him before he's forty. In either case, my key takeaway from this bit of reconnaissance is that he's crazy, and the people running him are even crazier.

"Quantico?" Bartelt says. He's looking directly at me. Santamaria is just coming up next to me, with Danny close behind, his stunner drawn and aimed at the cell. He's got no hope of accomplishing anything useful with it, but I understand his need to do something.

"Are you talking to me?" I say, hoping to distract and delay him while Santamaria figures out how to deal with this.

"You're in Operations," Bartelt says. "You've got the eye, a comms unit under your collarbone, and wireless implants in your torso. Where did you train in hand-to-hand?"

"Let me think," I say. "Yeah. That would have been last week, in a cheap motel near Miami Beach, with your mother. She didn't have great control, but she did some very interesting things with her legs."

This is not my finest hour. *I really hope you're thinking up a brilliant plan back there, Captain.*

The only reaction I get from Bartelt is a slow grin that spreads over his face like an oil slick. "Open this cell or I cut his head off."

I guess he's decided he isn't going to get anywhere talking to me. He's looking at Santamaria now.

"Then you'd be free," Santamaria says, "and you'd kill him anyway."

"Maybe," Bartelt says. "Maybe not. Can you afford to take that chance?"

I have no idea what Santamaria's thinking, and that's a problem. We didn't come in here expecting to deal with a hostage situation, so we didn't have a plan. Bartelt, on the other hand, has had hours alone in his cell to think up an escape scheme.

Escape. He wants to escape. That means—

Gotcha, you son of a bitch.

I move out of the corner, getting closer to Bartelt, upstaging Santamaria. "What do you know about the hijacking?" I ask.

Out of the corner of my eye, I see Santamaria shoot me a burning look. Yeah, he thinks I'm being an idiot, panicking and giving away information when we should be trying to get it out of Bartelt. I hope he'll catch on and follow my lead.

"Hijacking?" Bartelt says. "I don't know anything about that."

He's replaced his grin with a very convincing frown. Convincing, but not perfect. He wasn't prepared for me to volunteer such an important piece of information. I can tell he's lying. And if I can tell, the captain can tell.

Santamaria puts a hand on my shoulder. I turn my head and hope he can read my expression. *I'm not* really *an idiot, Captain. Come on, put it together!*

His eyes are dark, bottomless pools, and I can't read them. I raise my eyebrows and flick my eyes upward, as if looking through the ceiling, up where Jemison went to help with the evacuation. *Lifeboats. Escape. Come on!*

Santamaria leans in close to me and says, "I'll handle this." He's turned the right side of his face toward Bartelt, in profile, and he gives me a quick wink with his left eye.

I do my best not to exhale or otherwise show how relieved I am.

Santamaria turns to face Bartelt. "You know who I am. And I know who your boss is. Let's not waste time. What are his demands?"

Bartelt chuckles. "Wrong game, Captain."

"He's threatening to kill half of Mars," Santamaria says.

"Actually, you are," Bartelt says. "To no one's surprise, the hero of Elysium Planitia is still bitter about what happened on that battlefield. Your manifesto is quite eloquent. It'll be the top story on every news service tomorrow."

Santamaria grits his teeth. "So he's completely insane."

"Like many Independence War veterans, you disagreed with the terms of the armistice," Bartelt says. "You never stopped fighting for your beliefs. Even if it had to be in secret."

"And what beliefs are those?"

"Humanity united." Bartelt says it solemnly, like a pledge. "One people, many worlds."

"There's no guarantee Earth would win another war," Santamaria says.

"Once again, we disagree. But it doesn't matter." Bartelt grins. "The war's the thing, Captain. Have you forgotten all that history you studied? Armed conflict advances civilization. Nothing spurs innovation like the fear of violent mass murder. Everybody wins."

"I'm intrigued," Santamaria says. "Tell me more. Is it too late for me to switch sides?"

Bartelt stops smiling. "Open this cell or your man dies."

Mike's eyes are wide, and I can't tell if it's from lack of oxygen or fear of dying. He looks from me to Santamaria to Danny. His fingers haven't stopped scrabbling against the wire, but he can't get any purchase. The line is digging into his neck. Small droplets of blood are starting to form around the incipient cut. I don't know if the filament can actually slice through bone, but I'm sure none of us is eager to find out.

Santamaria takes a step back. "You'll have to release him before we can open the door."

Bartelt shakes his head. "No deal."

"Do you see any hinges on these panels?" Santamaria says. "They retract into the ceiling. If you've still got that wire around his neck, it'll drag both of you up."

"I'll survive," Bartelt says.

"You have to release the wire to exit the cell," Santamaria says. "That will leave you vulnerable to being stunned."

"No," Bartelt says, "because your other guard is going to give me his stunner."

"Why would he do that?"

I can see Bartelt's annoyance increasing. "He can't tag me through this Faraday cage anyway—"

"What's a Faraday cage?"

"Don't insult my intelligence," Bartelt snaps. "His stunner's useless. And I'll kill his friend if he doesn't hand it over."

Santamaria stares at Bartelt for a moment longer, then turns to Danny.

"Do it," Santamaria says.

Danny hesitates.

"Do it!" Santamaria repeats.

Danny flinches and lowers his arms. His hesitation wasn't long enough to merit a barked order like that, but I know what the captain's doing: he's creating the appearance of dissension within his ranks. I started it by seeming to volunteer information, and Danny's reluctance is continuing to sell our performance. I hope Santamaria's got a good finale planned.

The stunner leaves Danny's hands and tumbles to the floor.

"Good," Bartelt says. "Now open this door."

He's collected both ends of the garrote in his right hand, leaving his left hand free to grab the stunner. I briefly wonder how he's going to get through the Faraday cage, but then I remember that the conductive mesh isn't terribly sturdy. It wasn't designed to be used on its own; both in the cargo container and here in the holding cell, it needed structural support from another, stronger enclosure. Once the cell door slides away, Bartelt can just punch through the mesh and grab the stunner.

Santamaria makes a show of inhaling deeply and then sighing. He raises both his hands and says to Danny, "Go ahead."

"Yes, sir," Danny says in a tight voice. He swipes his thumb against the lockpad and enters an access code.

The next few things happen almost too quickly for me to follow.

First, the clear panel of Bartelt's cell hisses open. The door doesn't move very quickly, but it's fast enough to surprise me. Mike and Bartelt are both dragged upward by the wire around Mike's neck, just as Santamaria predicted, but Bartelt releases his hold on the wire before his own head hits the top of the cell.

As Mike bounces off the ceiling and falls forward, Bartelt dives toward the stunner on the floor. Santamaria, Danny, and I have also started moving. I'm the closest one to Mike, and I need to catch him and get his body out of the way of whatever Santamaria is planning to do. Danny behaves like a good security guard, going after his weapon before it falls into the wrong hands.

Santamaria rockets toward Bartelt, using his right arm to intercept Danny and knock him away. Santamaria extends his left arm and reaches the edge of the Faraday cage at the same time Bartelt rips through it.

Just as Bartelt's hand touches the stunner on the ground, Santamaria's fingers grab his hair and jerk his head backward. Bartelt grunts as both men fall away from me and crash into the back wall of the cell. Danny grabs his stunner. Mike slams into me, and I wrap my arms around him and spin myself backward, cushioning our fall.

Mike's weight knocks the wind out of me, and it takes me a moment to refocus my eyes and look around.

Santamaria has his right arm around Bartelt's neck in a chokehold. He's kicking and struggling, but the captain is holding him tight. I can see Bartelt's face changing color. He'll be unconscious in a matter of seconds—unless he's got some crazy body modification that lets him hold his breath for hours.

Fortunately, he doesn't. Bartelt's body goes limp, and I relax a little when Santamaria releases his head and lowers his left arm. But he keeps Bartelt in the chokehold, and then I see Santamaria's left hand come back up holding what appears to be an antique hunting knife with a ten-centimeter blade.

I'm too confused to say anything until Santamaria puts the blade to Bartelt's shoulder.

"Whoa!" I say. "We can't question him if he's dead!"

Santamaria shoots me the absolute epitome of a dirty look. "I don't murder people."

I hold up my hands. "Okay, then, what's with the knife?"

"I'm going to remove his communications package," Santamaria says.

I blink. "You're going to cut out his shoulder-phone?"

"Yes."

"With a hunting knife and no anesthetic."

"I need you and Danny to hold him down."

"With all due respect, Captain, you need your head examined." In my peripheral vision, I can see Danny and Mike moving closer, and I wonder if they'll agree with me. This is a civilian vessel, but it's still insubordination if they disobey a direct order. "If you want to keep him from using his comms, I can jam his frequency with my own transmitter—"

"For fuck's sake, Rogers," Santamaria says, "why do you think he wanted out of the cell?"

"To get off the ship, right? Because he knows—"

Santamaria frowns at me. "This was a suicide mission. Neither of these men expected to walk away."

"He wanted to get out of the Faraday cage," Danny says. "So he could use his comms."

There's only one person Bartelt could talk to via his shoulder-phone. And there's only one reason Santamaria would want to remove Bartelt's shoulder-phone instead of just jamming it.

Even I've never had an idea this bad before.

"He's going to know it's us," I say.

"Not if you do your job right," Santamaria says. "Danny, hold his legs. Mike, are you well?"

"Yes, sir," Mike says. His voice sounds hoarse, but there's no hesitation in his tone. "Want me to grab his arms?"

"Please."

Danny and Mike move into position, pinning down Bartelt's limbs. Santamaria drags the knife across Bartelt's shirt. The fabric tears open, and Santamaria rips it away to reveal Bartelt's skin underneath.

"Okay, let's stop and think about this for a second," I say. "That comms package is a very specialized piece of hardware. You can't just take it up to the radio room and plug it in. You're going to need something that can interface with—"

Santamaria's smiling now. It's really unsettling.

"I think we need to involve a medical professional at this point," I say.

CHAPTER THIRTY-FOUR

Dejah Thoris—Deck D, Sickbay
23 hours until we hit Mars and everybody dies

The surgery doesn't take long. After expressing strenuous objections on the record, Dr. Sawhney puts Bartelt and me in adjoining beds, administers a local anesthetic, and then makes matching shallow incisions in our shoulders. I flinch as nanobot-filled blood bubbles out of my body and the doctor siphons it away.

"Almost done," he says, misinterpreting my discomfort.

We're joined by a crewman with short brown hair, dark eyes, and a slim build. Santamaria introduces him as Fritz Fisher, the acting chief engineer. Fritz sets up a portacomp to which Sawhney attaches the data cables leading from the subcutaneous access ports on Bartelt's and my comms implants.

"How do you feel, Mr. Rogers?" Sawhney asks, setting the portacomp on a tray clipped to the railings between the beds.

"Like I've got a hole in my chest," I say. I look down at the bandage covering my left collarbone. There's a small spot of blood seeping through the gauze.

I really hope those nanobots aren't going to do anything weird in the trash. *Can't worry about that now. Ask Surge later.*

While Sawhney gets me closer to the enemy than I ever wanted to be, Mike opens an access panel on the wall next to me and attaches the device from Bartelt's closet to the network cables inside. The portacomp lights up, and I access the other shoulder-phone.

"Phones are connected," I report.

This is still a long shot. Bartelt does have an agency-standard comms implant, same as I do—the diagnostics confirm that—but it's entirely possible that he's not using any of our standard encryption keys. How paranoid is Sakraida?

The display in my left eye flashes, and then letters and numbers flash and scroll past my vision. I let out a breath I didn't know I was holding.

"I'm in," I say, and start sorting through the contents of Bartelt's data pod.

Santamaria orders Mike and Dr. Sawhney out of the room, then closes the door and asks Fritz to mirror my display on the tablet connected to the portacomp. I put a hand over the tablet before Fritz can grab it. "Are you sure about that, Captain?"

He nods. "I need to see what they were saying to each other."

"Yeah," I say, "but you have a dog, Captain." *This might blow your cover.*

Santamaria stares at me. "There are twenty million people living on Mars."

I hand over the tablet.

The messages between handler and agent are easy to pick out from all the comm logs. Bartelt's shoulder-phone hasn't been sending to or receiving from anybody else for the past few days. And all the messages are text-only—less data, easier to hide in a network stream. We learned that trick from the Martians during the war.

I scroll through the logs slowly, reading everything carefully, looking for any phrases that might indicate a code or give away some information about how Wachlin took over the engineering controls so quickly. It appears that Bartelt was feeding Wachlin instructions at each step. Either their recruit wasn't very good at remembering things, or the handler didn't want to divulge any detail unless absolutely necessary.

I allow myself a smile when I see Wachlin getting chewed out after setting the fire in his stateroom. That's what happens when you ask for obedience without granting trust. *Zealots need to be micromanaged.* But Bartelt doesn't hold a grudge; he stays focused on their mission. He tells Wachlin exactly where to hide to avoid the ship's security cameras, and when to move during the crew's shift changes.

A few seconds later, I have to stop reading. I look away to clear my head.

"Sick bastard," Fritz mutters. He's been reading over Santamaria's shoulder.

"No, Mr. Fisher," Santamaria says. "These men are professionals. They're executing a plan."

"This guy, maybe." Fritz jabs a finger toward the unconscious Bartelt. "The other one's a fucking psychopath."

"Stand down, Mr. Fisher."

"What exactly do you expect to learn from reading this crap?" Fritz smacks the tablet. "We're wasting time here. We need to figure out how to stop the ship."

Santamaria lowers the tablet and glares at Fritz. "Mr. Fisher, my offer to relieve you of duty still stands. Any time you feel you need to return to your quarters—"

"No," Fritz says. "I told you, I'm here until this is done."

"If you choose to remain on duty," Santamaria says, "I expect you to conduct yourself like a professional."

"I am giving you my best analysis, Captain," Fritz replies in a tight voice.

"No, you're not," Santamaria says. "You're angry. That's what they want. They want anger to cloud our judgment. This is not some random misfortune we're fighting. This is evil. And evil is predictable." He holds up the tablet. "We discover what they were planning, and we can stop them. We can make sure no one else dies today. Understood?"

Fritz inhales sharply. "Yes, sir."

Santamaria turns to me and nods. "Carry on, Mr. Rogers."

I force myself to continue reading. I remind myself how I got through my most gruesome analyst duties during the war, when I was processing raw troop helmet feeds from Mars. Don't empathize. Don't look at the individuals. Look at the big picture. Think strategically. Even if you hate yourself in the morning, you've got to get the job done.

I feel sick and furious and helpless, but I scroll through messages until I get to the end, when Santamaria knocked Bartelt unconscious. His last message to Wachlin was a string of numbers. Another code. I don't recognize the format. Neither does Santamaria.

"He could have told Wachlin he'd been captured." I stare at the glowing numbers, searching for a pattern, seeing nothing.

"That's unlikely," Santamaria says. "An abort signal would be short and simple. This is a large amount of data."

"Sixty-four digits," Fritz offers. "Could be a passphrase, or an encryption key."

"He already has access to everything in Main Eng," Santamaria says. "If it is a key, it unlocks something Wachlin brought with him."

"Bartelt was giving Wachlin specific instructions at each step," I say. "Wachlin could have been carrying a data payload—an encrypted file stored on his phone or some other personal device. It wouldn't be useful until it was decrypted with the key, but it also wouldn't be suspicious if he was searched."

"Fuck me," Fritz says. "It could be software."

I gape at him. "He can reprogram the ship?"

"Not entirely," Fritz says. "Critical infrastructure like the main reactor and life support are locked down. But he could interfere with other systems."

"Like what?"

"Public display walls. The touchscreen maps in the stairwells. Telephones. The PA system."

"The lockpad on his stateroom door?" I ask.

"Maybe."

"None of those things is life-threatening or crippling to operations," Santamaria says. "What can he do to make our situation worse than it already is?"

Fritz frowns. "I don't know."

Santamaria looks at me. "I guess you'd better ask him, then."

Fritz does a double-take. "Wait. *He's* going to pretend to be this guy"— he points at Bartelt—"and talk to the hijacker through their comms?"

"Now would be the time to suggest a better idea," I say, reviewing Bartelt's outgoing messages for repeated words or phrases.

"All their messages are text only," Santamaria says. "Rogers just needs to mimic his writing style."

"And he has some kind of special State Department training for this?" Fritz asks.

"Mr. Rogers is more than qualified to perform this task," Santamaria says. I'm not sure that's true, but I appreciate the vote of confidence.

"The messages will be buffered," I say, bringing up the messaging interface. "You two will be able to see what I'm typing on that tablet before I send it to Wachlin. Feel free to, you know, brainstorm."

"This is insane," Fritz says.

"We're ready when you are, Rogers," Santamaria says.

I place a timer in the corner of my left eye HUD to remind myself not to take too long crafting each response. Then I take a breath, exhale, and type: **Give me a status update.** I hit the send button.

It feels like forever before the reply appears: **About time you got back. Where hell you been?**

Was detained by crew, I type. **What is your status?**

Why detained? Wachlin asks after a few seconds.

Misunderstanding. Not important. I wait for Fritz or Santamaria to object, but they say nothing. **Status update. Now.**

Nearly fifteen seconds pass before Wachlin's next message: **Where are you**

"He's checking the cameras," Fritz says. "He wants visual confirmation that Bartelt's free."

"Well, that's going to be a problem," I say, looking at the unconscious man next to me.

"Tell him you're still hiding," Santamaria says. "You don't want anyone to see you sending these messages."

"Right." **Staying out of sight in restroom. No cameras. Give me a status update.**

This time, the delay's almost half a minute. **Tell me about the rabbits george.**

"What the fuck?" Fritz says.

"Must be a challenge phrase," I say. My pulse is racing. "I don't recognize it."

"I do," Santamaria says. "Type this phrase exactly." He spells it out for me.

They'll be a little patch of alfalfa, Lennie, I type and send. "Does this mean something to you, Captain?"

"It was his favorite book," Santamaria says. His tone of voice indicates he doesn't want to elaborate.

Wachlin's reply comes back. **Is david still alive?**

"His brother?" Fritz says. "He's going to kill everyone on this ship, but he's worried about his brother?"

"I'm going to lie to him," I say.

"Agreed," Santamaria says.

No. My finger pauses above the send button. I'm certain Bartelt would express no sympathy, but would he rub it in just to be mean?

No. He'd want to keep Wachlin focused on the mission. I hit send.

I watch almost twenty seconds tick past before Wachlin responds: **Its better this way. You understand right? Why I had to do it?**

"Really?" I say out loud. "We really need to do this now?"

"Stay on topic," Santamaria says. "Bartelt is single-minded."

"Right." I send: **Yes. Let's move on. Tell me your status.**

Wachlin doesn't buy it. **Tell me you understand.**

"What the hell does this guy want?" I say.

"He knows he's holding all the cards right now," Fritz says. "You saw how Bartelt was abusing him in those earlier messages. Now he's got control of the ship, he wants Bartelt to apologize to him. Just say you're sorry."

"No," Santamaria says as I start to type. "Bartelt wouldn't apologize."

"Yeah, that's not his style," I agree. "Wachlin knows that. So what does he want Bartelt to say?"

"Tell him he did the right thing," Santamaria says. "Wachlin wants acknowledgment. Give him that."

I nod and type: **Yes. You did the right thing.**

Wachlin replies: **I want you to say it**

"They must have talked in person at some point," Santamaria says.

"And we have no idea what they said to each other," Fritz says.

"We can figure this out." *We have to figure this out.* I stare at Bartelt's unconscious face. "Why *did* Wachlin kill his mother?"

"Um, because he's a psychopath?" Fritz offers.

"Even psychopaths have reasons," Santamaria says. "Best guess, Mr. Rogers."

I squeeze my eyes shut for a moment and concentrate. Alan Wachlin didn't *need* to kill his mother and frame his brother. What would have happened if he hadn't? If he and Bartelt had faked Alan's death only, using the cloned corpse and the spare PECC, then Emily and David would have thought—

"Got it," I say.

You spared your family, I type. **They didn't need to see any of this.**

"Sound good?" I ask Santamaria and Fritz. They nod. I hit send.

A few seconds later, Wachlin replies: **Yes. They wouldnt have understood our mission.** I hear Fritz exhale loudly.

"Speaking of the mission," I mutter. **What is your current status?**

Engineering compartment secure, Wachlin says. **Software uploaded.**

"Dammit. We need to know which system he's tampering with," Fritz says.

"Right." **Did you test the new program?**

How do I test it? Is there a different command?

"A little help here?" I say.

"I'm thinking!" Fritz paces in a tight circle. "Ask him what the output was from the reprogramming operation. What did it show on his screen when it finished running? Result code! Ask him for the result code."

"Got it." I type in the message as fast as I can, keenly aware of seconds passing, and hit send. "That'll tell us which system it was?"

"No," Fritz says. "We're just buying some time. We need to ask him something else. Let me think for a second."

"Think faster, please," I say.

The screen lights up again: **Result code was 0. That means it worked right? Thats what you told me**

"Okay, what are we doing here, Fritz?" He's holding his head with both hands.

"The test suite would depend on the system," Fritz mumbles.

"Is there something that would work on all systems?" I ask.

"Maybe. Yes! Tell him to run a memory diagnostic." Fritz spells out the command code for me. "Then tell him to transcribe its output precisely, word for word. That will tell us which system he's looking at."

I type the message and send it. Wachlin writes back: **Computer says 30 seconds to complete diagnostic**

"What if this doesn't work?" I ask Fritz.

He frowns. "It's just a diagnostic. If it doesn't work, it means his software bricked the system."

"No," I say slowly, "I mean, what if this doesn't tell us what we need to know? What do we ask him next?"

Fritz considers this. "Maybe ask him which console he's looking at."

"Good," Santamaria says. "If we know where he is in the compartment, we can plan our breach better."

"I thought we couldn't cut through that bulkhead," I say.

"There are other ways into Main Eng," Santamaria says.

Fritz shakes his head. "You know if we even attempt a breach, he's going to . . ." He doesn't finish the sentence.

"I can ask if she's still alive," I say.

There's a long pause before Santamaria says, "First you have to ask Wachlin if he took a hostage. Bartelt wouldn't know."

I steady my fingers before typing. **Did you take a hostage?**

Yes. Shes alive. For now, Wachlin replies.

A surge of emotion churns my stomach. I remind myself to stay in character. **Is she cooperating?**

She will . . .

Fritz bangs a fist against the wall. "For the record, Captain? I fucking hate this guy."

That makes two of us, buddy.

"So noted," Santamaria says.

I'm just about to ask what we should do next when my display lights up, as if I'm typing another message. But I'm not doing it. The screen fills with a single word:

AVUNCULAR AVUNCULAR AVUNCULAR

"What is that? Why are you sending that?" Fritz says.

"It's not me!" I reply. "I don't know what—"

I snap my head up and look at Bartelt. He's awake. He's blinking his eyes and moving his fingers. I yell this information to Santamaria and Fritz.

My tablet goes dark. Something flashes across the display for an instant, some kind of error message. I feel a warmth in my chest, kind of like heartburn, but not.

Before I can pull the data cable out of my shoulder, the portacomp connecting me to Bartelt sparks, and an unprecedented pain explodes through my torso. Through my suddenly hazy vision, I see Bartelt's chest belching smoke.

The next moments are a bit of a blur. The door slams open. I smell melting plastic and burning flesh. A high-pitched electronic whine joins a din of shouting voices. Someone yanks the cable out of my shoulder and slaps something cool over the skin there. I welcome the familiar numbing sensation of an anti-burn gel pack.

After I wipe the tears from my eyes, I see a charcoal-colored mess where Jerry Bartelt's heart and lungs used to be. His face is slack and lifeless. I might have allowed myself to be happy about that, if he hadn't found one last way to fuck us over before he died.

"You two actually thought that ridiculous plan would work?" Jemison asks.

She and I are back in the corridor outside the captain's quarters, waiting while he changes into a clean uniform. Dr. Sawhney has patched me up, though my shoulder's going to hurt like hell for the next few weeks.

"It did work. For a few minutes," I say. "We almost got what we needed."

"But you didn't," she says. "And now Bartelt is dead, and we have no way to communicate with Earth."

She doesn't say it accusingly—she's just stating the facts, coldly and efficiently—but I still bristle. "We have more information than we did before. We know Ellie's alive."

"She was alive fifteen minutes ago. We don't know what the current situation is."

"We verified the identity of the hijacker."

Jemison chuckles. "Yeah. Ex-military nutjob, willing to kill his entire family, prepped by the fucking D.Int. Good to know. Thanks. That helps."

"Look, *Chief*—"

The door opens, and Santamaria glares at both of us. "Status."

"We're loading all the lifeboats at once," Jemison says. "Blevins is on deck ten. He'll launch one boat as a canary. After we've verified that first launch, we'll send out the rest as quickly as possible while still giving the autopilots room to maneuver."

"How long until you're ready?"

Jemison checks her wristband. "Twenty minutes."

"Sounds like a good plan," I say, wanting to contribute something.

"Yeah." Jemison stares at the wall. "They're all good plans until they don't work out."

"Mr. Rogers." Santamaria turns to me. "Your Echo Delta out on the hull. Is it a standard X-4 field comms unit?"

"Yeah," I say, and rattle off the model number, which Oliver made me memorize months ago. "But it's useless without a working shoulder-phone keyed to agency encryption codes."

"Useless for talking to the office," Santamaria says, "but it's still a radio transceiver."

"Yes." I snap my fingers. "Yes! We can re-tune the hardware to other frequencies." My excitement dissipates slightly. "But how is that going to help? At this range, the transmitter won't have nearly enough power to cut through Earth's local radio traffic."

"I don't want to talk to Earth," Santamaria says. "I want you to re-aim the Echo Delta and send a distress call to Mars Following Trojan."

I blink a couple of times as his words sink in. "Oh. Right. I can do that."

CHAPTER THIRTY-FIVE

Dejah Thoris—Exterior, amidships
22 hours until we hit Mars

Standing on *Dejah Thoris*'s hull is just as starkly beautiful as it was the first time, days ago, when I went for that unauthorized spacewalk. Before I met Jemison. Before the ship was hijacked.

I don't have time to appreciate the view now. I'm working.

"All lifeboats are loaded," Logan says, his image moving in one of the two vid feeds on my spacesuit helmet's HUD. That camera is looking down on the briefing room table, where all the senior staff are gathered. The other feed shows Blevins and his security team standing outside the open doors of one lifeboat. "Ready when you are, Blevins."

"All passengers secured here. Deck ten, section twelve," Blevins says. "We're running one last hardware diagnostic now."

"Thank you, Mr. Blevins." Santamaria looks up at the camera—at me. "Mr. Rogers, what's your status?"

"Detaching Echo Delta now," I say. The last bolt whirs out of the hull, past the flange holding the dish down, and slips out of the front end of my multi-tool.

I grab for the bolt, but it escapes the fat fingers of my spacesuit gloves and spins off into the void, falling at point-nine gee.

"Oh no you don't," I mutter. I picture one side of a wrench and open the pocket on the far side of the bolt. It tumbles past the event horizon and into darkness.

I close the pocket, then think of the other side of my imaginary wrench and open the pocket again, rotated. *In through the front door, out through the back door.* The bolt flies up out of the pocket, slowing at point nine gee.

I catch it at the top of its arc, before it falls again, then tuck it inside my belt pouch.

"Say again, Rogers?" Jemison's voice sounds more shrill over the radio than in person.

"Sorry, Chief," I say, opening the pocket to a different location and stowing the radio dish. "Just packing up my tools. Moving to new location now. ETA five minutes."

I turn down the magnets in my boots so I can half-run across the hull, hanging off the safety line tethered to the airlock above me. The helmet HUD shows an overlay of my destination in green, plus a pulsing red circle in the black sky showing where I'm supposed to aim the dish: Mars Following Trojan, also known as Odyssey Base.

Odyssey is the free-floating OSS station where the peace treaty ending the Independence War was signed. It sits at a "Trojan" point trailing Mars in its orbit—a gravitationally stable position balanced between that planet and the Sun—and is the only Earth outpost close enough to have any hope of sending spacecraft to intercept *Dejah Thoris* before we crash.

The radio chatter continues as I get to the target location, open the pocket, and bolt down the Echo Delta again. More minutes pass while I program in the new sky coordinates and wait for the computer-controlled motors to re-aim the dish. This isn't complicated work—with the HUD overlays, it's pretty much paint-by-numbers. But I'm the only one who has the computer access codes for this equipment.

"Echo Delta is re-pointing now," I report. "Another minute and I can transmit."

"Thank you, Mr. Rogers," Santamaria says. "Do you have a visual on the first lifeboat?"

I tap the wrist controls on my spacesuit, and the HUD lights up with a yellow cursor, pointing me toward deck ten, section twelve. "Affirmative. Sending now." I open a live vid link back to the briefing room.

"Link is good," Jemison says.

"Question for the room," Santamaria says. "Have we thought of everything?"

Nobody speaks for a moment. This is what we're all afraid of: that we've missed something crucial, something that will endanger the thousands of civilians we're about to launch into open space.

"We ran full diagnostics on every lifeboat," Jemison says. "All clear. The bad guys couldn't have gotten to all of them unless they tampered with the firmware, and there's no sign of that."

After a pause, Santamaria says, "Very well. Mr. Blevins, launch the first lifeboat."

"Launching now," Blevins says. His tiny vid image turns to yell into the lifeboat: "Here we go, folks!"

He flips open a control panel and presses his palm against it. An alarm sounds, a light flashes, and the lifeboat doors hiss shut. Another set of airtight doors closes over those, and I hear muffled cracks.

Plumes of fire shoot up from the hull just before the vibration from the explosive bolts reaches me. The lifeboat tears free of its niche in the side of *Dejah Thoris* and sails up and away.

Something moves on the hull. I tilt my head down to see what it is. Another lifeboat?

Three bright lights flare up on the line separating the white hull and black space. The cloud of dust from the lifeboat launch glows with three sharp lines, lancing upward and converging on the lifeboat.

The pod changes color, from dull off-white to red to orange to yellow. Then it explodes in complete silence.

The shockwave taps the hull a second later. My boots vibrate again.

The lights on the hull disappear. Inertia carries the lifeboat debris away from the ship. I'm thankful that I can only recognize a few human body parts in the wreckage.

I hear Jemison screaming something, but I don't know what it is. My brain is burning again. Someone else is sobbing.

The radio crackles to life in my ear. "Chief! Egnor, deck three! My lifeboat doors just closed on their own! It's launching itself!"

Another tremor. I whip my head around, looking for the launch. It's behind me—above me. My HUD marks it as deck three, section six.

I turn off my mag-boots and pull myself up the tether as fast as I can. I need to get closer to use the pocket. I can open it fifteen meters wide. That's big enough to catch the lifeboat. But I need to get closer.

"It's the hijacker," Jemison says. Her voice echoes from the other vid feed. She must be broadcasting shipwide. "He's launching the lifeboats into the navigational deflectors."

I guess we know what Wachlin reprogrammed with his software update.

The second lifeboat disintegrates while I'm still half the ship away. I stop moving, reengage my mag-boots, and turn off my suit mic before screaming as loud as I can.

"Clear the lifeboats," Jemison says. "Get everybody out of the lifeboats. I repeat, clear the lifeboats. Clear the lifeboats! CLEAR THE LIFE-BOATS!"

Two more lifeboats launch at the same time. I can't catch both of them. I change the helmet HUD to paint the navigational deflector mounts. A blue stain bulges from the hull ten meters ahead of me. I pull out the heaviest multi-tool from my belt and start toward it.

The deflector mount is sturdier than I anticipated. It takes a good half dozen whacks with my multi-tool to smash the laser emitter. I don't need to destroy it completely; I just need to stop it from firing.

Another lifeboat launches and explodes while I run toward the next deflector mount. I'll never get to them all in time. But I have to do some-thing.

I can hear people shouting and crying in the background as reports come in. Jemison must have patched in the common security channel. The voices overlap, and the numbers become meaningless after a while.

"Deck ten, section one. All passengers cleared—"

"Deck nine, section ten. Forty passengers cleared. Eight lost—"

"Deck five, section four. All passengers cleared. If you can block the lifeboat doors, they won't launch!"

"Deck two, section twelve. All passengers cleared. Three injuries—"

I don't know how long it takes to account for all the passengers. The lifeboats never stop launching, with or without people in them.

"All stations checked in," Jemison says.

I trudge toward another deflector. This multi-tool is heavy. These boots are heavy. I'm tired and angry.

"How many?" Santamaria asks.

"Ninety-three passengers unaccounted for," says Jemison.

Another lifeboat explodes. The deflector is already disabled, but I keep hammering at it until the multi-tool breaks in half. I think I'm screaming again.

"That's our last lifeboat," Logan says quietly.

The shattered multi-tool drifts out of my hands. I only smashed up four deflectors. I didn't even slow them down.

"Rogers, this is the captain," Santamaria says.

I spit out another curse, then turn on my microphone. "I'm here."

"Get back to the Echo Delta," he says, "and send that SOS."

Jemison meets me at the airlock. I'm a sweaty mess. She takes my helmet while I strip off the rest of the spacesuit. If she notices me slamming things around with more force than necessary, she doesn't say anything.

"Control link with the Echo Delta is good," she says. "Erica's working on contacting Mars now. Were you able to—"

"Odyssey Base is scrambling an X-4 transport," I say, yanking off my boots. "Twelve spacemen and a plasma beam cannon. ETA ten hours."

"That should do it," Jemison says. A PBC is serious artillery. It'll cut through the containment bulkhead in less than a minute. And the Outer Space Service's Expeditionary Forces, nicknamed "X-4s," are well known as the toughest bastards in the entire Solar System.

She hands me a crew jumpsuit to change into, then updates me on the situation as we make our way back to the briefing room.

Dr. Sawhney is treating the various injuries suffered while passengers scrambled to get out of their lifeboats. Logan and the rest of the crew are doing their best to keep the passengers under control. I don't envy them that job. There are four thousand civilians on this ship, confused and scared, and we don't have any good answers for them.

I know how frustrating it is to feel helpless.

Captain Santamaria and Commander Galbraith are in the briefing room, waiting for Chief Jemison and me. I repeat my report to them. The radio button on Jemison's collar buzzes, and she answers it.

"Chief, Blevins. We've rounded up twenty engineers and mechanics from the passengers. Logan's cleared their background checks. We're pulling together equipment now. We should be able to get to all the turrets at once. ETC is two hours."

"Thank you, Blevins. Carry on." She closes the channel.

"You're disabling the navigational deflectors," I say. "You don't need fully qualified personnel because you just want to break the equipment."

"As you demonstrated earlier," Santamaria says.

"We don't know what Wachlin did to the NAVDEF system," Jemison says. "The only way we can be sure of disabling those lasers is by cutting their power."

"You want to make sure the X-4 transport can dock with us when it gets here," I say.

"Not just that," Santamaria says. "Odyssey Base also relayed a message from Mars Orbital Authority."

"They're sending six remote-controlled tugs to meet us," Galbraith says.

"Right," I say. "We can't use *Dejah Thoris*'s engines, so you're borrowing someone else's." Tugboat drones are used at most outer space facilities, to help guide large spacecraft that may lack fine maneuvering thrusters.

Galbraith nods. "The tugs aren't big enough to slow us down, but they can thrust from the side and push us off course. Just enough so that we miss colliding with Mars."

"When do the tugs get here?"

Santamaria looks at the clock on the wall. "Five hours. That gives us time to lock them down before the X-4s arrive."

We might actually be able to thwart this hijacking. Sakraida may have devised an elaborate scheme with multiple contingencies, but we have people and resources with which to improvise. Alan Wachlin is cut off now, completely on his own. He can't be smarter than all of us combined. Can he?

"The bad guys must have considered a lot of these scenarios already," I say. "Wachlin's got to be anticipating that we'll try some of these things, and he must have some countermeasures prepared."

Santamaria nods. "Wachlin's isolated. His handler's dead, and he has to guard a hostage plus watch every engineering control station—"

"If he still has a hostage," Jemison says.

"My point is, he's already off-balance," Santamaria says. "We just need to rattle him. Get him to make a mistake we can exploit."

"Is that wise?" Galbraith asks. "Chief Gavilán could still be alive. If whatever we try doesn't work, Wachlin might react by doing something rash."

"The hijacker is executing a plan," Santamaria says. "He's not acting on impulse."

"But you're talking about making him emotional," Galbraith says.

She and the captain continue talking at each other. It's not quite an argument, and I know how it'll end: Santamaria will either convince Galbraith he's right, or order her to stand down. I tune them out and stare at the countdown clocks on the tabletop display.

How do we make Wachlin uncomfortable? How do we distract him from whatever he's doing? Especially if he's doing it to Ellie?

The agency teaches us some standard tactics for "disturbing" an enclosed space. Bad smells are a good way to get people to leave a room without arousing too much suspicion. Spiking the temperature is also effective. The problem is, we can't get into this particular room to do any of these things.

Or can we?

"Excuse me," I say, then wait for Santamaria and Galbraith to stop talking and ignore their dirty looks. "How thick is that containment bulkhead? The one in front of main engineering?"

"Meter and a half," Jemison says. "Titanium alloy. I thought you didn't have any heavy cutting tools."

"I don't."

But I have opened the pocket on the other side of a crowded plaza, nearly ten meters away. And I didn't need line-of-sight to the portal. I estimated the distance from where I was standing to where I saw a grenade land, and I was able to suck it into the pocket before it exploded and killed dozens of people.

Let's hope my estimating skills are still that good.

"I have another idea," I say.

CHAPTER THIRTY-SIX

Dejah Thoris—Deck 20, engineering section
20 hours until we either hit Mars or celebrate not dying horribly

Even if I didn't have second-degree burns throughout my left shoulder, it would be very uncomfortable in this maintenance crawlway.

The circular shaft is barely big enough for me to fit inside to begin with, but I also need to move carefully to avoid dislodging the equipment I'm wearing. There's a lot of shielding here around the ionwell, making wireless communication unreliable, so I have an audio pack strapped to the work belt around my crew coveralls. Power and data lines from that pack are wrapped around a spacewalk cable leading back down the shaft to the hatch where I entered. If I run into trouble—or when I finish this job, whichever comes first—Jemison and her security detail will drag me out backward. That's something to look forward to.

"It's a good thing I'm not claustrophobic," I say out loud.

"Problem, Rogers?" Jemison's voice buzzes in my left ear, coming through the wired earpiece stuck there.

"I'm hot, sweaty, and I need to use the bathroom." The throat-mic band is also very itchy.

"Didn't I tell you to go before you left?"

"But you didn't *make* me go," I say. "So this is clearly your fault. I'm at section one alfa now."

"Just a few more meters," Jemison says. "You can file a complaint when you get back."

The crawlway ends abruptly at the emergency bulkhead, which closed when Wachlin took over main engineering. I swivel my head, moving the spot of light cast by the lamp strapped to my forehead. There are no markings on the slab of titanium alloy, but according to the directions Jemison gave me earlier and the location codes etched into the metal walls, this is the right place.

"I'm at the bulkhead," I say. "Seal is intact all the way around."

We spent nearly an hour working this out and practicing before I started my tunnel-rat impersonation. I don't need to close my eyes, but I do it anyway. Looking won't help me.

The bulkhead is a hundred and fifty centimeters thick. I press my head up against it, visualize a black-and-red roulette wheel, and open the pocket two meters away from myself—I hope. I make the portal about the size of my palm, no barrier.

"The pocket is open," I say.

There's nothing keeping the air in the engineering section from rushing through to the pocket universe. The emergency bulkheads also sealed the ventilation system, so main engineering has been recirculating its air supply. With at most two people breathing in there, it would take several days for the oxygen content to become too low for life support.

A ten-centimeter-wide hole into hard vacuum, on the other hand, will evacuate all the atmosphere in about two and a half minutes.

I put a countdown timer in my left eye HUD to distract myself from the dry-mouthed tension I'm feeling. There's a small chance that Alan Wachlin will look up at this corner of the engine room and see a wavy, disk-shaped mirror floating in mid-air, but even if he does, he can't do anything to stop me.

According to Jemison, a life support alarm will automatically sound when the passive sensors in main engineering detect less than twenty percent oxygen in the air, or atmospheric pressure below nine hundred millibars. We're hoping Wachlin won't know what the hell those lights and sounds mean at first, and will waste precious time panicking while Ellie—who will know exactly how long she has before she can't breathe— can get free of whatever restraints he's got her in and get to an emergency breather first.

I imagine what will happen to Wachlin when all the air vanishes from his locked room. If he holds his breath, his lungs will explode from the pressure differential. Meanwhile, his mucus membranes and most exposed capillaries will also burst. He'll be bleeding from his eyes and ears and nose and mouth before hypoxia renders him unconscious, fifteen seconds later. He'll have suffocated by the time the X-4s arrive and cut through the bulkhead.

I don't feel bad about any of that.

The timer in my HUD flashes. "Two minutes, thirty seconds," I say. "Air's gone."

"Copy that," says Jemison.

I wait a few more seconds, just to be sure, then close the pocket and prepare to open it again on my side of the bulkhead. Now comes the tricky part.

Let's see what you're up to, asshole.

One of my emergency gadgets is an omnidirectional spy camera, designed and built by Oliver. It looks like a casino betting chip, but hidden in its edge are multiple lenses feeding into an imaging array. Activate it by squeezing, then flip it up in the air like a coin. Accelerometers inside detect the spinning motion and turn on the cameras, capturing still images from all angles as the chip turns in midair. Catch it when it comes down, and you've got a panoramic, bird's-eye view of your surroundings.

Doing this completely blind, and in zero-gravity, will be a little different.

I think of a poker hand—five very specific playing cards—then open the pocket and push my hand through the barrier to grab the camera chip. I squeeze to turn it on, then flick the chip away from me. I've switched my left eye to EM sensing, so I can see when the cameras activate. I watch the chip tumble away for a second, check its speed, and then close the pocket.

Now I'm going to open the portal rotated around the chip and on the other side of the bulkhead, inside main engineering. The compartment should be airless now, so I can open the pocket without the barrier and not worry about the chip getting sucked back into the portal. Throw it in the front door, let it fly out the back door.

The trick will be making sure the portal is far enough from the bulkhead to give the camera chip a good view of the compartment when it comes sailing out to do its reconnaissance, and making the portal big enough to catch the chip after it bounces off the bulkhead at some random angle. I can control how I use the pocket, but it's not like I can dial in specific numbers. I just have to guess at what feels right.

I press my head up against the bulkhead and visualize the card backs of the same poker hand as before. Then I open the pocket, rotated, on the other side of the bulkhead. I count to ten with my fingers crossed and close the pocket again.

"Mission accomplished," I say. "Ready to—"

Something clangs behind me. The vibration ripples up the shaft on the left side of my body. I press myself against the opposite side of the shaft and tuck my chin down so I can look back along the crawlway.

The circle of light from my headlamp flashes across what looks like crumpled, dark blue cloth. The noise changes to a scraping, shuffling sound. I tilt the headlamp to the side and see a face—smeared with something dark, but still recognizable. I can't believe it.

"Ellie?"

She blinks and squints at me. "Evan?"

"Say again, Rogers," Jemison says in my ear. "It sounded like you said—"

"Ellie's here! Chief Engineer Gavilán! She's here in the crawlway!" I move the lamp so it's not shining directly in her face and shimmy backward toward her, stopping when my feet reach the junction she emerged from. "How did you escape? What did—"

She shakes her head. I realize the smudges on her face are dried blood. "Not now. You're on comms with Andie?"

"Yeah, but—"

"The hijacker is Alan Wachlin. He's not dead."

"We know," I say.

Ellie blinks. "He's overwriting our system software. Tell my guys to kill the network and run a full diagnostic on rack ten in the computer core."

I repeat her instructions to Jemison. "They're on it. Are you okay?"

"I'll be fine." Ellie frowns. "What the hell are you doing in here? No, tell me later. We need to move."

"It's okay." I'm almost close enough to touch her. "I just sucked all the atmosphere out of engineering. Wachlin's suffocating even as we—"

Ellie grabs one sleeve of my jumpsuit. "You *what?*"

I smile. "I took away his air."

I hear a high-pitched humming noise.

Ellie says, "Oh, shit."

My entire body seizes with pain, and then the world goes black.

I wake up zipped into a Sickbay bed. Jemison is on my left, tapping at a tablet. Fritz Fisher is on my right. I don't recognize the patients in the other beds, but they look like a mixture of passengers and crew, most with minor scrapes and bruises.

"What happened?" I ask. My mouth feels like it's been wicked dry by cotton balls and then scraped out with steel wool. "Where's Ellie?"

"We don't know," Jemison says.

I'm not sure I heard her right. "What do you mean, you don't know? She was right in front of me. I *talked* to her." *She touched me.*

"Calm down." Jemison stares at me. "Was she hurt?"

"There was—" My mission recorder's been going since the hijacking, but I don't want to review the vid right now. "There was blood on her face. Dried blood. I don't know if it was hers."

She was alive. She was alive*! Did I just get her killed? But we didn't know, I couldn't possibly have known—*

"Did she say anything else?" Jemison asks. "Other than what you relayed on comms?"

My head is pounding. "She said shit."

"Don't be an asshole."

"No, she literally said the word 'shit,'" I explain. "I told her we'd sucked all the air out of engineering, which should have been good news, right? But she said, 'Oh, shit.' Then I blacked out. What happened?"

"The crawlway walls double as electromagnets," Fritz says. "We can electrify them to clean out any loose metal debris or stray equipment."

"Wachlin figured out how to turn on the power and keep it on," Jemison says.

That would explain why I feel like I've been hit by a personnel stunner at close range. "But you didn't find Ellie?"

"We flew a cam-bot into the crawlway," Fritz says. There's an edge on his voice. "There was no sign of anyone else."

"I didn't imagine her."

"I'm just telling you what we found," Fritz snaps.

"We need to know what Wachlin's doing in Main Eng." Jemison pulls the privacy screen around my bed, with herself and Fritz inside. I suddenly realize they're both floating. We're in zero-gee again. "Let's see those pictures, Rogers."

"We're not accelerating anymore?" I ask.

"The hijacker finished his course change," Fritz says bitterly. "If we can't alter our trajectory, we'll hit Mars in just over eighteen hours."

"Pictures," Jemison says. "Now."

I look at Fritz. "I'm doing this with him watching?"

"What, are you shy or something?" Fritz barks.

"The captain briefed Fisher. He knows about your wormhole device," Jemison says. That's right, even the pocket has a cover story. Welcome to the agency. "We need those images."

I nod and focus. I have to use the barrier so I don't suck all the air out of Sickbay. Five playing cards. The pocket opens. Here's hoping I got all the variables right earlier.

I push my hand through the barrier. I don't feel anything at first, and I move my hand around slowly. Something touches my palm. I close my fist around it, then pull out my hand before it starts freezing. I close the pocket and realize I'm holding my breath.

"You got it?" Jemison asks.

I open my hand and see the camera chip. I exhale as Jemison plucks the chip off my palm and plugs it into her tablet.

"That's . . ." Fritz gapes at me. "How long have we had this tech?"

"It's classified," I say. It's not a lie. "The captain did make it clear how absolutely secret this is, right?"

Fritz makes a face. "Military intelligence. Right."

"We keep secrets for a reason."

"Doesn't mean they're good reasons."

"Both of you, shut up," Jemison says. "Look at this."

She turns her tablet toward us. The auto-composited image is dark and grainy, but it clearly shows a bulky figure standing next to a control station.

"He's wearing a pressure suit," Fritz says. "A goddamn pressure suit!"

"But—" I shake my head. "It takes at least ten minutes to put one of those things on by yourself."

"He was prepared for the worst," Jemison says. "He didn't know if we could tamper with his life support, but he didn't want to be caught off guard."

"Then you removed the oxygen," Fritz glares at both of us. "Chief Gavilán was still alive. The alarms went off, and the hijacker looked for her, but she wasn't there."

Jemison glares back at Fritz. "We couldn't have known that."

"We screwed up her escape," Fritz says. "You realize that, right? She might have made it out if we hadn't—"

"I'm not going to play this game," Jemison snaps. "We can only work with what we know."

"Fine. Let's review what we know." Fritz holds up a fist and extends his index finger. "We know the fucker's in a pressure suit." He extends another finger. "We know Ellie's not in the crawlway anymore." Three fingers. "We know that suit he's wearing is insulated against electricity."

He's wearing a silver ring on one of his fingers. Why does it look familiar?

"If Wachlin dragged Ellie back into Main Eng, she's already suffocated," Jemison says. "It's been two hours. No air, remember?"

"He could have put a breather mask on her," Fritz says, "or shoved her into a rescue bubble—"

"I'm getting tired of repeating myself. We only work with what we know."

"Everything he's done so far indicates he wants to keep her alive!"

"We do. Not. Negotiate!"

All this shouting is unproductive. And it's making my headache worse.

"Can't we can get another look inside engineering?" I ask. "If you put me in a spacesuit—"

"Not feasible," Jemison says.

"But you said the suits are insulated."

Jemison looks at Fritz. "You want to tell him?"

Fritz folds his arms across his chest. "The hijacker electrified every crawlway connecting to Main Eng. The shortest path is twenty meters long. Our suits aren't rated against that much contact with bare conductors." He finally turns to look at me. "You'd get zapped long before you got close enough to do your wormhole stunt."

"There's no way to cut the power?" I ask.

"That entire section is powered directly by the ionwell," Fritz says. "And we can't shut down the reactor from out here."

"So what do we try next?" I look from one scowling face to the other. "You guys did spend the last two hours coming up with a new plan, right?"

"We wait," Jemison says.

I'm confused for a moment. Then I blink my left eye HUD over to a clock.

"The tugs," I say.

Jemison nods. "NAVDEF is offline now. We've still got time to move the ship."

There's not much I can do to help with this part. One of the pilots on the crew will take control of the remote-controlled tugs and dock them with *Dejah Thoris.* Then, when they've been secured, the pilot will engage the tugs' rocket engines at maximum burn, pushing the massive cruise ship off course just enough to miss crashing into the planet. And once we're in Mars-controlled space, we'll be able to get more assistance from other vessels.

"No," Fritz says suddenly. "Oh, no."

I look around. Jemison also seems confused. "Now what?"

"We're rotating," Fritz says, looking at his wristband. "The ship is rotating."

"Why would Wachlin want to rotate the ship?" I ask.

"He's going to fire the engines."

"But you said—"

"The tugs," Fritz says. "He's going to fire them at the tugs."

Jemison curses like a sailor, yanks the privacy screen back, and tears out of Sickbay. Dr. Sawhney stops examining another patient and gives Fritz and me a curious look.

"What's going on?" Sawhney says.

"I need to get to the briefing room," I say, unzipping myself from the bed.

"I cannot allow that," Sawhney says, moving over to my bed. "You are still recovering from your injuries."

I give him what I hope is a threatening look. "Doctor, if we don't figure out how to take back this ship, nobody is going to recover from their injuries."

Fritz reluctantly helps me out of Sickbay and into the nearest elevator. He presses the button for the briefing room.

I suddenly realize where I've seen his ring before. Silver, segmented, inscribed with starbursts. It's the same one Xiao was wearing. It's their wedding band.

Fritz Fisher's husband is dead.

We ride in uncomfortable silence for a few seconds. Fritz's breathing is ragged. He's distracted, not thinking clearly. I know the feeling. But I need him to get past it. Everyone on this ship and in Mars Capital City needs his help.

"You can feel the ship moving?" I ask.

"Inertia," Fritz says, staring at the wall. "The hijacker's pulsing the RCS thrusters, changing the orientation of the ship. We're floating inside it, so we can feel it."

"*You* can feel it," I correct. "That's got to be a pretty subtle motion. And what's RCS?"

"Reaction Control System. Maneuvering jets."

He's definitely distracted. I need him to pay attention. I need him to focus. He can't think right now because he's using all that mental energy to hold back his rage. I need him to blow off some steam.

And so help me, I think I need to talk about this, too.

"I'm sorry about Xiao," I say.

Fritz continues staring at the display above the elevator door.

"Your husband was a hero," I continue. "He gave his life while performing his duty. I don't know if you've seen the security vid, but I think you should be proud of how Xiao protected everyone—"

Fritz launches himself off the other side of the elevator and pins me to the wall, one hand on the railing, his other arm against my neck.

"Ow," I say.

"His name is *Xiao,*" he says. I still can't hear the difference.

"Fritz—"

"Shut up," he says, spitting saliva in my face. "I don't care what you think."

I hate it when people spit in my face.

I work my arm inside his reach, push his elbow away from my neck, and slap his face as hard as I can. Fritz screams and hammers his fist against the wall. I take advantage of his backward momentum, turning him to face the wall and pinning him there. His screams turn to sobs after a few seconds.

"Feel better?" I ask after he quiets down.

"I'll live."

He struggles out of my grip. I let him go. At least he's not crying anymore. That might even have been a joke just now.

"How did you know?" he asks, wiping wetness from his eyelashes.

"Your wedding rings." I point at his hand.

A smile flutters across Fritz's reddened face. "He insisted we get matching rings. Everything fair and equal, that was his thing."

"He was a hero," I repeat.

"I didn't want him to be a hero," Fritz says. "I wanted him to stay alive."

"I'm sorry," I say. "But he's gone. We have to help the thousands of other people on this ship who are still alive—"

"I'm not blinded by grief," Fritz snaps. "But I *am* sick of everyone assuming Chief Gavilán is dead. She's not helpless."

"She's an engineer, not a soldier." And as much as I want to believe that Ellie's a match for Alan Wachlin—

"Eleanor Gavilán is still alive," Fritz says. "Because if she's not, then my husband died for nothing. And I won't believe that."

His red eyes look more angry than mournful now. I know how he feels. I've known too many heroes.

"Okay. She's still alive." I swallow the lump in my throat. "But best case, she's in a rescue bubble, which means she's trapped and can't do anything. She's counting on us now. She's counting on *you*. So tell me. What does she want you to do?"

Fritz glowers at me for another second, then blinks and looks at the wall. "She wants us to save the ship."

"Okay."

"And punish Xiao's murderer."

"Sure."

"I mean it." Fritz turns back to me. "Like the wrath of God."

I should discourage him from feeling vengeful. But if I've learned one thing from dealing with people, it's that vengeance can be a powerful motivator. Maybe not the best way to live your life, long-term, but I don't care if Fritz needs therapy next year. I want him to have the chance to worry about that later.

And *I* want to hurt Wachlin too.

"Good," I say. "Let's go smite this motherfucker."

CHAPTER THIRTY-SEVEN

Dejah Thoris—Deck B, officers' briefing room
18 hours until we might die and take half of Mars with us

The briefing room is as bright as ever, with the flat lighting common to always-on command centers everywhere. But the faces around the table—Santamaria, Jemison, Galbraith, Logan, and Fisher—are dark. We've now tried three different ways to foil Wachlin's plan, and been defeated all three times.

Galbraith plays back exterior camera vid alongside recorded radar displays. On the vid, a few faint points of light—maybe stars, more likely asteroids—streak by as the ship rotates, putting the approaching tugs directly behind the main engines.

The image ripples as the engines flare, lighting up the entire screen with a two-kilometer-long tail of white plasma. At the same time, the three nearest blips on the radar display disappear. The other blips veer off, but the ship rotates again, turning its pillar of flame to follow. Only one blip escapes.

Red lights, trilling noises, and we lose gravity again. I grab the conference table and brace myself for acceleration to resume, then stop when I notice nobody else doing the same.

"Why isn't he turning the engines back on?" I ask.

Galbraith gestures at the tactical display on the tabletop. "We're already at speed and trajectory. It's pure ballistic flight now."

"And if we have to chaperone passengers in zero-gee, we have fewer resources to do anything else," Logan says.

"I've moved the last tug out of range," Galbraith says. "It's on a parallel course, but we can't get it close enough for docking."

"Unless we can knock out both RCS and radar systems," Jemison says, "the X-4s don't have a chance either."

"We can disable the main avionics package at the top of the ship," Galbraith says, bringing up a schematic of *Dejah Thoris,* "but there's a backup rig in engineering that we can't get to. And the RCS mounts are hardwired to nav controls. We can send people out there in pressure suits, but there's no way we can disable all of them in six hours."

"What? It only took two hours to disable the navigational deflectors," I say.

"The NAVDEF lasers run on internal power," Galbraith says. "We just had to cut the lines inside the ship. The RCS pods are external, and each one has its own onboard computer and fuel supply. And they're all over the ship." She lights up the schematic with a constellation of red dots. "It takes a lot of thrust to turn this much mass."

All I can think to say is, "Shit."

"In six hours we'll be out of position for course correction," Galbraith says.

"So how many of these pods do we need to disable?" I ask.

"That's not feasible," Fritz says. "The RCS system can function with up to eighty percent of the pods offline."

"What about all those passengers you recruited?" I ask. "Didn't you have a whole bunch of civilian engineers taking out the deflectors?"

"Not enough pressure suits," Logan says. "We can't get the coverage we need in time."

"Even with service robots helping?" I ask.

"Serv-bots are offline," Galbraith says.

"What? Why?"

"We found a computer virus," Fritz says. "When we ran the core diagnostic. He was trying to reprogram our robots."

"Just like he did with NAVDEF," Jemison grumbles.

"And the lifeboat launch systems," Logan adds.

"We don't know how many bots were affected," Galbraith says. "We shut down all of them to be safe."

"What was he reprogramming the robots to do?"

Galbraith frowns. "We didn't really want to wait and find out."

"We need to disable the drive rockets," Fritz says. "He's using them as a giant plasma cannon. No ships can approach us without getting fried. If we can't get nav control back, we need to take those rockets offline."

"Agreed. Options?" Santamaria asks.

"The X-4s will have a fighter escort," Jemison says. "They can fire a missile into the main engines."

"Wait a minute," Fritz says. "I said 'disable,' not *destroy*—"

"Just one Fox," Jemison says to Santamaria, ignoring Fritz. "The blast will shove the ionwell up into the ship. That should crack the shielding."

"And it might also break open fuel lines or plasma conduits," Fritz says. "The explosion could compromise the superstructure and tear the ship in half."

"These guys know how to aim," Jemison says to Fritz.

"That's not the point, Chief." Maybe my pep talk in the elevator worked a little too well. Fritz looks like he's ready to ask Jemison to take this outside. "A detonation that close to the reactor will have unpredictable results. We can't risk it."

"Twenty million people on Mars are going to die if we don't," Jemison says.

"Stress fractures from an explosion could cause the ship to shear into pieces," Fritz says. "Then you're looking at *multiple* planet-killing objects."

"You're exaggerating the danger—"

"Hey, who's the fucking engineer here?"

"That's enough, both of you," Santamaria says loudly. "We have over six thousand souls on board. No missiles."

Jemison grumbles. "Yes, sir."

"Erica. Can we use that one remaining tug?" Santamaria asks, turning to Galbraith. "As a kinetic projectile. No detonation, just impact."

"Not enough energy," Galbraith says, changing the tabletop to a navigation display showing *Dejah Thoris* and the tug on parallel courses. "We'd have to send it away, then accelerate it back toward the ship. It won't have enough momentum when it hits to make it through the outer hull and the ionwell shielding. Plus, Wachlin's going to see it coming. He can still move the ship out of the way."

Move out of the way.

I remember Oliver yelling that phrase at me, right before a weighted projectile came sailing out of the pocket and hit me square in the chest. I was wearing a spacesuit at the time, but it still hurt like hell.

Move out of the way.

We were at Science Division, working on the rotation problem. Because the portal is locked to my physical location in space, I can't actually get away from it. The portal always stays where I open it, relative to my body, and I can only open it facing toward me.

But I can choose where to position the portal. I can make it pretty big. And it doesn't always have to be right in front of me.

Move out of the way.

Boy, is this a bad idea. But we seem to have run out of the good ones.

"Captain," I say, "could I have a word in private?"

"If this is about the wormhole device, Mr. Rogers," Santamaria says, "you can speak freely. I've briefed everyone here on that tech."

I blink at him for a moment. I guess his conversation with Paul covered many topics.

"What if you don't have to turn the tug?" I ask.

"I don't understand," Galbraith says.

"What if you had enough empty space to burn it all the way until impact?" I draw a circle on the display next to the tug, then an arrow pointing from the tug into the circle. "I open the wormhole and you pilot the tug through the portal. We let it accelerate for a few hours on the far side. Then I open the wormhole again, rotated around the tug, one hundred and eighty degrees." I draw a second circle with an arrow coming out of it, pointed toward *Dejah Thoris*. "The portal will be locked to the tug's position, but not its velocity. It'll come flying out again at high speed. Wachlin will never see it coming."

Her face lights up. "Maybe." She taps her keyboard, making numbers and trajectory lines dance across the tabletop. "Yes! That should work."

Understanding ripples through the faces around the table. It feels good to be able to provide some hope.

"Where does the wormhole lead to?" Galbraith asks.

"Interstellar space," I reply. "Light-years out. Plenty of runway."

"But where, exactly? I'm just curious—"

"That's classified."

"Wait," Jemison says. "I thought you couldn't open the wormhole facing away from you."

"I can't," I say.

"So when you open it that second time, the tug's going to be coming straight toward you at an extremely high velocity."

"That's the idea."

"How are you going to get out of the way?"

I stare at the radar map. "I'm working on that part. Might need a little help."

Captain Santamaria contacts the X-4 transport and explains the plan. They agree that it's the craziest thing they've ever heard, but they have no problems taking orders from Santamaria after he shows them the "1MB" tattoo on his right forearm.

Galbraith can't get me into a spacesuit quickly enough. I tell her I'll meet her in a minute and pull Jemison aside.

"No," Jemison says.

"You don't even know what I'm going to ask you," I say.

"Whatever it is, I'm sure it's ridiculous and unreasonable."

I open the pocket and pull out the therm-pack containing the duffel bag. Her eyes go wide when I unzip the bag and hand her the bottle of Red Wine.

"Please tell me you did not steal that," she says.

I'm flattered that she thinks I could. "Of course not. I paid for it."

"And how did you—never mind, I don't want to know."

"The nanobots are in here," I say, pointing to the bottle. "You need to get everyone who was exposed to the PECC radiation from the Wachlins' stateroom to drink this."

Jemison gapes at me. "You realize we'll all probably be dead soon, right? That it's not going to matter whether or not any of us will have increased risk for bone cancer?"

"Fuck that," I say. "We're going to save this ship. And you're going to have grandchildren."

She grimaces at the bottle. "I hate kids."

"The universe loves irony."

Jemison holds out a hand. I give her the duffel bag. She starts putting the bottle away, then stops, pulls out the cork, and puts it up to her lips and tilts back her head for a swig.

I blink my eye into sensor mode and watch as nanobots enter her bloodstream, outlining her limbs in a green glow.

"Thanks, Chief," I say.

"Did you get Ellie to drink this stuff?" she asks, not looking at me.

"Yeah. At dinner last night." The memory seems like it's from a different lifetime.

"Did *she* like it?"

I start laughing, then stop myself before it turns into something else. "She hated it."

"I'll get it done," Jemison says. "You get the hell out of here."

"I'll miss you, too."

"Save this ship." She puts the cork back in the Red Wine and shoves the bottle into the bag. "Then I'll buy you a real drink."

CHAPTER THIRTY-EIGHT

Dejah Thoris—Deck A, maintenance airlock
Approximately 10 minutes before I disembark

Galbraith and I wait in the airlock at the top of *Dejah Thoris* while Jemison sends a team to disable the avionics package. They're going to create a small blind spot in radar coverage that I can slip through. Nobody wants me to get fried by the engines. I can't die for at least another four hours.

It's a simple scheme, in theory: I jump off *Dejah Thoris* into open space. The X-4 transport picks me up. I open the pocket, and the tug flies inside at full burn. I close the pocket and wait. Three hours later, I open the pocket again, rotated, aimed at *Dejah Thoris,* and the tug comes screaming out to smash the ionwell before Wachlin can react. The X-4s board the ship and take down Wachlin, and other spacecraft push *Dejah Thoris* off its collision course.

Simple in theory, but a thousand different things can go wrong in practice.

Galbraith's voice crackles over my spacesuit radio. "Rogers, you are go for EVA."

Extra-vehicular activity. That's one hell of an euphemism for what I'm about to do.

"Copy that," I reply. "Let's do it."

"Good luck," Galbraith says.

"Oorah," I reply. She gives me a funny look, steps out of the airlock, and closes the inner door.

Atmosphere hisses out of the compartment, and then all I can hear are the sounds inside my spacesuit: my own breathing, the rustle of fabric as

I push open the outer door, the muffled clanging of my boots against the hull.

I'm wearing a jetpack this time, which makes it harder to move. I make my way to the top of the ship. I want to stay in the radar blind spot for as long as possible when I kick off.

"I'm in position," I say when I reach the nose of the spacecraft. I already feel like I'm in open space. I can only see the ship if I look down.

"You're all clear," says Galbraith. "Go when ready."

I bend my knees, turn off the magnets in my boots, and straighten my legs as hard and fast as I can. My muscles are still sore from my electrifying experience in the crawlway, and I'm sure I make a pathetic grunt.

I sail away from the ship. I look down and watch it fall away. It's only relative motion; I'm still hurtling toward Mars, that reddish speck in the distance, but it feels like I'm moving awfully fast in the other direction.

My shadow slides across the hull. That doesn't seem right.

"He's turning the ship!" Galbraith yells.

"That wasn't much of a blind spot!" I reply, fumbling with the jetpack controls.

"Go. Go! GO!" Galbraith says, unnecessarily.

I find the firing control and push my thumb down. "Thrusting now!"

A few short bursts of gas rotate me into position, and then the thrusters open up, pushing me up and away from *Dejah Thoris*. A timer pops up in my helmet HUD. Galbraith told me I would have fifty seconds of fuel at full burn, and that should be enough to get me out of range of the ship's engines. But we thought I'd have more time in the blind spot than—what was that? Four seconds? Five?

The countdown timer reads forty seconds. I look back and see the ship rotating, its egg shape turning, the shadows on its surface changing.

Fuck! Is there anything I can do to juice up this jetpack? If we were in atmosphere, I might try opening the pocket in front of myself and hoping that the vacuum sucks me forward—I don't even know if that would work. *Note to self: ask Oliver about it later. If you survive this.*

Fuck fuck fuck.

Thirty seconds. I'm looking down into a honeycomb of massive engine bells, glowing but not yet firing. On another day, I might marvel at the beauty of this engineering feat. Right now, I'm about to crap my pants.

"I'm looking straight into the damn engines," I say to the radio. "Am I clear yet?" I hear my voice cracking.

"Ten seconds," Galbraith says.

The white light glowing inside the engines starts expanding.

"Well, fuck," I say to no one in particular.

I'm dead. Nothing else to do. I close my eyes think about all the things I haven't had a chance to do with my life.

Well, at least I got to visit the Legendary Lands of Lore.

At least I got to meet Ellie Gavilán.

Everything around me seems to go quiet as I exhale. The blackness and silence and peace feel welcoming, as if they're telling me that I can stop worrying. Whatever happens now, it's out of my control.

Something cracks behind my head.

My eyes pop open instinctively. The noise was too dampened to have been inside my helmet. The jetpack? Maybe it's overheating or otherwise failing, from being pushed beyond its design limits.

Red text appears in the helmet HUD, covering my view of distant stars. It wasn't the jetpack—it was my life support backpack. I'm losing oxygen. Something must have struck the tank hard enough to fracture it. I could have run into a small rock or even a piece of dust. Speed kills out here.

"Debris impact," I say aloud. I'm not sure why it matters, but I'd feel remiss if I didn't report in. "I'm losing oxygen."

"You're almost clear," Galbraith says. I know she's lying, but I appreciate the effort.

My entire body lurches forward, and my nose smacks into the faceplate of my helmet. I wonder if the jetpack is malfunctioning or just running out of fuel. Then a jolt of acceleration pushes my stomach down into my crotch, and keeps pushing.

"What—the—hell—!" I can barely speak. This isn't the jetpack. Even with Fritz's modifications, it was barely putting out half a gee of thrust. What I'm feeling now is at least two gravities, maybe three.

Galbraith is yelling over the radio. I can't make out what she's saying, but she sure sounds—happy?

Below me, a dozen miniature stars flare into being as *Dejah Thoris*'s main engines ignite. A giant pillar of blue-white plasma fire surges toward me, disrupting my radio link with a burst of static. My faceplate darkens automatically to protect me from going blind, but I'm out of range. I can see that on the radar. Twenty-two hundred meters and increasing.

I'm in the dark except for the HUD readouts. Oxygen's down to eighty percent. Suit seals are intact. The thrusters cut out. More red indicators light up. Out of fuel.

But I'm alive. And according to my aching testicles, I'm still accelerating.

What the hell just happened?

"Rogers!" Galbraith shouts over the radio. Wachlin must have shut down the engines. Makes sense; he wouldn't want to push the ship too far off course. Just half a second in that fire would have vaporized me. "Rogers, are you there?"

"Still—here." I wonder if my words sound more like groans. "What—is—?" The acceleration crushes the end of my question before I can get it out.

"Hang on, Rogers," Galbraith says. "The cavalry just arrived."

It takes me a few seconds to stop hyperventilating and figure out how to override the helmet's auto-polarization filter. My faceplate clears just before the acceleration stops. I look around and spot two familiar, sharp-edged, gunmetal-gray shapes, the same ones I've seen countless times swooping over battlefields and patrolling around Earth colony outposts.

The X-4 transport and its fighter escort.

"Oorah," I say to no one in particular. I start laughing out loud. "OO-RAH!"

I wave at the two ships. The fighter dips its wings to acknowledge me, and the transport rolls until its airlock faces me. I don't think I've ever seen anything so beautiful in my whole life.

Galbraith gives me the frequency and scrambler code for the transport, and I switch over my suit radio. I'm drifting toward the boat slowly—at precisely half a meter per second, according to my suit radar. The pilot must have one hell of a good instinct for motion vectors.

I reach my arms behind my head and feel around for whatever struck my backpack and reeled me in. I'm guessing it's some kind of grappling claw. I see the cable going slack between myself and the front of the X-4 boat. Pulling on the cable until it goes taut again, I use it as a tether and rotate to put the boat below me.

"That was one hell of a stunt," says a voice over my radio.

"Speak for yourself, Colonel." I can see the detachment commander's stripes through the cockpit window. I do my best to salute him, trapped as

I am in a bulky spacesuit. "Did Chief Jemison give you the idea to harpoon me?"

He snaps back a salute and says, "No, Major. You've got friends on board."

"You can say that again."

"Spaceman Kapur will meet you out on the hull. We're going to maneuver the boat underneath you now."

"Go for it," I say.

Out of the corner of my eye, I see their thrusters firing, and the boat glides below me. It's almost dreamlike, moving in complete silence. I can see *Dejah Thoris* in the distance, what must be several kilometers away now.

Spaceman Kapur turns out to be a woman with an angular face and large, round eyes visible through her spacesuit helmet. She gathers up the cable that's been harpooned into my backpack, pulling me the rest of the way to the transport and grabbing my spacesuit when I get within arm's reach. She yanks me down hard enough to knock the wind out of me. I feel a click as she attaches a lifeline to my belt.

"Welcome aboard, sir," she says, spinning me to face her.

"Thank you, Spaceman," I say.

"If you'd like to engage your mag-boots, sir?"

"Right." I release my death grip on the jetpack controls and tap my suit wristpad, activating the boots. My feet hit the transport's hull with a thud.

While Kapur helps me detach the spent jetpack, I stare at *Dejah Thoris* in the distance. From here, it looks almost tranquil. A marvel of technology: a giant, manmade egg, carrying over six thousand souls.

And if that egg breaks against Mars, all the king's horses and all the king's men won't be able to stop the Solar System from erupting into open warfare.

Things have changed since the start of the Independence War. There are more planetary and sub-planetary colonies. Everyone's space fleets are bigger. How many simultaneous asteroid bombardments aimed at Earth would we be able to stop? How many ships could OSS commit to patrolling Jupiter's moons? How many civilians in the outback would get caught in the crossfire?

We need to stop this.

"Do you have control of the tug?" I ask Kapur.

"Yes, sir." She raises her arm and points off to her left. "Eleven hundred meters out. We'll be alongside in just a few minutes."

I switch my eye to radio sensing and find the tug's nav beacon. "I see it."

"Good eye, sir." She doesn't sound convinced.

"You know the plan?" I ask.

"Yes, sir. We were briefed on the way in. I'll deploy our canopy after the tug is in range. Do you need any assistance with the wormhole device?"

"No," I say. "My controls are implanted."

"Very well, sir."

"What's your security clearance?" I ask. I need to know which version of the "wormhole device" cover story to feed these spacemen.

"Everyone on this boat was read into TS/SCI Silver Sunflower, sir."

That's something I don't hear very often. My ability is not just Top Secret, it's "Sensitive Compartmentalized Information," and that particular code phrase means the X-4s are authorized to know everything about the pocket except the fact that it's not tech.

"May I ask something about the device, sir?" Kapur asks.

"Go ahead."

"Our briefing said there's a . . . parallel universe on the other side of the wormhole?"

"That's what they tell me."

"Is that why we built the device in the first place?" she asks. "For exploration?"

"We weren't trying to build it at all," I say. "It was an accident."

Kapur frowns. "So how do we know it's not just some distant part of this universe?"

"The cosmic background radiation on the other side is different. And there are no stars." It's nice to be able to talk about this with someone new. "As far as our scientists can tell, that universe is completely empty, except for whatever we send through the portal."

"Crazy." Something lights up in Kapur's helmet HUD. "Okay, here we go, sir." She points over my shoulder.

I turn around, and it's a good thing the mag-boots prevent me from jumping with surprise and launching myself off the hull. The tug has matched velocity with the X-4 transport and is now hovering barely a meter away from me, rockets blazing. Of course I didn't hear it approach; we're in hard vacuum. I can't feel the heat from its engines, either.

These remote mass drivers are only used in outer space, so it's not in the least bit aerodynamic. It looks like a big metal box the size of a small air-craft, with a giant shovel on the front and sensor pods bulging haphaz-ardly from every surface.

"Um, how wide across is the tug?" I ask.

"Twelve point eight five meters across the diagonal, sir," Kapur says.

This part is going to be tricky. The largest I've ever been able to open the portal is fifteen meters in diameter. And I can't open the pocket fac-ing away from me. The portal also moves and tilts with my body—my head, specifically—so I can't actually get out of the way. But I can posi-tion the portal off-center with respect to my body. I can move *it* out of the way.

When the tug is centered, it'll be just over one meter from my head. And that's where it'll come shooting out later, at about a thousand meters per second. If I can't open the pocket to the same size in a split second, the tug will take off my head, and possibly part of my torso.

Did I say this was a bad idea? I was wrong. This is probably the worst idea ever.

On the bright side, I guess that makes it a new personal record.

"Range is clear." Kapur taps her spacesuit controls. "Zeroing delta-vee and engaging stealth canopy."

The tug's rockets go dark, and the transport's hull vibrates gently as its engines stop. A metal stalk extends from the nose of the boat, and a matching stalk emerges from the stern, in between the main drive rock-ets. At the end of each stalk is a small gray ball. Once the stalks are fully extended, both balls pop open, revealing crumpled gray sheets that unfurl into two domes at the front and back of the boat.

The domes expand to sixty meters across—nearly twice the size of the transport—then stiffen and join together amidships, forming a sphere around the boat—like a drink bulb around a martini. But this ball is opaque, and it seals us inside total darkness. The lamps on our spacesuits provide just enough light for Kapur and me to see what we're doing.

"Confirm loss of signal," Kapur says. The stealth material absorbs en-ergy emissions, hiding everything inside but also cutting us off from the outside universe. "Your show, sir."

"Are we at all concerned about how this is going to look?" I ask. The canopy will conceal my use of the pocket from peeping telescopes, but everyone will see the tug when it comes crashing out again.

Kapur smiles. "If I understand correctly, sir, this tug's going to be moving faster than a speeding bullet when you deliver it. Let anyone watching think we're carrying the most compact railgun in existence." Railguns, which use electromagnetic force to accelerate metal projectiles to ridiculous speeds, generally require hundreds of meters of superconductor track. "They'll drive themselves crazy trying to figure out how it works."

I nod. "The wormhole opening is going to look like a white ring. I need you to send the tug through dead center, exactly perpendicular to the portal. Got that?" I hope the X-4 reputation for aiming very precisely is not undeserved.

"Yes, sir." Kapur taps at her wrist controls.

I think of a painted wooden shield—a reference object with two distinct sides, so I can rotate it later—then open the pocket as wide as I can and as far off-center from my body as I can. It takes more concentration than usual. A lot more.

A gaping black hole ringed by a white shimmer appears in front of me and above me, just inside the stealth canopy. I can already tell I'm going to have one hell of a headache after this.

"Kapur?" I say, staring into the pocket. I can't move my head, or the portal will move too.

"Yes, sir."

"Do you have the—ah!" I move my eyes to look up, and am startled by the sight of the tug directly above my head, even closer than before. I'm sure she's doing that on purpose.

I reiterate to Kapur the importance of having the tug centered in the "wormhole" and moving it forward exactly perpendicular to the plane of the opening. Then I stand very still while she walks around me, taking measurements with a rangefinder.

I've never held the pocket open this large or for this long before. Just as my neck starts to cramp up and my vision starts to blur, she finishes and gives me a thumbs-up.

"Good to go, sir," she says.

"Well, yes, go, then!" I say. "Now! Okay?"

"Firing tug thrusters in three, two, one, mark."

The tug glides forward into the pocket. I try not to think about how large the vehicle looks from here, or how quickly it's going to be moving when it comes out again. I can only worry about one thing at a time.

Once the tug is all the way through the portal, the main rockets light up, pushing the tug away from us at full throttle. It becomes a twinkling star in the void. I count down from thirty, to give myself some tiny margin for error later on, and close the pocket when I reach zero.

"Now we play the waiting game." I hope I'm not trembling too much. "Unless you'd rather play Hungry Hungry Hippos."

"I can check to see if that's in our database, sir."

Nobody gets my jokes.

CHAPTER THIRTY-NINE

X-4 transport, shadowing *Dejah Thoris*
25 minutes after I thought I was going to die in a fire

Kapur and I enter the boat through the dorsal airlock. Two other space-men help us out of our suits, bumping pretty much every part of my body in the process. After a week on a luxury cruise ship, it's going to be tough adjusting to these cramped quarters. Not to mention the smells. All spacecraft scrub carbon dioxide when recycling their air, but organic odors are harder to remove. And X-4s are loath to waste their precious liquid water on a luxury like showering.

Kapur leads me through the inner hatch to a narrow passageway. I'm so surprised to see a familiar face, I forget to address him by rank.

"Oliver?"

He looks like he hasn't slept for days. Come to think of it, that might very well be the case—if he was still in the office during the audit, when I spoke to Jessica, Paul would have needed to put Oliver on a high-gee military spacecraft to make this rendezvous. And it's hard to sleep when your chest feels like it's being crushed by an elephant.

"Good to see you, too, *Major*," he says, emphasizing the last word, probably to remind me that we're still under cover.

I check the stripes on his rumpled OSS uniform before responding. "Sorry, Lieutenant. I just wasn't expecting to see you here."

"We weren't expecting to be here," Oliver says.

"'We'?" Did he bring some kind of robot with him?

He shifts aside, and I nearly have a heart attack when I see Jessica standing behind him, also wearing an OSS uniform and looking exhausted. Or irritated; sometimes it's hard to tell.

She fixes me with a stare and gives her head the slightest of shakes, what seems like barely a millimeter from side to side. I get the message: *EQ doesn't know about the nanobots.*

"Commander," I say. "This is a surprise."

"Yeah. Funny story," she deadpans.

Suddenly, all the things the spacemen were saying make sense. *You've got friends on board. We were briefed.*

I actually want to give Oliver a hug.

"You saved my life," I say.

His face remains impassive. "It would appear so."

My urge to hug him disappears. "You shot a *harpoon* at me! At my *head*!"

"Just *behind* your head. And there was no danger. Your thrust vector was constant. The math was easy." He shrugs. "Besides, if it hadn't worked, you would have been unable to complain."

I make a mental note to kill him later. "Where's the radio?"

"Belay that," Jessica says. "Spacemen, clear the deck."

Kapur and the two other X-4s slide past us and out of the compartment. Jessica closes the fire door behind them.

"We're incommunicado," she says. "Lasher's orders."

I frown. "We need to talk to *Dejah Thoris.*"

"You're fine, Kay," Oliver says, "but Surgical and I have to stay off comms. Nobody else can know about us being here."

"Why not?"

"It's a security issue."

"Sakraida's in the wind," Jessica says. "We don't know how far his conspiracy extends. One lucky missile shot and the agency loses three-quarters of our department."

"Fine," I say. "I'll do the talking. Anything else you want me to not say?"

Oliver shrugs. Jessica says, "Just don't be an idiot."

"Thanks for the reminder."

Jessica and Oliver lead me up to the bridge. Colonel Brutlag welcomes me aboard, and I radio Captain Santamaria to give a status report. The X-4 transport and its escort fighter are flying on the spaceward side of the ship, so we can communicate with *Dejah Thoris* using my emergency comms dish.

According to the tactical displays here, we have just over three hours until *Dejah Thoris* passes "waypoint zero"—colorful X-4 terminology for the point of no return, beyond which no space vehicles in range can deliver enough thrust to deflect the cruise ship from her collision course. It'll take a full three hours for the tug inside the pocket to build up enough momentum to crash through the shielding around *Dejah Thoris's* reactor.

We're only going to get one chance at this. *Correction:* you're *only going to get one chance at this, Kangaroo. No pressure.*

"Very well," Santamaria says. "Thank you, Mr. Rogers."

"Any sign of Wachlin freaking out?" I ask.

"Not yet," Santamaria says. "Let's hope he thinks the spacemen picked up the tug." It's plausible—this boat is big enough to carry several smaller vehicles. All Wachlin would have seen from engineering was a radar blip disappearing.

"Has anybody come up with any more brilliant plans in case this one fails?"

"Maybe you should ask your friends over there."

Right. I'm just the blunt instrument. "Wait one." I mute my microphone and turn to Oliver. "I assume you've got something in the works?"

"We contacted Mars Orbital Authority," Oliver says. "They're evacuating all vessels from orbit and diverting incoming traffic. Four tugs, one frigate, and several cargo freighters are moving to intercept *Dejah Thoris.*"

I relay the information.

"Cargo freighters?" Santamaria says. "They pressed private spacecraft into service?"

I turn back to Oliver. He glares at me and points at the console. I mute again.

"Tell him they volunteered," he says.

I unmute and tell Santamaria.

"I won't put any more civilian lives at risk," he says. "Call them off."

"Hold on." I mute and prepare for Oliver's inevitable outburst.

"Does he understand the meaning of the word *volunteer?*" he says. "MOA ordered those freighters to evacuate. They refused. I don't think the entire US-OSS fleet could dissuade them. Or maybe the captain would like to speak to the Martians himself and explain, in his own words, why they should *not* participate in the primary effort to save their planet from mass destruction!"

"Okay, I'm going to paraphrase that," I say.

"Just wrap it up," Jessica says. "We need to talk. In private."

Really not looking forward to that. I turn back to the console without meeting her gaze.

"The freighter captains refused MOA's orders to evacuate," I say. "They're not going anywhere until they know their homeworld is safe."

After a second, Santamaria says, "Please give the Martians our thanks."

"You're going to do that in person, Captain."

"Very well."

The X-4 transport has four decks, not including the cockpit, and a sizable cargo bay. Oliver leads Jessica and me to the mess area while the X-4s prepare their part of our crazy plan to rescue an entire cruise ship and save the planet Mars.

I start to ask what happened with the audit back at the office, but Oliver puts a finger to his lips and pulls out a small, disk-shaped device. Jessica closes and locks both doors leading into the mess area while Oliver attaches the disk to one wall and fiddles with it.

I take a breath, preparing to criticize their paranoia, and my nose informs me that there are foodlike substances in the vicinity.

I don't know if it's stress, or if my constant overeating for the last week and a half has miscalibrated my body's sense of hunger, but I'm starving. I grab two packets of field rations out of a storage cabinet and scarf them down cold. When I turn back around, Jessica is holding out a bulb of red liquid.

"Electrolytes," she says. "Drink it."

I take the bulb and wash down my so-called food. A warbling, buzzing sound fills the room. It takes me a moment to recognize it as "pesticide": anti-eavesdropping masking noise. Oliver's device generates sound in irregular, unpredictable patterns, and also vibrates the surface it's touching to keep nosy neighbors from listening in.

It's unbelievably annoying.

"Is that really necessary?" I ask Oliver.

He stares at me for a moment, then says, "The *Director* of *Intelligence*."

I look at Jessica. She's pounding her fingers against a touchscreen computer tablet. "So what do we need to talk about?"

"How do you feel?" she asks.

"Fine."

"You're dehydrated. Finish drinking that bulb."

Of course. I always forget that Jessica has full remote access to my cybernetic implants. It always feels like a breach of privacy, until I remember that I don't have any privacy on the job.

"How big was that last portal?" she asks.

"Fifteen meters diameter," Oliver replies.

Jessica looks at me. "Fifteen meters is the widest you've ever opened the pocket, and the last time you did it, you fainted."

"Well, I'm fine now, as you can see. All that training must have paid off." Science Division loves to make me open and close the pocket in different simulated situations, for hours on end, while measuring my brain activity.

"You're dehydrated," Jessica repeats. She turns the tablet to show me a bunch of medical readouts. "Cortisol levels are still elevated, acetylcholine saturation is low. Drink two more bulbs of vitamin water, then go take a nap. You have less than two and a half hours to recover."

"I don't need to recover. I told you, I'm fine." I finish the red drink and stick the bulb to the nearest table.

Jessica lowers her tablet and nods. "Okay. Open the pocket."

"What?"

"Open the pocket."

I shrug. "What do you want me to take out?"

"Nothing," she says. "Just open the portal. Show me you're fully recovered."

"With or without the barrier?" I ask. I'm doing my best to stall, because I don't want to admit she's right, and I'm hoping another minute or two will make a difference.

"Open the damn pocket, Kangaroo."

I glare at her, then turn and look at the far wall. I concentrate as hard as I can on opening the pocket. Nothing happens.

"You know, that noise is really distracting," I say, pointing at Oliver's bug-killer.

Jessica nods at Oliver. He taps the disk, and the room becomes eerily quiet.

"Go on," Jessica says.

I put out a hand to focus my concentration and try again. Still nothing. I cycle through the first reference objects I can think of, attempting to pull each one: *pink elephant, blue elephant, orange elephant, white elephant . . .*

After a minute, I slam a fist against the table and curse.

Jessica opens a cooler, rummages through it, and retrieves a blue drink bulb. "Drink this one next." She pulls out a green bulb. "Then this one." She sets them on the table and removes the empty bulb.

"Is the goal here to get my tongue dyed completely black?"

"Each color indicates different vitamins and electrolytes," she says. "You need the variety to rebalance your system. And your body needs sleep to make that happen."

Might as well get this part over with. I take a big gulp of blue liquid and make a face. "I don't suppose you brought any alcohol with you."

She frowns. "No drinking on duty."

"I'm just saying, some liquid courage would make these more palatable. And a bit of the hard stuff would also help me get to sleep."

"You don't need to worry about that," Oliver says.

I've finished the blue drink and am halfway through the green one when I realize what he means. "No. Oh, no. What the hell did you—"

My muscles go slack before I can finish the sentence. Goddamn Surgical.

CHAPTER FORTY

I wake up zipped into a sleeping bag on one of the lower decks. I do feel better after my chemically induced nap, but I'm never going to admit that to Jessica.

Something pokes into my chest as I wiggle out of the sleeping bag. I unzip my jumpsuit and find an encrypted agency file tucked inside.

I instinctively hide the plastic document sheet and look around to make sure I'm alone. It's completely unnecessary—the display surface appears transparent to the naked eye, and will only be readable to someone with the right scanning implant—but it's a reflex.

Oliver and Jessica must have left it. Why didn't they just hand it to me? I blink my left eye into decryption mode, move my fingers to enter my passphrase, and wait for my implants to process the file. After a second, the agency logo appears overlaid on the sheet in my HUD, along with phantom controls for paging through the data.

I swipe over to the first page and have to read it twice to make sure I understand it.

When I get to page three, I realize I'm clutching the sheet so hard the plastic is starting to deform.

I take several deep breaths to calm myself and finish reading. Then I go to the bridge.

I find Oliver there with Colonel Brutlag and the pilot. I ask if I can have a word alone with Oliver, and wait until we're in the mess area and he's turned on his bug-killer before slamming him up against the wall.

"What the fuck!" I say, waving the file in his face.

"Lasher thought you should know," Oliver says.

"Lasher," I say, "is a deceitful, two-faced, manipulative bastard."

Oliver frowns. "And this is somehow news to you?"

"He lies to *other* people." I had resolved not to lose my shit, but I'm not sure I can hold it together. "He doesn't lie to *us*." *He doesn't lie to* me.

"You read the whole file?" Oliver asks.

"Who the fuck are you talking to? Yes!"

"Then you know he couldn't take the risk!" Oliver says. "Lasher knew there was a security breach within the agency, but he didn't know if it was a leak, a mole, or some kind of technology exploit. Not until you requested Alan Wachlin's service record. Lasher was able to pull that thread and discover Wachlin's connection to D.Int."

I feel a surge of pride. They wouldn't have discovered that without me. Score one for insubordination.

"And then military police arrived to escort Surgical and me out of the office," Oliver continues. "We realized we weren't actually in trouble when they strapped us into a high-gee US-OSS clipper, but we didn't know the whole story until we rendezvoused with the X-4s." He scowls at me. "At least you got to enjoy a seafood buffet."

It was a pretty good buffet. I shake my head. "Lasher should have trusted us."

"He *did* trust us. He just couldn't *tell* us. He didn't know who might be listening." Oliver points at the file. "He repositioned thirty-eight other operatives in addition to the three of us. And he moved everyone under nonofficial covers. That's a massive operational deployment, and he did all the paperwork himself. He must not have slept for a week."

"I could have exposed Wachlin and Bartelt sooner," I say. "I could have gone after the cargo immediately. I could have stopped them before they hijacked the ship." *I could have saved Xiao.*

I could have protected Ellie.

"You could have gotten yourself killed," Oliver says. "We couldn't prep you without raising suspicions. You would have been on your own, facing two trained killers. They would have made short work of you and anyone else who got in their way."

"You don't know that." *I could have tried.*

Oliver shakes his head. "How many contingency actions did Wachlin demonstrate after the hijacking, when you and the crew were attempting to re-take engineering? Sakraida has been planning this for years. Your biggest advantage was Bartelt and Wachlin not knowing who you were or what you could do. You had to wait until the right moment to use the pocket, for maximum effect."

"I don't know if anybody told you," I say bitterly, "but people have been dying out here."

"We didn't know what they were going to do. They could have tried to steal the ship, or destroy it, or ransom the passengers. We couldn't defend until we knew how they would attack."

I know he's right. That's the worst part. Paul's always right.

"*We* could have taken an educated guess," I say.

"Save it for the debrief," Oliver snaps. I guess he's had enough of me for once, instead of the other way around. "We still have work to do. If you're done with that?" He tugs the file out of my grip.

"Why tell us now?" I say, releasing the plastic sheet. "He must have known this was going to piss off every last one of us. Make us feel betrayed."

"I was curious about that decision as well." Oliver touches invisible controls at the corners of the document, and it shrivels up and vaporizes in a puff of acrid smoke. "Lasher said he wanted to notify everyone that they were, in fact, deployed on mission. To be ready for new orders at any time. And he wanted to remind you of your objectives and priorities."

I cough out an angry laugh. "My objective is pretty simple. Stop *Dejah Thoris* from crashing into Mars."

Oliver stares at me. "Your priority is Mars."

"What?"

"If a decision has to be made," Oliver says slowly, "it's twenty million people versus six thousand."

I didn't think I could get any angrier. I remind myself that Oliver's just the messenger. "I'm not very good at math," I say. "And I have friends on that ship."

"We will do our best to save everyone," Oliver says, "but if a decision has to be made—"

"Then I'll make it!" I bang my fist against a bulkhead and immediately regret it. Bulkheads are very solid. "It's *my* responsibility, *Lieutenant*."

Oliver exhales. "Perhaps we should stretch our legs."

We suit up and go outside on the hull. We have only an hour to rehearse what's going to happen when I open the pocket again.

I can't actually practice what I need to do. Opening the pocket with a fifteen-meter aperture takes a lot out of me. We just have to hope, based on my vital signs, that my body's had enough time to recover. All we can do is measure things, rig tethers, and talk through the steps until I'm sick of hearing them.

Colonel Brutlag gives us an update at one hour from waypoint zero. If this plan doesn't work, Mars Orbital Authority is prepared to use their planetary defense platforms to cut *Dejah Thoris* to pieces. There's no guarantee they can carve the ship into small enough sections to significantly reduce Martian casualties, but there would at least be a chance.

Spending six thousand lives to save twenty million.

Fuck that. I'm going to save everyone.

Or die trying.

Oliver calls for Kapur and two other spacemen to secure the cables attaching me to the transport's hull. It feels like forever while they check, double-check, and triple-check the rigging.

"Ready," Kapur calls, finally.

"I'm detaching myself from the hull," I say, disengaging my boots.

The transport has maneuvered into position for the delivery. *Dejah Thoris* is behind me, five kilometers away, looking like a toy. Our fighter escort has moved behind the transport, out of the line of fire. Past the fighter, I see dozens of other shapes. I blink my eye into radio mode and see the colorful pulses of spacecraft nav beacons—civilian, merchant, and military. All Martians. Ready to push *Dejah Thoris* as soon as we disable her engines.

The spacemen have set up a ring of marker buoys next to the X-4 transport, and Oliver has aimed it at *Dejah Thoris*. The ring is fifteen meters across. That's my target.

I reach the end of my tether, one meter short of hitting the ring, and stop with a jerk. I take a deep breath. One meter is not much margin for error, but I don't know if I can place the pocket any farther off-center from my body. Even this is a long shot. I've only been able to do it once in the lab.

Well, I'm only going to get one chance at this. I'd better get it right.

I sip some water from the dispenser in my helmet. It probably won't do any good at this point, but it couldn't hurt. And it feels vaguely useful.

"I'm in position," I report.

The engines cut out, and the stealth canopy deploys again, putting me in darkness except for the ring of blinking buoys.

"Vitals are good," Jessica says over the radio.

"You are go to activate the wormhole device when ready," Oliver says.

"Copy that."

This wouldn't be such a bad place to end. I'll have laid down my life in the line of duty. I'll have used my unique abilities to do something nobody else could. I'll have done it to save innocent lives.

But I don't want to die here. I want to live through this.

I want to capture Alan Wachlin alive.

"Delivery in three," I say aloud.

I want to make Wachlin pay for the murders he committed.

"Two."

I want to punish Wachlin for taking Ellie Gavilán hostage.

"One."

I want to hurt Wachlin. A lot.

"Now."

I stare at the center of the target ring and visualize the unpainted side of a wooden shield. I imagine it not directly in front of me, but above me, fifteen meters wide and lined up with the ring of marker buoys. *Right there. Up there.* Away *from me. Out the back door.*

I open the pocket.

Several buoys on the closest part of the ring disappear behind the bottom edge of the portal. The event horizon flickers less than half a meter from my face.

The tug has been accelerating at full burn for three hours. It comes tearing out of the pocket at over a million meters per second. It's a good thing we're in vacuum, otherwise the sonic boom would probably kill me.

I feel a shudder as the tug punches a hole through the stealth canopy. It closes the distance to *Dejah Thoris* in the blink of an eye.

The explosion has nearly faded by the time I twist myself around to look. The ruptured canopy has detached from the transport and is spinning away, giving me a clear view of the debris cloud expanding around *Dejah Thoris's* stern.

"Delivery confirmed!" Jemison shouts over the radio. "Ionwell is off-line!"

"Nice shooting, sir," Kapur says as she reels me back in.

"Thanks," I say, not trying to disguise my shaking.

"Spacemen, help the major back inside," Jessica says. "He's having a panic attack."

I don't love that cover story, but it sells. I touch down on the hull and feel like throwing up. Kapur grabs my shoulder and steadies me.

"Something's happening," says one of the other spacemen.

"We're getting gravity," says Jemison.

That's not right. With the main engines disabled, there can't be any significant acceleration.

I blink my eye to telescopic magnification. I see maneuvering thruster pods firing all over *Dejah Thoris*, turning the ship. It starts spinning on its long axis. Then the thrusters fire in a different direction, turning it end over end. The jets keep firing, increasing the spin rate and the rotation around all three axes.

"Oh, you have got to be kidding me," I say.

I hear Jemison cursing. Then the radio goes dead.

CHAPTER FORTY-ONE

Kapur leads us back inside to the situation room behind the bridge. Colonel Brutlag and the rest of his detachment are there with Oliver and Jessica. Nobody looks happy.

Brutlag stands in front of a wall-sized tactical display. *Dejah Thoris* is spinning madly. I wonder how much torque the superstructure can take.

"She's pulling up to three gravities with every new rotation vector," Brutlag says. "Anyone who isn't puking their guts out is having a hell of a time moving around."

"It's worse than that," Jessica says. "We're talking about four thousand civilians without variable-gravity training. They're getting thrown around like rag dolls. Broken bones, concussions, lacerations—"

"How often is the rotation changing?" I ask.

"Hesch?" Brutlag yields the floor to his pilot, a lanky man with pale eyes and stubble covering the lower part of his face.

"New vector every three to five seconds," Hesch says. "I doubt anyone can keep their bearings long enough to operate any controls."

The constantly changing rotation also makes it impossible for any ship to dock with *Dejah Thoris*. And we can no longer maintain line-of-sight with the comms dish on the hull. We're completely cut off from Santamaria and his crew.

"We're mapping the pattern," Oliver says. "The changes are very fast. The hijacker must be using a computer program, which means it's only pseudo-random, and we should be able to predict it. But it will take time to gather enough data to reverse-engineer the program."

"Four thousand civilians," Jessica says, staring daggers at all of us. "The longer we wait, the more serious their injuries become. Some of those people will die."

"There is another option," Brutlag says.

"Let's hear it," I say.

"We have two plasma beam cannons on board," Brutlag explains. "Each PBC disassembles into five separate components, and each part can be carried by one spaceman. We move to within half a kilometer of *Dejah Thoris*. Our fighter escort deploys countermeasures to jam her sensors. The spacemen jump in pairs, each pair carrying two of the same component, and latch on to the hull with grappling claws.

"Every spaceman who makes it onto the hull claws his way to an airlock and enters the ship. Once inside, they assemble the weapon, blast their way into the engineering section, and take out the hijacker."

I should tell him this plan is completely insane, but after what I just did, I'm in no position to criticize.

"We're fifteen minutes from waypoint zero," I say. "Is that enough time?"

"We don't need to deflect the ship that much," Hesch says. "We can still bounce it off the atmosphere. It'll be rough, but it doubles our time margin. We do the math right and we'll barely scratch the paint."

"And if we don't do the math right?"

Hesch looks at me. His mouth is a thin, determined line. "We lose one ship to save half a planet, sir."

This is the worst headache I've ever had.

"We need to contact all the spacecraft around Mars," Oliver says. "They need to coordinate their intercepts."

"And we need medical triage facilities for four thousand people," Jessica says. "Colonel, permission to open text communication links with Mars Orbital."

"I'll get you both set up," Brutlag says. "Do the math right, Hesch."

"Yes, sir."

When I got my spaceflight certification, I spent way too much time inside a "multi-axis trainer." It simulates the wild spinning of an out-of-control spacecraft. The goal of the exercise is to keep yourself from vomiting for fifteen minutes.

It took me a full week and eight different attempts to pass that test. I'm sure vomiting is the best thing that's happening to anyone aboard *Dejah Thoris* right now.

After issuing orders to our fighter escort and setting up Oliver and Jessica with text comms to MOA, Colonel Brutlag escorts me down below. He wants another pair of eyes on this unorthodox deployment. I hover inside the observation pod above the main cargo bay while Brutlag puts on a spacesuit and joins the ten already suited spacemen lashing artillery components to their backpacks.

I recognize Kapur by her size and graceful movements. All the spacemen act as a unit, with synchronized fluidity. After securing the PBC parts, they lock small arms into suit holsters. Then they move on to checking their other gear, including the comically large metal claws attached to their forearms.

The cargo bay doors open, and I look out to see the spinning mass of *Dejah Thoris* filling the view. From half a kilometer away, it dwarfs the transport. The cruise ship's thrusters continue firing, jerking the gigantic vessel this way and that. The cargo section rotates past us, and I can see that a few containers are missing. I hope the ship holds together long enough for the spacemen to finish their job.

Colonel Brutlag shouts an order that I can't hear—I'm not tuned in to the X-4 comm channel. The spacemen line up in pairs against the open doors.

Brutlag raises his arm, and two spacemen pull their way into the middle of the open bay along a scaffolding. They turn themselves upside-down relative to me, bending their legs, getting ready to literally jump out of the boat.

Brutlag's arm drops. The first two spacemen launch themselves out of the cargo bay. At the same time, bursts of light start flashing outside—our fighter escort's countermeasures.

I blink my left eye to radio sensing. I'm dialed into the spacemen's burst locator beacons, so I can see when each one reaches *Dejah Thoris*.

In less than half a minute, only Colonel Brutlag is left in the cargo bay. He turns and waves at me. "Can you see them, Major?"

"Yes," I reply, watching the red dots blinking in my left eye. "Eight landed so far. The last two are touching down—shit!" One red dot just bounced off the hull. "One's been thrown off. One spaceman has been thrown off the ship."

"Hesch, you got him?" Brutlag asks.

"Yes, sir. We're moving," Hesch says over the radio.

The view out of the open cargo bay changes as the boat rotates and moves. I watch the blinking red dot as we chase it. My eye makes its speed fifty-two meters per second. The spaceman must have been launched just as *Dejah Thoris* changed rotation. Not enough to damage him, but more than enough to shake him up.

Hesch maneuvers the open cargo bay around him. The spaceman grabs onto the scaffolding. His grappling claw is a mangled mess of metal.

"We got him," Brutlag says. "Let's get back into position."

"Yes, sir," says Hesch.

Brutlag closes the cargo bay doors and helps the spaceman down to the floor. After the room fills with atmosphere, I turn myself out of the observation pod and join them.

The spaceman's name is Lynch. He's sweating, and he grimaces as we pull off his helmet. The medical readouts inside show a lot of red lines.

"Looks like a cracked rib," Brutlag says.

I detach the claw from Lynch's suit and turn it over, surveying the damage. "Well, at least we know what went wrong."

"Yessir," says Lynch.

I switched my eye to medical monitors to make sure Lynch didn't have any internal injuries, and now I see his heart rate shoot up.

Brutlag starts helping Lynch out of his suit. I'm just about to put the claw back in an equipment locker when I notice something unusual. I take an extra moment to blink my eye into a different scanning mode and confirm my suspicions.

I don't say anything until we get Lynch secured in Sickbay. Then I bring Brutlag back to the cargo bay and show him Lynch's grappling claw.

"See here?" I point to the tip of one of the three digits. "That's too clean to have broken off due to shearing stress. He must have shaved it before jumping."

Hesch's voice buzzes over the radio. "Colonel, both landing teams are through the airlocks. They're inside the ship. Losing signal now."

"Copy that, Hesch, thank you," Brutlag says. He thumbs off the intercom and turns back to me. "I always knew Lynch was a short-timer. Thank you, Major."

I'm confused by his nonchalance. "You're not concerned?"

Brutlag casts an almost amused expression toward me. "That he was trying to sabotage this operation?"

"Well, frankly, yes, Colonel," I say. "He damaged his own claw. He didn't want to get onto that ship, which reduced the chances that you'd get the fifth artillery component on board by half—"

"If any pair of jumpers hadn't made it onto that ship, we would have picked them up and tried again. Lynch knows that. If he wanted to stop us, he would have tampered with the artillery itself, and we wouldn't have known until it was too late."

"What if he's planning something else? We're a skeleton crew here now. He could overpower us, take over the boat—"

Brutlag holds up a hand. "Are you always this paranoid, Major?"

"Well, no." But considering D.Int is trying to glass Mars, I feel pretty justified in my suspicions right now.

"I know my people, Major," he says. "Lynch is young. His wife just gave birth to a baby girl. He wants to go home. I can respect that. His inability to be open with this desire, I don't respect so much, but every man has his own way of dealing with things."

"And there's no chance he could have been compromised?"

Brutlag frowns. "I know my people. Lynch is not a security risk."

I sense it's time to drop this issue. "If you say so, Colonel." I can ask Jessica to keep an eye on Lynch.

"Humans are social creatures," Brutlag says.

Now I'm confused. "Yes?"

"We want to belong," Brutlag continues. "To have a tribe, whether it's family, race, or team. Not everyone is suited to the Expeditionary Forces. And allegiances change with time. Lynch's bond with his family is now stronger than his wish to continue doing this job."

"Okay." I wonder if anthropology lectures are common in this unit.

"I hear that this hijacker used to be in the military. Is that correct?"

"Yeah. Army Special Forces."

"And he was dishonorably discharged."

"For insubordination and theft."

Brutlag nods. "I've seen a lot of people wash out of X-Force, Major. A lot of angry young people wanted to fight the war with Mars. But being an X-4 is about more than fighting. It's about being part of a unit. I know that was the hardest thing for me to learn—harder than zero-gee close combat, harder than orbital mechanics. Some people don't have the skills to pass our training. Some don't have the intelligence. But others just don't belong."

"Colonel, I hope you're not suggesting that the military drove Alan Wachlin to hijacking and murder."

"No, Major," Brutlag says. "I believe that Alan Wachlin desperately wanted to belong in groups for which he was completely unsuited, and the military was merely more forceful in its rejection than most."

Which made him a perfect target for Terman Sakraida. D.Int could pretend to give Wachlin exactly what he wanted. The sucker never knew he was being played.

"Almost makes you feel sorry for the guy," Brutlag says.

I remember the only clear picture of Alan Wachlin I've ever seen, as he stormed into *Dejah Thoris*'s engine room and killed an innocent man.

"No," I say. "I don't feel sorry for the bastard at all."

Brutlag nods. "As you say, Major."

The next words leave my mouth before I realize they're going. "Get me in a spacesuit. I'm jumping."

Brutlag blinks. "Major?"

"You're down one spaceman," I say. "You need to get that last PBC component over to *Dejah Thoris*. I'm a trained astronaut. Get me in a suit."

CHAPTER FORTY-TWO

X-4 transport—Cargo bay
7 minutes from waypoint zero

"This is insane," Oliver says from the observation pod.

"What else is new?" I reply from the cargo bay.

"*Major*," Jessica says, standing next to him, "I strongly discourage putting yourself in harm's way yet again."

"Are you volunteering to take my place, *Lieutenant Commander?*" I ask. "We don't have time to debate this." Her cover identity doesn't outrank mine. I wonder if Paul did that on purpose.

"Helmet," Brutlag says, raising the last piece of the spacesuit over my head. I nod. He lowers it onto my neck and locks the collar into place.

"We know all nine other spacemen made it inside the ship," Oliver says. "They already have all the parts they need. They're probably cutting through the bulkhead right now."

"We don't know what's happening over there," I say as Brutlag circles me, checking my suit. "Some of the X-4s might be injured. One of the PBC parts might be damaged."

"The major's right," Brutlag says. "And if he's willing to jump, I'd rather give my spacemen every chance to succeed." He pats the side of my helmet. "You're good to go."

I nod and look down at the bulky PBC component attached to the side of my suit. It's easily half my body mass. I'm only able to move around with it because I'm in zero-gravity.

"You guys really run drills with those things?" I ask Brutlag as he guides me to the open cargo bay doors. *Dejah Thoris* looms below me, and it seems to be much bigger and moving much faster than before.

Brutlag smiles. "Major, if we're lucky, the only thing we ever do is run drills."

"Major!" Oliver calls. "For the last time. I am begging you not to go."

I look up at the observation pod. "This is probably the least dangerous thing I've done in the last twenty-four hours. Why are you being such a killjoy now?"

He glares at me. "Because this is not part of your mission."

"You're right," I say. "I'm not on mission. I'm on a fucking vacation."

I look from him to Jessica. She doesn't say anything. She can't say anything.

"Stand up as soon as you can," she says.

I think there's some dust in my eyes. That must be what's causing these tears.

"You're going to get thrown around pretty hard once you land," Jessica continues. "Lock your mag-boots, get yourself upright. Move slow." She turns to Oliver. "Lieutenant?"

"Bloody hell." He squeezes his eyes shut and shakes his head. "We'll be in your ear until you enter the airlock. Once you're inside, your suit will sync up with X-4 battle comms. They'll tell you where to go from there."

"Don't extend your arms," Jessica adds. "Your instinct will be to steady yourself against the rotation, but three gees can break your bones. You could snap a wrist when your hand hits the wall. Use your shoulders to cushion against impact."

"Protect your head," Oliver says.

"Thank you." I blink the wetness out of my eyes and turn back to Brutlag. "Let's go, Colonel."

"The heads-up display in your helmet has been programmed with *Dejah Thoris*'s deck plans," Brutlag says as he positions me on the scaffolding. "There are two airlocks on deck fifteen. They'll be outlined in yellow. I'll mirror your display to the observation deck for your team."

"Got it," I say. One glowing yellow rectangle whizzes past in the overlay. It's moving a lot faster than I expected.

The air inside the suit feels alternately icy cold and sweltering hot. My hands and feet tingle, and I curse at them and insist that they not go numb. *This is easy. Come on, Kangaroo, you just killed a nuclear reactor. This is, what, a little space-jump? This is nothing.*

Hesch moves the transport to within half a kilometer of *Dejah Thoris*. Brutlag gives me the signal to jump.

And my legs don't work.

"Major?" Brutlag says. "Is there a problem?"

"Just checking my suit," I say, finally convincing my knees to bend. "Safety first."

"You're good to go," Brutlag says. "Any time you're ready."

I hear the impatience in his voice. Before I can have a second thought or a fainting spell, I launch myself off the scaffolding, out of the cargo bay, and into open space.

I barely have enough time to enjoy a clear view of Mars off to my right before it's blotted out by a burst of countermeasures from the X-4 fighter. Then the bulk of *Dejah Thoris* rushes up and slams into me.

The right side of my suit scrapes along the hull for a second before I manage to stab my claw into the hull. Three gravities of acceleration pin me down. Just as I get my bearings, the thrusters fire again, spinning me sideways. The side of my face pancakes against the inside of my helmet. Sunlight blinds me for a moment. The rotation changes again, and the ship falls away from me.

I'm glad this claw is holding on tight, because I sure as hell couldn't. The rotation flips in the opposite direction, and ninety thousand metric tons of spacecraft smack into me. Again.

"Goddammit!" I shout at no one in particular.

"Get your feet under you," I hear Jessica say.

"Mag-boot controls are in your palmpad," Oliver's voice says.

"I'm working on it!"

This is worse than any training. I drag my boots against the hull until I can place them flat, locking the soles to the hull. I triple-check my footholds, making sure I'm stable, then release the claw and stand up.

"I'm on my feet," I say.

"Airlock at your two o'clock," Oliver says, "range three meters."

"One step at a time," Jessica says. "Take it slow. Slow is smooth—"

"And smooth is fast, yeah yeah yeah, I got it."

Now that I'm standing, it's easier to brace myself against the changing acceleration. I find the airlock in my HUD and stagger toward it slowly, carefully, taking one step after each rotation change, ignoring the wrenching in my gut every time the ship lurches.

After what feels like hours, I reach the airlock. The spacemen left their override gadget stuck to the hull. I slap the device to open the outer doors.

"I'm at the airlock," I say. "Going in now."

"Remember, *shoulders*," Jessica says. "Hands at your sides."

"And loss of signal after ingress," Oliver says. "Time to waypoint zero is—"

"Don't want to know." I lean down, turn off my boots, and pull myself inside the airlock. "I'll see you on the other side. Over and out."

I smack the control panel to cycle the airlock. The outer doors clang shut. A few seconds later, the inner doors hiss open. I wobble out into a service corridor and wait for my suit to sync up with the X-4 battle comms.

After a few seconds, the helmet HUD shows me a red stripe glowing on the wall to my left: battlefield smart-dust, sprayed on by the spacemen to provide wireless comm relays inside the signal-blocking superstructure of *Dejah Thoris*. I move into the corridor, following the trail of high-tech breadcrumbs and bouncing from side to side.

"X-4 teams, this is Major Rogers," I say. "Spaceman Lynch was injured during the jump. I've taken his place. I have the second PBC firing coil with me. What is your status?"

"Welcome aboard, Major," says Kapur, her voice ringing over the audible groaning of metal every time the ship's rotation changes. I can feel the vibrations through my boots, and they don't feel good. "I'm afraid you're late to the party. We're in main engineering, and the crew has control of the ship again."

I have to know. "Who's in charge down there?" I ask. *Did you find Ellie?*

"I think it's the chief engineer."

"Fisher?"

"I don't know her name, sir. Do you want to speak to her?"

My voice catches in my throat. "Yes. Yes, Kapur. Affirmative. Yes!"

I'm feeling lightheaded. I stop walking. The radio crackles.

"This is Chief Engineer Gavilán." Her voice is the most wonderful thing I've ever heard. "Whoever you are, we don't have time—"

"Ellie, it's Evan," I say. "Are you okay?"

Static hisses back, and for a second I'm afraid I've lost her. "Evan? I thought—Andie said you were off the ship."

"Well, I'm back. Are you all right? Why aren't you in Sickbay? It looked like you were bleeding—"

"I don't have time for Sickbay. Where are you?"

"I'm coming to you." Rotation slams me into another wall just as I start moving again. This is really getting old. "Did the X-4s get Wachlin?"

"What?"

"The hijacker. Is he in custody?" I'm secretly hoping the answer is *No, he put up a fight and they put a bullet through his head.*

"He got away."

I'm not sure I heard her right. "What do you mean, 'He got away'?"

"I mean he ran when the X-4s blew the bulkhead."

"Okay, where do you need me to search?"

"Forget him," Ellie says. "We have bigger problems. You might have noticed we still don't have RCS control."

My nausea and headache are both getting worse. I stop and brace one shoulder against a wall. "So we catch Wachlin and make him undo whatever he did."

"I know what he did!" Ellie says. "I was watching him the whole time. He overloaded the ionwell ignition batteries to trigger an EMP. Fried all the electronics in Main Eng. And right before that, he flushed drive plasma into every cable bay in this section, so we can't load new software from the network. We're moving backup hardware now to reinstall navigation controls."

This is absurd. I feel like laughing. "So you're pulling parts from the computer core and dragging them through this crazy funhouse."

"Yeah. We could use your help. Where are you?"

"Sure." I unstrap the PBC component from my spacesuit. It clatters loudly back down the corridor. "Let me find a fucking sign or something."

"Which airlock did you enter through?" she asks.

"A yellow one." Maybe I don't feel like laughing. Maybe I feel like crying. What's the difference?

"Evan—"

I switch off the radio.

I should be happy. Ellie's still alive. She knows how to fix the ship. The X-4s are helping her do that. We're almost out of this crisis.

Except I didn't get what I wanted. I didn't get to punish the bad guy.

It shouldn't matter this much. But it does. Why am I doing any of this, if we can't catch the villains and make them pay? What's the point of saving this ship if Wachlin and Sakraida can just run away and do it all over again next month?

When do I get to fucking punch someone in the goddamn neck?

I take two steps forward, toward a T-intersection with another hallway, and stop. I turn to the wall, tilt my helmet down, and thump it against the wall repeatedly.

"It's not fair," I mutter to myself. "It's not fair. It's. Not. Fair."

Emily Wachlin and Crewman Xiao are dead. Alan Wachlin is going to get away with murder. And I'm probably going to puke inside this spacesuit pretty soon.

I slam my head against the wall one last time and hold it there.

It's not fucking fair.

I realize that I'm still hearing a rhythmic thumping noise coming from somewhere, and it's not me hitting my head against the wall. I push myself back and start looking around just as another spacesuited figure comes charging into the intersection.

The other person skids to a halt. I stumble backward. I see his face through the helmet—it's one of the standard cruise ship suits, with a clear bubble dome—and I recognize his eyes. Just his eyes. Why do I know his eyes? Why not the rest of his face?

No fucking way.

I blink my left eye into radiation scanning mode. The center of his chest lights up with an unmistakable purple glow.

"Alan Wachlin," I say out loud.

He can't hear me, of course. But he can see that I'm wearing an X-4 spacesuit. He charges me before I can raise the assault rifle clipped to my chestplate.

Wachlin slams me backward. We both go flying just as the ship changes rotation again. We crash headfirst into the ceiling and tumble over. He's trying to yank the rifle off my suit. I get my feet between us and kick him away. He rolls back into the intersection.

"The hijacker's here!" I shout before remembering my radio's off. I unclip the assault rifle from my suit and fumble with it. I don't recognize this model.

The ship lurches again. Wachlin launches himself at me. He uses the ship's rotation to his advantage and sends us careening down the hallway. He raises one arm and brings a metal baton down on my helmet. The faceplate cracks, and my HUD blinks out.

I yell something that probably isn't words. My arm is pinned to my chest. I can't find the trigger on my weapon. My faceplate crunches and spiderwebs as Wachlin strikes it again and again.

What the hell is he doing? He must know he can't smash through this helmet with a puny baton.

Then I realize: he's blinding me. Or trying to, anyway.

He doesn't know about my eye.

Another spin change. My back slams into the wall, or maybe the floor. I blink my eye into wide scan mode. Wachlin appears as a blotchy outline of colors.

He raises the baton again. I grab his baton-wielding forearm before he can bring it down again.

"That's enough, asshole." I wish I could see the expression on his face.

The ship rotates. I turn his arm into the same direction we're flung. He emits a muffled shout when we hit the wall, and I feel something break in his hand. The baton falls out of his grasp.

I jerk my right arm up and use the length of the assault rifle to pry him off me. With my left hand, I yank the emergency release on my helmet. Both the helmet and Wachlin fall away and smack into the wall directly in front of me. Wachlin grabs a handhold just before rotation changes again, and the helmet tumbles off down the corridor.

It's a lot louder without my helmet, and the air is foul. The contents of the Barsoom Buffet must be covering just about every interior surface by now. I'm sure other foodstuffs have emerged from the stomachs of many a passenger over the last half hour.

I have a clear view of Alan Wachlin. I've found the safety on my assault rifle.

My boots lock to the floor. I aim the weapon at him.

Nobody will question why I shot and killed this man. There are no witnesses here. And even if someone did see an X-4 spaceman gunning down a terrorist? Just part of the job. *Oo* fucking *rah*.

So why aren't I pulling the trigger?

I step forward. I have the rifle pointed at his head. He's yelling now, his face red and contorted. I can't hear him through the helmet. His left hand grips the handhold on the wall. His right arm is limp and flopping at his side.

Good. I want this guy to hurt. I want him to suffer.

But that's not why I haven't fired yet.

He's a murderer. He's dangerous. But he didn't do this on his own. He couldn't have.

Wachlin's just a pawn. And you don't kill pawns.

You capture pawns, on your way to bagging the king.

I move closer. Wachlin stops yelling for a second. He looks confused. His lips start moving again. I'm not paying attention. I'm looking at the life support readouts on his spacesuit's chest monitor.

Six hours of air remaining. More than enough.

I swivel to my right and squeeze the trigger. A burst of bullets tears into the wall next to Wachlin. He totally falls for it, flinching and releasing the handhold. Now he's floating in space, untethered.

I think of a stubby black chess piece and open the pocket.

I open it without the barrier, directly behind Wachlin. I make it as wide as the corridor is tall, so the event horizon touches both ceiling and floor.

The expression on Wachlin's face as the void sucks him in is priceless.

I lean forward with the air rushing into the pocket. The breeze cools the sweat on the back of my neck. The man in the spacesuit tumbles away, shrinking until he's just a dot in the middle of a yawning black emptiness.

"Welcome to Waypoint Kangaroo," I say. "Don't enjoy your stay."

I close the pocket.

My mouth is dry. I feel lightheaded. The edges of my vision start to blur. Yeah, that was a larger portal than usual. And right after those two fifteen-meter jobs? Plus all this additional stress lately? Probably not a good idea.

I'm just thinking I should sit down when an X-4 spacesuit sails into view. The spaceman kicks off the far wall and flies toward me. Impressive, considering the ship is still spinning wildly. The suit stops half a meter away.

I see Kapur's face in the helmet. I smile and wave. Her mouth is moving. Were they worried about me after I went radio silent? How touching.

"Wait one," I say. I turn away from her before throwing up. Then I pass out.

CHAPTER FORTY-THREE

I wake up in the medical bay of the X-4 transport, strapped into a bed and surrounded by blinking lights and soft beeping sounds. There's an IV cuff around my left arm. Amazingly, my splitting headache is not accompanied by world-class nausea. That must be thanks to whatever pharmaceuticals the IV is pumping into my bloodstream.

I raise my right arm to scratch my nose and almost punch myself in the mouth. *No gravity. Are we in orbit?*

A flicker of light off to the left catches my eye. I turn my head and see a tablet attached to the side of an open drawer, playing a silent newscast. The vid shows the familiar bulk of *Dejah Thoris* with a swarm of other ships covering her cargo section, their engines glowing white-hot. The headline superimposed across the bottom of the screen reads LIVE: MARTIAN FLEET STEERS DISABLED CRUISE LINER OFF COLLISION COURSE.

But that can't be right. The timestamp is just minutes after waypoint zero. They couldn't possibly have repaired the engineering controls, shut down the RCS system, gotten the Martian ships into position, and also moved me back to the X-4 boat that quickly. Am I dreaming?

I pinch myself, and it's really painful. *Okay, not dreaming.*

The tablet screen blinks to black for half a second, then plays the same vid segment again from the start. It's a recorded loop.

Oliver. He couldn't just leave a note like a normal person. I laugh until tears shake free of my eyes, drift away, and get sucked up by the ventilation system.

The Sickbay door opens, and Jessica floats up to my bed.

"Congratulations," she says. "You didn't get anybody killed."

Coming from her, that's high praise. "How long was I out?"

"About forty minutes." She grabs Oliver's tablet, stops the vid, and taps the device against the medical monitors next to my head. "*Dejah Thoris*'s security chief had a message for you. Jameson?"

"Jemison."

"Right. She said the officers and crew celebrated their safe recovery with 'a very small bottle of red wine.'" Jessica looks sideways at me. "Does that mean what I think it means?"

I risk a smile. "Yeah. She delivered the nanobots. Let's hope your new program works."

"You get me a list of names and I'll flag their medical records for surveillance."

"How the hell are you going to get Paul to approve that?"

She taps the tablet screen with her fingers. "I'm going to lie to him."

Fair enough. "Have you been in touch with the office?"

She nods. "Lasher's putting our house in order."

The audit. I can't believe I didn't make this connection before. "That wasn't a coincidence, was it? Us getting investigated at the same time all this was happening?"

"No. The auditors bugged out as soon as Sakraida went AWOL. Lasher and State traced the paper trail back to Intel, but Sakraida commandeered a fighter group from Andrews and broke orbit before Ops could intercept."

"I'm sorry, did you say fighter *group*?"

"Twelve birds. They entered a stealth tunnel just outside Lunar orbit." OSS has several large, open-ended, energy-absorbing structures deployed throughout the Solar System. These "tunnels" can be remote-piloted to meet spacecraft and conceal their maneuvers. The spacecraft in question deploy their own stealth canopies before leaving the tunnel, and they're impossible to track until they need to use their engines again. "Smart money says they're headed for the asteroid belt."

No-man's-land. "So when you say 'putting our house in order'—"

"There's going to be some demolition first."

"I have something that should help," I say. "Or, should I say, some*one*."

Jessica frowns. "What are you talking about now?"

"I have a package I need to deliver, planetside, in less than five hours."

She shakes her head. "Mars isn't exactly welcoming Earth ships with open landing pads right now."

I grab her forearm. "I've got the hijacker."

"You've got—" Jessica's eyes widen. "You mean he's in the pocket."

"His spacesuit had six hours of air."

"We thought you threw him out the airlock."

"This was easier."

I can't read her expression. She nods. "Five hours."

"Yeah."

She pushes off the wall and flies out of Sickbay. The door hisses shut before I can ask her to leave the tablet behind. With my shoulder-phone fried and only the transport's internal comms available in here, my entertainment options are limited.

The door clangs open, and two spacemen tumble into Sickbay. The one in front is Lynch, the fellow who failed his space-jump earlier. Behind him is Kapur. She shoves Lynch into the bed next to me.

"For the last fucking time, Lynch," Kapur says, pulling restraints closed around Lynch's shoulders and hips. He winces as she clamps an IV cuff around his arm. "You're injured. Colonel says you stay put until we reach base."

"But I can help—"

"You can go the fuck to sleep," Kapur says. Lynch gives me a desperate look.

"I'd listen to her, Spaceman," I say.

"But I need to . . . ," he slurs before his eyelids close and his entire body goes limp. I look over to where Kapur is tapping at a medical console.

"Man, I love sedatives." She turns to me. "You want something to help you sleep, Major?"

"No, thank you." I hope I didn't puke on her earlier.

"Very well." She checks Lynch's restraints, then whirls around and leaves.

Peace and quiet gets boring pretty quickly. Also, Lynch snores. I'm just starting to consider disengaging my IV and wandering out to look for some so-called food when the door opens again.

It's Ellie.

I don't know what to say. She drifts into Sickbay, grabs a handhold, and stops herself a good meter away from me. A bandage covers the left third

of her forehead. The right side of her jaw is bruised. Her left arm is in a
sling.

She's still beautiful.

"Andie said I shouldn't come over here," Ellie says.

It's not the worst greeting I've ever encountered. "Did she say why?"

"She said I'd have a lot of questions you couldn't answer."

I nod. "I can't tell you any technical details about the wormhole device.
That's classified. I can't tell you who I actually work for. That's even more
classified."

"So what *can* you tell me?"

"We're the good guys," I say.

"Yeah, I figured that one out on my own."

She's staring at me. Do I have something on my face? "I'm sorry."

"You're sorry you're the good guys?"

"No, that's not—I didn't mean—" Finding the stupidest possible thing
to say, that's my other superpower. "I'm sorry I ruined your escape. In the
crawlway."

Ellie shakes her head. "You were trying to retake Main Eng. Same
as me."

"What . . ." My mouth feels dry. "What happened in there?"

"I don't want to talk about it."

"Sorry."

"Stop apologizing," she says.

"One more, then I'm done." I stare down at the floor. "I'm sorry I
couldn't save you."

She laughs out loud, just for a second, then gives me a forbearing look.
"I don't need anyone to save me, Evan. I don't want that. I can take care
of myself."

"Look," I say, "we're probably never going to see each other again after
this. I just want to make sure our last conversation isn't awkward and
uncomfortable." *Yeah, great job on that so far, Kangaroo.* "I just want you to
know. I was on vacation."

She gives me a squint. "Like every other *Dejah Thoris* passenger? Not
really news there, Evan."

I can't stand it. "That's not my name."

"I suspected as much."

"I wasn't working," I say. "You understand? I have to protect my identity at all times. I wasn't on a mission or an assignment or anything like

that." I resist the temptation to turn on my left eye so I can get a better read on her emotional state. "I wasn't using you, Ellie."

"Not even to steal a centrifuge?"

I catch myself before apologizing again. "That's also classified. I, uh, regret I can't tell you any more than that. Don't worry, I'll return the centrifuge. I didn't break it."

She's smiling.

"What?" I ask.

"I'm going to kiss you now," she says.

Ellie flies across the room before I can respond. Her lips press into mine. Either she's getting very good at kissing, or I am, or these IV drugs are severely mood-enhancing. I let my eyelids droop shut and put one hand on Ellie's waist to bring her body closer.

Maybe I should go on vacation more often.

All too soon, she pulls back. I open my eyes. I will never get tired of that smile.

"So," she says, "what's your real name?"

ACKNOWLEDGMENTS

It's been said that "art is made by the alone for the alone," but this book wouldn't exist without the efforts of many people besides myself.

Thanks to my literary agent, Sam Morgan, who answered my many noob questions with a straight face, and to all the JABberwocks who helped find a good home for Kangaroo.

Thanks to my editor, Pete Wolverton, the most adorable pitbull in publishing, and to everyone at Thomas Dunne Books who helped turn my manuscript into an actual novel with an amazing cover. Any errors are mine alone.

Thanks to Janet "Query Shark" Reid, the best agent I never had, for believing in Kangaroo from the very beginning.

Thanks to my parents for making my whole life possible, and to my sister for always thinking ahead to the next meal.

Thanks to all the wonderful writers I've met through Viable Paradise, Clarion West, SFWA, Codex, Rainforest Writers Village, and NaNoWriMo who helped me stay on target. Extra shouts out to Charlie Jane Anders, Jennifer Brozek, Tobias Buckell, John Crowley, Hiromi Goto, Camille Griep, Jason Gurley, Randy Henderson, Claire Humphrey, Kij Johnson, James Patrick Kelly, Marko Kloos, Mary Robinette Kowal, Fonda Lee, Ursula K. LeGuin, Ian McDonald, John Scalzi, and Alison Wilgus for showing me the way.

Thanks to my numerous alpha, beta, and gamma readers, especially Chris Carlson, Stephanie Charette, Nadya Duke, Shannon Fay, Michael

Hernshaw, Steve Kopka, Julia Reynolds, DeeAnn Sole, and Peter Sursi for their steely-eyed insights.

Thanks to Folly Blaine for making me look good in photos.

Thanks to Corby Anderson and Larry Hosken for helping with the puzzles. (*What puzzles*, you ask? Take a close look at the spacesuit, then visit www.waypointkangaroo.com to find the rabbit hole.)

Finally: thanks to you, dear reader, for joining me on this journey. Yes, Kangaroo will return. And no, I won't tell you his real name. Not yet.